PRAISE FOR FAITH O'SHEA

Faith O'Shea is a contemporary women's literature writer who loves writing about romance, magic, conviction, and loyalty, with strong women and the friendships they build. She has created many series of stories to make us laugh, cry and feel empowered and writes in a voice that speaks to women of all ages. Faith believed there were subjects and life that needed to be written about. ~ Loyce M.

I truly love the Everyday Goddess series. The strong, leading women characters, in this day and age, are inspiring to me and keep me coming back for more! The books are light, fun, extremely relatable and I can't put them down! ~ Kathryn B.

I just finished the Fire and Ice series. It had romance, strong friendships between the women characters and complex stories that were clearly very well researched. Loved all of them and looking forward to the goddess series next! ~ Gail N.

Books by Faith O'Shea

The Greenliner Series
Thrown for a Curve
League of Her Own
Clutch Hit
Out in Left Field

The Scalera Family Series
Cold Sweat
Edge of Forever
Thin Blue Line
Coming Home to You
Finding Joy

Fire and Ice Series
Consumed by Fire
Skoli on Ice
Heart on Fire
Heart of Ice
Tendril of Ice
Rekindling the Fire

Everyday Goddesses Series
Magic Bean Café
Once There Was a Tree
Tipping the Scales

Fire and Ice

One law firm, six partners, friends to the end

Consumed by Love

Nell Warren has just won a Supreme Court victory but it comes at a cost in the form of Congressman Jack Adams. They've got a past, and he wants to resurrect it, but she's not sure. There's a problem still lingering in the shadows. Will he be able to convince her, he's in it for good this time?

Skoli on Ice

Camille Bissonnette's expertise is asylum, and she's done some work, for the FBI. When they drop Maksim Skolikovsky in her lap, she's not sure if he's a spy, a journalist or someone more dangerous. The Russian trusts no one, for good reason. Will she be able to prove she's his fighter, or will he cut her loose, in fear for his life?

Heart on Fire

Emilia Spenser-Ronan deals with families in crisis, and her best friend, Nick Katsaros's is a mess right now. He calls her his lifesaver, but she's feeling like a two-pound whirly sucker. She drops him flat, just as he's seeing her in a new light. Will the college besties find their way back to each other?

Heart of ICE

Jelani Ramirez has been looking for love in all the wrong places, but there's no way Alec Cleland is in the right one. He's a member of ICE, part of Homeland Security, and she's sure he has a heart to match. Will it take more than his smile to melt away her misgivings?

Tendrils of Ice

Arianna Woodley, original partner of Woodley and Fisher, has spent her life nurturing the firm since her divorce but when her ex-husband, Evan Cox, makes a run for governor, she throws her hat in the ring. When time spent together begins to heal the fractures in her heart, he asks if she's willing to go back and change the ending. Can she trust him enough to try?

Rekindling the Fire

Mia Fisher's life is unraveling and she's ready to leave it all behind, and that includes her husband Nate, an FBI analyst. He's inattentive, work-driven and useless when it comes to keeping the home-fires burning. When he realizes she's serious, he commits to doing whatever it takes to keep her in his life. Will he be able to keep his promise?

SKOLI
ON ICE

Fire & Ice
Book 2

FAITH O'SHEA

Cover Design by Jaycee DeLorenzo at Sweet 'N Spicy Designs
Formatted by Woven Red Author Services, www.wovenRed.ca

Skoli on Ice/Faith O'Shea- 1st edition
ISBN eBook: 978-0-9996806-2-9
ISBN print book: 978-0-9996806-3-6

www.faithoshea.com

Printed in the U.S.A.

TO MY READERS

This story line came into being soon after I heard about the foreign intervention in our elections. The topic interested and intrigued me, and I wanted to learn as much as could about the how and why behind it.

Knowing nothing about hacking, bots or the dark web, I began researching everything I could find on it. The books were both fascinating and frightening at the same time. I didn't realize there was a different kind of war being waged, this one in cyberspace.

As Skoli on Ice is a love story, my job was to take what I learned and weave it into my plot as a backdrop, not as a primary theme. Once Maks and Cami came into being, it was easy. Their love transcended time, even though they were culturally world's apart.

I hope you enjoy reading it, as much as I enjoyed writing it.

Please feel free to contact me at my website www.faithoshea.com and follow me on Facebook and Twitter.

Faith

PROLOGUE

November

He slid the plastic key into the slot and pushed open the door.

After calling out and hearing only the silence that enveloped the room, he took tentative steps across the threadbare carpet, into the darkness. The heavy drapes were covering the windows and the early morning sun was being denied entry. Nina didn't like the light. It's where her monsters lived.

He felt his way to the bed, the smell arousing an unspoken fear. It was strong enough to cut through the thick, stale cigarette smoke. He sought her form with his fingers. When he found it, he groped, trying to distinguish where she lay. He snatched them back, the body he'd found, wet and slick. Flipping on the lamp by the bed, he all but gagged at the picture illuminated in the shadows. Bile rose in his throat and he swallowed the foul taste down.

Nina lay on her back, the cut across her throat, deep and wide. Her head was barely hanging on to her torso. Blood was everywhere—the walls, the body, the bed linens, the comforter, the rug. With shaking limbs, knowing there was nothing he could do for her, he searched the room. Everything was gone. Her computer, phone, satchel, purse, and the notebook she'd been writing in before he left. Unwilling to be found with a corpse, he hurried out, the door slamming shut behind him. There would be too many questions if he was found here, and it would give her murderers a shot at the mark they'd missed. If Nina hadn't sent him out on an errand, he could very well be lying in the same pool of blood. Shoving his hands in his pockets, the red substance evidence of where he'd been, he pushed the elevator button with his jacket and stepped in as soon as it swished open.

Leaning against the wall, as the rumbling cage made its way down to the lobby, he breathed in, trying to relax his nerves. It had the opposite effect and he started to hyperventilate. He squeezed his pocketed hands into fists, knowing they could be after him. And they would be if they knew he had most of her notes. If they knew what else he had, he'd be a marked man for sure. Once the doors opened, he was more in control and strode out as if he had nothing to hide.

Checking what was around him from every angle, he hurried out of the hotel and onto the busy street. As he tried to blend into the throng of pedestrians, he continued to glance behind him. There didn't seem to be anyone following him, but he couldn't be sure. There were eyes and ears everywhere.

Stopping in at a restaurant, one he'd never been in before, he made his way to the men's room at the back. He needed to clean himself up, wash the blood away, maybe get himself a stiff drink. He lathered up his hands, washed away the evidence, but no matter how much soap he used, he couldn't get rid of the stench. Yanking at the towel, he dried off as best he could, a sliver of red still beneath his fingernails. He washed again and again, feeling like he'd never come clean. Stealthily, he opened the pockmarked door, surveyed the area, and stepped out.

His hands were still trembling when he sat at the bar and ordered a vodka. He had to think. He had to figure out where to go from here. He looked around, paranoia settling in, and he saw the enemy in every face his glance fell upon.

After shooting the clear liquid down in one gulp, he ordered another.

That's all the time he'd allow to calm his nerves.

Back on the street, he hailed a cab to take him the short distance to his apartment. He had to chance the stop, needing to collect the valuable material stored there. Then he'd head to the train station, hoping his luck would last, and leave the city. There was nothing for him here anymore. Death was everywhere, a war of terror being fought by those in control. And they were cunning. They rarely chose the most obvious dissidents, which kept everyone guessing who would be next. Through the chaotic noise in his head, a picture of where he could go emerged. He knew what his next step would be.

Nina's editor would help him, he was sure of it.

After the stop, another cab.

He entered the clean and well-lit space and he walked the terminals, waiting for service to St. Petersburg. Train tracks dissected the areas. He could hear doors as they slid open and closed, passengers getting on and off in the interim, talkin loudly, announcements being made over the intercom, the outside traffic competing with whistles and engines, wind whistling through the doors as they were whipped open and slammed shut. He squashed his cigarette under his boot, the concrete littered with used butts, a garbage can nearby overflowing with cans, paper wrappers, and Styrofoam. He pulled his coat more securely around him, the air thick with frost. He paced until the blare of the horn and the clacking train on the tracks alerted him that he would soon be aboard. As the engine screeched to a halt, and opened its doors, he scrambled in and fell into the first available seat.

He was almost safe.

CHAPTER ONE

Camille Bissonnette glanced up to see her assistant, Sikha Rangsey, about to enter her office. She all but crept inside, leaned over the desk, and whispered, "Call on line four. It's Nate."

A sense of foreboding shot through her. Matching the volume and tone, Camille asked, "Did he say what it was about?"

"Just that he needed to talk to you."

A hundred different reasons for her to dismiss the call flew through her mind, but she collected them all and put them in the back-drawer compartment. Closed and locked.

Nate was married to one of the founding partners of the firm, and his wife Mia knew her husband was dropping some of his cases into Camille's lap, although she didn't know the exact nature of what they entailed. Mia thought it was more about filing paperwork, conducting basic interviews, and appearing in court for the decision. She was unaware that a few had been cloak-and-dagger. It had started innocently enough with the first request. The FBI had needed an attorney for a high-profile foreign politician who'd been swept into the country upon threat of death. Mia had asked if she'd be willing to take it. When it had gone well, Camille became Nate's go-to at the firm.

"Thanks, Sikha."

Taking a deep breath, she picked up the phone and punched the button to connect her to the man who was waiting.

"Camille Bissonnette."

"Camille, I was hoping you wouldn't avoid my call."

"It did cross my mind but what was the point? We have too long a history and I know you. You would have hounded me until I had no choice but to talk to you."

"I'm glad I've set precedent."

"You've been listening to your wife. I'll have to let her know. She thinks you tune her out most of the time."

"I only miss the unimportant details. Words like precedent, Nell Warren, Supreme Court I hear."

"Probably a million times. We're still waiting to hear the outcome."

"I know that, too."

Swiveling in her chair, Camille looked out over the city. Her office was one of four along this wall of windows, the others occupied by the other three women who'd won partner at the firm Woodley and Fisher, all within a year of each other. Arianna, one of the co-founding partners and matriarch of the group, joked that they'd have to start sharing their digs soon with new hires if the calls for business didn't slow down. They knew she was kidding. Their view of the plaza was one of the perks, and they'd each earned their suites with the hard work and sweat that came from long hours and little social life. There very well could be an upswing in clients if Nell won her Supreme Court case. The opinion would be out by the end of the week, and they were all checking daily.

She watched the pedestrians scurrying along the sidewalks like mice in retreat. At least they looked that small from the fourteenth floor.

"Why did you call, Nate? I told you I needed a break."

The last one had thrown her. She had an aversion to getting killed.

"You've got persistence down to a science. You uncovered it all, in time. You have a knack for digging until there's nothing left to left to find. It can't happen like that again."

She slunk down in her chair, crossed her legs, and closed her eyes.

"Isn't there someone else the FBI can pull in for this?"

"No. It needs your finesse. And your background. We're still trying to work out the logistics, but I'd like you to meet with him today. We're in a time crunch and I don't want to waste any."

She refused to work with anyone from Saudi. Or Pakistan. Or sadly, with French nationals.

"Where's he from?"

"Russia, as far as we know."

She sat up. There was a niggle of interest that she tried to tamp down. "His story?"

"Says he's a journalist. He's handed over some damaging information on the Kremlin...among other things...and we're trying to ascertain its veracity."

That would be considered treason from where the man came from, and would mean certain death. The Russian government didn't condone freedom of the press and snuffed out anyone who had a liberal slant of what was happening there. It sounded like the application process would be a slam dunk.

"Where'd he acquire the information?"

There was a pause, as if Nate was looking for the right words.

"He's not giving away his sources. He's told us point-blank that journalists are being killed for the type of information he gave us and he's not putting anyone else at risk."

Picking a dead leaf from the African violet that sat on her credenza and throwing it in her waste basket, she said, "They are. Began with Anna Asaulchenko back in 2006."

"See? You're already up to speed."

"When you work on the kind of cases I do, you know more than you want about gang violence, terrorists, and hit men."

It also came from her interest in all things Russian, sparked early on because of her ancestral roots there. Her curiosity had peaked in college when she chose Russian studies as a major. It included the literature of Dostoyevsky, Nabokov, and Tolstoy. Her dog-eared copy of Solzhenitsyn's, *Archipelago*, one of her favorites. She'd begun to learn the language, studied their history, culture, and the national identity that emerged after the fall of the Soviet Bloc. Once she'd switched her major to political science, and gone on to law school, she was readily able to compare and contrast their politics and forms of government with her own. Her curiosity wasn't satiated yet, and she still read all she could about the civil war fermenting within the country. She'd read most of Asaulchenko's books, which slanted to dark and oppressive stories about the suffering going on there. It hadn't surprised her when Anna had been shot just outside her home. Nate's Russian was facing the same fate.

His voice cut through her mental wanderings.

"The thumb drive we sent over has material collected by a reporter who was killed a few weeks ago, in addition to what he gave us on...other things. I need you to look at this guy. What he has looks impeccable, but I need to know for sure if I can trust it. Him."

If she was reading between the lines correctly, picking up on the things Nathaniel Fisher wasn't saying, the man in question could be a spy. Assassins were masquerading as reporters these days, and they had to be damn sure this Russian didn't have murder on his mind. Just this past June there was an attempt on the Ukrainian interior minister's life. It was the third high-profile assault, and rumblings were that it'd originated with the Russians. It seemed the government had legalized the killing of people abroad. The United States fit that category.

"What's his name?"

"Maksim Skolikovsky."

"It reminds me of vodka. Makes me think fake."

They were all struggling with fake news these days.

"I trust your intuition. Will you take the case?"

"The goal being asylum?"

"If he's who he says he is, yes."

"Can I have time to think about it?"

"No. I'm getting him underground within the hour. I want you, kid."

Her slender fingers massaged her forehead. Underground? Of course they'd keep him underground if they wanted to keep him alive. Without her conscious permission, she heard herself asking, "Where and when?"

"Another FBI agent is the operative handling the case. I told him I'd call and get you in place. He'll be your contact from now on. His name is Alec Cleland. As always, the less Mia knows the better."

"Are you admitting she wouldn't like some of the cases you've given me?"

"She'd be more pissed than a hornet's nest if she knew I was putting one of her lawyers in jeopardy."

A shiver of fear raced along her nerve endings.

"What are you telling me?"

"If he's the real deal, there could be a hit out on *him*. I don't want you getting any closer than you have to."

Nate wouldn't have to guess about that, he'd have to already know the man was wanted or not. That he wasn't coming out and saying it told her he was.

"I can promise you that I won't. If I take the case."

"You have five seconds, four, three, two, one. Is that a yes?"

"This goes against my better judgment. I haven't given myself time to rebound. I hope you know what you're doing."

"I do. And thanks. Alec will be in touch with your rendezvous point."

The dial tone buzzed in her ear. Nate had hung up.

She slid gracefully from her seat, walked to the glass wall.

What the hell was she doing putting herself in another risky situation? The flashbacks still had a way of numbing her, and she was still easily startled by sudden movements in her peripheral vision. The intrusive memory came at odd times and in odd places. If it had occurred during her first case, she would have stopped working with the federal agency and never looked back. They'd come knocking on her door almost three years ago when one of their on-staff attorneys had jumped ship to the district attorney's office. She was pulled in to help protect the interests of a political refugee with a high profile. There had been several other cases since then, and up until her latest, they'd all been routine except for the preponderance of paperwork required by the government agency.

The last one could have killed her. All but signing off, she'd gotten a funny feeling somewhere in her gut that told her to put it off one more day, find another avenue to pursue. There was something she didn't like, and her intuition had paid off. The French national was a terrorist, using the system to gain a foothold in the United Sates, something that had come to light at the very end of the discovery process. That was her job as an adjudicator for the FBI, to determine whether the asylum claimant had a well-founded fear of being persecuted. Hala Al-Fakeeh looked like the poster girl for asylum. Well-mannered, articulate, Hala had played her part well, and she'd almost fallen for it. If it hadn't been for a surprise visit, a glimpse at an open laptop, and an angry confrontation that put her in a compromising situation, she might have let her slip through the system. There was a moment she'd feared for her life, a knife, a slash, and blood seeping from her wounds before the agent outside in the hall heard the signs of a struggle and interceded. If she hadn't insisted on being accompanied by one in service, she could have been killed and Hala could have escaped. Instead, Hala was arrested as part of an underground terrorist cell. The backlash was the immediate removal of the clandestine group, all seven being deported out of the country. The traumatic experience had shaken her to the core and she'd made an oath to herself that she wouldn't accept another case until her injury had healed. And her psyche. It had never escaped her that these types of cases carried a grave responsibility, but the danger to her life put it in a new perspective. She wasn't sure she wanted to continue in the role Nate Fisher had carved out for her.

It looked like she was being handed another one.

Her fingers sought the scar hiding beneath her shirt. The abject terror and anger knotted inside as she wondered again why she'd taken this on.

Her hand stilled when Emilia Spencer-Ronan came barreling into her office, a huge smile on her face. She was her best friend in and out of the office and they had worked closely on several cases that had put the firm on the map. Originally from Australia, Em had come to America when her parents died, their will leaving her and her sister to an aunt and uncle who lived on the outskirts of Boston. She still had an Aussie twang and they all kidded her about it. She'd been living here long enough that she should have picked up the linguistic quirk Boston was famous for. She still wasn't dropping her *r*'s.

"I'm already packed for our ski trip this weekend. Two whole days without a frantic phone call. I am psyched."

The look Camille gave her had the smile melt away.

"What are you telling me?"

"I can't, Em. I'm sorry. I just got a call. I wasn't even thinking about Cannon Mountain."

Dropping into her seat, deflated with the news, she whined, "You promised."

"I did. And I meant to keep it. I thought I'd convinced myself I wasn't going to take another one of these cases. Seems I was wrong."

"Now I know how Bill felt. How many times did you cancel on him?"

Too many to keep track of. They had never gotten to a third date. It was no longer a problem. She hadn't even noticed his absence from her life.

"You better not let this happen with the trip to Marrakesh. That one I won't forgive."

For the last couple of years, since they'd made partner and got a month's vacation as one of their benefits, the pair had traveled. Breaking the four weeks up into two-week packages, they'd already been to Paris, Barcelona, Berlin, and Athens. Their scheduled trip to Morocco was set for April. The skiing trip was to get them over the winter hump. Now, there'd be no break. And she desperately needed it.

Em cracked her knuckles, a habit that didn't usually annoy. For some reason, it did today.

"Is it FBI? You wouldn't cancel unless it was one of Nate's."

"Yeah."

Em knew some of the basics but not any of the in-depth work she did. No one knew she'd been hurt during the last one. Being unable to share the burden was beginning to wear her down.

"Why couldn't he find someone else?"

"I asked the same question. He didn't have an answer that satisfied but I went there anywhere. Why don't you ask Liz to go with you? She might like a short vacation."

Liz Somersworth was Em's assistant and a good friend.

"She started seeing someone and I doubt she's ready to take time away from him."

Jelani Ramirez peeked her head in.

"You guys want lunch? We're ordering in."

Em asked, a forlorn look on her face, "Want to go skiing this weekend with me?"

Taking a step inside, Jelani asked, "What happened to your partner in crime, here? I thought you were both taking the weekend off."

"Nate Fisher is what happened." Turning back to Cami, Em said, "I really think you need to talk to Mia about his taking advantage of you."

"These types of asylum cases aren't like normal ones. If the feds feel the need for a fast turnaround, it means there's a lot riding on it. They turn up when they turn up."

Em looked up at Jelani.

"So, do you want to come with me?"

"I've never been on skis in my life. I will probably be able to say that on my deathbed. If I can't wear shoes, it's outside my comfort zone."

"Fine. I'll go alone. It's probably just as well. I need to think some things through. I think it's time I made some changes."

"Nick?"

"Among other things."

The phone rang, and Camille snatched it up, her eyes suggesting that it was private. Em and Jelani hurried out and shut the door.

There goes lunch.

⌒

Maksim Skolikovsky paced the confining area.

He'd arrived at the Boston field office of the FBI earlier this morning after the late-night flight out of France. Accompanied by the agent assigned to him, his file already in process, he was being given consideration for asylum in the United States. He still wasn't sure he'd made the right decision. He could have picked out of a half-dozen countries that would have been interested in his story. Coming here had seemed the most expedient.

He was a marked man for all intents and purposes, but he was not going to let the risk of death keep him from passing the information on. Or unearthing more on what the Russian government was up to. No one saw the danger. All the players on the world stage were fools.

Here, at least, he'd have protection. Something he'd begged Nina to get. Her mother was an American citizen and she would have been welcomed but her heart was with Russia, the home of her birth. Wanting to prove the brutality of the oligarchy that ruled the state, she had asked questions, interviewed people, marginalized the leaders, criticized the systematic killing of individuals and the cleansing of large groups of ethnic partisans. In the end, it had killed her. His soul still shuddered at the loss. She had been at the center of his life and now? It seemed even in death, she kept him close. Where would he be now if they hadn't talked about the possibility of that outcome after the first attempt on her life? She'd made him swear he would take the information to the United States. It was critical in the country's own pursuit of the truth, a truth most were just coming to terms with. She was sure that they would know what to do with what he'd found.

He'd do as promised, no matter the cost.

He stopped pacing when the door opened, and Alec Cleland walked in.

His handler looked and acted the part of FBI agent. Dressed in a dark suit, a conservative tie, and oxford shoes, he was a large man. Gruff and detached he didn't give away much in the way of information. At least he hadn't until now.

"We are moving you to a safe house this afternoon. You'll be interviewed there by one of our attorneys who's being given the task of filing your paperwork. Her name is Camille Bissonnette and she's also been tasked as a member of our discovery network. She'll help us determine that you are who you say you are. Is there anything you want to add to your dossier before we hand it over?"

He flicked his eyes in Alec's direction, his nerves humming in anticipation. "No."

"You are aware that any misleading information will be looked upon with suspicion and might affect your chances of staying here."

"I have given you all information you need to determine fate."

"It's compelling."

"It is death-provoking. It is this type of pursuit of truth that earns you death squad where I come from."

"We will do what we can to keep you alive."

"I am not so sure. The government has long reach. But I am prepared for what comes."

"No one knows you're here."

"That is not the truth. You know, and other members of team do. Now, this attorney."

"We trust Camille. And I believe you will come to trust her, as well."

"I do not give it lightly."

He got a grunt for an answer.

If you came from where he did, you trusted no one but yourself. Only if you were lucky did you find someone you could share things with, and he'd been lucky. He'd not only worked with Nina, they'd become intimately involved. He had respect for her courage and her integrity. He doubted he'd ever find someone he could trust like that again.

He followed Alec to the underground garage and got into car. The grey concrete pillars made backing up difficult, the vehicles squished together like red caviar in a can, but Alec reversed the black sedan with practiced hands. It was like the cars the military police used in Russia. He had visions of being led to his execution. Wasn't that the way they did it here? In his home-land, you were slaughtered on the street, in a hotel room. Very few had the guts to speak for the dead.

⌒

Maks sat, looking out the car window. He hadn't seen much in the last few weeks but safe houses, train stations, and airports. He was fascinated with the snarling traffic in and around the city, the sidewalks packed with pedestrians, the multi-lane American highway system. The buildings were tall and in contrast to his homeland, new. His country had over a thousand of years of history, and the architecture showcased it with a multitude of styles from plain wooden structures to huge architectural complexes with domes and spires. There were also soulless buildings that were built with totalitarian efficiency. His first taste of America was disappointing. It was dirty, congested, and without warmth.

Was there much difference between this country and his own?

His question reverberated when he was shown into his temporary home. It had no breathing room, no aesthetics. The kitchen was small, the living room claustrophobic. He could have been in Kiev.

Alec was scanning the interior.

"It's not the greatest location but we wanted to keep you as well-hidden as we could. We're going to move you around soon, so don't get too comfortable."

Maks scanned the interior again wondering how that could happen.

"I would think this is how most of Americans live?"

"I'd say some. Not most."

Alec must have taken a second look because he changed his assessment. "Okay, most."

"I can go out?"

"Within limits. There'll always be a member of the team within reach. I don't want to take the chance that someone finds out you're here."

"They already know I'm in country. Do not be fooled."

Alec had placed his suitcase by the door. He put down his satchel and computer bag on a table in the living room.

"We've stocked the place so you won't starve. Look around. If there's anything you need, just ask."

"I will do that."

"Camille will be by this afternoon. Don't let anyone else in. We have an agent out in the parking lot as surveillance but...things can turn to shit quickly if we're not careful."

"I've survived this long. It proves I'm not stupid."

Although he still wondered how. He'd never thought he'd make it to Finland, never mind to America. Were they playing a cat-and-mouse game with him?

Time would tell.

As soon as Alec closed the door, leaving him alone in the space, he dropped down on the sofa. He couldn't relax yet. He might have achieved the first phase of his objective, but there was still a lot to do.

CHAPTER TWO

Camille left her office soon after hearing from the FBI contact. The only one who knew where she was going was her assistant, not that Sikha had any details. Never without her phone, she'd be open to communication but only for emergencies. When she agreed to work with the FBI on these kinds of cases, she became something of a covert operator. It wasn't what she'd planned on doing after law school. Fact was, she hadn't even thought about going to law school until her sophomore year in college. It had taken a crisis to make the life-altering decision, but when she'd taken the class in immigration law, she was hooked, and she knew she could affect more change in that field than in Russian studies. She'd taken the LSAT test and applied at several colleges in the area. When she was accepted to New England School of Law in Boston, she'd enrolled, knowing she'd be graduating not only with her degree but with a staggering debt that would take her years to pay down. She'd lucked out after graduation, by being in the right place at the right time, and was offered a job at a newly formed law firm in the city. It'd become the best of the best due to the legal minds of the partners, and she'd been able to pay off her loans after the first year. Living with Em that year had helped. They'd shared expenses and everything else. What she'd earned since then was gravy. Or maybe gooey, sweet icing on the cake. She'd been able to purchase a condo in South Boston that even her sister had ahed over. Camille was the baby of the family, a rebellious teenager, and a princess to boot, and they had all been pleasantly surprised when she'd done so well. Would they still be happy with her job if they knew she took risks that probably weren't prudent? The risks weren't necessary for her financial security. Asylum was her specialty, and she'd pursue it for anyone who warranted protection by the United States.

Everyone at the firm had one. Nell was a constitutional wizard, who dealt with immigrant civil rights, Em represented immigrant families, doing her best to prevent children from being separated from their parents, Jelani got the most of the DACA cases since Obama signed the Deferred Action for Childhood Arrivals and spent most of her days in court fighting to open pathways to citizenship. And they all seemed to be called on by various members of government to represent the vulnerable. Nell offered her services to immigrants at a congressman's office. Em worked with children's services. Jelani worked more in the business community where the clients were, bumped into Immigration and Customs Enforcement more than the rest of them. She didn't work with them so much as in opposition to.

⌒

Camille straightened her posture as she rode the elevator down to the lobby and walked through the elegant glass-walled space, but her legs were shaky. Without the time to begin the discovery process, she was going into the interview blind. The zip drive Alec Cleland had messengered over was in her brief case. She'd have to spend some time going over it tonight. Nate hadn't given her much to go on, just the fact that he was somehow tied to a journalist in Russia and he had some damning information that the intel community could use. If it was accurate.

Part of her job would be picking apart fact from fiction.

She might be apprehensive, but the juices were flowing. If it wasn't for the sheer black fright sweeping through her, she'd be looking forward to it. The client was Russian, so the case would involve a culture she knew almost intimately. The good and the bad. Meeting a Russian journalist who was willing to hand over information on his country would satisfy a decades-long fascination with people who defined human consciousness, those who testified to the truth in the face of death. Who was this Maksim Skolikovsky? Was he who he said he was? Was he an imposter with an agenda? A spy? A murderer?

She had to remain on guard.

With address in hand, not one of the best in the city, she drove over, her mind working the threads of what she knew. It wasn't much. For now, she'd have to count on her intuition. She wished she had more to go on than that.

After she climbed out of her car, which she'd parked in one of the slots behind the building, the agent on duty stopped her and asked for ID. Once he was satisfied, she knocked on the back door, announced herself, and waited.

The man who came to the door all but stopped her breath.

The man wasn't tall, maybe a couple of inches shy of six feet, but he had a muscular build, from what she could tell, with penetrating black eyes in an oval face. There was the beginning of a beard and his hair was on the long side with riotous curls that she envied.

It felt like she'd been hit by a hammer. She didn't have time to recover from the blow before he was telling her, "Come in."

His accent was thick, his English passable, his manner surly.

She squeezed by him and muttered, "Thank you."

She stood just inside the doorway, taking in the space. It was run-down but clean. She'd seen some of the safe houses the FBI used, and it was no better or worse than the rest.

He didn't invite her to sit down, just stood staring at her, scowling.

Not willing to let him intimidate her, she scowled back. He was the first to break the face-off.

"Alec tell me you will be asking questions. He calls it discovery. What exactly are you trying to discover?"

His voice was deeper than she'd expected, and she wasn't sure if the tingles running down her back were from fear or something else. She'd go with fear, although she couldn't show it. In her most severe tone, she asked, "Who you are, why you're here and what you want."

"I am Maksim Skolikovsky. I am from Moscow and I want asylum."

She already knew that, and she considered her next question carefully before simply asking, "Why?"

He closed all expression and her nerves tensed. Her gut was telling her there was something more going on here, and the fear began a new journey.

His answer was terse and not what she wanted.

"I have already informed FBI. Why do I need repeat it?"

This was a new experience for her. He was being contrary. Most of the people she dealt with were more than willing to share their stories if it meant gaining a visa or green card and becoming an LPR, lawful permanent resident. She often walked a delicate path, listening sympathetically while coaxing them through their tale of terror and persecution, but they were willing to walk it with her. It seemed that Maksim Skolikovsky was not.

Was he being coerced into this? And if so, by whom?

She shrugged out of her coat, laid it down on the worn sofa.

"May I sit down?"

"If you must." His tone was irascible.

While studying him, trying to determine if being rude was an aspect of his nature or some part he was playing, she sat, pulling her skirt closed over her legs. She wished she was armored in a suit. She would have felt more in control. With no court appearances today, she'd dressed down. This interview was an unexpected turn of events and she felt ill-prepared on many fronts. Part of her job was getting his story. If she could slip beneath the veneer, she'd have a better idea of how to work him.

She pulled her briefcase onto her lap and lifted out the file she'd started. The twelve-page application would expand over time to become a monstrous paper trail of where he'd lived, worked, played, suffered. Extracting a pen, she balanced the folder on her lap and looked up.

His arms were crossed over his chest, and her heart sank. He'd erected an impenetrable wall in one smooth motion. This was not going to be easy. She should have been better prepared. She knew where he came from. The country was run according to lynch law, which consisted of retaliation, corruption, and murder. He probably trusted no one with his pound of flesh. He'd be out of his mind if he did.

Deciding the best way to handle this would be more conversational in nature, she put the file back in the side compartment of her briefcase and asked, "Why don't you tell me a little bit about yourself?"

"Like what? Name, rank, and serial number?" His tone was distinctly mocking.

"You are not a prisoner. If I have it right, you contacted us; we didn't reach out to you."

He glared at her, the scowl back in place. He didn't refute it.

"Has Alec explained the application process?"

"He says I will be interviewed. By you, I assume."

"I'm the first in a long line of interrogators. You'll have to talk to Homeland Security, Immigration, someone from the Department of Justice, and the list could expand from there."

She had a feeling there'd be even more interrogations before this was over. There was a rampant flow of Russians coming in and out of the country, but due to the election hack, the long arm of the Justice Department was taking a closer look at them all.

"That seems like waste of time."

She couldn't disagree but that's the way it was done.

"My job is to fill the application out, send for all pertinent documents that would justify asylum. There are three basic requirements. I must establish that you fear persecution, that you'd be persecuted on one of many grounds such as race, religion, political opinion or I can try to establish that the Russian government is involved in the persecution. If I understand your situation correctly, you'd be eligible for asylum due to the fact that the FSB is seeking to redefine the definition of high treason to include sharing any information with a foreign state that they deem hurtful to national security."

His eyes burned into her.

"You know this."

"I told you, I read everything I can get my hands on. I've represented Russians before. I know personally how the authorities use the tax-evasion threat as often as they can. They know it works. People back down or get dead."

He paled, his hands becoming fists.

"They pass law so anyone who obtains information through open sources can be accused of treason. They want nothing to get out. My punishment for bringing it here will be no more severe than if I stay in Moscow. I have no fear of death."

There was a shimmer of admiration. He hadn't flinched even knowing what happened to people who told the truth in his country.

"Once you left the country, they lost the ability to exile you. They could issue a red notice, but I don't think any of the countries in NATO would move on it. Especially if we can get you granted asylum here."

"Only important people are exiled. Like Kasparov. The FSB can arrest and convict in absentia."

"But they wouldn't dare touch you here."

"If you say that, then you do not know them as well as you think you do."

His stare was unsettling her, so she dropped her eyes as she thought about what he'd just said. He was probably right but she wouldn't dwell on that right now.

"Have you suffered at the hands of the Russian government in the past?"

"Many have. But I have not in way you imply."

She had to be careful when phrasing the next question. She couldn't use the word *fear*.

"Is your...need for asylum based on what you've uncovered?"

"*Ja.*"

"Because you're a journalist?"

He turned away, giving her the impression he didn't want her to see his face. Was he about to lie?

"I am...I worked for one of papers that prints truth. It is in Ukraine. Several...peers have been killed over the last several years. I thought it time to take the story to another agency."

One just recently. She remembered reading the article in the *Times*, not front page, but then she never bothered with headlines. The woman had been a journalist for the newspaper *Reform,* based in Ukraine. The name of the newspaper wasn't what it suggested. It had become the word synonymous with crime, hunger, and rampant inflation. Democracy had lost its appeal when violence and corruption became the norm.

"There was a woman killed there a few weeks ago. Nina Cherepnev. She was found in a hotel with her throat slashed. They said it was a suicide."

He spun around, faced a wall. Had he winced? Gagged? He was slightly bent over, his hands on his hips.

She gave him a moment to compose himself before asking, "You knew her?"

She had a feeling he more than knew Nina. Had he seen the body? The article mentioned that it was a bloody death scene.

Or had he perpetrated the crime?

When he turned around to face her, he wore a grave expression; his complexion was white like glue. "We worked together. Your FBI already know that. If any of you believe it was suicide, I've come to wrong place."

She began to chew on her nail but caught herself, clasping her hands in her lap to stop the urge. It was a nervous habit that had no place here. She couldn't let him see she was unsettled. There was still a lingering reservation about his complicity in Nina's death. He was acting the part of aggrieved friend but...

"Most of the deaths today are suspicious and not what they seem. Do the police have you down as a person of interest?"

"There are no suspects. The government kills with impunity. They never bother to investigate own hits. Would be waste of time. Besides, they cannot tie me to Nina. Not to say they wouldn't if it serves agenda."

"She was taken out on purpose."

It wasn't a question. She didn't have to ask. She knew more than most about what was going on over there.

"It is as plain as nose on your face."

Her eyes were drawn to his nose. It was straight, almost aristocratic. He wasn't what she'd expected when she knocked on the door.

Shaking the thought out of her head, she asked, "Did she work on the stories you've supplied the FBI?"

Nina was well-known in journalistic circles, in human rights circles. She'd won awards from various news agencies. It was no surprise that she'd been silenced. What did surprise her? That this man was here telling her story. Nina concentrated on her own country's barbarity. Her main thrust was stories concerning Crimea, the peninsula that had been part of Ukraine until Russia annexed it. The area was in turmoil, with protestors jailed, tortured, and killed. She'd also written about the Kremlin-backed party in power, exposed the corruption, and dissected how they were betraying their people. She'd been willing to die to disseminate the information. Nothing would have stopped her except the cold-edged steel of a knife. What would the United States do with this kind of information?

He studied her before he began to pace. The rangy body was mesmerizing, and she had to snap herself out of the hypnotic spell he put her under.

What the hell was wrong with her?

When the voice became a growl, she was able to put her mind back on why she was here.

"She worked on own."

"Why did you bring her notes and unpublished articles here?"

"She suggested before her death."

"I've read some of her work. She was formidable."

His eyes shot up to meet hers as if surprised at her admission.

"You have read her?"

She studied him with a cool stare, examining his movements, his facial expression. She didn't think he was a danger to her, but she couldn't let her guard down.

"Yes."

He stopped his pacing and met her eyes with his own.

"Why?"

She could feel his eyes boring into her, as if to read her soul. She offered him the truth and hoped he knew it when he heard it.

"My great-great-grandfather was born in St. Petersburg, fought in World War I and the revolution before immigrating to France in the 1920's. It piqued my curiosity about the culture, the reasons he left his homeland. I study up on the current laws when I get a client from that part of the world. I read anything credible that comes out, more so now since it seems the Russian government interfered in our election."

He cautiously moved away from her, running his hands through his hair.

"You say you are attorney, that you represent Russians. What kinds of cases you handle?"

"Mostly asylum. Not all of them come from the FBI. We have thousands of people coming here to avoid persecution and I seem to have an aptitude for that. It's all in how you answer the questions on the application."

To win asylum, she had to prove that the applicant had a well-founded fear of reprisal if returned to the country of origin. The file had to contain sufficient collaboration to support the claim, no matter the veracity. It had to go through multiple agencies: Homeland Security, federal immigration, varied courts of appeal, and the State Department. Embedded in the process were systematic problems that had not been smoothed away in decades, and reform was still no more than a whisper of an idea in the most liberal of minds. It was a technical and complicated process, one that she'd learned to mine with intuition and perseverance. She would have to spend hours with this man to document his story and prove his vulnerability.

"You are closing borders."

The percentage of applicants who were ultimately granted asylum was small; the numbers of undocumented persons being allowed in for it were dwindling.

"We haven't yet."

There was a spreading sneer on his face.

"Your government is as corrupt as ours."

"I wouldn't go that far but it's more corrupt than people admit."

"Heads in sand."

"Or up their ass."

She caught what she said and blushed.

"I'm sorry. That's not something I should be saying to someone interested in living here, especially if they're clients."

"I am client?"

She stood, her eyes meeting his. They were darker than she'd first thought. "You are."

Picking her coat up, she put it on before grabbing her briefcase by the handle. Before she moved toward the door, he asked, "What do you tell Alec? Everything we talk about?"

Studying him for a minute, she saw something akin to fear. Maybe he was more afraid of what could happen to him than he was letting on. Reassuring him in part, she said, "No. That's confidential. I have a fiduciary relationship with you as of now. I will be exploring whether you have the right to be here. That's part of the job and those aspects will be shared, but if I find that you pose a threat to the country, then my fidelity reverts to the government, and I will do what I can to get you sent back. If I discover that you are telling the truth, then I will fight as hard as I can for you to be granted asylum."

"I am not here because I want to be but because of promise I made."

"Nina?"

"Her, *ja*. And to...myself. Those who took—her life will be punished in one way or other. If I can, I will take down everyone in Russia who had hand in it, from top down."

"I have a lot of information to sift through tonight. I'll be back tomorrow, and we can talk some more."

She showed herself out without another word.

CHAPTER THREE

Camille sat in her car without moving. Maksim Skolikovsky was not what he appeared.

That was the voice in her head, her gut telling her there was something else going on. Did she think he might be in danger from something? Yes. Did she think he was a journalist? No.

She'd seen them, talked to them, knew them. One from the *Washington Post* was a good friend of hers. They lived life in questions. The ones he'd asked hadn't been probing, open-ended.

And there was anger. Deep-seated anger at Nina's death—or something he wasn't telling her, and if revenge was on his mind, the question became, who did he want to punish and how? Was he blaming the West for lack of outrage, for allowing the Russian government's brutality, their intrusive and unlawful occupation of Crimea, or the ease with which they were killing those speaking out against the tyranny?

These were the questions she'd have to find answers to and she'd begin by reviewing the material Alec had given her.

After starting her car, she eased out into traffic and headed home. On the way, she planned on stopping for take-out and a bottle of good wine. Her cooler was empty, and she needed it after the interview. Maksim was a striking man and she didn't like how her body had responded to his. She was not going to fall into a false sense of security like she had before. Friendship was not part of the equation here, and she had to keep that fact front and center. Although it wasn't friendship on her mind but something much more dangerous. When the Blue tooth signaled a call from her sister, she hit answer and let Solange's voice fill the interior of the car.

"Can you come for dinner?"

"Unfortunately, I'll have to take a rain check. I have a lot of work waiting for me at home."

"That's the third rain check this month."

She took the exit that put her on the Mass Pike, maneuvering the BMW into the swell of cars.

"I just saw you at Thanksgiving. Doesn't that cross one off?"

"No. That's a family day and we don't get you for Christmas. That one's owed us."

"I didn't know you were keeping track?"

"I have to. You work too much. And I miss my little sister. We didn't get to talk much that day."

Her extended family made the day more a circus than a holiday. Aunts, uncles, cousins filled her Aunt Aline's home in Lowell and there was never the time to have an in-depth conversation with anyone.

"Soon. I promise."

"After your ski trip?"

"I had to cancel that. Something's come up that I've got to work on over the weekend. Em's not happy with me right now."

"It seems you've got rain checks out all over the place."

After looking in her rearview mirror, making sure there was an opening, she moved to the exit lane and yielded, merging into South Boston traffic.

"I'm almost home. I'll call at the beginning of next week."

"I'm keeping you to that, Camille. I thought once you made partner, you'd get a break from the grueling schedule."

"The election has everyone on edge. We've had more calls than Arianna knows what to do with. She's been interviewing and we've got sit-downs with some of the potential hires next week. It should help."

It was something else she'd have to add in her day book. It was too full as it was. Now, with Maksim Stolikovsky, she'd have time for even less. It helped that the case intrigued her.

"I guess I'll talk to you next week. I love you."

"Love you, too. Bye."

She pulled into her driveway and shut off the engine.

Shit.

She dropped her head to the steering wheel. She'd forgotten all about the food and wine. Now she'd have to make do with what was in her refrigerator. Or pantry. Grocery shopping was never high on her list of priorities and she'd be lucky if she found anything more than crackers and cheese. She'd cut around mold a few times to get something in her stomach before an all-nighter.

And tonight would be that. The zip drive was probably full, and she'd have to ingest a lot of information before she met Maksim again tomorrow. She wanted to be fully prepped for her next go-round with the Russian.

⌐

After changing into a pair of jeans and a sweater, she uncorked an open bottle of wine left over from a few nights ago when Em had brought over dinner. Her kitchen was sleek, with clean lines, and stainless-steel appliances, and she was sure a cook would be in heaven. She'd never invested much time here. It's not like she couldn't cook but would rather spend her time doing more important things. Taking a sip of the dark red merlot, she compressed her lips at the flat taste, shrugged her shoulders, and carried it and a bowl of soup to her desk. The can of soup that had been way back in her pantry. She'd checked the expiration date before heating it up, satisfied it was still good. The date, not necessarily the flavor.

She booted up her personal computer, digging into her overstuffed brief-case for the zip drive while waiting for it to come up. After inserting the thumb, she moved the mouse to open the file.

It read like a journal and she could tell it was Nina's work by the writing style.

Had Nina had plans to publish it as a book? Was this what had gotten her killed?

Nina's missive explored the troubled political spirit of the Russian peoples over the centuries. There was a more lethal and hypocritical aspect to the current regime. They spoke as if they considered themselves a democratic society while doing all in their power to bring democracy to its knees. For several hours, she read about the atrocities going on in both Ukraine and Chechnya, all at the Russians' hands. A re-iteration on what was going on in Putin's Russia. The press was muzzled, as fake news pumped out of the state-held media, elections were abolished, with cronies being assigned political positions, nationalism was thriving as citizens tried to figure out who they were and how they fit in the world's hierarchy, corruption was eating up a third of the state budget, judges were practicing telephone justice, rubber-stamping the directive as to how to resolve a case. The Kremlin was forcibly taking the country back to their glory days of the 1930's when Stalin ruled with an iron hand.

It was scary to see how closely the incoming president resembled in thought and deed the persona who was leading Russia on its backward journey in time. He was using deflection, blaming others, censuring those who disagreed with him, turning truth on its head, rambling about inconsequentials like rally size, and applying a braggadocio attitude on how he was going to make America great again. The president-elect was taking them back to the fifties, when racism and radical nationalism were at their peak. Instead of offering condolences to the families of those dead at the hands of the police, rioters, and white supremacists he was ramping up the divisive rhetoric that had gotten those balls rolling. His base didn't care how violent it got, even voted in a candidate for Congress who'd assaulted a member of the press. First Amendment rights, civil rights, and women's rights were being vilified, the interests of the people ignored, and there was no outline for policies that would improve lives. The president-elect was shamelessly lying to the public, and the election had plunged much of the country into a deep depression. The oppositional party was doing nothing to promote their agenda, instead willfully ignoring those disenfranchised, being painted as elitists whose political correctness had reached absurd proportions.

Russians had passed the point when someone could have stopped their trajectory into the past. She had to believe her country would save itself in time.

Nina had outlined it all, compared and contrasted the slippery slope they were sliding down. It was nothing she hadn't read before, but this time she read it as a precursor to where America was headed. It still shocked her that people could be so easily seduced by a conman, one who had ties to the evil empire. To find out that Russia had been complicit in turning her country's election on its ear, doing what it could to undermine democracies around the world was repulsive. That they'd been successful, even more so.

Deciding to take a break, her neck sore, her eyes strained, she took her dirty dish to the sink, washed it, and left it to dry on the side-board.

She poured herself the last of the wine and drank it down in one gulp.

She'd taken in a lot for one night, but none of it told her why Maksim Skolikovsky was here. What she'd read were Nina's perceptions. Where was

Maksim's contribution? Had Alec given her the wrong thumb drive? Nothing so far had given her a reason Maks' life was in danger. She couldn't start the application process until she had more facts. Which meant she'd have to try again tomorrow, get in touch with Alec if she couldn't pull any information out of Maks. With nothing more she could do, she stripped down and climbed into bed. Beginning to shiver from the chill of the December night, she dragged her duvet up under her chin and fell into a deep sleep, with visions of a dark-eyed Russian. She was dancing away from the glint of steel he held in his hand.

⌒

Maks got up from his makeshift desk, stretched his back like a cat might, then rubbed his burning eyes. Sitting and trolling for hours, he'd popped in and out of sites, searching for any other information he could find. He had assembled a dossier that was as thick as an ancient Russian oak. And it continued to grow. He wasn't nearly done. He would spend the rest of his life, no matter how long that was, uncovering the duplicity of his government. That was wrong thinking. It was his no longer. Would he be able to find a home here? Did he even want to? Betrayal lurked in every country's history. His had gone through many sieges through the centuries, invasions, poverty, brutality. When the Communist Bloc shattered, there had been hope that they could find the road to freedom, but the people were tired. They had let the unthinkable happen when they'd re-elected a former member of the KGB as their president. When Yeltsin had handed the country over to a brute, it was a cataclysmic event in the making. The current leader would never shed the cloak of secrecy, corruption, or power he'd worn throughout his military life. Not only his countrymen were paying but the world, as well. Dirty fingers were in every pie, contaminating all he touched. It had become a Mafia state. When would the world wake up? Why did every head of government appease him?

There had been one who hadn't. Maks had seen the picture on-line and had been instantly impressed. A snapshot of a staring contest between two world leaders, the United States president not amused. Strength, intimidation in reverse, on course to condemn and deny.

But that man would soon leave office and in his place would stand another fool. Maybe the biggest of all. Would these Americans care that the man had worked closely with the enemy to secure his position? Would all the work he had done over the last two years go for naught? Would he want to live in a country where this could happen? Was he swapping one homeland for another with the same kind of limited thinking and the same disregard for the rights of others?

He looked around the cramped space. It wasn't that much different than the one he'd left. The one he'd returned to, to pack a few of his things before going on the run.

It had taken only a few hours after finding the dead body for the process of immigration to be put in place, even though it had taken weeks to put it into action. Leaving Moscow, he'd rushed to the newspaper agency Nina had worked for. Huddling in the editor's small office, he'd cried as he told the story of finding the body, his grief at the waste of life unbearable and a reminder of what else he'd lost. She would be missed, like all the other journalists who had gone before, over twenty killed since Putin took office, shot, strangled, poisoned, butchered. No one had yet been convicted of murder. News agencies were afraid to report on any topic that could anger the Kremlin. Reporters were becoming puppets. How many more would be willing to sacrifice their lives to tell the truth of what was going on?

After debating the pros and cons of staying in country, Nina's boss had decided that Maks would bring his story to light in another part of the world, where there was less likelihood of getting killed for it. The editor had made a call to one of his sources. A woman had shown up close to midnight, picking Maks up and transporting him across the border into Finland. What he'd taken with him was everything Nina had collected for the next round of articles, what he had uncovered, and a few personal belongings. He'd hidden in Helsinki for close to two weeks, living in the American Consulate, while the CIA and FBI put his papers in order, checked out his story. Once they'd given the green light, he was sent to France, accompanied by one of the ambassador's aides.

It was the first time he'd flown, and his agitation had multiplied.

There were crowds of people, and the sickening fear of being detected was amplified. He searched each face, looking for the assassin sent to take him out, frustration of being visible mounting with every step he took, causing his thoughts to blank. He'd tugged the scarf he'd worn off, overheated by the mass of bodies, and blindly followed the aide assigned, into a private waiting room. The chatter in his head telling him to calm down was incessant. His nerves had settled into a jitter when he was able to avoid the line longs at the counter and the people scurrying between gates. His anxiety level had risen

again as he was escorted to the gate by several airport security guards, the loud
noises from the intercoms creating havoc, scrambling his brain. Gratefully he
was moved through security without pause, his computer satchel, instrument
bag, and small suitcase having already been searched upon arrival. He'd spent
the flight clutching the armrest, his eyes riveted out the window, following
the endless sky until he could see the lights illuminating the runway. The airport in Orly was bigger than the one he'd left. On debarkation in Paris, there
were thousands of travelers weaving back and forth between terminals, coffee
shops, bars, and restrooms, and it would either make it safer for him, or he'd
be less apt to protect himself. He didn't know what was around any corner.
He'd never seen so many people gathered in one place. Alec Cleland, the man
they were calling his handler, had escorted him off the plane. He didn't look
like the thugs in the FSB, the acronym for the Federal Security Bureau, which
was a renamed version of the KGB. They killed with impunity. Alec was more
mild mannered, although he was built like a tank, and he knew he'd be well
able to protect him. He just hoped it wouldn't be with his life.

He'd been mildly surprised they'd gotten here safely, even though they
were taking every precaution to keep him alive. There was an agent outside
the apartment and a new one would arrive every few hours.

He peeked outside to make sure the man was still on guard. He was and it
should have re-assured him, but he was still on edge, still worried that the
strong arm of Russian law would find him and expunge his entire existence.
As long as they waited until he'd given testimony—

His stomach growled. With the intention of satisfying his hunger, he
moved to the tiny kitchen. There was a steak from the supermarket wrapped
in plastic that he'd seen earlier, so he prepped the broiler, scrubbed a few potatoes. He'd already inspected the appliances, had experimented with how
they worked. He was impressed with how quickly the flame came up, how
modern the machinery was. Growing up in a small town under Communist
rule, with antiquated appliances and only three restaurants, all offering the
same fare, he'd become accustomed to going without. Moving to Moscow
was like moving to another country. The bloc had crumbled by then and all
the satellite states were scrambling to find their own identity. Parts of the
country did well; others did not. He was beginning to think that here, no matter how poor, you had the necessities, a stove, heat, food. Where he came
from, nothing was a given. People were pulled out of their homes, tortured

and killed for no reason. Journalists were gunned down in the streets. Lawyers were hanged or dismembered. Assassins were around every corner.

He shut down the stove, put away the food when the image of Nina, blood pooling everywhere, congealed and already dried, came rushing back into his mind. He forced the bile that threatened back down, as he had done when he'd knelt by the bed. He'd known immediately there was nothing he could do to save her. She'd stared lifelessly at the ceiling, when only hours before it was where they had made love. He wiped his clammy forehead as he reviewed that day again, still wondering why he'd gone off that afternoon. She'd asked him to run an errand and he'd done her bidding, as always. Could he have stopped the bloodbath, or would he have died beside her?

He'd never know.

Needing to wipe away the grizzly scene from his memory, he stripped down and stepped into the shower, letting the hot water pound against his skin. After lathering his body, he scrubbed until he hurt in a different way. He'd never hear her laugh again, never be able to listen to her view of the world, never look into her eyes and see determination and grit shining there. He let the emotion and grief wash over him as well, the overwhelming feeling of powerlessness mind-numbing.

After wiping himself down, he put on sweats and a jersey, all provided for him by the U-S of A. He could tell they weren't government standard issue. They were more comfortable than his own clothes, and he sunk into the sofa and tried to get his mind off his misery.

It turned to Camille Bissonnette. She'd said she had ancestors born in Russia but Bissonnette wasn't a Russian name. Had she told him that to get him comfortable, to get him to talk? He had to remember to trust no one. There were people who infiltrated positions such as hers. Was she an attorney or an assassin? No one knew who was who anymore. But she faintly resembled Nina. Blond hair, round face. Where Nina's hair was short, Camille's had long, flowing tresses that he thought would feel like silk. Fumbling over that thought, he moved on to her personality. She was more reticent, less self-assured even though she tried to hide that fact from him. He'd lived with a strong woman, could read her moods, knew when she was battling diminished confidence in her abilities. He'd regarded her with a critical squint. She hadn't looked like an attorney. Her long, blond hair was wavy and cascaded in disarray down her back. Her neck was long, her button-down jersey leaving enough exposed skin to make his attention wander. Grey-blue eyes were penetrating, her lips well defined and tempting. Was she a Mata Hari sent to unravel him and his story? He had to beware. He'd heard stories about the people here. Some of them he knew were outright propaganda, but the others? He would have to go on what Nina had told him. That the First Amendment, freedom of speech, was at the root of their liberties. That it was protected and revered. Would these people believe what he had found? What Nina was collating for print for him? Or would he find that it was just lip service with no basis in fact, like in Moscow?

He had taken some time and explored Ms Bissonnette on-line. She was accomplished. Her bio read like a textbook on asylum. She gave talks at colleges in the area, at lawyer conferences, at immigration centers. Alec might be correct when he said he could trust her, at least as far as naturalization. It would take more than a five-star rating on Yelp for him to trust her with his life.

His stomach rumbled again but there was nothing he could do for it. It had been almost twenty-four hours since his last meal, right before boarding the plane in France, but he was still too nauseous to eat.

He sat in the dark, in an old recliner, and let the strangeness of the place move through him. He had no lover, no friends, and no one to trust. His world had been a cold one. Since arriving, the ice was setting in.

CHAPTER FOUR

Camille got up early, thoughts of the Russian still consuming her, and she didn't know why. She'd never been consumed by a case, or more truthfully, a man before, and it was playing havoc with not only her mind but with her body. She had a full and busy day ahead, and she knew that if she didn't talk to him before her first appointment, she'd be working at half efficiency. She was only one cog in the governmental machinery that would be examining Maks' life from birth to his arrival here, and she had to assume she knew the least of any of them. In the past, she'd been given what she needed to do her job, but this time around had been different. She was sure she didn't even have his real name, never mind birth date, passport information or any background to base her discovery on.

The why was bothering her.

Who was he? And why was the FBI keeping him so closely guarded and under wraps? It spoke to a bigger investment than a journalist would yield. Nate had said he had handed over damaging information on the Kremlin. Where had he gotten it? From Nina? From another source he refused to name? Or had he scored it on his own? What would that mean if he had?

There was a possibility that he was one of the many who'd been hired by the Russian government to flood the internet with fake news. Was he one of the election hackers? Was he one of the bot trolls? Convinced that his name was bogus, she had proven her impression correct when she'd googled Skolikovsky and got nothing. The only sites that came up related to vodka. It would be a fitting pseudonym.

As she sipped her coffee, she went over the conversation she'd had with Nate, to see if there was something she'd missed or if there was something she could read between the lines.

The journalist story just didn't ring true. She'd bet her life it wasn't.

The material she'd gone over last night didn't hold the key as she'd hoped it would. She'd learned nothing about him from Nina's notes.

Most of the journal resembled a day-to-day account of corruption, names and places damaging and credible. There had been a brief passage in the hundreds of pages she read that dealt with the American election, that it had indeed been sabotaged, but it didn't amount to more than a few sentences. There was a mention of Guccifer 2.0, an entity that dumped stolen information into an open Word Press page and the phrase *three-dimensional chess*. It wasn't the kind of article Nina was known for, but she had no idea how it brought Maks into the mix. Unless those passages were Maks' contribution. Had he found evidence that would prove the theory that Russian hackers were behind all the leaks? Would it lead to congressional inquiries? Or would it be swept under the rug like all the other things that had come to light? It didn't seem like there was anyone in charge of damage control. For as much as the Democrats were screaming foul, the Republicans were going about business as usual.

If this was the kind of thing Maks was dabbling in, he would be in even more danger than she'd initially thought. And not just at the hands of the Russians. He'd be under a microscope here in the States as well. The difference: he wouldn't be facing a firing squad. They hadn't started murdering whistle-blowers here yet.

Her curiosity was heightened by the time she left her condo, and she couldn't wait to see Maks again. Although some of the reasons were not what they should be.

⌐

Camille rang the doorbell. And waited.

She knew he was here. When she'd called Alec to tell him she was going over, he said he appreciated the early-morning detour, that Maks would be on FBI time every afternoon.

She must have startled him awake, because he was rubbing an eye when he peeked through the thick curtains that covered the window.

Apparently, he was still half-asleep. He let her in without thought or grumble.

She rushed through the door as soon as he opened it. And stared. His chest was covered in nothing but swirls of dark hair, his jeans unsnapped. His feet were bare, and he looked...mouth wateringly good. She caught herself before she gave him a head-to-toe examination, her gaze faltering when she got to the waist band of his pants. The gut check snapped her out of the haze of desire and she shifted her eyes to his.

"Sorry if I woke you. I picked up coffee. I've heard Russians like it strong, but I can't promise anything. I got a Robust but just how robust it is, you'll have to tell me."

She set the tray down on the counter and shrugged out of her coat, still a little shaky from the way he looked. She'd thought she'd be in better control than yesterday, more prepared for the meeting even though there were lingering reservations about who he was and what he wanted. She'd taken time with her morning ritual, pampering herself more than usual, lounging in the bath, slathering her body with the lotion she'd purchased in France, applying her make-up with a skilled hand. Dressed as the professional she was, she'd felt more in command of the situation. Until he'd opened the door.

After extricating her cup out of the paper four-hold carton, she took a sip, skirted by him, and went straight to the room they were in yesterday. She felt his hot eyes boring into her back.

"Please. Make yourself at home."

He'd finally woken up. His tone was more of what she was used to, patronizing, but she brushed it off as she smoothed the surface of the sofa before taking a seat.

"Thank you. I will. There's a bag with some donuts in it. I didn't know if you'd be hungry."

"Donuts for breakfast? Is that how you start your day?"

"I don't usually have time to make myself breakfast."

"I do. And before I sit through third degree, I will eat."

He disappeared from the doorway and into the kitchen. She heard the refrigerator open and close, a pan set to the stove, and her curiosity drove her to get up and investigate.

She lounged against the wall as he cut up some ham, peppers, and onions and inhaled the aromatic mixture as soon as it was sautéing in the pan, her stomach growling in anticipation. Would he make enough for two?

"You cook?"

"If I want to eat."

That was where they were different. If she wanted to eat, she picked up something from the local organic grocery store. This morning's donuts were an anomaly. She'd prefer some delicate French pastries, but that bakery wasn't on her way.

He cracked almost a dozen eggs into a bowl and scrambled them with a touch of milk, salt, and pepper before pouring them over the other ingredients. It sizzled.

"Make yourself useful. There is bread there. Put pieces into toaster."

She straightened, hoping the invitation to help was an invitation to share and followed his directive.

"This beats out the canned soup I had for supper last night."

He shook his head and she felt sufficiently chastised.

She watched his movements, surprised at his wiry build. He had more muscle than she'd originally thought and there was unexpected rippling of his shoulders. She didn't know many journalists who had such a solid core. They ate on the run, chasing headlines. It was another piece of this puzzle that didn't fit.

As soon as he handed her a plate, the toast now buttered and sitting at the edge of the omelet, she followed his lead and sat down at the tiny table.

With a gruff voice, he waved his fork in her direction and commanded, "Eat."

As she took a bite, her taste buds came alive. The eggs were fluffy, the ham and onions giving them all the added flavor they needed.

"This is good. Thank you."

All she got was a grunt in return for her gratitude.

On closer inspection, she thought the non-answer might be due to sleep deprivation. He looked tired. His eyes were bloodshot, his stubble more than a day old, his skin on the pasty side.

"Didn't you sleep well?"

"Have not slept well since— for a few weeks."

That would put it around the time of Nina's death. She could relate to that. After her assault, it had taken her weeks to sleep through the night.

She broke apart the toast, and held a small piece in her hand when she asked, "Where did you go when you left Russia?" before popping it into her mouth.

"Left Ukraine. Went to Finland."

She pondered that. It rode the border of western Russia and would have been a neutral site. At least for now. Finland was bracing for an invasion, unsure that Russia would leave them to their own brand of government. It seemed it wasn't safe anywhere in Europe. If it wasn't terrorists, it was a country poised to take over parts of the world.

Would there be no one to stop them?

"How long were you there?"

"Couple weeks. Waited for...what you call red tape to clear."

"Then to France?"

"*Ja.*"

If this is how the interview went later, with one-word answers, it would take months for her to uncover his secrets. If he was willing to give them up. Maybe this was just his way of stalling, thinking she'd surrender. He'd soon learn she wouldn't.

"What made you come *here*?"

This country rather than another. This city rather than a bigger one more inclined to harbor this kind of refugee. Boston was not the usual locale for cases like this. She knew of only a half-dozen detainees housed here out of hundreds of FBI directed cases. She'd handled a few of them personally and there was a reason for everything the agency did. They left nothing to chance.

"I did not choose. You must ask Alec."

"I will."

He moved his fork in the direction of her plate and asked, "You liked?"

Her plate was empty, so he wasn't going out on much of a limb.

"Yes. I think I already thanked you. You grunted back, which I assumed was your way of saying, you're welcome."

She'd folded her arms against her chest. She'd show him she could be surly, too.

It might not be the honey she'd need to sweeten him up, but she had a feeling it would take more than honey, and she wasn't wasting her time or energy. She'd meet his sour mood with one of her own.

He sat back, his fork still in his hand, inwardly amused.

She'd come back cockier this morning than she'd been yesterday and seemed willing to go toe to toe with him down the road of irascibility. The scent of lavender and rosemary floated around her, her pale pink wool suit bringing out the blue in her grey eyes. She was feminine but certainly not delicate.

His opinion of her had shifted. He didn't like that it had.

He scraped back the chair, reached over to take her plate, put it on top of his own, and took them to the sink. He'd started the coffee before they began to eat, and the aroma assured him it would be as strong as he liked it. The robust she'd brought him was laughable. After dumping the brew out of the paper cup, he poured himself a new and improved serving. Turning to her, he asked, "Refill?"

"I don't need hair on my chest, but thanks for the offer."

His brow furrowed.

"Hair on chest?"

She found herself staring at his chest again and dipped her eyes before she began to drool.

"It means it's a manly kind of brew. Too strong for the likes of me, a mere female."

"I think you are not mere."

"You think right. It is kind of a chauvinistic saying."

Her eyes sparked when they met his, a hint of a smile on her face. It lightened her features, the crinkles proving she didn't take life as seriously as she let people think.

"Will you be coming here every day?"

"No. Only until I can get the right framework for the application. I need to gain an understanding of who I can contact for your defense, amass concrete evidence that it would be disadvantageous to send you back."

"Is certain death disadvantage?"

"It is. It's up to me to prove it and convince the courts that I'm right. We need to give intricate detail on the disadvantage. Have you been tortured?"

"*Nyet.*"

"Threatened?"

"*Nyet.*"

"Imprisoned?"

"Not yet."

"I know you're involved in some kind of espionage, at least the Kremlin-sanctioned kind. Have you participated in any protests or any other event that might put you on their watch list?"

"*Ja* to the first."

He was standing against the counter, one foot on top of the other, thinking.

"I haven't attended protests in long time. I might be on watch list but I'm not sure. The FBI might know. They provided me escape."

"And they need an attorney to put it all into the legal language the courts love. I've been tag teamed."

"Tag teamed?"

"They hired me to pick up where they leave off."

"Hand you baton. Like in relay race."

"Exactly."

He was rinsing off the dishes as he talked, not wanting to look at her directly. There was something about her he was beginning to like. It was not smart to drop his guard. He still didn't know what her agenda was. It could be what she explained. It could also be something else entirely. Lawyers where he came from circumvented the law too often for him to trust this one.

"I need shower. You wait?"

"I will. I'll be in the other room. Do you have Wi-Fi here?"

"*Ja.*"

"I'll do some work while you're gone."

"You do not waste moment."

"I don't have any to waste."

"What other case are you working?"

"Cases. I have a dozen I'm filing. A couple dozen more interviews lined up. There's never a shortage of persecution taking place in the world."

He studied her as he backed out of the room. There was something about her that called to him. If he was smart, he'd ignore it. Not only because he didn't know if he could trust her, but because Nina was not even a month in the grave.

⌒

Nate was comparing notes with Alec in his office. It was cramped, the treadmill taking up a good portion of the closet-size space. He leaned forward in the one good chair. Alec got the metal back. It was uncomfortable to say the least. The government didn't spend money foolishly on things like that.

Alec held the thick file, leafed through the pages, the highlighter indicating key points in florescent green.

"I still can't believe what's contained in this dossier."

"He's spewing out reams of information every day."

"I know. I can barely keep up. Was he pissed you had to terminate *Matrixiator*?"

"I think he understood we couldn't take the chance of someone picking up that trail."

They'd told the subject to choose several user names and utilize them all. He'd laughed. Called them amateurs. Told them it wouldn't take long for those following him to figure it out.

Alec knew he was right.

"Where are you moving him to next?"

"The house in Brighton should be ready for him within the next forty-eight hours."

Hefting the thick dossier, Alec asked, "Are you going to give Camille the details?"

"No. It's on a need-to-know basis and she isn't in need yet."

He disagreed. He might be the agent handling Maxim Skolikovsky but he answered to Nate, so the decision was not in his hands. It didn't stop him from voicing his opinion.

"We're leaving out some key pieces. Is that fair to her?"

Nate chuckled as if this was some joke in the grand scheme of things.

"When did we ever consider being fair?"

"I think we owe her that after the last detainee. She didn't choose this kind of life. We did."

"She'll get what she needs for her part in this. We need paperwork filed."

"She'll need to prove he's in danger. She can't do that unless—"

"He *is* in danger. If only as Nina's co-conspirator."

He was more than that and Nate knew it. They finally had a living witness and a first-hand account of what was going on in cyberspace, with details that could help them shape a case against Russia and some American co-conspirators for their intervention in the election.

"We haven't even given her his name. How can she find anything on a man who doesn't exist? I don't like it."

"Are you getting soft in your old age, Alec?"

"No, just getting sick and tired of the games we have to play."

"That why you're putting in for a transfer?"

"I need a break from all of this. The world is going crazy. And for as much influence as we have, we can't affect the kind of change to...—change anything."

"One small step at a time. Being in Homeland Security won't take you away from the bullshit, you'll just be feeding another form of it."

He knew what Nate was saying was true, but he was still putting his application in for the job that had recently been posted.

"Who knows about the file?"

"Everyone at the top. CIA, FBI, DOJ, NSA, all IC supervisors, the president."

"Why wasn't it leaked?"

"Republicans didn't want any distractions for their run at the White House."

"It makes them complicit."

"It certainly does. And if what's in that dossier is true, we'll have to tap the Designated Survivor for the oval office."

"This is nuts."

"The world's become a giant jar of peanut butter."

Thick, sticky, and it could choke you if you weren't careful.

CHAPTER FIVE

When Maks returned to the living room, his hair was wet, his flannel shirt unbuttoned. Camille dropped her eyes from the open display of chest. The tingling was back with a vengeance. Wanting her mind focused on something else, she asked, "Did you work for *Reform*?"

"Not directly. Not on payroll."

"Were you feeding Nina the information?"

He disappeared into the kitchen and came back out within minutes with what she assumed was a refill of coffee, the steam suggesting it was hot. After taking a seat opposite her, he asked, "How would I do that?"

"I don't know. I'm asking you."

He looked thoughtful for a moment, as if weighing what to say.

"Nina had all sources she needed."

She leaned forward, wanting to press her point.

"You must have played some part or else your life wouldn't be at risk."

"You can say I did research."

"On what?"

"This and that."

"There were some vague passages in the file I read last night that spoke to an entity called Guccifer 2.0. Do you know who that is?"

"Anyone who follows Twitter knows who he is."

His voice was filled with contempt.

She looked at him abashedly.

"I guess I don't follow the right people then. I've never heard of him."

He stood staring at her as if he couldn't believe his ears.

"He was thief who stole information from Democratic National Committee."

"The information that was leaked?"

"*Ja.*"

"So that wasn't something you uncovered?"

"No. Well-known fact in cyberspace."

"Since when?"

"Spring."

"Are you working in cyberspace?"

"I work here in apartment."

He was being blatantly ambiguous. She let it go, beginning to get the bigger picture.

"What will happen to you if people find out?"

"You already know. You told me yourself. I will be killed."

"Can you prove it?"

"Probably not."

She flopped back against the sofa. He wasn't giving her anything she could use in granting him the protection he was asking for. She'd need to do a full biographical report, so maybe she could start at the beginning, and build from there.

"Where you were you born?"

His eyebrow arched as he considered her.

"This is important?"

"Questions about your background are part of the application. And it might give me some insight into who you are."

"I am man in need of a new country. I have chosen here."

"Why America?"

He got up and began to pace, slow steps rather than frantic ones, back and forth over the brown tweed carpet.

"Nina's mother was American citizen."

"Have you talked to her since coming here?"

"No. Never met."

"Then what is the correlation?"

"The...correlation? What is this word?"

"If you've never met her, then what does she have to do with why you're here?"

He stared at her, his expression one of contemplation. After a brief hesitation, he said, "I have hope America will take revenge for one of their own."

"Nina never lived here, did she?"

"No. Mother met father in Moscow. They married but got divorce when Nina was teenager. She chose to stay in what was home."

"Then why should we care?"

He crushed the empty paper cup and threw it against the wall. It was too light to go far and never reached its destination. Pushing his hands through his hair in frustration, he bellowed, "People should not be dying for speaking truth. Someone should care. Why not you?"

He was right, of course. But her job wasn't to defend Nina's right to justice. It was to make sure he didn't forfeit his life in the same way. She had to determine whether he would if he was sent back, and he wasn't helping her reach that conclusion.

She rose and walked to where her coat was and slipped into it.

"People should not be dying for that. I can't change the outcome of what's already happened. I can only try to change the outcome for what happens to you. Think about that, and when I come back tomorrow, I'll be looking for you to help me do that."

He saw her to the door and watched as she pulled out of the slot in back.

The agents made him promise not to give away why he was here. There would be repercussions if he broke it. Not that it took a lot of persuasion. If the truth got out, lives would be even more at risk than now. The Russian government had long fingers and could reach him no matter where he was. He had to get Camille off his back so he could accomplish what was still left to do. If he wasn't granted asylum here, he would seek it someplace else. There would be a country that would take him in. For now, he would do all he could to topple the governments that were causing the world so much chaos. It used to be just one, but soon, two leaders would be collaborating, and it was up to him to blow the whistle, sound the alarm. After striding over to the table he was working at, he sat down and began to dig.

This was a new experience for him. He'd always kept a low profile, writing computer code in his apartment, selling some of his work on an anonymous segment of the internet known as the dark web. It was where Nina had found him. When she had reached out, he hadn't a clue as to who she was. They'd met secretly a few times, discussing what he had uncovered, what she was looking for and they'd come came to a meeting of the minds. He would root around in cyberspace, tracking intelligence reports and she would expose it to the world at large. What he had stumbled on in the process was a story of significance. He began collating the evidence, turning over to Nina what she wanted on Chechnya, Crimea, and Ukraine, retaining the mass of material he collected on a cyber war that was accelerating for some future date. Over the two years they'd known each other, he had come to admire her, especially her courage in the face of mounting pressure to stop what she was doing. She'd been stalked, intimidated, poisoned and finally slaughtered. They'd become lovers a few months before her death, more from being together so often than some grand passion. Nina was not someone you could get close to, keeping all her emotions in check, unable to give more of herself than her body. Even so, when she'd been killed, he'd been devastated. And horrified. When he'd found her, he promised, to seek retribution. The way was clear in his mind. He would turn over his handiwork to a higher power. From what he could see, they would have a vested interest. Once he got to Finland, he'd contacted the American embassy and had taken the steps necessary to see it done. He didn't yet know who he could trust and who he couldn't. He'd continue to use his wiles to stay alive, using those who could help him achieve his goal.

Before he even got started, there was a knock on his door. Swearing to himself that he was being distracted from his objective, he hoped it wasn't Camille backtracking with more questions. She was a distraction with her feminine looks, long blond hair and changeable eyes.

When he got to the door, Alec was standing there, another man close at his side.

He swore again.

How many people were going to know about his existence?

As he let them in, he snarled, "What are you doing here? I thought I was to be left alone to work. And who is he?"

Alec didn't seem to mind the animosity he was going for.

"This is "Boog". He's part of the Bunker Hill Group. They're a team of eccentric computer geniuses who help me out, occasionally. He's here to move things along. We want this done as quickly as possible."

Maks looked him over. He was about thirty, wore jeans, a tee shirt that read, "YOU'RE LOOKING AT A LEGEND", an earring, and long brown hair.

The surliness was back in spades.

"I don't need help."

Alec, still sickening agreeable, said affably, "Not with content, I'll give you that. Time, though, is, as they say, of the essence."

Boog took his computer bag off his shoulder and carried it over to the table he was working at.

"I've read the dossier. You've discovered some holes that haven't been patched yet. I want to help you take advantage of them before they're sealed off."

Exploiting the zero-day vulnerabilities in a system was key to gaining information for both spies and hackers.

Maks let his guard down a half an inch. Here was someone who knew his language.

"I was surprised how easy it was."

After sliding his computer out of the bag, Boog set it down on the table, across from Maks'.

"The packets of data you've pulled out prove spot on what's been going on between your country and mine. It's my patriotic duty to work on this with you."

"My country no longer."

"Whatever."

Boog took his seat, booted up, and began typing.

Alec, seeming pleased with the way it was going, took his leave.

"Boog, or some member of the group, will be working with you for the next couple of weeks. It's why you were brought to Boston. We knew we'd get the information we need quicker with their help."

Maks watched him leave, a frown still lingering on his face.

"So, tell me. How'd you find that hole?"

Maks glanced over to see Boog's fingers flying across the keyboard. He moved to the table and sat down before answering his question. They discussed decryption, remote spying, and reverse engineering. After the small talk wore down, they both worked diligently, coding, stalking, retreating, pulling packet after packet of intelligence from the air.

⌒

Camille walked through the double doors of Woodley and Fisher later than usual. She'd be spending time with Mr. Skolikovsky every morning until she got something that could help her with the paperwork. She got the sense he didn't care as much as he should.

She needed to uncover why.

If he didn't care, then maybe Nate and Alec were blowing this all out of proportion.

She heard the squeal coming from down the hall. The flurry of activity, the voices raised in congratulatory praise told her the opinion had been posted and Nell had won. The partners were streaming out of the offices, congregating around Nell's. She scurried closer, a huge smile on Em's face. "She did it."

Jelani was all but jumping for joy, Arianna was like a proud mama, Mia was high-fiving Hani, Nell's assistant. Fist bumps went all around.

With the Supreme Court down one justice, due to Scalia's death and the Republicans denying a hearing on the outgoing president's nominee, it could have ended in a loss or a tie, but it seemed Nell was able to persuade the chief justice that her client had a right that was unalienable. She'd gotten justice for the daughter of an undocumented woman. Ramona would be getting out of detention and going home, her family back intact. They were able to celebrate until the congratulatory calls started coming in. Then they dispersed, leaving Nell to her adoring public.

Em followed her into her office and took a seat opposite the desk.

"This is huge."

"Did you ever doubt Nell would win? That woman could convince the pope to switch sides with the devil."

"This will open up so many more doors for us to use for our clients. Especially for me."

Camille sat back, a smile on her face.

"It is pretty cool that it was one of us who did it."

Em agreed before asking, "Where were you?"

"With a client."

Needing to get Em off the scent, she picked up one of her folders and flipped through the papers as if needing to check something and asked, "Have you found anyone to go with this weekend?"

"I cancelled it."

Glancing up, now feeling guiltier than ever, she asked, "Why?"

Tucking her hair behind her ear, Em looked away as if she didn't want to face her.

"Um, Nick asked if I could watch Teddy this weekend. He wants to take Saban away for a couple of days."

Feeling her blood pressure rise, wishing Em would stop answering Nick's every beck and call, she clenched her teeth so she wouldn't say something she'd regret.

"Em."

Her friend flashed her a look.

"You know I love having Teddy with me."

Teddy was Nick's four-year-old son. Em seemed to spend as much time with him as his parents did.

"I do but Nick takes advantage. You said you were going to rethink this relationship."

Em got out of the chair and headed to the door. Looking over her shoulder, she admitted, "The one with Nick, not the one with Teddy," before vacating the premises.

Camille pursed her lips. Em would have to figure it out herself. Until she did, they'd all be there with support and a shoulder to cry on.

She got down to work, pulling out another of her cases that was going to court in just over a week. The woman she was representing was from Uganda. Arrested, detained, and beaten for opposing her government, Engemu Nakato had arrived in Boston over a year ago and was still waiting for a hearing. The growing backlog in the immigration courts was making it impossible to get a speedy decision. Most of her clients were languishing in detention or living in limbo, unable to make a new start. In November alone, there were over twelve thousand asylum cases filed and only four thousand interviews had been granted. Just yesterday she'd gotten a date for Engemu's appearance, and it was set for the beginning of next week. The judge assigned was middle-of-the-road, meaning it could go either way. She'd have to fine-tune her paperwork, making sure the language was exact and there was no doubt Engemu's life was in danger if deported back.

Camille had made some rookie mistakes on her first few cases and had lost them. In one case, the judge ruled that a man named Juan, claiming persecution, was being threatened because of his position in fighting a terrorist group in Peru, not his political opinion. His request for asylum didn't meet the standards set by immigration policies. After taking the time to attend other hearings, studying the way the more successful attorneys argued cases, she'd begun to realize that the wording was key to gaining a judge's favor. Since then, she'd been able to craft the application in such a way she won more of-ten than not. Deciding to set aside the next couple of hours for a review, she hunkered down, blocking all other thought out.

It was only when she heard the buzz going on in the lobby that she put down her work. Ambling out of her office, Arianna waved her over, a bottle of bubbly in her hands.

"We're toasting the opinion and our woman of the hour before sending her out to face the press. She'll need a shot of something."

Everyone knew Nell's aversion to publicity. She liked working behind the scenes, waging her wars in the courtroom. She skipped most of the network-ing events that the rest of them attended but no one could fault her. She pulled in more business than most of them, and although many of her clients were unable to pay for her services, there were many more who could.

"Is that what all the commotion is out there?"

"It's a full house and we need our waiting room back."

After following Arianna into Nell's office, the bottle got passed around, the close-knit group discussing what it all meant.

And then Nell dropped a bomb shell.

After, Em was shaking her head as she and Camille walked the short dis-tance to her office.

"I never saw that coming."

"Me, neither. Still waters sure do run deep."

Nell had finally come clean about her eleven-year-old daughter's paternity. Chloe's dad was none other than the infamous Jack Adams, the man they'd all campaigned for since his first run for Congress.

Still stunned by the news, Em added, "She never once let on while we were hounding her to support him."

They stood just outside the doorway of Em's office, Camille ready to move into her own right next door.

"She works with his staff all the time, doesn't she?"

"She once told me she worked around his schedule. I didn't know why back then but now...—I understand."

"With him being an eleven? She has the will-power of a saint."

Camille took a breath, a sense of sadness washing over her.

"An eleven. I wonder what that's like."

She hadn't met anyone who made sex and love gel for her. Even with her college boyfriend there hadn't been the explosive coupling that could be measured an eleven. They were young and had plenty of energy but...it had never scaled that high on the sex Richter. Since then, the sex might be good, but there had never been love involved. Maybe she hadn't even been in love back then. She'd never felt the earth shake or her heart hammer. She wondered how Nell could have given it up. She'd grab on with both hands, no matter how many outside distractions there were. At least she hoped she would.

The women looked at each other and read each other's thoughts. They were both still waiting for Mr. Right to show up. The difference was: Em had found hers but he was already taken. Camille had given up looking for it.

CHAPTER SIX

Boog had left just under an hour ago and Maks already missed the comradery. It was a strange feeling. He rarely let his guard down anymore. Living in a corrupt society had made it difficult relaxing around people. Being cautious was a strategy that worked for him. It had gotten him here. There'd been an instant kinship with the computer geek, a sharing of the minds. It felt good to talk the same language, something he'd missed being a hermit.

They'd made some good progress, found a hacker who was stalking packets of political data and stealing it. Boog had created a "honey pot", which was a set of phony files. They'd spent the afternoon coming up with directories, user names, and passwords to fill it with, hoping to lure the interloper to take the program so they could trace him or her back to an address. Find out where the hacker was from. He'd helped Boog devise a worm with a beacon and tucked that inside the pot as well. Their efforts were rewarded when the pot was taken, the digital beacon leading them to an address in Moscow. It could have been a hopping point, but it gave them another source to investigate. He was pleased with the afternoon's efforts.

Now it was time to eat that steak, his hunger finally taking a more important space in his head than memory. Turning on the broiler, he waited for the coils to turn red before placing the beef under them. He popped a potato into the microwave and set the timer. While he waited, he poured himself a vodka. Alec had made sure he had a couple of bottles, at his request. It was his drink of choice. Had a tumbler full while working. It had given Boog the idea for a nickname: As a newly minted part of their group he'd be known as Skoli from now on. All the members went by pseudonyms.

He'd changed his username to Skoli.on.Ice.

He chuckled to himself. It sounded rusty to his own ears. It had been a long time since he found the humor in things.

The name fit. Being on ice, here in America, meant he was being kept safe which translated to alive.

There was something comforting in that.

Taking the meal, once it was finished, to the living room, he set up a tray table and clicked on the television. Scrolling through the stations with the remote, he was amazed at how many stations there were. There were hundreds. He settled on a show called *House Hunters*. Wanting to get a feel for Americans, he thought this would give him insight into their personalities. He watched show after show, eating the steak slowly, wanting to savor the taste and flavor. There were so many different styles of houses across the country. Cape cods and colonials in New England, Spanish style and stucco in the Southwest, mid-century modern, ranches, contemporary in the rest of the contiguous states. Some were updated, some needed renovation, some were millions of dollars, some only a couple hundred thousand. The clients seemed to look for open concept, hardwood floors, and stainless-steel appliances. These were not rich people, just average. Most in Russia thought Americans were arrogant. He was beginning to think they were more spoiled than self-important. There was still middle class here, although from what he'd read, it was shrinking.

What would they do if their country was like his? It wasn't too much of a stretch to ask. They were on the same path. The difference? Americans were fighting back, protesting, standing up against the tide that was growing. Oligarchs ruled Russia. The ultra-rich were taking over this country, as well, but freedom to speak was still available here. He would do all he could to make sure it was always so. Not for them, but to see the leaders of the nation-state come to their rightful demise.

He switched channels to find murder movies, cop shows, comedies, and sports and left on a soccer game that would at least be familiar. After the kitchen was clean, he sat back down in front of the TV and began to strum the instrument he'd brought thousands of miles with him. It soothed his soul.

Em conned Camille into going out to eat. After the soup last night, it wasn't hard to do.

She was hoping a night out with her friend would also banish some of her frustration with her latest case. Before leaving the office, she'd pulled out Maks' asylum application and, with pen in hand, stared at it, using her mental powers of persuasion to change some of the questions. Like name and age. She didn't know his point of origin, his parents names, his employment status. He said he wasn't on the payroll at *Reform*, but he must have been working somewhere to support himself. Or maybe he lived at home? She had to guess he was around her age, early to mid-thirties, but in Russia you lived with family far longer than here.

She shivered at the thought of still living at home. It had been hard when she'd been younger. Today? Impossible.

She could probably put down he was from Russia but from what district? Russia was a huge country and she couldn't begin to guess what part he came from.

Current address? He was being moved around a lot and didn't have one.

Was he married, divorced, single? She didn't want to dwell on the fact there might be a spouse.

The only box she could check was the one for gender. There was no doubt about that. He was all male.

This was becoming an addictive pursuit, one she couldn't seem to put away, but she forced herself to as soon as Em asked about supper. Checking her emails before leaving, she tied up the loose ends she'd left dangling while staring at his empty application form.

Standing inside the door of a semi-fast-food restaurant they frequented, the ambience trendy and casual, Em chatted on about the family she'd just put back together after the dad was picked up for deportation.

"The little girl was so cute, Camille. Your heart would have broken if you saw how sad she was that he was gone."

If anyone wanted children, it was Em. She lived for the day she'd have a family, was why she took Teddy so often. She didn't play a passive role, either. She took him everywhere, the park, the museum, anywhere kids would want to be. She was kind of a big kid herself. She'd boasted how much of a tomboy she'd been growing up, even before moving here. Played all kinds of sports in high school, was on the volleyball team, the basketball and softball teams, and still climbed trees. Camille's heart had been in her throat the last time Em had reached the top of the old elm in her parents' yard. Her brother Stephen's son had gotten stuck up there and Em was the one who'd played monkey to retrieve him.

It was one of the reasons she gravitated to family immigration law.

"She must have been happy when you got her father out of detention."

"I know I was."

The hostess seated them and left the menus although they knew what they wanted. They picked the same thing every time. Camille fingered the tri-fold, thinking maybe it was time for a change. After perusing the meats, pastas, and salty pig offerings, she thought better of it and went with her favorite pork dish. It reminded her of the cuisine in Spain. One of the things she loved best about traveling to different parts of the world was the food. That and experiencing different cultures. Her palette was more varied than Em who seemed to lean towards more American fare. One of these days she'd get to Russia, but there were so many worries in that part of the world, she knew it would be a few more years before it would happen. Europe wasn't any safer, if she thought about it. The bombings in France and England were becoming more and more frequent. She wasn't going to let it ground her. Then the terrorists would win.

After they placed their orders and their wine was brought to the table, Em rubbed the rim of her glass and asked, "Is there something going on with you? You've been kind of...preoccupied lately."

She shouldn't be surprised Em had noticed. They knew each other well. She could always tell when Em was feeling depressed about her relationship with Nick. Or her non-existent one.

"It's that case Nate handed me."

"Not your run-of-the-mill FBI asylum seeker?"

"No. There's too many pieces missing, and I think Alec, the guy handling the process, is keeping me well-misinformed."

Em had started picking at her appetizer, finger food that was messy but good.

"Have you interviewed the guy?"

"I've tried. All I get are one-word answers. I'm beginning to doubt he's who he says he is."

"Whoa, Cami. That's not good."

Em didn't know the half of it.

She didn't know about the Hala episode or that her confidence had disappeared in a flash of steel. Since then, there were moments when she felt heart-pounding fear. She'd never experienced those kinds of feelings before, so it was hard to analyze them or know how to re-act. Did they come from disappointment in herself that she'd that frozen at the first penetration, had been unable to defend herself? Was it guilt? She'd almost let a terrorist slip through the discovery process? Maybe it was nothing more than coming to grips with the fact that she was going to die one day.

Up until she saw the glint of the knife, she'd never thought much about it. Not even when someone she cared deeply about was killed when she was younger.

The case she was handling brought it all back. Nina's death and all the unknown factors regarding Maks were making her nervous.

It didn't help that there was a crackling energy that filled her when she was with him. She didn't understand *that* emotion, either. When he'd opened his door yesterday, her whole being had melted. There was the sensation of being burned; licks of fire penetrated every cell.

She could get swept away if she wasn't careful. If he was a cold-blooded killer—

There were too many mixed up feelings that she was unable to define or articulate.

"I think I'm just tired. I needed Cannon as much as you did."

"Do. Changing our minds doesn't negate the need. Would your parents mind if we rescheduled?"

"Not at all. But I know they've got some Christmas events going on and they'll be using the condos for their overnight guests. It won't be possible until after the first of the year."

Mountain Man Winery, named after the Old Man in the Mountain, which had fallen away a few years ago from centuries of rain and erosion, was opened back in 2002. It had garnered a great reputation over the last decade, and more and more people were being drawn to the wine-tasting festivities and daily tours her brother, Steph, had started when it first opened. Skiers, in for a weekend at Cannon Mountain, were partial to sipping wine at the vast outlet rather than sipping hot chocolate at the lodges that dotted the area. The restaurant was housed in what resembled an open cask, the ceiling high, the lighting soft, and the food excellent. She was sure they'd be booked solid through the holidays and wouldn't even bother to ask. This weekend was the one free one open until mid-January. They had to take it or leave it. They'd taken it but...—it hadn't worked out like they planned.

Her fault.

She glanced up and asked, "Would you have cancelled on me if Nick had asked you to watch Teddy?"

"The only reason he asked is I told him you'd cancelled on me and I wasn't going. So, no. Your guilt can fester."

She took a sip of wine, gulped back a lump at the back of her throat, and said, "I am really sorry, Em."

She got a pat on the hand and a sad smile telling her she was forgiven.

"I know. We'll have make it up in Marrakesh. I wonder what the men are like."

"You've yet to sample any of the foreign fare."

"I'm getting there. Maybe this will be my lucky break."

"What? Fall in love with a man so far away? Don't you already have one of them? Distant is distant."

"If Nick was distant, I'd be fine. He keeps popping into my life too often for me to move on."

"You've kept the door open. He sees the opening and whoosh, he's in like Flynn."

"Who's Flynn? Is he good-looking? Available?"

They laughed as the waitress came over with their dinner. As each took up eating, Em asked, "Who's the guy Nate fixed you up with?"

Camille's heart began pounding, like a hammer hitting a thousand nails. They hadn't been fixed up although the way her heart was racing she thought maybe—

"I can't tell you much."

"You can tell me where he's from. If he's good-looking or has a toad-like face. If he's sexy and has the potential to be an eleven or a swamp boogie."

"Russia. Good-looking. Potential for an eleven."

"*Russian?* Like Jean Valjean?"

Camille took a sip of her wine, amusement breaking through the melancholy.

"He's French. Dr. Zhivago would be a better ethnic comparison."

"Your Russian looks like what's-his-name?"

Her Russian? Why did that term stoke a growing fire? He could never be hers. First off, she never dated clients. Never. Second, she didn't dare get too close. Not after the last fiasco. And third—there was no reason for a third reason. The first two were enough to keep her from dancing into that tempest.

"If you mean Omar Sharif, no. The actor who plays the part is more like the men in Turkey. He was Egyptian, same locus."

"I could so do one of them."

"You are so full of it, my celibate friend."

"I can fantasize, can't I?"

"You're going to fantasize about your fantasy? That's two degrees from separation."

"It's better than fantasizing about something that can't come true. This at least has possibilities."

"Only until we're there. Then reality comes rushing back."

"That gives me a couple of months to think of a hundred different ways to love a lover."

Camille shook her head and smiled.

Maybe she'd do a little of that herself later. Not that she'd have to work at it. Maks was there behind her eyes when she closed them last night. The knife in his hand might have been off-putting, but if she could get rid of that tiny detail, she might be golden.

CHAPTER SEVEN

Maks glanced at his watch.

If Camille was a creature of habit, she should be arriving within the next fifteen minutes. He'd already showered and changed and had gone back to the computer, drifting in and out of sites Boog had shown him yesterday. For as much as he didn't want to admit it, the guy knew his stuff and he'd been able to access more data with his help.

The dossier was growing. SIGINT, or signals intelligence was keeping up, and he was sure the back channels would only add to the information being breached from foreign sources. Boog's group had devised software that could alter the cyber war race. He'd always worked alone but having someone who knew what he was doing, could speak his digital language, was more than agreeable. They chatted as they worked, and he found a comrade in arms. Boog strongly suggested the people here didn't know there was a war going on. Past presidents had underestimated the consequences of cyberspace and, in the process, diminished the legitimacy of tailored access and the ability to wage a different kind of war. The Russian nation-state had been tapping into all kinds of American grids and networks for years. Military networks among them. It was hybrid aggression, with a mix of on-the-ground fighting, cyber warfare with a lot of *kompromat*, where everyone had the goods on one another, thrown in. America had been lagging behind the country he'd left, even though their spy agencies had penetrated deeply into the Soviets' military complex back in the 1980's. It wasn't until the current president was elected that the top military brass began to understand how critical it was to scan for data and find suspicious traffic patterns. Now the motto seemed to be *Get everything, even the un-get-able*. It was a different kind of war that it seemed America had only recently learned how to wage. The thing about America, though? They were quick learners. The National Security Agency had gone through several leaders, each successive one adding his own brand of sophistication, building a solid foundation of intelligence-gathering methods. Today, the NSA and other intelligence agencies had top-gun cyber fighters in the trenches. Even with their expertise, nothing had been done to staunch the damaging data coming from the foreign bots. They were wreaking havoc on personal media sites such as Facebook and Twitter. It was how elections were lost.

It seemed the Rubicon had been crossed. Some self-proclaimed patriots on Twitter were swearing vengeance for Putin's role in the election hack. There was one group he'd been following since he got here, and they were threatening the same thing as he was. They were now at the point of no return, and Maks was steering one of the boats. The destination? The ultimate destruction of that nation-state he had once called home. They'd started the war. It was up to people like him to end it.

He packed up his computer, and stashed it away in his bedroom, and within minutes, there was a faint knock on the door.

Camille was right on time.

He walked over and opened the door, blocking her entry as he stared at her.

Today she was tucked into a fitted white knit dress, vee neckline, that expressed her curves better than what she'd worn yesterday. The snow hadn't stopped her from wearing open-toe brown heels that matched her blazer. His gaze fell to the creamy expanse of her neck. The tingles that accompanied it were new, and his body didn't know what to do with them. If she was Mata Hari, he was in trouble. There was something about her that made his palms sweat, and he had to watch his step.

He took one to the side and let her slip by him.

"No donuts?"

She faltered, then regained her footing.

"Why bother? Would you have eaten them?"

"No."

"Then why should I waste my money?"

"You could have at least brought coffee."

"So, you could dump it out like you did yesterday? I don't think so."

She was scanning the room as if she was looking for some damaging information to take away with her. She wasn't going to find it.

"You will try again to ask me questions?"

"I will. And if you want to get rid of me, you'll answer them."

She walked into the living room, smoothed the dress down under her, and took a seat. When she crossed her legs, his heart thumped in his chest. He busied himself in the kitchen, and soon the coffee maker was dripping steaming black liquid into the pot. He waited until there was enough for a cup and filled one before returning the carafe to the hot plate. It also gave him time to put his hormones back in place.

He was sipping it as he returned to the living room.

Her voice was seductive to his ears when she asked, "What did you do yesterday?"

The hormones came racing back out. He gave her a tight-lipped smile.

"How you say it? Hung out?"

"Did anyone come by?"

She could not know anything. Could she?

"Alec."

"What are you going to do to pass your time?"

"I'm not allowed to go for walks in neighborhood. Many guns here."

She couldn't argue with that. This town on the outskirts of Boston was known for its drive-bys and murders.

"I have books with me, computer. And balalaika."

The word that penetrated her brain was the instrument mentioned.

Like in Dr. Zhivago?

Her tongue was swollen and tied.

"You play the balalaika?"

The words came out garbled.

"Since I was boy. I have played American banjo. It is much like it."

The fantasy took a sharp curve, making her breathless. Instead of concentrating on the instrument, wishing she could ask him to play it, she asked about his childhood. "Where did you live when you were a boy?"

He straddled one of the chairs, leaning his chin on the back edge. He studied her for a minute before answering.

"I was born in town outside St. Petersburg. Moved to Moscow when I was teenager. Lived in two-bedroom apartment. Went to school there, worked with Nina there."

"Did you go to university?"

"I didn't finish. There was nothing I could learn that would do me any good. They don't let you think, and they teach only propaganda now."

"No military service? Doesn't the government force inscription?"

"Not always. Some get...passed over. I was lucky one. The generals are barbaric and many die at hands of countrymen. Others fight to reclaim territory lost when USSR fell."

"Is that what's going on?"

"Yes. Economy crumbles as oil prices drop, rich get richer, everyone else gets poorer. Without nuclear arsenal, they are second-tier power. Leaders need to be aggressive, are driven by fear that they will be left out at table. They miss past glory."

"They want the USSR back. Interesting theory."

"This is why it destabilizes their neighbors, commit terrorist attacks in Crimea and Chechnya. They now wage war against countries democratic, like yours, Britain, France."

"Not one with bullets and bombs?"

"No. It is hybrid. They mix cyber with fake news and special forces. They hack into networks to weaken your systems, create chaos, and share false information. It has worked, yes?"

"It has worked, yes. Was that the kind of stories that Nina was working on?"

"She uncovers truth and spreads it like butter on toast."

"And gets killed for it."

"Like many others. And no one fights back."

She leaned forward.

"Is that why you're here? Are you fighting back?"

There was hope in her expression, that maybe this would be the answer she was seeking.

He could not give her what she was looking for. Not yet.

"How would I do this? She is gone. *Reform* or some other news agency will print her articles, and someone else will die."

She dropped back against the sofa, frustration written on her face now.

"What was Nina to you? Associate, friend, lover—"

Before his eyes dipped, she saw pain flash in them.

"Lover."

Disappointment fluttered through her for some reason, one she wasn't going to delve too deeply into. He'd been in love with a woman who was an icon in Russian journalist circles. Probably still was.

"I'm sorry for your loss."

His eyes were dark and menacing when he looked up at her.

"Not only mine. The world's. Upon her death, Nina became a symbol of what Russia has become."

She gasped inwardly. Was that why he'd left? To escape what his country had become? That wasn't grounds for asylum. There were thousands, hundreds of thousands, maybe millions who felt the same way about their country. America couldn't give a home to them all. What the hell was Nate thinking? Why had Alec gone to France to escort Maks here? There had to be something missing, something they were withholding from her. Did it have to do with this Guccifer?

She rose from the sofa, grabbed her coat on the way out, didn't even bother saying good-bye so lost in her tunnel vision.

When she got to Nate's office, she was still steaming. It turned to a rapid boil while she waited for him to give her some time.

⌒

As soon as the door closed behind her, Maks felt loneliness sneak into his heart.

He didn't understand it. He was used to being alone. Even when he was with Nina, they'd lived such separate lives that they were never really a couple. More bedfellows and co-conspirators. He'd worked in his cramped apartment; she'd worked out of the newspaper office. He'd chased after proof of fraud and corruption; she'd chased after the atrocities that were occurring more and more frequently in the old satellite countries. Their work had meshed from time to time, but she'd refused to report on things close to his heart. He'd wanted her to take up the gauntlet for the individual deaths that were going unnoticed. There had been so many. The most significant one in terms of coverage was Sergei Magnitsky. He was an attorney who had been imprisoned and tortured for uncovering a massive fraudulent scheme, dying because he refused to lie. Many had fought to clear his name, on both sides of the Atlantic, trying to break through the massive cover-up from the bottom up. By 2013 the American Congress had introduced a bill that was supported by highly visible Russian-American citizens, and although it took some time, the Magnitsky Act was finally passed. It was meant as a punishment for the Russian officials who took part in not only Sergei's death but the deaths of eighteen other men, killed for similar reasons.

The American law declared that all participants in the murders of these men were blacklisted, no longer allowed into the country and their assets were frozen. Maks' father's name didn't make the list. Petrov's death came one year later, along with several others, proving that nothing had changed, that nothing could stop them.

Nina had played to a larger audience, bearing witness to group annihilation, describing the acts against humanity going on in Ukraine. The people needed to know, but the growing awareness wasn't changing behavior. Putin was playing the bully, proving he was strong and in charge, fighting enemies abroad to cover up the problems at home. What the FSB was doing was also wrong. Freedom was being stolen from the citizens one benefit at a time. Things might look like they'd improved since he took over, a boon in oil and gas, improvements in social services and pensions, but it was an illusion. Corruption was booming, as well. It was happening inside the borders, not outside. High-ranking officials were stealing money from the citizens and anyone who had the courage to call them out, was silenced.

Someone needed to stop them.

It appeared it would have to be him.

It had been a lonely business over the last couple of years, one that came with risk.

Camille brought a ray of sunshine into the dark world he lived in. He missed it when she took it away. It was an odd feeling, one he'd never felt before, but such an attraction would be perilous. He still couldn't trust her. Still couldn't trust the people he was working with. Propaganda might play a part in what he was anticipating, but if the FBI was anything like the equivalent agency back in Russia, they had a hidden agenda, and he was merely a means to an end. Once his work was done, who knew what they'd do with him. Would he be granted asylum as promised, or would he be facing certain death? Or prison at the very least. How did they treat political prisoners here? Were they tortured and killed like they were in Russia? His thoughts turned to his father. A lawyer, he'd represented people convicted of trumped-up charges. The government didn't like legal minds like Petrov—

The knock on the door helped him put those debilitating thoughts out of sight.

Alec was there, with an unfamiliar face. Letting them in, he waited for an introduction. Another member of the Bunker Hill Group was going to be working with him today. His user name was Smokey and Maks found out why when he first stepped outside for a cigarette. Smoking where he came from was a given. That and vodka. It was probably why twenty-five per cent of men in Russia were dead by fifty-five. He figured the odds of reaching that ripe old age weren't good anyway, so he imbibed as often as he could.

Smokey seemed to be more talkative than Boog, and he heard all about Silicon Valley, which is where Smokey was from. Most of the high-tech companies were housed there, tucked into the San Francisco Bay area, and it's where Smokey had learned how to keep back-door channels open. Together, as aggressors, they began their attack on the site in Moscow he'd found yesterday, breaking passwords, sniffing out the network, burrowing in to see what information he could extract. He could have inflicted some damage, but his primary role today was to see what was in there.

⌒

When Nate came out of his office to claim Camille, she was sputtering.

"Slow down. Tell me what the problem is."

He stepped back into his office. She was following, already in the middle of her tirade.

"Why are you giving Mr. Skolikovsky the red-carpet treatment? There must be something you're not telling me. As it stands, there's nothing for me to base an application for asylum on. Did he come here to escape persecution or just to escape his form of government?"

She watched Nate's face move through several different emotions as he decided what to give her.

Feed her was the better phrase, and she wasn't going to let him feed her bullshit.

"It's a top-secret operation. I can't say more than that."

What the hell?

"Is it related to Nina's death?"

"That prompted the initial contact."

Maks had told her someone had to pay for Nina's death. Maybe he'd given the FBI bogus information to get an entrée visa into the country, with revenge his true intent. That wasn't a plausible explanation for why they should grant him protection. She'd been told he'd brought information on the Kremlin, but what kind? Did it have to do with the hacking and the election? How could she determine the veracity if she wasn't allowed access? Why couldn't Nate just tell her? Maks might be risking his life, but she couldn't be sure. The thought of that sent a shiver down her spine. She needed to get to the bottom of this not only for Maks but for her, as well.

"If you remember correctly, I didn't want to take this. You all but coerced me into it, and now you're stonewalling. I've got to have something more concrete than it's *top secret*. That doesn't cut it on the application. I'm a lawyer, for God's sake. I know how to keep things confidential."

Nate had taken a seat behind his desk. Now his hands were steepled, his chin resting on them. He let a few moments of silence fill the space.

"I'm sorry, Camille. It's way above your pay grade. There are reasons I can't give any information away right now."

She leaned her hands on his desk, got into his face.

"I know he's not a journalist. Doesn't fit the mold. If I had to make a guess, I'd say hacker, one who's going to deliver a shit load of information on the Russian intervention. That would make him valuable."

"Can't say anything more than he is valuable."

After backing away, she dropped into one of the metal chairs. Had he just confirmed her guess, in a back-door kind of way that was so typically FBI? Don't just spell it out, let the shadows cast doubt and suspicion. Frustrated, she asked, "Is he one of theirs?"

"Theirs being, did he work for them and turn? There's no evidence of that."

"Five eyes?"

The five English-speaking countries shared all kinds of intelligence. They included the United States, Great Britain, Canada, Australia, and New Zealand.

"Supports our assumption."

"What is he working on?"

"He's important. That's all you're getting."

She gave up, got to her feet, and moved toward the door. A cold knot forming in her stomach.

"Is he being hunted?"

"He's still alive."

"Which means you're not sure."

"We've got agents covering him twenty-four seven, just in case."

"Is that why he's here, in Boston? Less visibility?"

"In a way, but nothing I can share."

"What is my job here? It can't be the application process, because you're not giving me anything to move that forward. You mentioned I was good at digging. Is it my job to get you information?" Her eyes flashed up and into his. "Do you even know what's going on?"

"I know. I just can't share. I want your perceptions of him, your counsel."

"Without any help from you I don't even know where to start. Can I at least have his real name?"

"I'm afraid you'll have to get that from him. The better you get to know him, the more he might trust you enough to reveal himself."

Sheer black fright swept through her. She'd gotten her answer, but she'd also been handed a plateful of worry.

"Am I in danger?"

"Not presently."

The answer should have relaxed her, but waves of apprehension were still rippling. She might not be in any physical danger—yet,—but she there was another kind that just might prove more lethal. Getting to know him better might be a problem. She liked him, felt drawn to him. It was as if the hammer hit, and the reality of what she was feeling raced up her spine.

CHAPTER EIGHT

After her meeting with Nate, Camille was hard-pressed to concentrate on her other cases. She was able to accomplish the mindless job of collating some of the documents that had come registered mail earlier in the day.

One concerned a woman from Sri Lanka. The Liberation Tigers of Tamil were wreaking havoc there. Mihiri had been raped multiple times by multiple men when the insurgents came to her home. They'd repeated the brutality every week for over a month, making her husband watch at gunpoint. Her husband had succeeded in smuggling her out of the country, hoping to follow later. Her first application for asylum had been denied. The judge had decided that there was no evidence that the rapes would continue if Mihiri was returned. That's when Camille had taken on the case. She was determined to prove that one of the perpetrators was a uniformed soldier and there was no sensible possibility that the state would protect her. Some of the documents she needed to support her case had arrived this morning, along with a certified statement from the neighbors bearing witness to the assaults. The other packet contained the documents on a couple from Iraq. Shiite Muslims who had been threatened by the militia. An uncle had already been killed, which proved there was an objective expectation of death if they were returned. It was a well-founded fear based on a tangible past action. Camille could add the uncle's death certificate to the file, which already held the threatening note that had been pinned to their door. It read, "YOU ARE NEXT."

After stacking the sideboard report binders on the side of her desk, she threaded her hands through her hair.

There was so much evil in the world. She knew the United States couldn't take in every refugee, but it broke her heart every time she had to turn someone away who didn't meet the standards. For every case she took on, there were thousands she couldn't.

Her thoughts drifted back to Maks.

Would his case meet the protocols in place?

She had no idea given she had no credible information to go on.

The burden of proof would have to come from him. Her job was to ascertain and evaluate all relevant information and express it in such a way that a judge decided in their favor.

She needed to spell it out for him. Let him know how crucial his cooperation was. She couldn't fight for his right to freedom without his help.

After trying to talk herself out of what she was thinking and failing miserably, she drove to Dorchester. Grabbing the take-out bag, she exited the car, hit the lock button, and deposited her set of keys in her pocketbook.

It took him a couple of minutes to come to the door, which told her she might have interrupted something, and a sliver of fear almost chased her away. She glanced back to see the agent in the car, as unobtrusive as possible, if a man sitting out in his car in twenty-degree weather was unobtrusive.

Before she could move, the door opened, and her breath caught. He was dressed in jeans and a tee, and his hair was now in a man bun, which accentuated his cheekbones and his deep-set eyes. The thought *He's gorgeous* ricocheted around her mind for far too long.

"It is not morning. Why you here?"

"I...picked up something for supper and I guess you could say I didn't want to eat alone. If you don't want me here, just say so."

She held her breath, not knowing which way it would go. Not knowing which way would be smarter.

"I have yet to eat. It is good timing. Come in."

She slipped by him and placed the big brown bag on the counter.

He opened it and sniffed while she took off her coat and boots.

Taking one of the containers out, he asked, "What is this?"

"Chinese. Have you eaten it before?"

"I have. Russia is no longer back water country. There are many good restaurants in Moscow. Americans think we are peasants."

"Not all of us do. I'm looking forward to experiencing the country someday."

"You never been?"

He had busied himself with plates and cutlery, setting the small kitchen table as she emptied the rest of the contents.

"No. It's on my bucket list, though."

"Bucket list?"

"It's a saying here. The things you want to do before you die."

"Me, I want to live before I do."

He wore a serious expression, as if he wasn't sure he'd have that chance.

"I guess we all want that."

"You have nothing to be afraid of. You will get to this bucket list."

She'd always thought so. Now? She was a bit more vulnerable than she'd been before. And from what Nate confirmed, this man was on a very short leash for his own safety.

"I didn't know what you'd like, so there's probably enough food for an army."

"The Red Army. Millions in line."

She offered him a cautious smile.

"I brought wine for me, but I thought you might want something more potent. There's Skoli in the other bag."

"You know my likes?"

"I saw a bottle on the counter when I was here this morning."

"I can suffer with wine."

"It's from my parents' winery. It's pretty good."

"Your parents own winery?"

"Yeah. It's in New Hampshire. About twenty minutes south of Cannon Mountain."

"I thought wine must come from...valley."

"Napa. It's in California. Some do. There aren't many in New England but they're gaining a good reputation."

He was looking in the cabinets, moving things around.

"No wine glasses. Will have to drink from vodka glasses."

"Regardless of my brother's opinion, it will taste the same."

"You have brother?"

"Yes, and a sister. Do you have any siblings?"

"No. I was born in the 1980's. Was not good time for economy. When things turned around, too late for another."

"There were some days I wanted to be an only child."

"Lonely life at times."

He sat down and began to inspect the offerings.

"There's chicken, shrimp, beef, pork, some appetizers, vegetables and lots of duck sauce. I kind of hog it."

He pried open the container, stuck a finger into the tub, and tasted it. She almost laughed at his expression.

"Very sweet. You can have all."

"I probably would have taken it all, anyway. You saved me from being rude."

He picked up an egg roll and took a bite. He inspected the crunchy delight as if trying to figure out what was in it.

"Taste is different."

"Good or bad?"

"Neither. Just different."

Once he'd finished the finger food, he used a spoon to scoop some of the main dishes onto his plate.

"What do I owe this pleasure?"

His gaze traveled over her face and searched her eyes as if looking for truth. In the hope that she could set some groundwork for trust, she gave it to him.

"I'm not getting as much in information from your handlers as I'd like, or need, to do my job. I'm hoping that if I get to know you, I can at least fill in some of the blanks."

"Know me how?"

Why are you here? What do you have on your countrymen? What is your fucking name?

"What was it like during glasnost? Going from the Soviet Union to varied autonomous states?"

His forehead creased as if he couldn't figure out how an answer to that would help.

Shrugging his shoulders, he said, "Chaos. It was like earthquake, everything shaken up, and we were left in rubble."

"It wasn't better?"

"How could it be? All government-owned factories, businesses, utilities were now owned by no one. Someone had to fill void."

"Were you living in Moscow by then?"

"Still living outside St. Petersburg. It included apartments, and hospital that had to be privatized. Gangs were formed. They preyed on everyone."

"How long did it take things to get better?"

"Moscow saw improvement first. Money was there. We moved there few years later."

"What did your father do for a living?"

His face clouded, his eyes glazed.

"Not important."

"I'm going to need his name, and your mother's. It's all part of the—"

"Yes, I know. Application."

He rose from the table, his vexation with the topic obvious. He picked up her plate even though she wasn't finished, and brought everything to the sink. He yanked up her coat and shoved it at her, saying briskly, "You must go now."

He didn't even wait for her to be on the top step before he shut the door.

His heart rate was off the charts.

What was she doing?

What did his father have to do with any of this?

There was no way to bury all memory with the man's body, and there was much that had escaped the tomb.

He began to pack up the leftovers, his shaking fingers making it a more difficult task than it should be. He should have sent it home with her, but he'd had a dire need to get her out.

It had been such a surprise to see her standing outside his door that he'd let his guard down. Dressed down in jeans and a black, red, and yellow multi-colored shirt with fringe that sat at her waist, she'd looked so desirable he'd let her in without more thought than that. It had been a grave error on his part, and he needed to stop thinking with his dick. The irony was not lost on him. He'd never felt like this about a woman before and now—he wasn't going to do a thing about it. Couldn't. She was after something and he had to protect himself.

He unscrewed the cap on the vodka bottle and poured a generous amount into the glass that had he'd rinsed out.

He shot it down in one gulp. Next, he grabbed his pack of cigarettes and stepped out to the front stoop to satisfy his other addiction. The agent sitting in the car opened the window and asked, "You good? Camille sure left in a hurry."

"She had to go."

"Okay. Don't stray too far."

"I won't."

He stood looking up at the sky. It was dark, and the stars were there, just like they were where he came from. After taking the elastic out, he shook his hair, letting the curls blow in the biting wind. It was cold here, and it felt like home.

Home.

Waves of nostalgia hit him like a riptide, pulling him under. No matter how much he wanted to, he couldn't change the past. Or the stupid men whose greed had ruined his life. Brits, Americans, Greeks, who'd moved to Russia when the Communist Bloc fell apart, buying up all the cheap stock they could find, not unlike many in Russia. They'd destroyed everything around them for the sake of a dollar. Police were picking up citizens and charging them with pedophilia, their new and improved excuse to arrest and imprison, tax-evasion still their fallback position. Gay culture was being demolished one law at a time. Anyone behind bars was still receiving starvation rations and working sixteen-hour days. It was the gulags of yesteryear just repurposed to look differently. Protests were raging in Ukraine, the citizens there wanting to be part of the European community, to break free of Russian influence. People drank more if that was possible.

His father had kept up his protests of all these things, continued to dabble in politics. The Kremlin had kept showing him the error of his ways, and he'd spent years in and out of jail, until he was silenced for good. He'd refused to take their message to heart. Others who'd walked with him were sentenced to prison colonies, some were still awaiting trial, others forced out of the country, one assassinated with a car bomb.

Petrov Zhernova had been a man of honor and refused to back down in his pursuit of justice. That honor and integrity had cost him his life. Just as it had Nina. There was no room for honor now. Only truth.

And he would shout it out to the world, no matter the cost.

He stepped back into the warmth of the apartment, looked around. This wasn't home. He didn't have one anymore. In limbo, caught between two different cultures, he had a month to decide if this was where he wanted to stay. It shouldn't take longer than that to finish what he'd started.

After rummaging around for the disposable cell they'd given him, he punched in Alec's number.

When the agent answered, all Maks said was, "I need to speak to her."

"You can't do it from there."

"Find someplace."

"I'll have someone pick you up tomorrow and bring you here."

"I hold you to that."

"You have my word."

When the call ended, he was satisfied for the moment.

He retrieved his computer from the bedroom, sat down at the table, and got back to it. He called himself a special-ops soldier. And this was his battle-field. He might not be able to beat them at their game, but he could beat them at his.

Camille was thunderstruck.

Maks had all but kicked her out. She hadn't even made it out before the door slammed against her back.

She'd hit a nerve.

His father had something to do with his immigration, but she saw no way to uncover what it was without a name. Firmly believing he was using a false one, she was already at a dead end, and she hadn't even gotten out of the start-ing gate. Alec might know what was going on, but he wasn't giving away state secrets. The only other place she could look for answers was the newspaper Nina worked for. Someone there might be willing to co-operate with her. It was after midnight in Ukraine and too late to call, but she had a new avenue to pursue and she was going to run with it. When her cell rang, she hit the Blue tooth to answer Alec's call.

"What?"

"Can you do me a favor tomorrow?"

"I don't know. It's not like I owe you one. You're giving me nothing."

"Can you bring Maks to my office? If a woman picks him up, it might look less clandestine than one of the other agents bringing him in."

"Aren't you moving him soon?"

"Day after tomorrow."

"Where's he going this time? Hopefully, a better location."

"We've got a couple of places in the city. We should have more, but it gets expensive."

"When did the government worry about expenses?"

"When we began getting far too many asylum seekers whose lives were im-minently in danger."

"And you want me to drive him in? Thanks for having my back."

"Will you do it or not?"

She wasn't sure Maks would get in a car with her after showing her the door tonight, but it might be the way to get him talking again. She'd just make sure there'd be no mention of his father. She needed to get inside of him.

Figuratively speaking. The shimmer that sent sheets of lightning through her made her amend that, but silently.

"I will. What time?"

"Early. Have him here by seven thirty. I'll need you to stick around and drive him back."

"My schedule won't allow me to stick around. I have other clients who need my attention. I can pick him back up after my mid-morning appointment."

"I guess that will have to work."

"You could always drive him back yourself."

"I'm too busy."

As soon as she began stuttering, he ended the call.

She was still seething when she got home. Who the hell did he think he was? She was doing him a favor taking this case on.

Throwing her briefcase and pocketbook on her kitchen counter, she stormed into her bedroom and began ripping her clothes off. The FBI was a bunch of arrogant jerks who thought they were—

She flopped down on her bed, letting the anger fizzle out.

They had a job to do. Same as her.

All thought fled her head except one that screamed in neon lights.

Maks was in imminent danger.

She had to change that, and the only way she could affect that kind of change was if she was able to successfully get him granted asylum. Not that living here would guarantee his safety, but he had better odds here than being sent back to Moscow. Or so she'd been led to believe. It would be her number one priority. She'd begin her in-depth research tomorrow. Talk to Nell if she had to. Constitutional rights might play into it somehow. And if not, maybe she could just talk to Nell about what she was feeling. It seemed three of the female lawyers in the firm wanted someone they couldn't have. She had only recently joined the group, and she didn't know what to do with the emotions rocking her world.

She needed that vacation, needed time to process the electrical currents Maks seemed to touch in her. She might not be willing to open her heart again, but her body was telling her in no uncertain terms that it didn't give a shit. Couldn't she work at the lodge as well as here? She'd already cleared her schedule. Two days away might be just what she needed to sort this all out. It didn't look like she was going to get any pertinent information out of them anyway. All her work would have to be done on her own.

After calling her parents and making sure the condo was still available to her, she snuggled under the covers. She was happy with her executive decision, even though she couldn't stay with them. They had some of her father's family from Canada for the weekend, but she'd be able to see them, relax, work, and try to expunge the hum that vibrated inside of her.

CHAPTER NINE

Camille was surprised he'd been outside waiting for her when she swung by to pick him up.

He climbed right into the passenger seat and he buckled himself in.

"Alec told me you would bring me to office."

She breathed a sigh of relief. The anger she'd seen in his eyes before he showed her the door last night seemed to be gone. After pulling out of the space and onto the street, she caught him inspecting the dashboard of her car, looking in every nook and crevice.

"Where is video cam?"

"Video cam? What do you mean?"

"To support insurance claim."

She glanced over to see him staring at her. The seismic shift tilted her again and her eyes darted back to the road.

"What insurance claim? I haven't had an accident since the first year I started driving?"

"In Russia, every car has video. Accidents always happen. Five a day outside apartment."

She vaguely remembered reading that somewhere. His reaction seemed to amuse her, and she couldn't help but laugh. "Not here."

He slouched down in his seat, as if trying to assimilate what she'd told him.

Wanting to fill the silence, but intent on keeping the conversation safe, she figured the weather would be a good place to start.

"It's supposed to snow this weekend. I decided to go visit my folks for a couple of days and fresh powder is always good for the slopes."

Without taking his gaze from the scenery out his window, he said, "I thought they own winery."

"They do, just outside one of the ski meccas of the Northeast."

Now he showed some interest, turning to her with a gleam in his eye. "You ski?"

"Since I was a kid. Even before they bought the land for the house and the vineyards we used to go every winter. Have you ever skied?"

"A couple of times while—a couple of times."

His expression clouded, and she felt the door close again. She wanted back in but didn't know how to get there. It seemed there was no safe subject that didn't revert to his life in Russia.

She weaved through the downtown traffic, picked up the thread of the conversation.

"It's the only sport I enjoy. I can tolerate watching a hockey game here and there, but that's about it. Do you like hockey?"

"I play a little. We have good teams. It is good to watch. That and football."

"That's your version of soccer."

"It is real football. You play inferior version."

She took the risk of glancing over again. His grin was devastating. She couldn't help herself from giving him a return smile.

"What team do you follow?"

"Sputnik. They win ten championships. They are best in country."

They had moved well, until they got to Purchase Street, where the early commuters were battling for position and she had to inch her way towards Seaport Boulevard and Atlantic Ave. She was grateful it wasn't far from her office, because it meant she wouldn't fall too far behind with her appointments for the day. Luisa's case was near closure, and she wanted to get it finished. They'd be doing her exit interview before her court date, which was right after Christmas. Later this afternoon, she'd be meeting with Maybelline de Alvarado, an El Salvadorian who was here due to the continuing violence in Central America. As she was processing what she could do for her, she pulled into the underground garage and spiraled around until she found an empty space. Pleased that they'd made good time, and she wouldn't be late for her first interview, she was also glad she'd stuck to neutral topics with

Maks. Once the car was locked and they got out, the low ceilings, cramped space, and open air spooked her. She glanced around, fear skittering up her spine. This would be a great place to assault someone. Her eyes sought out the man beside her, wondering if he felt the same kind of trepidation. With hands in his pockets, his shoulders hunched, she got the sense he was trying to make himself appear smaller. Less of a target? She picked up her pace, and only when they reached the lobby did she relax. Once she'd checked in with the receptionist, who sat behind a bullet proof glass, they took the elevator up to the ninth floor, her body still humming. When the door swooshed open, she stepped out and accompanied Maks into the vestibule to wait with him until Alec came out. She was relieved when she saw him walk briskly through the double doors. Hefting her pocketbook to her other shoulder, she turned to leave.

"I'll be back in a couple of hours."

As Alec began to lead Maks away, she said as an afterthought, "I'm going to be gone for the week-end. Just in case you need me for anything, I'll have my phone, but I can't play taxi."

"Where are you going?"

Alec looked overly interested and she didn't like the evil twinkle in his eye.

She had the urge to lie, fabricate something rather than give him the truth. If she knew why he wanted the information, it would have made the decision easier.

"Skiing."

"Did you rent a place?"

Now that the truth was out and she couldn't take it back, she stalled for time.

"Well?"

"No, I'm staying at one of my parents' condos just outside of Franconia Notch."

"Come with me, will you?"

He had moved forward so quickly she didn't have time to evade him. When he took her arm, she eyed him suspiciously.

"Why are you asking and where are you taking me?"

Maks was right behind them as he led them back into the bowels of the government building.

"The safe house had an electrical problem and we haven't found another place to stash Maks. I'm thinking you could take him with you for a couple of days, until we can sort this out."

An alarm bell sounded in her brain. If Maks was there, the weekend would no longer be the balm she needed for her overwrought senses. All she needed to reinvigorate herself were the icy slopes, not the kind of danger that Maks offered.

"No, I wouldn't. This is a mini-vacation. I'm not spending it babysitting one of your cases."

"Camille, this is perfect. No one will look for him at a ski resort. And he'll still have an agent with him."

"As body-guard or babysitter?"

They had entered an open area where dozens of personnel were sitting at cubicles.

Maks all but yelled, "I do not need babysitter. And I do not want to go with her."

The men and women in suits couldn't help but hear the outburst and she noticed some raised eyebrows.

Alec took both by the arm and led them away from the central artery.

"Let's take it someplace more private, shall we?"

Both Camille and Maks kept their mouths sealed until they were behind closed doors and then began to talk at once.

"That was not agreement."

"This is not in my pay grade."

Nate looked up from the paperwork on his desk, startled by the invasion. Alec informed, "We found a place for him for the weekend."

She shot that down immediately, looking at Nate to be sure he understood when she said, "No, you haven't."

Alec ignored her, and the seething started again. He was speaking to Nate as if she weren't even in the room.

"Where?"

"Franconia Notch."

"That's a little far afield, don't you think?"

"Camille's going to be there."

Nate's eyes moved to her, and he took a minute before asking, "I thought you'd cancelled your vacation?"

"Nothing gets by you, does it? Mia would be so pleased. I changed my mind. I need the time off. Time off. Do you know what that means? No work."

Her voiced dripped with sarcasm. She could hear the agitation. It was surging along her nerve endings and spilling out of her mouth. She was going to work up there, but they didn't need to know the extent of her plans. As they say in the FBI, this was on a need-to-know basis.

The one thing bothering her was Maks' insistence that he didn't want to go. She'd obviously ruined everything with the mention of his father last night. How would she know it was a touchy subject? She might be rusty, not having been on a date in a while, but there were a few questions you asked when you wanted to get to know someone. What do you do for a living? What are your hobbies? She'd never once had to ask if parents and siblings were off the table.

"You don't have to work if he's with you. You can do anything you want. As long as he has a bedroom and there's a couch for an agent, we're good."

"I am not entertaining anyone. I want to be alone."

"Who are you? Greta Garbo?"

She turned her eyes to Maks who'd just been standing there since his pronouncement.

"Jump in anytime you want."

As if needing permission, he strode right in.

"It is not good idea. How will I—"

"I'm sure she has internet service there and she'll be skiing most of the day. You'll have plenty of time to...do whatever you want."

He didn't want to be alone with this woman. It seemed like she felt the same. He would miss working with the group. He'd have to watch what he did, what he said. And he didn't want to sit through anymore third degree.

"I can do better...here."

Nate closed a file and handed it to Alec. He also handed them his decision.

"It's settled. Just ignore each other."

Alec was leading Camille to the door and seeing her out.

Maks watched as his fate was sealed, his appreciation of the woman out in the hallway far too much for comfort. She looked professional this morning, in a camel-hair suit with a silk blouse, her pearls a throwback in time. Her short boots sturdy yet stylish. Her hair was streaming down her back, waves of sunlight gold.

Ignore each other?

How would he do that? He felt like the walls were closing in around him, his heartbeat stuttering, his breathing more labored than the day he'd found Nina. Camille Bissonnette did funny things to his system, and he wasn't looking forward to being confined with her in a condo in whatever a notch was.

Or was he?

There was a two-pronged fork prodding him here. One, go with the danger, the other protect yourself at all costs.

He looked back at Nate, wondering...Could they force this? If he complained with more vigor? If they could, he was in no different place than where he'd left. Enforced imprisonment for speaking out, for protesting, crooked judges who went with the money, ignoring justice, unethical lawmen who trumped up charges, sending many to prison, where beatings were measured by how much was paid in bribes. He'd gone into debt paying the guards to treat his father well. He might as well have flushed his rubles down the drain. Would they put him in jail if he didn't agree? What would happen to him, to—

He would have to go along, unwilling to find out.

It was one more strike against these Americans, so smug in their all-knowingness.

He'd heard they were ignorant about the rest of the world and had a very low opinion of Russians, thinking them crude and backwards. He had to admit there was an outlook of fatalism that came from hundreds of years of fear. The current president was doing nothing more than his predecessors had. It was all about control, and his people had spent so long being told what to do, how to think that they had lost the ability to think for themselves. It's why they found themselves back under someone's thumb. Willingly.

From what he had read, there was more resilience in Americans. More fight. They had revolution in their blood and on their minds. Unwilling to let their freedoms be taken, they were in the streets, calling their representatives, affecting the kind of change that should come with a government of and by the people. He had to admire that.

And here, brilliant minds were birthed by offering incentives and allowing innovation within a free society, not ordered it up as if it were on a menu. The Bunker Hill Group was an example. They were on the cutting edge of technology and the outer limits of cyberspace. Instead of crushing them, the government worked with them, using their talents and skills for good instead of forcing them underground. That was why he was here. He had the freedom to do what he was doing without worry or fear.

Or so he'd thought.

According to Camille, they were giving her nothing to work with. Did it mean they weren't going to honor their agreement? That he was not going to be given amnesty?

He eyed them suspiciously, wishing there was someone he could trust, someone who could help him understand how things worked here.

Nate asked, his eyes revealing nothing, "Do you want to make that call?"

"*Ja.* I do."

"I have a secure line here. We don't have any reason to believe the encryption's been breached. I'll go grab a coffee, give you some privacy."

Maks watched as Nate closed the door behind him and lifted the receiver. Taking a wrinkled slip of paper out of his pocket, he dialed the number written there and waited.

When she came on the other end of the line, he heaved a sigh of relief.

"You are there."

"I am. They are treating me well."

"Good. I needed to hear your voice."

"It is good hearing yours, as well."

"I have uncovered many crypto findings. I work with a group here who are very good."

Those findings belonged to the men he was following, tracking, the intention to take them down as strong now as it had ever been. Maybe more so.

"I will be here waiting for you to finish. I will come when you call."

"I will hurry so we can be together again soon."

It was another reason he hadn't complained about working with others.

"I trust you that you will."

"Be well."

"Please stay safe. I couldn't bear to lose you."

When the call was disconnected, he stood looking at the receiver, wishing they were still talking. It was the only connection left and he was afraid it would be severed if anyone found out about what he was doing.

He dropped the phone back down when Nate returned.

"Is everything okay?"

"It is fine. Thank you. For that."

"Camille isn't going to be back for a couple of hours. I'm going to send you down to our computer programmers. You can work down there, let them get a sense of your skills. We're working to put you in place at one of our defense department facilities once this is finished. It will give you a way to support yourself if you decide to naturalize. You won't get within an inch of it unless you swear loyalty to this country. It's something you are going to have to decide."

He knew that. Changing loyalties had been easy once he realized how corrupt his country had become. He needed to make sure that the country he took as his own, would deserve the loyalty he was willing to give. He wasn't quite sure yet that this was the one.

When the door closed at her back, Camille sighed. This was the second time in two days that someone had thrown her out.

Why was she letting this happen? She could be as forceful as the next person, more forceful if push came to shove.

Was the undercurrent of desire for this mystery man stronger than she'd admit? Spending a week-end with him...wasn't such a bad thing, was it?

She took the elevator down, weighing the pros and cons, the cons tilting it into menacing territory. Snow was falling gently when she exited the building and she stood there letting the silence hiding beneath it calm her. She loved this weather. Loved the cold, the snow, the season. The thought of being on top of the mountain, ski poles in hand, pushing off, feeling the freedom of movement as she went barreling down the slope brought such happiness it overshadowed all else. What did it matter if he was there? It wouldn't stop her from seeing her family, relaxing, spending the days outdoors in the clean, crisp air.

Let him stay in the condo. Left to his own devices, whatever they were. He'd have the agent to make sure he was safe.

Her time could still be her own.

As she drove to her office, she let the gloominess go, knowing she'd feel free as soon as she was barreling down the mountain. She hoped that Em would understand her reversal. For as much as she loved her friend, she would have spent the weekend talking about Nick. If there was going to be a man present, it might as well be the one she drooled over.

"Hey, Camille. You have some messages."

Their receptionist was holding up some slips that she went over to collect. As she sifted through them she asked, "Is Nell back yet?"

"Yeah, she got in about an hour ago."

"Thanks."

After dropping her briefcase in one of the visitor chairs, she grabbed the file she'd started for Maks and went next door. Arianna was in there, so she knocked on the doorframe. When Nell looked up, she asked, "Do you have some time for me? I'd like to talk to you about something."

"Sure, check with Hani. See when I have a free moment."

"I'm going to need it ASAP. There's someone waiting underground. I'm not sure how to handle it."

The partner was willing to give her twenty minutes then and there.

As soon as Arianna left them alone, Camille got right to the point, going over some of the details, knowing she shouldn't be breaching protocol, and not caring. Nate and Alec deserved it for leaving her out of the giant loop they were tying her hands with.

Nell, astute as ever, agreed with her.

"He's not a journalist. He sounds more like a computer savant."

"I can buy that. But what specifically is he doing on the computer?"

"I heard some of the Russian hackers were working for the government, putting things in place to steal our election. Could he be one of them, one who turned?"

"I asked. Nate said he wasn't one of theirs."

"Do you want me to run it by Jack the next time I see him? He's on the Intelligence Committee and might have heard about a rogue computer analyst."

"Are you talking to each other?"

"He recently found out I run some appointments out of his office, so I have a feeling I'll be bumping into him more often."

She couldn't tell if Nell was happy or not with this latest development. She'd have to save that question for another day. The one that was foremost in her mind was, "Will he share classified information?"

Nell's eyes settled on her while she thought about it.

"We've been dancing around so many other issues I doubt it. But it might be worth a try. Maybe this guy, this Russian isn't as top-secret as Nate's leading you to believe. That would answer a key question, wouldn't it?"

"It would, actually."

"I'm sure you'll get to the bottom of it. You always do."

"Yeah, right. The man is as tightlipped as a clam. Not that I blame him. It's not like he's learned how to trust people. If I just knew his real name—"

"If he was involved with Nina, someone will know who he is."

"That's the avenue I'm pursuing. I have a call in to the paper Nina worked at. So far, nothing."

"There's something else, though, isn't there? You don't usually get this...involved. Not with Nate's cases anyway."

"They're usually much more cut-and-dry than this one."

She wasn't going to let anything about the last one slip out. She'd given away enough classified information.

"And...?"

"He's fucking gorgeous."

Nell sat back, fiddled with a charm on her bracelet. Then smiled.

"Oh."

"And they insisted I take him with me this weekend. How do you ward off an attraction that's got the force of a magnet? A very strong magnet."

She'd read there were some, strong enough to break bones. What could they do to a heart?

"Distance and time."

"I won't have either."

Nell leaned forward, a questioning look on her face.

"What the hell is wrong with us? We are strong, resilient women. Why do we fall for the wrong men?"

Had Nell just admitted that she wanted a relationship with the congressman? Now that Jack was going to meet their daughter, Chloe, Nell's emotions must have resurfaced. The past and future had merged, and she'd run out of time and distance. None of them had known, except maybe Jelani, as close as they were. Em was the one who used Camille as a sounding board, not that the other partners didn't know the reason for her underlying sadness.

"I always have such great advice for Em. Seems I'll have to follow some of it myself. I'm beginning to know how she feels. Wanting someone you know you can't have is hard on the soul."

She got up to leave.

"Thanks. I don't have to ask that you keep this confidential."

"No. And if you ever need to talk, I'm here."

"Thanks."

CHAPTER TEN

When Camille finally got around to looking at the pink slips that were still in her hand, she swore under her breath. The appointment that kept her from waiting around for Maks had been cancelled, but not by Luisa Ruiz. Homeland Security, those fuckers, had picked the refugee up at home and had her transferred out of Boston to another facility. Frustrated with a system that had no rules or order, she spent wasted time tracking her client down, making phone call after phone call to several Homeland Security offices on the Eastern Seaboard, trying to get her sent back. Co-operation was in limited supply when dealing with the agency and it took longer than it should have to find her. Once she tracked her to New Jersey, there were reams of paperwork needed to be completed for the transfer, to reschedule the cancelled interview and the court date when she'd go before a judge.

Once that was done, not caring that Maks would have to wait longer than anticipated, she spent some time rooting around on the computer digging into Nina's life. There was no mention of a man named Maks, or Skolikovsky. There was a full bio on the journalist, her marriage, her divorce. She'd worked for *Reform* for several years before her death, and there were articles Camille had never read before, but they all contained the same kind of information as those she had. All about the wars, the brutality of the military, the corruption. Ukraine was a hotbed of violence, chaos being spread—as Maks said about Nina's truth, like butter on toast. No matter how much she scrolled, how many sites she visited, she could find no mention of an accomplice, no mention of another journalist who matched Maks' description.

Which brought her back to the same question she'd been asking herself since the minute she'd met him.

Who was he and why was he here?

She had decent computer skills but lacked the ability to invade and track. It wasn't required for the job she did, and she left hacking to those more qualified. There was a person on staff at the law firm who they used for more tech-savvy work, but she couldn't bring him in for an FBI case. That was one of the rules Nate had put in place when she took her first case. Any classified information had to be handled at the agency's clearance level. She was supposed to get what they had but they'd given her nothing to go on.

The FBI worked over fifty avenues, all including information-gathering services, handled so many different types that she had no idea how to figure out which category Maks fell into. They dealt with counter-terrorism, which struck at the heart of terrorist prevention, counter intelligence, which dealt with espionage, and cyber intelligence, which was becoming the most significant national security threat of the times. Protecting cyberspace had gone to the top of the agency's agenda. They hadn't done a great job over the last few years. WikiLeaks had proved the point when they'd leaked information they'd stolen from various government sites.

Was that where Maks fit in? Was he part of that network? Had he have a hand in the election hack? She wouldn't put it past Nate to lie to her about Maks' involvement.

It was just another reason to avoid any entanglements there. No matter how attracted she was, she'd have to stifle any desire to taste until she knew the whole story.

What the hell are you thinking?

Did she really think she'd start something with him when she knew the story? As if that would make them compatible in any way. And what the hell difference did it make if they were compatible? She wasn't going to let anyone in. She didn't deserve it.

Getting up from her computer desk, knowing she'd put off telling Em about her change of mind long enough, she stepped out to the hall and peeked in her friend's office. If the door was open, it meant the partners were available for either brainstorming or a brief chat.

Knocking, she waited for Em to look up before moving into the room.

"You taking a break?"

"I've got to run an errand, but I wanted to tell you something before I leave."

"Okay. Sit. I'm at a good stopping point."

She sat at the edge of the upholstered chair across from Em and leaned forward, her hands clasped in her lap.

"I...I changed my mind about this weekend. I'm going to my folks' for a couple of days. Please don't be mad."

Em began to chew the end of her pencil.

"I thought you had to work?"

"I do but I can do it there as easily as here, and the mountain is calling my name. It's hard to hear anything else over it."

With her elbows on her desk, the pencil now held in her fingers, she asked, "Are you going alone?"

She'd decided to tell her the truth. She didn't want Em finding out somewhere down the road and thinking she'd lied to her, even though she was supposed to do that. It was rule number two when working for Nate. But he wasn't being very co-operative, so she didn't feel she owed him anything, and she knew the women here could keep a secret. Even one classified as national security.

"Alec, the agent I'm working with on the latest case, asked that I take the client with me. Something happened to the safe house he was moving to and Alec wants him out of town for a few days until they can figure something else out."

Em leaned back in her chair, studying her.

"And you agreed?"

She felt a momentary panic at the thought and she closed her eyes before answering.

"Yeah, I guess I did."

Gentling her expression, as if Em knew exactly what she was feeling, she asked, "Who is this mystery man?"

Answering as if it wasn't personal, as if he was just another case, another client, she said, "I have no idea. They're not giving me much. Neither is the client. He's a stone."

Em wasn't buying it. "This might be a way for you to get to know him."

"Don't want to."

"He's Russian. I know you do."

"That's why I can't. Want."

"But he could be your eleven."

"He might be that high on the scale but never mine."

"Cami, you do deserve to find someone to love, you know. More than most of the people I know."

Cocking her head before shaking it, Camille volleyed, "So do you, Em. Please don't lecture me on this."

Emilia raised her hands in supplication.

"You're right. I have no right to tell you how to run your life. Not with the way I live mine."

"Are we good?"

"Of course. I'll spend the weekend playing with Teddy and you'll find a hundred reasons not to get to know your Russian. Even though that's what you've been hired to do."

"I need to uncover the reason he needs asylum. I don't have to uncover who he is as a person. Besides, what if I find out he was working for the other side? Then what?"

"Then I guess you can tell me you told me so."

Standing up, she smoothed down her skirt and turned to leave.

"Cami, what if he isn't? What if he's a great guy? What if it's worth getting to know him?"

Camille didn't answer. She couldn't. It was a question she'd asked herself dozens of times. She still didn't have an answer.

⌒

Maks was sitting in a room filled with computers, men and women behind individual cubicles, a wall unit flashing red and yellow lights. It was high energy, without any talk, but he could see the intensity on faces totally focused on their screens.

He wasn't given access to anything of import. They still didn't know his true reason for being here, and the material they were dealing with was sensitive and highly classified.

They sat him at a lone desk against one of the walls, and he was asked to invade a site they'd put in place for training purposes. He knew anything he found would be bogus, but he played along, siphoning off the information they'd planted. If the exercise was to give them a good idea of his skills as a hacker, they'd gotten in it spades. He broke through in no time at all.

Impressed with his talents, the supervisor in charge stood over him, a slight frown on his face.

"How did you do that?"

"It is basic."

"Can you write a program that would be more difficult?"

"I could."

It was said without cockiness. He was confident in his abilities. He'd worked hard during the empty hours between jobs, evolving from an amateur to a full-on expert in the field of cyberspace. He didn't have an education in the sciences, but he steeped himself in the core components, learning all he could about radio signals, fiber optic transmissions and internet packets. It was hands-on learning and he'd excelled. It'd began as a foray into the dark territory concerning the Ministry officials who'd arrested his father. He'd amassed pages and pages of wrongdoings, wanting to support the claim that Petrov's imprisonment and death were part of their plan to stay above the law. Then Nina had found him, and his window opened wider. They fed each other information, and to reciprocate, he gave her a technical collection of proof to support her findings, pulling from emails, hacking into government sites. He'd pressed forward on his own search and his reputation grew among the other insurgents, fighting their battles on a different field. Dubbed the Matrixiator, he'd found ways to stay underground. He'd gone rogue, and the heads of different agencies were scrambling to find out who and where he was. Only with Nina's death had he realized they were zooming in. She'd been killed due to her constant protests about how the government conducted itself and its activities, but she had become linked with him through his work underground. The signature gave it away although they'd never tie him personally to the Matrixiator. He'd made sure of it. Even if the FBI hadn't made him erase all evidence of his existence, he would have anyway. He'd needed a new handle and he'd gotten one he was happy with when Boog assigned him Skoli.on.Ice.

That had been another reason he'd been devastated by Nina's death. She'd supported his drive to open Pandora's box, letting all the country's secrets out. And there were plenty. The country defied human rights activists with impunity. The directive to kill Petrov Zhernova, just like all the others, had come from the top. It had to have. Nothing was done in the country without the president's consent. Nina's death had been another nail in the coffin, provoking him to tell all and sealing the fate of the FSB and all related activities.

Today, at the FBI offices, he'd almost used one of the alternate usernames he'd taken on when he first arrived, after Nate had forced him to expunge the Matrixiator. It would be a flagrant signal to any enemy translator that he was alive and well. He could bounce it off enough signals that they'd never find where he was transmitting from. Being more circumspect, he used the code name that he honored. It was Petrov's initials and inmate number. PMZ367547809. It was indelibly etched in his mind, tattooed on his arm, a brand on his heart.

As he wrote the program the supervisor had asked for, he thought about Boog and what the group was doing. He wanted to be with them, not here.

When would Camille be back to get him? He was wasting time with this silly exercise. He didn't need to prove anything here. He could get a job anywhere doing what he did. He'd gone online, Googling technical security jobs, and there were thousands out there. And if he wanted out completely, when his task was finished? He could go back to his old job, the one that had filled his days with a different kind of creative art.

Just as he hit the last stroke, the supervisor came over to tell him it was time for him to leave.

"I leave program open?"

"You're done?"

"Yes."

Don Pressman was bending at the waist, scrutinizing the screen. He could clearly read what was written there in code, but he'd have to go deeper to see the quality of work he'd done.

"Phenomenal. When you get clearance, please consider coming to work for us. We could use another of your caliber. There's a war going on out there and we need all the soldiers we can get."

"Boots on ground?"

"Fingers on the board."

He shook hands and took his leave to find Camille waiting for him in Alec's office.

⌒

He climbed in her car and leaned back.

"Your appointment go well?"

She didn't answer. Couldn't. She was still seething at the way her client had been forcibly taken from her home and imprisoned in New Jersey. She'd warned Luisa that asylum seekers faced an uncertain future, that there was no guarantee she wouldn't be arrested and detained before the decision was handed down. ICE hadn't let her down. It was always a crap shoot. She never knew what would set them off. The Immigration and Customs Enforcement teams were aggressively targeting people like Luisa, and it made her sick to her stomach. The family had already been through so much. Arriving a couple of months ago from a location in Central America, they were fleeing a gang that threatened her and her family with violence. When the gang had destroyed their home and slaughtered their farm animals, they'd sought refuge here.

Camille had taken the case on Nell's recommendation and, after the initial interview was bound and determined to see her settled here. Luisa had a well-founded fear of being persecuted and there was evidence that proved her claim. Luisa's brother had had the prescience to take pictures of the wreckage. She'd hoped the immigrant's cycle of traumatization would be coming to an end soon. She'd already spent hours building a case, had all the documentation she'd needed, her case file over a thousand pages. Now, she'd have to file a request for Luisa's extradition back to the Suffolk facility so she could continue as her legal representative and advocate. She'd spent the morning in that pursuit.

"Actually, no."

"What happened?"

"ICE."

"Frozen water, ice?"

"No. Homeland Security, ICE."

"Remind me of FSB."

"Now that you mention it, I guess they would."

She wouldn't tell him that the conditions in the detention facilities could be compared to Russian prisons, as well. Isolation, beatings, lack of medical care, death. Not here in Massachusetts. There were too many human rights groups here and the citizenry would not allow it. There had been protests at the local facility to demand lesser stays, barbed wire. Nell had almost been arrested during one she participated in.

She told him the gist of the story, leaving out names to protect the privacy of her client. Her frustration must have showed because he commiserated with her.

"I am sorry. This happens everywhere."

"It shouldn't happen here."

"At least you can do something about it. There are places where people are thrown in jail for speaking truth. Lawless countries where there is lack of judicial order."

"We are not supposed to be one of them."

The people she represented might not be citizens, and yes, most were here illegally, but they were human beings and deserved respect and civilized treatment.

Wanting to be done with this conversation, knowing she had more work to do regarding Luisa and it couldn't begin until Monday, she asked, "How did your day go?"

"Waste of time."

"Third degree?"

"No. Alec gave me job."

"What kind?"

"Sorry. As you say, not in your pay grade."

The anger about Luisa was still simmering. There was a woman who wanted to stay and here was a man who—

"You are infuriating. I've been given the task of keeping you alive and I get bupkiss."

"What is this bupkiss?"

"It means nothing, *nyet*thing, not a damn morsel of information. I will uncover it all. I have my ways."

He slanted a glance at her.

The way he was staring set her nerves on edge. They'd be together this weekend, and she needed to stay far away from the condo or she might be willing to extract the information in a very unprofessional way.

CHAPTER TWELVE

After she dropped him off at the safe house he'd be leaving soon, he watched her pull away. Had she been warning him that she'd set out to seduce him? There was an erratic beat to his heart. If he was honest, he wouldn't mind her trying to extract what he had to give by physical persuasion. She would be a nice diversion from the relentless pursuit of truth.

They would be together this weekend. Not alone...but...

With a jolt of sexual energy that went bone deep, his rock-hard body was telling him he wouldn't turn it down. He was hungry for her, and although it wasn't safe or sane, it was there.

He opened the door to find Boog sitting at the table as if he'd never left, a can of soda sitting next to him, completely focused on what he was doing. Without taking his eyes off the screen, he said, "That guy, I think his name is Shane, let me in, said to pick up where we left off the other day. I'm fired up about this back channel. Hope you don't mind."

Shane was another agent, just assigned to his detail. He didn't seem prone to sit in a car in sub-degree weather and had made himself at home in the safe house.

After getting himself a tumbler of vodka, Maks took a sip and proceeded to his spot at the table, his computer ready and waiting.

"Not at all. It has been helpful."

"I penetrated another source but stopped short of feeding it false information. I wasn't sure it was a good idea. Don't want them spooked."

"Disrupt but don't destroy."

"I'm probing the perimeters for weak spots, already found a few."

"Where?"

The enemy was hiding everywhere. So were the fault lines where an invader could sneak in and create havoc. There were threats to the grids, to intelligence networks, and to multiple government agencies that were not color-coded like the perceived danger from terrorist attacks. Those threats could be countered but that wasn't his job here. He ignored them, spending his time spying on the men and women who were trying to disrupt the American systems, retrieving material on what had already occurred during their election. Facebook was a big offender although no one knew that yet. Russians had bought advertising and targeted those states where they could turn the tide, where they could make an impact. WikiLeaks was still causing problems, and classified documents were being sold to the highest bidder. People thought elections couldn't be rigged. But any digital device could be attacked. Remote viewing was commonplace; analytic tools that processed data had been developed. It was a free-for-all where anybody with a talent for hacking could access the most sensitive of information.

Maks sat down and began to work, keeping the chatter to a minimum. By dinnertime they'd covered a lot of ground and had amassed another hundred pages of material. When would it be enough? They were following the money now and it had taken them into a dozen different countries. There were no rules out in space, no one telling them what they could or could not do. Because of this, the volume of traffic around portals was increasing every year and the damage being done to the financial sector was measured in terms of millions lost. It had become a game for him and he was one of the best out there. Sort of like a chess master, each of his moves was methodical and debilitating. There would be nowhere to hide once he was finished.

He sent Boog off with a promise to pick up where they left off once he got back. There'd be other sites in cyberspace for him to track in the interim, and they didn't want to duplicate efforts. Packing up for the trip to Franconia didn't take long, and he was ready and waiting, all his worldly belongings zipped away in his carry-on. He was vacating these premises and wondered where he'd be going once he returned from this mini-retreat. He'd done due diligence and knew "they" still hadn't found him. He just needed a little more time, a few more documents, a couple more gaps, and he'd be free. What that truly meant, he didn't know yet.

⌐

Maks was driving up with Camille. Shane would follow behind making sure they weren't being followed. It was a two-hundred-mile trek straight up Route Ninety-three and she'd been able to keep steady at seventy miles an hour. Thankfully, the weather was co-operating. Maks' personal belongings were stowed in her trunk, along with her overnight case. She'd let Alec determine her fate, and she had to admit she wasn't entirely bummed. Scared shitless, but the rapid heartbeat was almost welcome after all these years.

"How long till we get there?"

She'd hadn't forgotten there was someone in the car with her, not with the way her flesh prickled at his presence, but they'd been on the road just under an hour and it was the first time since she picked him up that he'd said something.

"We're probably half way there if traffic holds."

She'd glanced over to find him studying the sandwich she'd picked up for them to eat on the way. He didn't seem thrilled with the selection but that's all they had time for. He kept lifting the top of the sub to sniff at the filler before taking another bite.

"What is this?"

"It's a chicken teriyaki. If you don't like it, take the other one."

"What is other?"

"A plain roasted turkey. I wanted something that wouldn't leak."

All she'd eaten so far were her fries. If Em was with her, she'd have her rip a part of the sandwich off so she could eat it piecemeal. She thought it was much too personal a request for the man sitting next to her.

She noticed the frown before she heard the question.

"Why put with cucumbers?"

"It's the way they make the sandwich. Just take them out if you don't like them. What are you, a food critic?

"I know good when I taste it." She detected a bit of censure in his tone.

Rolling her eyes at his petulance, she said, "Eat the cookie."

"Not warm from oven."

She couldn't help the laugh that bubbled up.

"If I had known you were such a food snob, I would have stopped someplace else."

"Not snob, just more discerning in taste."

Her eyes strayed from the road from time to time to see him wrestle with it. He'd removed the offending cukes and the tomato was next to go. When it was half-eaten, he wrapped it back up in the paper and shoved it in the bag. After wiping his face with the napkin, he leaned his head back, seeming content with the companionable silence.

They were making good time. She'd left after nine to avoid the backlog of cars that would be on the road around dinnertime. Her estimated time of arrival was close to midnight.

She let a memory bubble up.

"My grandfather used to warn us about driving through the notch after dark. It became kind of a ritual before anyone arrived or left."

It was Gaston Bissonnette who had introduced her to skiing. She'd accompany him on his yearly pilgrimage to Quebec to see the family left behind. His father had made him promise he'd keep in touch with grand aunts and uncles, and he had until his death. On the way back from the family gathering, they'd stop at one of the lodges in the White Mountains. It's where he'd taught her how to slalom. They'd spend two days together, and she had loved every minute with him. Out of all the Bissonnettes, she was the one who loved family, kept the photographs handed down, had begged for Gaston's desk when he died. She'd sanded it down and refinished it, and it'd found a home in her second bedroom. It's where she did all her work. She swore he was there with her, prodding her in different directions when she was probing for information. Maybe he'd help her with—she glanced over to the man sitting next to her—her Russian.

"What is bad about driving through Notch after dark?"

She scanned the dark countryside before admitting, "Nothing, really. It's kind of deserted up here and it goes down to a single lane the closer we get. There are a lot of moose up north, and you can't really see them that well. Until they're right in front of you. You don't want to tangle with one of them. They'd win."

"Do you come up a lot?"

"A couple of times a winter. If I want to ski, I usually go somewhere closer to home. My home."

"Where is that?"

"South Boston."

"You live in house?"

"No. A condo. There's no point living in something bigger. There's only me. And I'm not there much."

"Open concept?"

She glanced over at him, giving in to the beginnings of a smile.

"I guess so. Everything nowadays is open concept. I didn't care one way or another. Sometimes definition is a good thing."

"I watch Hunters for Houses one night. That is what everyone looks for. And stainless-steel appliances."

She chuckled at the way he remembered the show.

"It's *House Hunters* and I have them, too. The appliances. They collect smudges like bees collect honey. Just sayin'."

"You are true American."

There was that grin again. The one that set her heart racing.

"God, I hope that's not what we're known for around the world. It makes us look somewhat shallow."

He shifted into the corner as if he wanted to see her better. He'd taken his coat off a hundred miles back, and the sweater set off his dark, mysterious eyes.

"These hunters seemed to have big, what they call it, wish list?"

She felt a flush of color at his intimation.

"Maybe we do seem that shallow. We always want more, bigger, better. It's what manifest destiny was all about."

"What is that?"

"We continued moving west when we got bored. Sometimes we did bad things in the process."

"Like kill all natives."

He knew more about her history than she'd expected. He was smart, although it was in a cagey sort of way.

"We didn't kill them all, although we tried to kill their spirit. I think every culture has episodes like that in their past, don't they?"

"Yes, but do not make themselves look superior."

His expression had turned serious, his eyes darkened even more. She couldn't help but feel disappointed that he had such a low opinion of her, them.

"You don't like us much, do you?"

"I don't know many. I only know what I hear and that is not something to trust. The jury is still out. This saying, you know?"

"As a lawyer, I know first-hand. Would it help my cause if you knew my ancestors weren't from here?"

"Where they from?"

"Quebec. If I still lived there, I'd be considered something like royalty. My who-knows-how-many-times grandmother was from France, came over as a fille du roi or daughter of the king. It would be comparable to an American with Mayflower ancestors. That was the boat that came over with the first group of British citizens to settle in Plymouth, just south of Boston."

He didn't have to know she'd acted like a princess right through high school. It was only when she got to college and life became more difficult that she'd decided to become a warrior instead.

"Why did they leave?"

She'd learned over the years that people migrated for different kinds of reasons. Many today to escape the death and destruction going on in various countries around the world.

"Economics. The agricultural climate had changed; the industrial revolution had an impact. A large group moved en masse to a city north of Boston. That's where I grew up."

"You didn't live in this Notch."

"No. My father and mother moved there when I was in college. It was always my dad's dream to own a winery. My brother had just graduated from a local college in botany and went with them."

Her father had been a science professor at the local college but didn't like the politics that went with the job. He'd been granted tenure but was expected to write papers and books on his subject, knowing it held very little interest for anyone other than those in his field. He'd come to dislike the students, as well. On their phones during his lectures, they talked, ate, ignored what he was feeding them. He complained how disrespectful they'd become. He couldn't wait to save up the money to get away from it.

"You have other sibling, right? Sister?"

"Solange. She lives in Tyngsboro with her husband and two kids. She teaches fourth grade at a catholic school in the same town."

"You are Catholic?"

"Raised that way. Attended a French elementary school. Catholic high school."

"You must speak the language?"

"I do. My mother is from France and she made sure we learned. Thus, the school. When Em and I went to Paris, I appreciated it more than ever."

She wasn't going to tell him she had a rudimentary grasp of the Russian language. She'd only taken it for the first three semesters in college, before changing her major. After that it seemed a waste of course selection. She had too many to make up if she wanted to graduate on time.

"You say raised that way. Are you Catholic no longer?"

"I don't think it's anything that goes away. I don't practice it anymore, though."

"You must practice?"

"No. I...I stopped going to church. There's a lot of hypocrisy in what they teach. The law makes you more sensitive to justice and the truth. There were a lot of things swept under the rug. I didn't like that."

"I feel same way. Church collaborated with whoever in power. It has long history, deep roots, and was useful to state. They conformed to restore wealth, became nationalistic arm to government, stood for nothing they preached."

"Today the religious groups are for the strangest things. I swear if Russia did want to subvert our way of life, they'd target them first."

He nodded as if he knew something she didn't. It got her thinking...the evangelicals had jumped on the campaign train of the incoming president...

Not wanting to think too deeply about that, she looked at him when he asked, "Do you travel a lot?"

Almost absently she replied, "A couple of times a year."

"With this Em?"

"Yeah. We do a lot together."

"BFF?"

"You know what that is?"

"I am on internet a lot."

She wanted to ask him if it was for researching things, but she hesitated. They were having an actual conversation and she didn't want to ruin it.

The Blue tooth barged in.

Hitting the button, she said, "Hello, Mama."

"Bonsoir, my Cami. Are you almost here?"

Maks listened intently. There was a French lilt to Camille's mother's voice and it echoed inside the car. Camille glanced over, put her finger to her lips, as if she had to tell him to be quiet. He had no intention of saying a word.

"Sorry, but no. I left late to avoid the traffic."

"We will see you in the morning, then?"

"I plan to be on the slopes by eight."

"We will plan breakfast for seven. We are looking forward to seeing you, my love. I'm glad you changed your mind. Why isn't Em with you? I don't like you driving up here alone in the dark."

Her eyes stayed on the road, but she compressed her lips.

"Mama, I am fine. Em is watching Teddy this weekend."

"I see. I won't keep you. I just wanted to check on your progress. Be safe and I'll see you in the morning."

She ended the call and he heard the soft sigh she emitted once it was done.

"I thought I was going to have to lie. I don't do it well."

He wondered if that was true. If it was, he'd be more inclined to trust her. At least with some things. He would watch and wait a little longer before he made that decision. It wasn't some small detail he'd be trusting her with, but his life.

Quiet descended again, and his gaze went back to the inky blackness of night. Camille was right. It was a deserted stretch of road. He was almost glad he'd been forced into this. It got him out of the small, cramped space of the apartment and into the wilderness. Here he could breathe the cold, clean air without worry or care that someone was watching. Except for the agent who'd been assigned to him. He was younger than the others, but with the same stern demeanor. Was that something they taught you in FBI school? Along with the skill of blending into the background so people forgot you were there.

Camille was a different story. She could never blend into her surroundings. Fresh and feminine, her scent alone would make her stand out. He turned his head to peer at her. Her hands rested easy on the wheel. The relaxed appearance was at odds with the slight frown on her lips.

"You are worried?"

"I don't know how I'm going to keep you away from my family. There's a handyman that is always on site and will see our comings and goings, and a maid who cleans the rooms every morning. I'm going to have to tell her not to bother with mine. We did not think this through well enough."

"I stay in bedroom."

"And what about Eliot Ness back there?"

"His name not Eliot, it's Shane."

She shook her head, as if remembering he was from a different world.

"Ness was FBI—Just a figure of speech."

Almost absently, he asked, "What made you become lawyer?"

"Long story. And I'm not giving you anything until you give me something."

"I give you my name."

"No, I don't think you did."

She was right, of course. Nate and Alec had it. The background checks while he was staying in Finland had made it a necessity. No one would get access unless he had no choice but to reveal himself. Thinking about Boog and the group, he said, "People call me Skoli. Like your mother calls you Cami."

"Skoli, huh?"

"I like."

"You would. You drink enough of it. Oh, and FYI there's no smoking in the condo. Or outside it. Or anywhere around it. My parents would have a fit if they smelled even a hint of it."

"Not outside?"

"I'll find you a place if you can't live without them, but that will be the only place you can do the dirty."

"Everyone smokes in Russia."

"That's what I've heard. Here, not so much. I'll pick you up a vape. Maybe that will get you through the night."

"Vape is—?"

"A smokeless alternative."

He grimaced, not wanting the alternative.

There were lights beginning to illuminate the road. They must be getting close to a town and this place of her family. He would like to meet them. See where she came from. Maybe he could sneak a peek if they dropped by. Did she look like her mother? Her father? What were they like? This curiosity was not smart, and he had to detach himself from it. It would not be a good idea to go there. Was she plying her wiles on him? Was this situation pre-ordained by the FBI and their lawyer to get him away from safety? Was the agent with them an assassin?

No matter what his body wanted, he'd thought better about giving in to any seduction on her part. He would have to keep his wits about him. *Trust no one* had become his mantra, and he needed to listen to that warning voice.

It could be a matter of life and death.

⌐

When they pulled into a parking spot that had been plowed right down to the asphalt, he took in the building in front of him. It was a rambling three-story colonial with balconies, set atop a small hill. It looked like it had been plunked down in a pile of snow, fitting perfectly amidst the white powder.

"This looks like house."

She had put the car in park and shut off the engine.

"It used to be. My parents broke it up into six condos, so they could accommodate their visitors. They sell packages to the winery that comes with a ski-lift pass and condo suite. They kept one open for me this weekend. I'm costing them a thousand dollars a night."

She was glad they hadn't rented it out when she cancelled. Knowing her mother, she'd probably arranged this whole thing with the universe. Michelle had some pretty powerful juju.

She popped the trunk, got out of the car, and took her bag out, waiting for him to do the same. After she'd checked on the agent to make sure he was following them, she led them up the stairs and into the first door on the right. It was expansive, with an open concept, high ceilings and lots of windows.

As she walked towards one of the doors down the hall, she pointed to another and said, "That's your room. Shane, you get the couch. There are pillows and blankets here in the hall closet. Help yourself. I've had enough people here to know it's comfortable. My parents bought the best, wanting each suite to sleep six. Good night, all. See you...whenever."

And with that she disappeared behind door number one.

He entered and stood inside his room. The bed looked inviting. It was covered by a white duvet, and four goose-down pillows were fluffed and waiting. Immediately going to a window, he unlocked and opened it, letting the raw winter wind in. It felt glorious.

He put all worry aside for tonight. This was the kind of elegance and comfort he hadn't experienced in a while. After stripping out of his clothes, he slid beneath the covers, the cool cotton feeling good on his skin.

Maybe because of the cold night air ruffling the curtains, or because he felt safe for the first time in a while, in no time at all, his slight snores alerted those around him that he'd found slumber.

CHAPTER THIRTEEN

Camille wandered out for some water before going to bed, found Shane in a darkened room except for the glow of the television. When he glanced up at her, she said, "Help yourself. They stocked the refrigerator with drinks and some food. It's one of the perks that comes with the rental."

He signaled with a finger to his forehead and went back to the show he had on, the sound low enough so only he could hear it.

On her way back to her room, she paused outside Maks'. She could hear him through the wall. The snoring didn't meet buzz saw levels, but was the gentle sounds of someone fast asleep.

Her body tingled at the thought of him so close. There was a smoldering flame that she hadn't felt in a long time, not that she had let herself get that close to anyone again.

A face appeared, one that hadn't changed over the years. He was still nineteen, blond hair, blue eyes, soft smile.

She hadn't thought about him in a long time.

After closing herself in behind her door, she went to the balcony, pushed open the slider, and stepped out. The night was cold, but the wind had died down, so it was bearable without a coat. She looked up at the stars, her arms crossed over her chest.

Michael Evans.

The name floated through her body, the sadness no lighter today than it had been back then. It had colored everything in her life since.

He'd been majoring in pre-law. Was serious, studious, kind.

She was the exact opposite. Selfish, willful, spoiled.

It was a part of her history, one she couldn't shake, part of her personality she'd buried deep inside herself. She was quite different today, the metamorphosis complete the night he died.

Her rebellious streak had caused her own demise. Had it come from the strict upbringing, or was it a defect she was born with? Reckless not only with her life but with others' as well, she'd driven too fast, lived too large, partied too hard. She'd talked back, acted out. After she'd almost gotten tossed out of school her senior year, her mother had somehow talked the nuns into keeping her, but it hadn't stopped the antics. She just made sure to keep them contained in the hours after school got out. She'd drive to downtown Lowell and hang out with her friends, smoking and drinking. Homework was a burden that she didn't carry well, and her grades had reflected it. Following in the wake of two of the school's A-plus students, she'd figured she'd never measure up, so she didn't bother to compete. At least not for honor roll. She counted on her charm to get what she wanted, and usually succeeded. She had it in diamonds. The only reason she got into college was her father's position there.

When she'd started going out with Mike sophomore year, she settled down a bit, but she was frivolous in her choices, took courses that interested her, avoided a study track that would lead to a good-paying job.

Then, one night a party. Too much to drink. Having too much fun to leave. A boyfriend who had a test the next day and went home early with one of his friends. An accident that killed. Not only him but the driver. Two deaths on her conscience.

As soon as she'd heard about it, she'd broken down into hysterics, rushed to the scene, sat by the side of the road in the broken glass shards that were evidence he'd been taken out of the world. The asphalt was spattered red with his blood, the telephone pole freckled blue from the impact of the car, the smell of burned rubber still thick in the air.

And she'd cried. The crying hadn't stopped for weeks. She took the blame for it because it was all her fault. If she'd stayed sober, if she'd left with him, driven him home, if she'd been a better girlfriend...he might still be alive today.

Her social-butterfly days had ended that night.

She'd shut off the affection, shut down the outgoing personality. She'd switched to pre-law and become a hermit. She'd known she could never be the lawyer he would have been, but she wanted to fill the slot he'd left open. Try to make it up to him. Took up asylum cases, represented those who faced death, as if she could refund his life.

And she'd never seriously dated again. Put work before her social life, put work before play. The only time she let her guard down was on vacation with Em, or when skiing. Not that she went wild. She wouldn't know how to anymore. But her spontaneity resurfaced in the different locales; her runs down the mountain gave the feeling of freedom she no longer allowed herself, a taste of danger that she missed.

There was danger down the hall.

It was in the form of a man she didn't even know. How could she stay safe if her job was to uncover who he was? The few things she'd learned were chips of magnet that were clinging to her heart. She'd glimpsed a deep soulfulness. Sadness hung over him like a dark shadow. Was it Nina? Or something more? His Russian nature, or his country's slide back into a constricted form of government? But when he smiled, the warmth of it reached out and touched her. He was willing to give his life to whatever cause he had taken as his own. Would she ever know what that cause was? As she lay in bed, aching for sleep, the answers refused to come.

⌐

The room was dark and Maks was disoriented when he awoke, trying to remember where he was.

Franconia Notch. Camille Bissonnette.

As her name came to mind, so did her face. There was a tightening in his gut, and he couldn't ever remember feeling this tight from need. It was a madness he didn't know how to ignore, his arousal throbbing and rock hard.

He threw off the covers when he heard her walk down the hall. After climbing out of bed, he inched to the door. Opening it up a sliver, he peeked out, to see her dressed in a heavy parka, snow pants that fit her lean legs, leaving no curve to the imagination, with her hair tucked under her hat. She moved with such feminine grace that his gaze lingered too long, and she caught him at his perusal.

Her eyes changed to quicksilver. Her lips puckered in what appeared to be disapproval.

"I'll be gone all day, possibly most of the night. Make yourself at home."

He stepped out, now that she knew he was awake, forgetting he was clad only in his boxers. "There is coffee?"

"There is. Shane's up already. He's taking a shower, but he made it earlier. I showed him the spot where you can smoke so please, not in here."

"I promise. No smoke inside."

"Thanks. There is a bottle of vodka behind the bar. It's probably not your preferred label but I can pick some up later if you want."

"No. What is there will be fine."

She dropped her eyes at his steady gaze and backed away. She was out the door without another word.

He poured himself a cup of coffee, hoping that Shane made it strong. He needed a shot of something other than adrenaline, which was already pumping fast and furiously.

What was it about her that disturbed him?

The way she looked...moved...spoke?

Feminine in an earthy sort of way, sensual in the way she expressed herself, her voice silky, and the underlying sexuality of it captivated him.

Taking a long swallow of the deep brown brew, he closed his eyes in appreciation.

Once the coffee had satisfied one of his needs, he went to his bathroom to fulfill another before getting his clothes on to rectify his third. As soon as Shane had given him directions to his hiding spot, he took a cigarette and a lighter and moved towards it. It was tucked away behind a large bush where he would go unseen. The only thing that might give him away was the streaming smoke rising from the greenery. It was a good vantage point from which to watch the morning's activity. Cars were being packed with ski gear, voices were raised in revelry, the smell of approaching snow hung in the air. How he would love to be part of it all.

He had been once, when the carefree days of youth were his. He'd skied more than he let on. Not that he'd gone to any place like this. It was one of the things you did during the Moscow winters. There wasn't much else to do during the cold, dark days. There was a short window of time when the people had been liberated. Glasnost was supposed to last. Students, people his age had grabbed onto it, not realizing how entrenched their elders were in the past. The Russian spirit was too long controlled to find release. Before they knew it, they were back under the thumb of the government and all things changed once again, but not for the better. When a personal tragedy had struck, the hopes he had for his future there had been dashed. He'd lost his love of country the day his father was arrested.

It didn't take much for the memories to take hold.

⌒

The knock on the door came early, before he'd left for work. It was a week after one of the major protests in the city, right before the most recent election. Four members of the Interior Ministry, an arm of the police, were standing outside. Barging in, without an invitation, they began to take apart the apartment, room by room. After six hours of searching, they confiscated everything they'd found: computers, family affects, DVD's, and all his father's personal papers. They were only done with their task when they'd handcuffed Petrov and arrested him.

His father whispered to him before they carted him away, "It is all right. We still have the right to protest. I will be fine."

But he was wrong, underestimating the radical turn his country had taken, ignoring what had already happened in the past to people like him. His father had failed to observe the new rules in the game of politics. None of them knew that authorities had put extensive restrictions in place and self-identified activists were now breaking the law when they came together. You couldn't speak out about corruption anymore. If you participated in any way, you could be arrested and charged as dissidents who were destabilizing society. The FSB was given the power to pull them out at the root. Petrov was sent to a detention center, and over the course of the next year, he was systematically tortured, his living conditions increasingly worsened, his requests to see family consistently denied. The journal his father had left behind spoke of his deprivations, each cell worse than the last. No heat, no food, no privacy. All done with the intent to break him. Why hadn't Petrov listened to the advice of his lawyers? They'd warned him that something bad was going to happen. But Petrov had thought the law would protect him. His naiveté had put him on the fast track to death.

His crime?

His steadfast refusal to recant the truth. At first, he'd acted as his own attorney, filing motion after motion but every level of the government denied him release. As his health deteriorated, Petrov's requests for medical treatment rejected, he'd endured a nightmare of pain for continuing to speak out against the corrupt government for what it was. The lawyers who'd offered their assistance could do nothing to save him. He'd died in that pitiful prison for those things he held dear: truth and integrity. His death certificate claimed he'd died by his own hand. Maks knew it was a lie. The condition of the body told the truth. The guards had found a way to silence him. They had beat him to death.

That's when Maks had begun his work in exposing the duplicity of the legal system. He'd taken up the cause, but not in the same way. What he'd found along the way was what had brought him here.

His father's journal kept him focused. And he read passages when he needed the motivation to keep going, to keep up his work, in spite of the danger.

Was he a coward for doing it underground? Would his father be ashamed of his methods?

He'd been told Petrov would be proud.

He didn't know if that was true, but he would keep his promise to avenge that death with his last breath.

After crushing the cigarette stub under his booted foot, he returned to the condo to get back to the job that had become an obsession. With Camille gone, he could work. There would be no distractions, no woman competing for his attention.

He settled himself at the make-shift table in the breakfast nook and picked up another thread.

⁓

As she approached her parent's house, Camille was still sucking in her breath at the way Maks had looked, dressed only in his boxers, a thick gold chain and cross hanging around his neck. He was a specimen. His abdomen was tight, his legs muscular. There was a tattoo on his arm, but she hadn't been able to see what it was. It looked like letters and a number. A very long number.

What did it signify? What did it mean to him? If she could figure it out, it might give her something on which to base her discovery. These were the small details she had to pick up if she was going to do her job without help.

When she walked through the door, she didn't even get a hello out before her mother asked, "So who are the young men you have with you?"

Camille had prepared for this but didn't expect the news to spread so quickly. The handyman had gotten word to her mother before first light. He must have because she'd been up close to it.

After unzipping her jacket, she shrugged out of it and tossed it on one of the chairs in the kitchen.

"They're just some guys I know who wanted to get away. When Em couldn't come, I invited them along. They'll be staying at the condo, so they won't interfere with family time."

"You must bring them to dinner tonight. You know I love meeting your friends."

She could tell by the look on Michelle's face that she was overly interested and hopeful. Her mother often complained about her obsession with her job and the fact she'd shut down her emotions. Her mother understood where it came from but didn't like it and spent many an hour trying to convince her that she needed to give love another chance. It fell on deaf ears.

Camille was convinced she had everything she needed. She had her associates at the law firm, and it was all for one and one for all there. She trusted them enough to let her real self sneak out from time to time: her mischievousness, her playful side, her sense of humor. She'd limited her field of play and she had every intention of keeping it that way.

"One of them is kind of a recluse. I don't think he'd want to."

"You'll call and ask. It's the polite thing to do, Cami."

Ignoring her mother's request, she went over and hugged her brother.

"What's going on around here today?"

He had the newspaper open and was checking the sports page. He was a huge hockey fan, and any knowledge she had of the game came from him.

"You have to ask, with Christmas coming? We're booked solid until after the New Year and we're still getting calls for gift cards and pre-paid packages."

She went to the sideboard and began taking some of the foods being served buffet style. Standing at the counter, she tasted the eggs benedict. It was delicious.

"The restaurant?"

"We just got our fourth star rating."

"Congratulations. I can understand why." She lifted her plate in a symbolic salute.

Small talk filled the space as she ate. It always felt good being here. They were close, and it was easy to be wrapped in the intimacy of family. After the grave thoughts that had consumed her last night, she needed the loving atmosphere. Thoughts of Michael had led her to thoughts of Maks, and she was deathly afraid of what he represented, afraid that her heart was opening after all this time. She was doing her best to close it. The creaks and groans suggested it might not be as easy this time as it had been in the past.

Once she deposited the empty plate into the sink, her mother came over and handed her her cell.

"Call."

She stared at her mother, her heart beginning to canter, her stomach beginning to ache. How could she get out of this? She couldn't pull Maks out of hiding. And what about the agent? Would he have to check with Alec? What if Alec said no?

And she knew her mother would give her the third degree if she met Maks.

Where had she met a Russian? Was he a client? A friend? A lover? Michelle knew she was drawn to the culture. Or maybe her parents would give him the third degree. That would be even more problematic. She knew Maks would go on lock down.

Her mother was giving her the mother look, one eyebrow arched as if daring her to dismiss her and her request. How could she explain that bringing Maks out in public wasn't on the to-do list for the weekend?

Taking a deep, cleansing breath, she dialed the number of the landline, praying no one would answer.

When someone did, it reinforced the fact that prayer was for the foolhardy. That it was Maks proved humiliating. His voice was soft and accentuated by his accent and a fragile flame sparked inside of her.

"I'm at my folks' house and they wanted to know if you want to join us for dinner. Seems the guy who works for them noticed I had guests. I understand if you don't want to."

When she heard Maks' response, she swallowed hard.

"Good. I'll let them know. We'll have to be at Stone Soup around six."

"That is Russian fairy tale."

"It is. My contribution. It's suit and tie."

"Didn't bring. Don't even own."

"Then I guess you'll have to take a rain check. Do it some other time."

"Shane cane take me to town to buy?"

"Not a good idea. There are a lot of people out there."

"Who will be looking here?"

"You never know."

"If they were, I'd already be dead already."

A whisper of unease teased her senses.

"Why don't you talk to Shane. He might have another suggestion."

"He invited as well?"

"Of course, the two of you. Leaving one behind would be rude."

"I call back."

There was nothing left to say. He'd hung up the receiver.

"It seems like you were right. They might want to come along."

Not waiting around to see her mother's look of smug satisfaction or how else she'd meddle in her life, she headed out to the slopes.

⌒

As she approached the ski resort, Camille could see the open trenches between rows of trees from the car. The hillside was decorated with dozens of trails. They looked tiny from this far away. She knew they weren't. Some of the best skiing she'd ever done, was here. To the left, lay the backcountry, the snow fresh powder, the trails unchartered, the passages narrow. Unless you knew your way through the forest, it would be stop and go, something she wasn't settling for today. She was going black diamond, wanting full-out speed, the steepest and most harrowing trails, on the mountain.

Once the car was parked and locked, her skis and poles tucked under her arm, she approached the gate, her year pass stapled to her jacket, and she was waved through. It was the perfect day for this, and it showed as hundreds of people gathered in various poses, some milling around the bottom of the hill after a run, others standing around an instructor or snow-plowing down the beginner slope. There were dozens shushing down in a zig-zag formation, snowboarders descending in sweeping curves. Tingles of anticipation shot through her as she waited in line for the chair lift. There was something about this that never failed to thrill her. Soon she'd be standing at the top, staring in the face of an unopposed force that she'd become one with.

CHAPTER FOURTEEN

By late morning, Maks had a new suit, tie, and shoes. Shane had called Alec before running the errand and had gotten permission for them to accompany the Bissonnettes tonight. Alec thought that it would be a good way of acclimating him to his new country. They were unsure of his intentions to stay, and rightly so. He'd made no secret of the fact he wasn't sure he liked the country enough to make it his home. They had plans for him, or so they'd said. There was a government agency that had the most elite computer geeks in the world, and they felt his skills would be well used there. He'd have to take a test, make sure he was up to their caliber, but he had no doubts he'd pass it. He might not have a college degree, but he'd been working with computers since he was a kid. Taken them apart and put them back together, built his own several times, his latest the one he was using. He could fight a cyber war with the best of them. He just wasn't sure he wanted to do it here.

Then where? What were his options? No place called to him. No place was safe right now. Democracy was going through a crisis, fueled by nationalism and a need to be governed. People didn't want the responsibility of governing themselves, being knowledgeable, being up to speed on what was happening. They wanted to live in their own little worlds and be taken care of. Here? He'd seen signs of resistance, of protest, but he'd also seen signs of division and racial tension. He knew better than most what had happened to cause it and was doing his best to bring it to light.

He'd be killing two birds with one stone, as Alec had told him.

He'd already put in a couple of hours work, and decided to take a break for lunch. As he was rifling through the refrigerator, the doorbell rang.

Shane jumped up from his chair, his hand on his weapon, and made his way to the front door, signaling him back and out of the way until he determined who it was.

Hiding behind the wall in the kitchen, Maks listened to the verbal exchange.

"Hello. I'm Michelle Bissonnette. I thought I'd drop by and make sure everything was to your liking. You are a friend of my daughter Cami, aren't you?"

Maks had eased away from the wall and peeked around the cut out as Shane backed away from the door and invited her in. Maks didn't miss his eyes sweeping the perimeter before closing it.

"Yes, ma'am. It's nice to meet you."

"Likewise. There were two of you from what I heard. Is the other one hiding?"

Maks inhaled sharply.

"No. He's in the kitchen."

He heard Shane call out, "Hey, Maks. Camille's mother is out here."

His body was tense. He hated not being able to trust. It meant he had to think everything through, before acting. Hoping the person on the other side of the wall wasn't holding a Glock, he stepped out.

And let his breath out.

It was obvious why Shane had relaxed his stance. Camille was the spitting image of her mother. The same blue-grey eyes, the same small nose, the same type of feminine beauty that seemed fragile. He knew it to be an illusion.

"Mrs. Bissonnette. It is pleasure to meet you."

He could tell she was...intrigued?

"A Russian. How very interesting."

"It is problem?"

"Not at all. It's just Cami has always been...intrigued by your culture. That girl is all about family and it started with an interest in her ancestors. When she found my grandfather's dog tags she was hooked on everything Russian."

His great-grandfather had fought in the revolution as well. He no longer had the dog-tags. The goons from the Ministry made sure he would have no ancestral artifacts to prove his family had been grown in Russia before Stalin, Lenin, communism and the latest in a long line of bullies. They had taken everything the day his father was arrested. The only thing left was the solid gold cross his father had given him on his twenty-first birthday. It had been handed down to the first-born son for a hundred years and he'd never taken it off.

He was staring into space, fading into the past, but the soft voice called him back.

"Where did she find you?"

When he couldn't find his voice to answer, Shane interjected, "He's a friend of mine. We met Camille through the husband of one of her partners. Nate Fisher."

Flicking some of her chin-length hair back, she remembered. "He's married to Mia."

Shane was still standing by the door, as if protecting him from every angle. "That's right."

"Are you FBI?"

Shane walked back into the room, addressing the older woman.

"I am. Maks will be working for one of our other agencies soon."

"You're not one of her cases, then?"

"Cases?"

"Cami is an immigration attorney who handles asylum cases. Where you're Russian, I thought—"

Not wanting to give away he knew exactly who she was, he fired back, "No. As Shane says, I work for American government."

It wasn't a lie. What he was doing would go a long way towards gaining indictments for espionage and treason for a few highly placed individuals. And hopefully, an Interpol notice for another for crimes against the motherland. Would the world finally pay attention? Stop pandering to a global enemy?

He was brought back by the lilting accent of Michelle Bissonnette. The timbre was a match for her daughter's.

"Are you going to ski this weekend? Or did you come to relax? Of course, Cami would say they are one and the same."

"I have no...what you say? Gear."

"You can always rent. We have an agreement with the management there. All you have to do is tell them you're staying at the winery."

"Maybe I take you up on that. It has been years since I have skied but maybe it come back."

Michelle was studying him, examining him from every angle, and he became discomfited. Was this a trap? A set-up? It would be safer if he just stayed here, did his work, and didn't want for anything more. Maybe he could become American. He did want more, wasn't willing to settle for what his country offered. He was surprised to admit he was optimistic. It wasn't a natural tendency where he came from.

"Good. If you want, I can take you over. I'm hoping to join Cami at some point today. I don't get to see her often and I like to take advantage of it when she's here."

Alec stepped forward as if to cover him. "That's not necessary, Mrs. Bissonnette. I can take him over later if he wants to go."

"Please, call me Michelle. And take advantage of the offer. There's nothing like a run down the slope to clear your head. They've got some excellent trails."

"We will think about it."

When Michelle turned to go, Shane added, "It was nice meeting you. We'll see you at dinner, if not before."

Her eyes were back on Maks.

"I hope we get to know you better, Maks."

What did she mean? Why would she want to?

Shane once again moved into the breach. "We're only here for the weekend...Michelle. Then it's back to Boston and our jobs. Your daughter was kind enough to offer us a break. We took her up on that."

"We'll see, Shane."

Maks was the one who answered, thoughts of her a jumble in his head.

"You want to get to know us better, why?"

"I'd like to see my daughter play a little. She does it so rarely. If you can help me in that, I'd appreciate it."

She opened the door to see herself out.

Maks turned to Shane and asked, "What did she mean?"

"If I'm reading this right, she thinks you and Camille might be dating."

He felt his blood flood to his groin at the suggestion that they were together.

"What makes her think that?"

"You're Russian. I think it's that simple."

"That is crazy. To date you, would need more than nationality as starting point."

"Maybe. Maybe not. Did you bring your guitar?"

"It is balalaika, not guitar."

"Whatever. Did you bring it?"

"I had to bring everything remember? Not going back to other place."

"I have a feeling Camille would love to be serenaded."

He was not going to serenade her but thoughts of getting her to play were dancing in his head, and the dance was being done amidst tangled sheets. Was that what Michelle wanted? It could only be for a night or two. That's all he could give her. He'd have to think long and hard on that. His focus had to be on the work at hand, not some woman. Even if the woman did funny things to his metabolism.

He stopped himself. He wasn't going there. Thinking that the cold winter air would be a good way to clear his head, he asked. "Can we do this? Go skiing?"

Shane shook his head.

"I've never been on skis in my life. I wouldn't be able to keep up with you, which translates to no."

Maks stood thinking. Could he ski with Camille? He might not be able to keep up with her, but he could tag along and see. What if there was a foreign agent here, following him? He'd be putting her in the line of fire. He couldn't do that to her. Not thinking about who else he put in danger with his presence at the lodge, he asked, "Can we go and watch? That would not put us in different locations."

"You'd be satisfied with that?"

"I must be if I want to get out."

"Alec left things to my own discretion. If you promise to stick to me like glue, I'll agree. I'd prefer to stay here where I can be in control, but it will look strange if two young, single men stay in with all that action out there."

When he'd agreed with the terms, they drove to the ski area, and as they approached the lodge, Maks took in the scene. He'd never been to a place like this before. Only the rich had comforts like this in Russia. Smoke was streaming from the stone chimney, boots crunched on icy snow, kids were squealing, people were laughing, calling out to friends, members of the ski patrol making their rounds in orange vests. Walking into the building at the foot of the slopes, he was awed by the high ceilings, the wooden beams massive and sturdy. Light flooded into the space through walls of glass. Chairs were littered with hats, mittens and jackets. The scent of freshly brewed coffee filled the air, along with the smell of wet wool and wood smoke. He was entranced as he followed Shane to a table by the window, a vodka in front of him, a soda in front of his body guard.

The scenery was stunning. The snow glistened in the early-afternoon sun even as white vapor streamed out as people breathed, speaking to the subzero temperatures. Maks was peering into the distance, looking for Camille, hoping to catch sight of her, gauge her skill as she came down the mountain. He knew what she was wearing, but there were so many skiers it would be by luck that he found her among the hundreds here. As he sipped his vodka, ate the sandwich ordered, he envied those who had such freedom of movement. It was nice here. People were friendly, offering smiles if they caught his eye, and there was a feeling of optimism that trickled though him. The heaviness that hung like an albatross around the inhabitants of all the Baltic states was debilitating. It kept them emotionally stressed, aggressive, vigilant.

The hum of the televisions caught his attention. They hung from the walls, the volume down. One showcased the skiers on the mountainside; the other was broadcasting the news. A weather report for the area came up. The colorful maps with swirls and arrows forecasted snow for the next few days. Reporters were describing what was happening in the towns surrounding the Notch. Others were giving a run down on more national news. The election over, the coverage was now centered on what to expect. They didn't have to try to avoid conflict here. They could offend anyone who disagreed.

The reporting in Ukraine had been shoddy. Nina was one of a few who'd fearlessly told the true story, but she'd become an example of what could happen to those soothsayers. Fearmongering was everywhere. Fewer and fewer were ready to die for the cause.

Battles were waged on the streets, in the prisons.

Advertisers were the hidden persuaders, using psychological warfare on their audience.

Freedom. Capitalism. Democracy.

Good, yes. But good for him? He didn't know.

"What do people here do for living?"

Shane looked up from his newspaper, scanned the area, and shrugged his shoulders. "Most of the guests are fairly well off, so upper management, finance, CEOs. The day trippers come from all walks of life. Skiing is a popular sport in the winter and attracts every day kind of people."

Maks went back to his scrutiny of smiling faces, warm clothes, expensive equipment.

He jerked forward, to see Camille coming toward the restaurant, her cheeks chapped from the cold and wind. There was lightness in her step as she walked seamlessly in her ski boots, as if she'd been doing it all her life.

He stood as she entered and smiled when she noticed him, a shocked look on her face.

"We come to watch. Your mother insisted."

"My mother?"

Shane said, without even glancing up, "She stopped by. Wanted to see if we had everything we needed."

The groan was from the gut.

"I'm so sorry. She's hoping that I brought a boyfriend—."

The pink in her cheeks turned a mottled shade of red. She looked even more beautiful.

"Do you bring one often?"

"Never. That's why she's being so...forward? Intrusive? Take your pick."

"You never bring man here?"

"Nope. Don't want to waste my time introducing them to someone they'll never see again. I'll leave you two alone. You shouldn't be forced into keeping me company."

"No force. Pleasure."

Shane took a sideward look at Maks, his eyebrow arched.

Getting up, tucking the paper under his arm, he said, "I'm going to sit over there. I'll be able to see the perimeter better. You take your time."

Camille wanted to stop him, but she knew it would look even more obvious that there was something going on here between her and Maks. She wasn't sure what it was, but it was definitely something.

"I'm just going to grab a water."

She made her way over to the wall unit that housed the cold drinks, took a bottle out and over to the cashier. She had to make this short and sweet. She wanted to spend as little time as possible with the man who was making her rethink her vow. The one that said there would be no involvement with clients. It was teetering on the edge of insanity.

After giving herself fifteen minutes of light conversation, she excused herself and left. As soon as she stepped out the lodge door, her breath hitched. The transition from hot to cold was never an easy one and she shivered at the brutal chill in the air. After clipping her skis back on with quick and efficient movements, she headed for the lift that would take her to one of the paths hidden in the backcountry, now that the craving for speed was satisfied. The quiet beneath the falling snow never ceased to amaze her. As she wound her way down the mountain, it was as close to a spiritual experience as she came. She maneuvered the skis in the soft mound of snow, catching herself often from sinking or falling, all thoughts consumed by the man she knew she could never have.

She gave herself just enough time to get back to the condo, to shower and dress for dinner, so she wouldn't be bound to carry on a conversation with Maks. When she came out of her room, the men were waiting, dressed in the suits they'd purchased that morning. She hadn't forgotten how good-looking Maks was, but dressed up he was even more delectable. Her nipples tingled, setting off quakes in another part of her body. What would it be like to kiss him? Be touched by him? Seduced? She rolled her eyes at the unruly thoughts, knowing how unrealistic it was to want something she couldn't have. Wouldn't allow herself.

Grabbing her coat, she headed for the door and the cool winter air. It had gotten far too warm with him so close.

"Come on. We can't be late or I'll get scolded."

"Your mother still scolds?"

"All the time."

She went to unlock her car when Shane directed, "We take my car. I need to be at the wheel."

Of course he did. Camille had forgotten Maks could be in danger. And here she'd let her mother manipulate them into dinner. In public. With dozens of people around.

"Are you sure this is safe?"

"I cleared it with Alec. He seems to think we'll be fine. No one was following us on the way up."

"What if they planted someone here?"

Maks gave her a grin. Shane asked, "How would they know to?"

"I don't know. I'm not an agent. I'm a worrier."

Maks climbed into the back seat and left her the front.

"Don't worry. Let's enjoy the night."

They followed Camille's directions, the streets dressed in winter's finery, church steeples standing at attention, until they came to a dirt road that inclined upward towards the hilltop orchard. It bisected rows of barren ice-encrusted stalks. Small fences stood protecting the dormant crop until spring arrived. Green and red lights were strung along wooden posts, helping to illuminate the long drive, and a spotlight swung back and forth across the sky, guiding them forward as they slowly made their way toward their destination. It was completely different in the summer, the vines green, holding the precious fruit that was picked by seasoned farmers, their wide-brimmed hats offering the only shade they'd find. The pungent scent of blossoming flowers would fill the air, tempting the visitors forward so their palates could be satisfied.

Shane asked, "How many acres?"

Glancing over at him, she gave him the standard tour guide pitch.

"Just under fifty. There are a couple roads of the main track that lead to different parts of the winery. There's the distillery, a couple of wine-tasting cottages, the storage facility among others. Everything you need, from farm to gift shop."

"How did your father get into this line of work?"

She twisted her head around so that Maks could be included in the conversation, giving him a sense of where she came from and who her family was.

"He is a chemist at heart and wanted to try his hand at it. The French love their wine as much as Russians love their vodka. He's done a great job. It's state of the art and his reputation gets better every year. My brother plays an important part in it all."

Maks asked from the back seat, "Never thought about joining family business?"

In Russia, people were encouraged to stay in the family business. There were generations of doctors, lawyers, scientists, children following in the footsteps of their parents and grandparents. Was he following in his father's? Had he picked up where Petrov had left off? He'd never meant to. It was too stressful. It took a lot of time and energy to spit into the wind.

"As what? Tester? That's about the only job I would have excelled at. I'm not the scientist in the family. Neither is Solange. Everyone agreed we were better suited to other fields of endeavor."

They pulled up to the restaurant, the brilliant lights sparkling in welcome. Shane was adverse to letting the valet park his car, so Camille directed him to the family parking area. As they walked towards the entrance, taxis were lined up in a queue, waiting their turn to let their passengers out, the parking attendants doing their best to keep up with the influx of customers who kept arriving.

⤙

As soon as they entered Stone Soup, Maks turned in a circle, admiring the dome. It had metal strips crisscrossing the ceiling with rivets at various points. The dining area itself was enclosed in an arc and the tables were oval rather than round or square. A Christmas tree sat majestically in the corner, antique decorations hanging on the green boughs, lights and popcorn strung around its girth. She inhaled the scent of Scottish pine. It brought back memories of her childhood.

Maks looked significantly impressed.

"This feels like inside barrel. Cool yet warm. Interesting architecture."

She couldn't help but admire his appreciation. Her parents and brother had worked hard to make this a success, the building taking almost two years to complete.

"Let my brother know. He loves to hear what a good job they've done."

Their table was far back along one of the walls, tucked away, at a discreet distance from the other diners. She was relieved they'd reserved their usual table. They could talk freely here without the regulars stopping by to chat. It would also take Maks out of any line of fire.

Her father got up from his seat as she approached.

"Camille. You look lovely as usual."

He gave her a peck on the cheek and looked eager to meet the men with her.

"And who do we have here? Your mother said you brought a real Russian with you."

He seemed thoroughly amused.

"Dad. These are my friends, Shane and Maks."

Her hand landed on Maks' arm and the shock effect was immediate. Keeping her voice moderate as the shock waves kept shooting straight to her heart, and other secret places, she said, "This is my father, Steve Bissonnette. My brother, Steph, and his wife Patsy."

Finally able to remove her hand without giving what she felt away, she added with an exasperated frown, "You already know my mother."

"It's so nice to see you both again. I hope you took me up on my offer of skiing."

"I'm sorry but no. We did go over to watch for an hour but that was it."

"Tomorrow then. I insist. I wasn't able to get out there today, but I have every intention of being out there with Cami the whole morning."

She took a seat, Maks taking the one next to her, the only one left to him. There was a spurt of anger at her mother's match-making, that she was trying to keep from showing. Her mother had to stop. Now.

"Mama, let them be. It is not what you think."

"Fine. If you say so. I just don't want them, or you, to miss a chance to have some fun."

Having fun was what had gotten her into trouble when she was younger. She didn't want to live with any more of the repercussions that came with it. She'd closed that chapter of her life and she had no intentions on going back.

The waiter came over, and announced the specials, took their drink orders and left them with their menus. As they were looking them over, Michelle asked, "So Maks, what did you do before you moved here?"

He heard Camille's intake of breath.

He patted her hand, letting her know it was all right, that he wasn't going to storm away. He let his hand linger a little longer than he should have. She'd worn a navy-blue dress that made her eyes a darker color blue, her curves so alluring his pulse had begun a rapid beat against his temple. Her hair was pulled back and tied, the curls that escaped softening her features. She was too mesmerizing to leave. Besides, this was something he could talk about. It held no memory that could hurt him.

"In country, career ladders don't exist. Nothing has really changed from communism. Workers aren't motivated to do more than their allotted tasks. And as I get bored easily, I could not sit and do nothing for long periods of a time. I became sous chef at restaurant in Moscow. There I was always busy."

What he didn't add was the place was a hotbed of political intrigue. All the city's movers and shakers regularly congregated there for lunch or supper. He'd met a lot of interesting people, made a lot of contacts, and garnered the kinds of information he put to good use when hacking became his prime occupation.

Michelle seemed fascinated.

"Then you will appreciate even more so what my son has done here."

"I will, yes."

"What was the name of the place?"

"Name was Seiveri, part of Hotel Galopolis."

Steph leaned forward, showcasing his competitive edge.

"How well did it do against the others in the area?"

Maks laughed. "It is one place where competition is. With a corrupt economy, skilled workers are not needed, except in food industry. We hold own."

"How long did you work there?"

"A couple of years after I graduate from high school, I start at other, a stolovaya. This is inexpensive Soviet-style café. From there I go to another and another before I am hired at Seiveri."

Camille's arms were across her chest as if she'd been insulted somehow.

"No wonder you turned your nose up at Subway."

He grinned that grin that made her stomach drop to her toes.

"You do not put cucumber with hot chicken."

"Maybe not in Russia but here—"

The waiter brought over the wine and stopped her as he handed Michelle the first glass poured. She was the family's tester.

She swirled the wine around the glass, held it up to inspect the color before inhaling the aroma. Only then did she sample it.

"This is delicious, Marcel. Thank you for digging it out."

The waiter poured glasses all around and the diners toasted the night. Shane took a sip, then pushed it away. She noticed he'd ordered water, once again being reminded why he was here.

Everyone else seemed oblivious.

Her brother asked, as if overly interested, "What kinds of signature dishes was the restaurant known for?"

"Lot of duck. Salmon. Borscht. Caviar and herring in large amounts."

It was typical Russian fare, caviar given out as freely as bread and butter here.

"Maybe you could give us one of the recipes."

As if to rain on her brother's parade, she grumbled, "Caviar's on the expensive side, you know."

"We already use it as an ingredient in one of our dishes. We set a good price and make money."

Michelle tried to glean more information and asked, "Was it in Moscow?"

"*Ja*. In downtown."

Camille began to stew. She'd been asking Maks questions since the minute she'd met him, and he was as close-mouthed as a clam. With her family, he was willing to spill his past out as liberally as he poured vodka from a bottle. Maybe she could give her mother a list of questions to put to him. He seemed somewhat enamored with the older woman. Courteous and complimentary.

She sat back and half listened to the conversation, trying to come up with new angles that might get the background on him that she needed. She now had a place of employment that she could contact, and knew it was in the city itself, not that it meant she'd learn anything. She hadn't gotten anywhere with *Reform's* management. The editor denied ever knowing a man who fit the description, quickly got her off the phone as if her question was dangerous. Maybe they were. If Maks was a wanted man, they couldn't take the chance of being linked with him. Were they being wire-tapped? It was possible. If that was the case, she might have made an error in judgement in even making the call. Those listening in would now know Maks was in the United States. Boston to be exact.

She shook off the apprehension. It was bound to come out. Documents required per the application would be sent for, so the Russian government would know soon enough where he was. And what he was seeking.

Should she tell Alec what she'd done? Give him a head's-up?

Nate was the one who'd told her she was on her own, so she didn't owe them anything.

The spoiled teen was emerging, and she slapped her down as soon as she saw the familiar face. Her willfulness could get Maks hurt, and she would not allow that. How would she walk that tightrope? Do her job while keeping everyone safe in the process? She took a gulp of wine, unsure as to what her next step would be. Or where it would lead her.

When the waiter came over and began serving, she could tell Maks was impressed. His eyes widened as he scanned each dish.

"These are well designed plates."

When he was presented with his roasted goose, ordered at her brother's suggestion, Maks leaned in to inhale the aroma. The apricots would sweeten it; the herbs would add the French flair that the chef, Georges Barbot, was known for. He had come from France, and his menus always reflected the nationally renowned cuisine. This month they would serve more traditional Christmas dishes like the goose, scallops, foie gras terrine, and roasted capon.

Maks pointed to her brother Steph's meal. "Already serve caviar. With scallops. Interesting."

Silence settled over the group as they ate, each savoring the delectable food in front of them.

The vodka kept coming, as well as the wine.

She reined herself in, trying to be careful. She couldn't afford to be inebriated around a man, especially this man. It had proven deadly. And the way Maks affected her system, there was the possibility she'd throw caution to the wind.

When the *buche de noel* was served for dessert, the touch of brandy only added to the feeling of light-headedness.

She glanced over at him between bites and shuttered lashes.

The need to get to know him better made her ache inside.

CHAPTER FIFTEEN

Her mother seemed bound and determined to help her.

"So, tell me again how you met?"

Michelle was swirling her after dinner brandy, watching it coat the sides of her glass, as if the answer held no consequence.

Shane began to answer for them, but Michelle obviously wanted it from the horse's mouth.

"Maks?"

"We met through Nate. Just like Shane tell you."

"At a party? At his office? How?"

The silence was telling but her mother waited patiently for an answer from someone. Camille stepped in to supply it.

"Mama, Nate mentioned to Mia he had some friends who needed to...get away for a couple of days. Mia mentioned it...at a staff meeting and I offered to let them tag along."

"Why would she bring that up at a staff meeting? Was she trying to fix you up?"

She gave her mother a fixed stare and said, "Mia doesn't interfere in my life like some other people."

There was a warning look attached but her mother waved it aside.

"He is the first man you've brought here, and we've owned the winery for ten years. There must be a reason."

"Um, Shane is here, too. How do you know that he's not the one I brought along?"

Michelle's mouth pursed.

"Is he?"

The heavy sigh couldn't be helped.

"Neither of them are. They are friends. Plain and simple."

Her father put his hand on Michelle's arm.

"Why don't you let this go, Misha?"

"Because Cami needs someone, and if she refuses to put herself out there, she'll never find him."

"I don't need—"

"You've lived in a one-dimensional world since Michael—"

"Mama."

That one word shut that topic down. It didn't stop her mother from adding, "I wanted you to be less defiant, but I didn't want you to give up who you were completely."

Her father countered, "She hasn't given up who she is at all. She still questions authority, pushes boundaries, argues for a person's rights, and fights for personal freedom. She just does it in a more responsible way. That's the only thing that's changed. She will always be our rebel."

Camille could feel her cheeks flush. She didn't want to be the center of conversation tonight. Especially not in front of Maks. Trying to lighten the mood, she said, "Someone had to play that role. Mama was too much the disciplinarian."

"And you gave her the fight of her life."

Michelle refilled her wine-glass and announced, "I'd say there was a draw. No one really won."

Her mother was right. She never backed down from arguing in her own defense, disobeyed rules she thought stupid or just plain antiquated, and ignored her mother's attempts to bring her to heel. Nothing had changed. She was still doing it only on a different stage.

"Mama, it seems like we're both still fighting. Don't you think it's time we stopped?"

"A mother wants her children to be happy. You are not. There is an underlying sadness that prevents you from finding joy."

Maks gave them a sad smile. "I thought that was Russian trait."

Michelle countered, "Unfortunately, it's circumstances more than nationality that causes that."

Maks looked at Camille, as if wondering what the rest of the story was. There was no need for him to know.

"I find joy every time I win a case."

"I'd say you find relief, not joy. There is a difference."

Her father must have felt it was time to end this age-old discussion, because he shifted the conversation.

"What part of Russia are you from, Maks?"

"Born in northwestern part of country."

Michelle's eyes showed interest.

"Near St. Pete's?"

"Near."

Cami's father had pushed his chair away from the table, crossing one leg over the other.

"Isn't that where your grandfather was from, Mish?"

"Yes. He was born in Shlisselburg. Back then it was called something else." She waved her hand in the air, trying to come up with the name but unable to. "Anyway, after the war, the Russian Revolution, he immigrated to Paris."

"Petrokrepost."

Camille said the name out loud as if thinking had produced sound.

Maks did a double take.

"You know this?"

Her voice was soft when she answered, thinking about her great-grandfather's history.

"I do."

"Why?"

"The day I found my great-grandfather's dog tags in an old chest Mama had in the attic, I had a sudden urge to know everything I could about him, where he came from, why he left."

"Was he farmer?"

"He was a Bolshevik, but when Stalin came to power, he was repulsed by all the killing. He came to appreciate a more balanced form of government when he got to France."

Maks leaned forward, his arms on the table now cleared of the meal.

"It was violent revolution. My great-grandfather survived World War I, only to fight again to overthrow tsar. He fought for a better life, died from his wounds less than a year later. He would not have liked what came after. First

Lenin and then Stalin. Now—I understand why your relative left. I sometimes wish mine had, as well. What was his name?"

"Fyodor Gorokhov."

He sat up as if this came as a shock and peered at her intently.

"You are part Russian."

She peered back, his gaze deeply sensual. In a hushed whisper, she said,
"You knew that before."

"Name puts it in better light."

She couldn't help but notice her mother's smug smile and quickly finished
off her brandy, her head spinning.

⌐

Camille was Russian. Part Russian. Her ancestors had lived only miles from
where he was born, grew up. Had there been no immigration to Paris, he
might have met her there, might have known her before...Would he have been
this interested? Would she have stood with him when his life turned upside
down? The events in his past tested a relationship. Those that weren't strong,
crumbled. Or maybe it was the woman who'd been weak. Too afraid to stay.
She married soon after. A man in government. He had come to hate her and
all she stood for. His mother had warned him that Marya was not who he
thought she was. She was a beautiful woman and he'd made an error in judgment, his hormones taking over all rational thought. After his father's arrest,
Marya was afraid of what it would mean for her. Not wanting to be associated
with a convicted felon, she ran away from what his family represented. She
wasn't the only one who'd ostracized him. Many of those citizens who wanted
the glory of Russia returned to them, had cast him aside. The steadfast and
loyal to the president ignored the atrocities that were part of daily life. It was
Petrov's associates who'd stood firm at their side, eyes wide open to the nasti-
ness going on around them. They'd continued their fight and he'd joined
them. His mother had, too, was steadfast in her devotion. She'd gone to the
jail on visiting day every week for over a year, sat for hours, only to be denied
rights to see her husband before being sent home. The ordeal had almost
killed her, too. He'd been shown what true love was and how it worked. Next
time he'd choose more wisely. Trust and loyalty were imperative.

He glanced up to see Michelle staring at him and his thoughts drifted in
another direction. Here was a woman who'd left her country behind. What
had it been like for her?

"How is it that you met Stephen?"

"He came to Paris for a science convention and was staying at the hotel where I worked."

Stephen smiled at her. "It was love at first sight. I took one look at her and that was it. I wasn't going to leave until she at least had dinner with me."

Michelle laid her hand against Stephen's cheek. "It was the same for me."

Turning her attention back to Maks, she said, "It is like that when you find the one. It's magic from the moment you set eyes on him...or her. After he left, two dinners later, I applied for a visa and moved to Boston. We were married before the year was out."

Taking his wife's hand in his own, he kissed it.

"I would have moved to Paris if I had to. I wasn't letting her get away."

Maks asked, "Do you like living here or do you wish you had stayed in France?"

"Once I became a citizen, I left France behind. My children were born here, our winery is here, there is freedom. I would not go back to live, although a winter home in Tuscany would not be such a sacrifice."

He gave her a small smile at her intended joke. At least he thought it was. He needed to know more about her immigration, what kind of impact the total change had on her.

"You were young then. Would it be hard for you to do it now?"

"If I was leaving for something better, I would not hesitate. My grandfather never regretted it."

He could understand that. Each successive generation had lived with the kind of freedom that didn't exist where he was from.

Michelle asked, "Are you thinking about naturalizing?"

"Thinking about it. Haven't decided whether I will stay here."

"There are some problems with where we're going. I have faith that the people here will right the course. Cami could help you if you want to stay."

"So I have heard."

"She's one of the best although she handles mostly asylum cases. Someone in her office could fill out your paperwork, petition the court. If you're working for a government agency, I'm sure it would be an easy enough process."

⌐

Shane rose from the table, suggesting it was time to go. He probably thought the talk was straying into classified territory.

Camille looked around. The huge clock on the mantel said it was close to midnight. Where had the time gone? All through dinner her mother shot her looks that suggested...what? That she'd done well. Choosing Maks? She'd never brought a man here before and her mother was reading far too much into it. There were secret smiles during the on-going conversation. Maks seemed so at ease with her parents, and they drew him out, got him to talk about himself in a way she hadn't been able to.

There was a deeper problem beginning to simmer. She liked him. She'd felt drawn to him in some inexplicable way from the minute she'd met him, but now...?

She had to get out of here. She had to get this feeling of vulnerability to go away.

Unsteady on her feet as they left the table, she held herself tightly as she walked the short distance to the car, making sure to put one foot in front of the other, in a straight line. When she felt Maks' hand on her back, she stumbled. The reaction was immediate—a spike of heat arced in her gut. It wasn't the wine but what this man made her feel. Instead of stepping away as she should have, she leaned back into the contact to feel his hand slide around her waist.

Her eyes sought his out, as she was no longer able to deny the delicious feelings he evoked. What she saw made it even more powerful. She read the same flicker of desire.

Shane was trying to be as unobtrusive as he could, all while staying close to his charge.

"Okay, folks. Let's get us home for the night."

Maks climbed into the front seat as soon as Shane had opened it. She tilted her head at him as if to ask, "What about me?" when he pulled her onto his lap before closing the door. She sat stiffly, still unwilling to give in, but the motion of the car as Shane drove them the few miles to the condo was enough that she relaxed against him. His hand rested lightly on her hip, the contact making her itch from the inside out. To feel this again, the thrumming sensation that came from physical need, was like a heat wave. Hot and sultry. She'd forgotten what it was like. Had kept herself contained, forbidden herself from getting entrenched in something that had proved so dangerous. She wasn't good girlfriend material. She still spent too much of herself on her own pleasure. The pleasure today was not what it had been in the past, but the total immersion into her client's lives. Nothing came before that. No one had been able to infiltrate her space.

She hadn't let anyone get that close. When a pang of longing shot through her, she knew enough to be scared. She wanted this man, for a night, for a month…

Squeezing her eyes shut, she pushed out all thought of forever just as the car pulled up to the condo.

Maks opened the door, scooped her up in his arms and carried her to the front door. When she fumbled the key out of her purse, Shane opened it and let them in.

"I've got to make some calls. I'll be in soon."

With her arms around Maks' neck, she hung on as he delivered her to her room and let her slide gracefully to her feet, while still holding her against his body.

She felt so good in his arms he didn't want to let her go. She fit like no woman before, and he wanted to see what kind of passion lay buried beneath. Threading his hands through her hair, he bent his lips to touch hers, the feel like flower petals, soft and inviting.

With each caress, the kiss went deeper, the taste of her sweet yet overpowering. He couldn't get enough, and when he stroked her lips with his tongue, she opened to him and he invaded. She met him thrust for thrust, the warm interior of her mouth tasting like brandy, intoxicating him more than the wine, more than the vodka. His lips left hers to nibble at her neck, the skin so soft, the hint of perfume still hiding behind her ear. As he seared a path downwards, his hands roamed the curves that had enticed him all evening, pulling her closer so that she could feel how much he excited him. Her willingness to participate enflamed him, her fingers sinking into his hair, before cupping his cheeks and reclaiming his lips with hers. He was on fire. Never had he been this turned on by a woman, never had he felt this burning need to become one. As he found her breast with his hand, she jerked away. Turning her back on him, she cried out, "No. I can't do this. I'm not good at it."

The shock of that statement froze him in place.

What was she talking about? She was *too* good at this, tempting him in a way he'd never been tempted before. He didn't trust her yet, didn't trust anyone and suspicion clouded his judgement.

Did she mean she couldn't go through with her seduction? Was it preplanned and now she was having second thoughts?

Now the questions came like rapid gunfire.

Why had Shane left them alone? Why had her mother plied her with drinks? Why had they suggested he come here with her?

What the hell was he doing?

He backed out, closing the door in her face, taking the steps needed to reach his own room just as he heard Shane come back in.

Deciding he needed a shot of vodka, he went to the wet bar and poured himself a liberal dose. It might not be the remedy for what ailed him, but it was his go-to when things got crazy.

And what he'd almost done was crazy.

Shane went to the refrigerator and grabbed a soda and made for the sofa.

"Alec was happy to hear we got back safely."

Maks backed up, keeping his distance and protecting his own space.

"Why did you not call from in here?"

Dropping down, reaching for the remote control, Shane clicked on the television and surfed the channels.

"Reception isn't great, and I thought I'd give Camille time to compose herself."

That made sense. He had seen Shane take a call outside for the same reason before. He relaxed his stance, took a sip of the clear liquid, the memory of how Camille had felt in his arms rushing back at him. Closing his eyes, wanting to shut desire down, he murmured, "She is fine."

Shane settled on the news. The headlines over, the station having gone to commercial break, Shane muted the sound.

"Glad to hear it. Her mother seems excited about the prospect of you two pairing up."

"We will disappoint her. That will not happen."

"Why? Do you have someone waiting for this to be over?"

He did but that wasn't the reason he was not making another move in that direction.

"It is not right time to get involved with anyone."

"I've noticed that's usually when it happens."

"Not this time."

He had to make sure of it. Being this close to such a distraction was tempting fate. He had too much work to do, there was danger all around him, and he was not putting himself at that kind of risk.

"What we will do tomorrow?"

Shane asked, "Do you want to ski?"

"I want to go back to Boston."

Glancing up at him, Shane reminded, "We don't have anywhere for you to stay."

Maks was standing, his eyes on his bodyguard.

"I stay anywhere. You will come with me. I will be safe."

"I'm off duty as soon as we return. Someone else will take my place."

A fissure of fear traveled through his body.

"Why? I have to learn to trust all over. I want one agent. I want it to be you."

He liked Shane's unobtrusive presence. Shane didn't push or prod, didn't give the third degree, never strayed into personal business, kept the conversation light. He also did his job well, and Maks felt as safe as he could, given the circumstances.

Sitting forward, he studied Maks with narrowed eyes.

"I'll talk to Alec. I wouldn't mind. I want to see if Michelle is right."

"Right at what?"

"There is something going on between you and Camille. Whether you like it or not. I can't say Nate or Alec would be thrilled with it but what they don't know won't hurt them."

The sound came back on, the announcer giving a run down on the sports scores and Shane went back to watching.

Maks gulped down the vodka and hurried to his room. He didn't want to think about Camille. It brought him too close to doing what Shane suggested. One night. He'd take one night. He couldn't take more than that or he'd be in danger. Camille knew nothing of his past, didn't even know his real name. He didn't want her to take her fight to the streets, but to wage battle for him in a courtroom. He'd see how the judicial system worked here and then decide whether to stay or go. Then...maybe...

CHAPTER SIXTEEN

As soon as Maks closed her door, Camille plopped down on the bed. Her fingers strayed to her lips as if they were changed somehow by the kiss. Except for the slight puffiness, they felt the same. The rest of her body had been transformed. There was an ache of longing that had settled in every cell, a need that had come bubbling up like hot lava, threatening to rupture the ice she'd encased herself in. This was the reason she didn't imbibe. She wanted to be in complete control of her emotions. Normally she declined any more than two drinks when out, but she'd let her father refill her glass every time it was empty. At her mother's subtle or not-so-subtle signal.

She felt light-headed, intoxicated, more by the man than by the wine. His black onyx eyes, with the glacial silver streaks, captivated her. His mouth was perfectly sculpted and had left hers burning with fire.

She touched them again, fighting the conflicting emotions that were waging a war inside. She wanted him with every fiber of her being. But she couldn't do this no matter how fascinated with him she was. He was her client. He was an unknown quantity. She knew nothing about him, or what he was doing here. What if he was playing a charade? Trying to worm his way into her bed for a reason that had nothing to do with desire?

He could be her enemy. Dressed up in wolf's clothing.

She could be hurt, maybe killed.

What if he was the harbinger of death?

He made her heart beat to a rhythm she'd never heard before which made him even more dangerous.

Was this what Nell felt for Jack, Em for Nick? If so, she could no longer gloss over their feelings.

It was an emotion you felt at the core of your being. It became a part of you, a memory tucked away in your heart that couldn't be exorcised. Michael's memory had stayed with her because of what had happened, not how she felt about him. It only added guilt to the mix. She had loved him as much as she'd been able to back then, but not like...He didn't make her melt with a look, didn't make her want all there was. He'd been a nice boy. Maks was a dangerous man.

Her breath caught on a rush of longing so intense it felt like pain.

She might manage to deny herself the gift of his body, but she would never forget the way he made her feel. It was the yardstick for who came after, and she knew no one would measure up. She was glad they had only a limited time together. She didn't know what she'd do if he was an everyday fixture in her life. She was going to have to give Em a big hug next time she saw her. Her friend had been living in hell since the day Nick had chosen Saban over her.

She closed her eyes, stifling a groan. She hadn't been a very good friend. Had she shut down so much of herself that she couldn't feel another's pain anymore? Her mind was stumbling around, searching for truth. She felt for every one of her clients, felt their fear in a tangible way. Wanted to fight for them with everything in her. Why couldn't she feel Em's?

Maybe it was merely the fact that her clients were fighting along with her. Em refused. She stuck herself in a victim role and refused to abdicate it. Was that what Michael had done? Poor me, Cami doesn't want to go home? I'll go without her?

She scrubbed her face, her mind shifting like the beads in a kaleidoscope. Making patterns and shapes that were distorting her perception of everything real.

Wiping her nose with the back of her hand, the sniffles the precursor to the tears that threatened, she was not going to let herself be led by her emotions.

She had to find out who Maks was so that she could walk away.

Her mind wandered back to the application tucked away in her Skolikovsky folder. She had taken it out, numerous times, the first line preventing her from going any further. She couldn't even fill in his name. Now she knew he'd been born in or around St. Petersburg, worked at a restaurant named Seiveri out of the Hotel Galopolis. Another avenue for her to pursue. She would go on the assumption he'd kept his first name, Maxim. It would make sense for him to keep to a partial truth. How had a chef come to have the kinds of skills needed to help Nina in her journalistic pursuits? It didn't equate. Who was he? What did he have that was so important to the FBI that they brought him here, were seeking asylum for him?

Then her mind wandered in other directions. His body, his looks, his accent, his intelligence.

She'd caught herself staring at him many times during dinner, watching his facial expressions, a muscle quivering in his jaw, his lips drawn in thoughtfully, his accent oddly arousing, his voice husky and smooth. Even knowing better, she'd kept drinking. She'd wanted to stop the spasms from pulsing, wanted to numb all feelings. It hadn't worked.

If there was an upside to drinking so much, it was the lethargy that came with it. She was sleepy, from the wine and from chasing her racing thoughts. As soon as she shed her clothes, she slipped under the covers and let visions of Russian sugar plums dance in her head.

⌒

She was up bright and early. She'd texted Em first thing to check in. See how she was doing with Teddy. She didn't give away her new perspective—she would have had to explain why she'd gained it, but she offered more of a shoulder to cry on when Em told her about Nick and Saban's itinerary. Took an extra minute to let some of the sadness seep out.

Then she took to the kitchen.

Her father used to make her and her siblings a treat several times a year. It was a recipe that had come down from Quebec with his grandmother. He used to call them roll-overs, but they were actually crepes with bacon, topped with butter and sugar, rolled like a cigar with all that sugary sweetness melting out.

Shane had already devoured three before Maks came out to claim some coffee.

"I'm chef this morning. Would you like one?"

He leaned over her shoulder to smell the bacon, see for himself the sizzle as it browned. It wasn't the only thing that sizzled, and she had to keep her heartbeat from pounding out of her chest.

"What is it?"

His breath tickled her ear and she shivered from the contact. Her voice was huskier than she wanted. "A family tradition."

He stood against the counter as he watched her pour a small amount of batter over the bacon and twirl the pan so it covered the flat surface. His perusal was more intimate than the kiss they'd shared last night.

Not quite, but right up there. She shivered from the thought of his lips on hers, and when the crepe began to bubble, she quickly flipped it before it burned. When it was done, she slid it out of the pan and onto a plate, spread the softened butter, sprinkled white sugar over the surface and rolled it up. Handing him the plate along with the utensils, she said, "See? I can cook."

"It looks good. Thank you."

Shane put his hands on his stomach and rubbed. "It's too good. I ate too much."

She watched Maks from the corner of her eyes as she made herself one. Waited for him to taste it, see his reaction.

He ate it with gusto, a smile on his lips before he licked them.

"I will need recipe. This could be Russian dish."

"Do you want another?"

"*Ja*, please."

She handed over the one she'd made for herself before going back to the stove, scraping out the last of the batter.

Taking a deep breath, not knowing how he'd respond, she asked, "If you decide to stay in the country, will you look for work in a restaurant?"

After carrying her plate to the table, she took a seat and waited. She was relieved when he seemed inclined to answer.

"I don't think so."

Shane shook his head, and she thought he was going to say something but thought better of it and stayed mute. After getting up, he brought his plate to the sink.

"I'm taking a shower. Let me know what you decide you want to do, Maks. I'll have to let Alec know, so he can come up with an alternative."

"I'll take shower as soon as I'm done. I want to go back to Boston."

"You're sure you don't want to ski?"

He glanced up at Camille, took a moment in her eyes before saying, "I'm sure."

Last night must have shaken him up as much as it had her. He was taking advantage of the fact he could leave. The fact that she'd miss him when he did was not something she wanted to dwell on. There would be no repeat of his lips on hers, no overwhelming feelings bringing her to the edge of a very fine line she feared crossing.

It would be the smart thing for him to do. She just didn't like that it was.

After Maks excused himself, she heard the front door open. She knew he'd gone out to grab a smoke and wished she could join him. She'd quit during college but there were days that the smell, or even the thought of them, made her dance with indecision. They could be a friend when you needed one. It was one of the bigger fights she'd had with her mother. Michelle detested the odor and would always lecture Camille when she came home smelling like an ashtray. The nagging had done nothing to stop her. It was her own decision that made her give them up. Studying long hours in the library during law school, she got tired of having to stop, get up, go outside to satisfy her craving. She'd lose her focus, her rhythm, or her study group would move ahead without her. She'd ordered a case of gum on Amazon and chewed her way to nicotine free.

Today she'd give her right arm for one.

Walking down the hall to make the bed and get ready for the slopes, she passed by Maks' room, and peeked in. She felt a buzz. Her heart started beating fast. Her hands became clammy.

His satchel was sitting on his bed, unzipped, and it was calling her name.

She looked around, her nerves now on overdrive. Did she have the nerve to go in and investigate?

As if to answer her own question she felt her feet moving in that direction.

Was she really thinking of doing this?

This was a total invasion of his privacy. Went against every principle she held dear.

All these thoughts were racing around in her mind as she took the final steps needed to reach the bag. Her ears perked up, and she listened.

There was nothing to indicate he was returning from his smoking spot.

She slid shaking fingers into the side compartment. It was the bag that contained his computer and if he was who she thought he was, it would be his most valuable possession. If he was caught in a crossfire, he'd save this one. It would make sense that his private papers were here, as well.

She held her breath hoping she was right, knowing if she judged wrong she wouldn't have time to search further.

When she felt the stiff leather, she knew she'd hit pay dirt.

Gingerly, she pulled out his brown colored passport, the Cyrillic print easy to read. It looked similar to her grandfather's, the one she had stored in her high boy at home, along with his dog tags. It's where she'd gotten the data she needed to delve deeply into his life, follow his movements from country to country on the ancestry website. The leather was cracked from age and the ink inside faded. The one she held in her hand was new, as if never used before.

Looking around, making sure she was still alone with no witnesses, she bit her lip as she began to open it.

A voice inside told her to stop, and from somewhere outside her consciousness, she heard the front door open.

It was the sign she needed telling her she was crossing a line. She pushed the passport back into the zippered compartment, yanked her fingers away from the bag, and backed out, her lungs constricted, her breath shallow.

When she made it into the safety of her room, she was ready to close the door when she heard Maks' footfalls.

Turning back, she called out, "There you are. I peeked in to your room thinking you were there. Knocked on the bathroom door. I forgot about the smoke."

The lie almost choked her.

She had been ready to push boundaries again to get what she wanted.

How could she expect him to trust her if she'd been willing to break the first rule of attorney conduct?

Maybe her father was right. Maybe if she hadn't heard the door...maybe she hadn't changed at all.

Maks still felt tension seeping through him. He'd seen a ghost retreat from his room. A specter shadow, and he knew it was Camille slinking along the hallway toward hers and he wondered what she'd been doing in there. The disappointment didn't catch him off guard. It was what he'd come to expect from those in the legal profession. Why wouldn't she be like the rest? He'd learned not too long ago that people in the judicial field thought they were above the law, above suspicion. The police were the worst offenders but lawyers? A close second. Or most of them were. What were the chances that Camille was as honest and upright as his father had been? Not high in his estimation. Was she telling him the truth, or did she suspect he'd seen her? He'd hoped he could come to trust her but now...well, now he'd have to be on guard again. They'd just taken two steps backwards.

He hurried into his room, scanned it, but found nothing amiss. He lifted his satchel, patted down the sides, making sure everything was still in place. He pulled out his passport, which was right where he'd stored it. Was it a little higher up than it had been before? Closer to the zipper? As if she'd had to hurry to get it back in place? If she'd seen it, she knew who he was now. His name, where he was from, his birth date, his identification number. She would have found that out at some point, he assumed. Otherwise he'd never get his case filed with the courts. It was what she planned on doing with the information that made his blood pressure hitch. Nate had left the decision of telling Camille who he was up to him. After last night, with her in his arms, he'd been tempted. Tempted to bare his soul, tempted to trust her with who he was. He was glad he hadn't given in. She wasn't who he'd hoped she'd be.

Hope.

It had betrayed him.

He'd hoped his father had been right. Hoped his country was not so corrupt it would kill its own for their purposes. Hoped that Nina would survive the attempts on her life. Hoped that his father would be released and his life would go on in some semblance of order. Hoped that this country would be different.

It seemed the laws here were not any more sacrosanct than Russia's. Civil rights ignored by the willful disrespect of privacy and common dignity. And with the way he felt about her—?"

He was more convinced than ever that he had to leave here.

Closing his door, he undressed, showered, changed, and packed his dirty clothes for the ride back down the mountain.

When he came out to the living room, Shane was there, sitting and chatting with Michelle Bissonnette.

He hoped she wasn't here to talk him into staying.

The smile she offered was a replica of Camille's, and he understood how Stephen Bissonnette had been bedazzled. It's how Cami made him feel.

"Maks. How nice to see you again. I came over personally to escort you to the slopes. I called ahead, and they have some skis, boots, and poles put aside for you. From what I understand, Shane doesn't ski, so it will just be the three of us."

He narrowed his eyes at Shane, who imperceptibly shrugged his shoulders.

"This offer is kind, but we have decided to go back to Boston."

Michelle eased up out of the chair, stepped toward him, her hand going to his arm.

"Let us give you the Mountain Man treatment. I won't take no for an answer."

Camille entered his sphere of vision, dressed similarly to how she was yesterday, ski pants, a bulky sweater, and a winsome smile.

He tried to talk himself into believing it was fake, but he couldn't manage it.

She stopped short when she saw her mother and the smile faded. Annoyance was clearly written on her face.

"What are you doing here? I told you I'd meet you out in front of the lodge."

"I had a feeling you wouldn't invite your friends. Seems I was right."

This kind of interference was what she'd fought against when she was younger. Her mother just wouldn't leave some things alone and it drove her crazy. She'd learned to handle her differently as she'd gotten older. No more raising her voice, no more screaming to be heard. She went to her current default. She spoke with quiet emphasis.

"They know they are invited. They decided to go home early. It is their decision to make."

Her mother was determined not to let it go and said in the same cool tone, "I've learned that if it's something you want, Cami, you never hesitate to force the issue."

She felt the blush creep into her cheeks. Her mother was right. She'd just proven it. She might have wanted the information for a good cause, but it didn't take away the fact that she was ready to steal it from him. There was no good defense for it, but she gave one, anyway.

"Seems I've inherited that proclivity from you. You do it all the time. I do it only when I'm at odds with the people working against me. And I always have my clients' best interests at heart."

She glanced over to see Maks' eyes were hooded as he listened to the back-and-forth.

What was he thinking? Had he figured out why she'd been in his room? If he had, she'd have a snowball's chance in hell of getting him to confide in her. Even though she hadn't gone through with it, his perception of her might have changed. She was stuck now. If she had opened the passport, she'd know who he was. His name would have been indelibly inked in her mind, and her fingers would have been itchy to dig and find out everything about him. She wouldn't have needed his cooperation. Instead, she'd backed away, leaving herself suspect in his eyes. She could only hope the bits of information she had would get her what she wanted.

Shane was standing in the midst of the small group now.

"Maks, let's go have a smoke and talk about this."

Camille knew what was going on. Shane was trying to keep Maks from making a public display of his displeasure. Her mother would understand none of this. Safe houses and bodyguards were not in her purview, and there was no need for her to know about any of it.

She could feel her mother's glare. It was something she was used to. And she knew what would follow: a lecture about good manners even though this was about something much more sinister. Her mother was match-making again. Had been doing it since both her other children married and settled down. Michelle had the romantic notion that love found you in the oddest of places. Steph had married his childhood playmate, whom he'd known he'd marry at the age of ten. When his wife's family had moved across the country a few years later, odds were that the promise wouldn't be realized but they'd reconnected at the University of Virginia as freshmen and married right after graduation. Solange had met her husband, Matthew Smith, at a funeral. During her sister's first year teaching, a student's father had died and at the graveside, the day of the burial, she'd offered her condolences to the man's brother. They'd spent the night talking and they were married less than a year later. It would make sense to Michelle that when a Russian came into Camille's life, it had to be fate. Her mother wasn't one to turn her back on it. She didn't expect her daughter to, either.

When Maks didn't seem to take the hint, Shane grabbed him by the elbow, picked up their coats, and handed Maks his on the way out the door.

They slid down the icy walkway on their way to Maks' spot.

"I don't want cigarette. I want to go back."

"The house still isn't ready. We have to stay."

Maks' feet were planted wide, refusing to budge another inch.

"I will stay at hotel like I told you."

"I can't get that okayed. Alec was clear about this. Why don't you take the day, go skiing, and I'll spend the afternoon in the lodge figuring out our next move."

"Will not be what I want. I have no more freedom here than I did at home."

"That's not true and you know it. You'll have a place of your own one day and you'll be able to come and go as you please."

"Will always be looking over shoulder."

"Your odds of staying alive are better here. Besides, you'll get to spend the day with Camille."

He narrowed his eyes at his bodyguard.

"This is dangerous."

"Only if you look at it that way."

He stood still, the complexity of his feelings causing an unruly effect on his mental processes. Could he look at the situation with Camille differently? Could he see the day as just another one in the long line of unsettling ones? The image of Camille pushed through all thought and he reconsidered.

"We leave right after."

"If I can work something out."

They made their way back up the embankment, boots crunching on the frozen snow, stomping their feet when they got to the door. When they entered, Maks could feel the tension. Camille was standing stiffly not three feet away from her mother, but the body language told him they were miles apart.

Frowning, Michelle asked, "What is the problem?"

Shane must have given the only answer that came into his head. "Maks has been staying with me since he got here, and my place is being...fumigated and I can't get back in until tomorrow."

Maks gave him a knowing look. Blinded by his need to get back to Boston, he'd forgotten that Michele didn't know why he was here or why he wanted to leave. Shane obviously hadn't and wasn't willing to share. By the looks of things, neither was Camille.

It gave Michelle an opening.

"It's settled then. I'm not letting you leave without spending a few hours on the slopes with us. Then if you are intent on going back, you can stay at Cami's tonight. She'll be here until tomorrow."

Camille almost gasped out loud. Her mother obviously wasn't giving up yet, and she was getting tired of this fight. She'd spent her life rearranging the pieces Michelle forced into place for her. Would she never stop her meddling?

She clenched her teeth so hard she thought her jaw would break.

"I don't think that's a good idea, Mama."

"Why not?"

Her finger went to her mouth and she began to nibble.

"I have a lot of confidential files in my office. Clients trust me with their secrets. I can't allow anyone access."

"What would they want with your files, Cami? I thought they were your friends."

She was stumped now and scrambled for a legitimate reason for her hesitation.

"If they go to my condo, I have to go with them. I have an obligation—"

Michelle looked straight to Maks.

"Will you tamper with her files?"

Camille was watching him, and he didn't know what to give as an answer, so he gave the obvious one.

"*Nyet*...no."

Camille gulped, images of him roaming around her apartment too stark to dismiss. She tried to picture what she'd left behind, left out in her rush to get on the road. She'd stayed late at the office, wanting to get things in order before leaving for the weekend. There was a mug on her sideboard, but it was clean, her coffee pot in the dishwasher. Had she put it through the cycle before vacating the premises? Her bed was unmade, but the sheets had just been washed. The woman who went in once a week to clean had stripped and remade the bed as part of her weekly tasks. What had she done with the suit she'd taken off before getting more comfortable for the ride north? Was it in a heap on the floor waiting to be put out for the dry-cleaning pick up?

As her thoughts swirled, Shane became a moderate voice in a sea of chaotic feelings and he admitted, "It would solve one of our problems."

Maks glared at her, his voice directed to Shane.

"Hotel would be best."

He apparently didn't want to have anything to do with her. She tried to tell herself it didn't matter. The end goal was asylum. It wasn't to fall in love with him or have him fall in love with her. This, was why she never got involved with clients. It got messy. The problem? She'd already gotten involved. It was a finger-painting mural in primary, bold colors.

CHAPTER SEVENTEEN

They took separate cars, Shane driving behind Camille, Michelle behind in hers. It was as if they were boxing him in, so he couldn't change his mind. Not that he would have. He'd come around and was now anticipating how it would feel at the mountain top.

He could tell Shane was anticipating problems, his checks in the rear-and-side view mirrors happening in minute cycles.

"Are you worried?"

"Not really, but I can't let down my guard."

He could understand that. It had been years since he'd felt free enough to move without thought. Arrests in Russia happened every day, but no one knew who the next victim would be. Leaders of the protest movement went untouched, while rank and file were gobbled up by the military machine. Keeping everyone off guard was how the government tried to neutralize the citizens. The people like his father, who couldn't be subdued were silenced in other ways. The ones left behind, like him, were hard-pressed to wrap their brains around what was happening. As a result, he'd taken up the cause, as if driven by some kind of death wish, a destructive force within that refused to fade away.

Camille was the only curative he'd found. The mere action of watching her sent the demons that were shredding his humanity away. Getting lost in her allowed time to stand still. He forgot about the past, his father, his mother, and the need to move faster, work harder.

It was one of the reasons he was glad he'd been forced into another day with her.

As he stood at the ski shack with Michelle, Camille was hustling toward the chair-lift and disappointment filled him. She had left him in her mother's care, not waiting for him to join her, and Michelle seemed inclined to take over. Was this what Camille fought against so vigorously? He had to admit, it would feel suffocating after a while, but for now he was glad. It gave him the time to study Camille's movements, the way she moved in skis, as if she'd been born wearing them, the graceful push and pull on the poles as she propelled herself forward. There were several lifts scattered across the terrain, and he squinted into the distance to see which one she chose. When she came to a stop in line, he followed the moving cables to the top of the mountain. Could he blame her for aiming for the farthest point away from them?

She'd stated quite emphatically that she wanted to be alone this weekend. Between him and Shane and her mother's interference, she'd been railroaded. He should be feeling bad, but as he scanned the area, watched the skiers flying down the mountain, he was exhilarated by the thought of being one of them. He was glad Michelle had talked them into this even if it meant he'd be skiing solo. He hadn't been on skis in years, too busy foraging the internet for bears and trolls. He took in the beauty of his surroundings, the white-tipped peaks, and a feeling of serenity washed over him. He couldn't keep his eyes from straying to a figure growing smaller and smaller as she rode into the sky. Would he have to go to the top to see her full run? He wasn't sure he'd be up to it, but he was stubborn enough he'd give it a try. Defying gravity necessitated one hundred percent engagement, and it would feel good to be that free for a couple of hours.

Maks listened to the chatter between Michelle and the rental clerk as his eyes took in the scene, trying to find a trail that converged at the bottom with the one Camille would take. He planned on meeting her at the end. She wasn't going to get away from him that easily.

After Michelle had signed the contract for his rentals, insisting it was her treat, she handed over the skis, poles, and boots just as a bright pink parka caught his attention. Camille was roaring down the slope, her body a blur as she zigged and zagged across the course.

Michelle followed his gaze and smiled.

"She's quite good and she knows this mountain like the back of her hand. She was on the ski team at college and this is where they competed. We thought she had the talent to—"

Her hand made a visor over her eyes as she continued to watch her daughter. Camille had reached the bottom with a swoosh, pushing her goggles up over her hat and looked their way. Her mother gave a short wave and turned to him.

"She quit during her sophomore year, didn't ski for the rest of the winter. She'd changed her major by then and spent all her time studying. Didn't come back to it until after law school."

"Why she quit?"

Making sure that Camille wasn't coming toward them, she answered, "For the full story, well, that's for Camille to tell. The shorter version? She said she had to play catch-up with her political science and history courses. She was taking six a semester so she could graduate on time, studying for the LSAT. Like I told you, she gave up having fun. Come on, you can put your things in the lodge. They have lockers. Or you can leave your boots with Shane."

They began to walk the short distance, weaving between others who were coming and going.

"The reason is secret?"

"It's not something she likes to talk about. And for as much as I meddle in her life, or so she thinks, I do respect her privacy on certain issues. This is one of them."

She stopped short of going in with him.

"You go ahead. I'll see you on the slopes."

"Thank you. For your help."

"The way you can thank me is to take her mind of off things. She's a good woman, Maks. One of the best I know. And if I'm honest, I had very little to do with it."

After patting his shoulder, she walked to the rack where she'd left her skis and began to put them on.

Shane was sitting at one of the tables, facing the slopes. He looked edgy, binoculars in hand.

"I'm not crazy about this, Maks. Are you sure you don't want to hang out with me instead?"

"Maybe before, but now?" He took a deep breath. "I am feeling good. Don't worry."

He went back out and got busy clipping on his skis before making his way to the lift. Camille was only one ahead in line, her mother a few chairs up.

He tapped the man in front of him. "Excuse. May I join friend?" He pointed to Camille's back and the man gave a nod in answer.

Skirting in next to her, Maks announced, "I am glad I stayed. This is good for soul."

The air was bracing, the company unparalleled, the freedom inspiring.

"How often have you skied before?"

"Often enough. More when I was kid. Not so much in last couple of years. It's what one does in Russia for sport."

"Do you want to start out easy, difficult, or...more difficult?"

"I did no easy when I first start but it has been years, so I guess difficult."

"Okay. Come on."

They stepped up to catch the next chair lift. She got on with ease. He didn't but she grabbed hold of his arm and balanced him against her body. He didn't mind in the least and took his time righting himself.

Once he had, she said, "We'll take Middle Cannon. It's a straight-forward trail, not a lot of moguls, and with all the new snow, it's packed well. It should give you what you want."

He was enthralled with the vista, the sky blue, the sun like a muted ball, tree-dotted mountains as far as the eye could see. When they reached the jump-off point, he did a better job than when getting on, and he skied over to the top of the slope, using his poles to guide him. He wasn't as rusty as he'd thought, the skis fluid beneath him.

After flipping her goggles down, she asked, "You ready?"

He grinned as he mirrored her action, and yelled, "*Ja.*" He pushed himself off the shelf, leaving her behind with a surprised look on her face.

She didn't waste any time catching up with him and stayed by his side as he picked up speed, crisscrossing the trail like he had when he was a kid. Shouting back and forth, they carried on a conversation as they descended the mountain. Then, he lost his flow and his footing, his arms flailing, one ski up in the air as he tried to regain his balance. They laughed like kids until he wiped out, tumbling a few feet before he stopped himself. She stopped short and came edging up to him, a concerned look on her face. When she checked him out to find he was all in one piece, he didn't let her curtail him as he pushed his way to the bottom. He hadn't felt this carefree in a long time, hadn't realized how much he had missed it. He let himself go today knowing he'd get back to his more serious pursuits tomorrow. Michelle joined them for the next couple of runs, almost as good a skier as her daughter, before bidding them farewell. She had to get back to the winery and the event Mountain Man had scheduled for the night.

Over the next couple of hours, they tested out every trail but the most difficult, and he was proud to say he'd kept up well. It was close to dusk, the sky pink and dark grey, the sun just making its descent before he agreed to give one he'd avoided all day a shot. He figured it would be a great way to end the day. And it was. He'd managed to keep both skis on the ground, but it was the woman beside him who continued to take his breath away. It was a good thing he was leaving. He might want to take the kiss they'd shared last night a step or two further, and he wasn't ready for that kind of wild ride.

Camille had changed into more comfortable clothes, and had a book in her hand when she came out of her bedroom. She'd hoped after the day they spent together Maks would change his mind about leaving but he'd been more determined than ever to get back to Boston. When her mother began to push her suggestion about the condo, she'd acquiesced, which was highly unusual. It wasn't her mother's persistence that changed her mind but the raging lust flooding her system that had prompted her to hand over the keys. If her mother thought she had won that round, she'd let her.

Shane had the security code, and she'd explained where everything they might need was stored, coffee, vodka, extra blankets, and pillows. Her second bedroom didn't have a bed, so Shane would be stuck on the couch again. It was her home office replete with desk, computer, file cabinet, and other touches she'd acquired in her travels. Family pictures were framed and scattered over bookcases, walls, and credenza. Maks would know her inside and out after spending the night there while she still had little on him.

Shane's bag was over his shoulder, his hand on the door knob.

"Thanks for the hospitality, Camille. It was a nice break. Now it's back to the gold mines."

Maks wore a perplexed look on his face.

"We go to Cami's."

"Just a saying Maks. Say good-bye."

He was hesitating, lines of concentration deepening along his brows. It was as if he was having second thoughts. She held bated breath seeing which way he'd turn. When the muscles in his face relaxed, he expressed his gratitude and he followed Shane out of the condo.

As soon as the door closed, she felt an acute sense of loss. She'd wanted quiet, and it seemed she was finally going to get it, but now...—she began to pace, swallowed the despair in her throat.

After wading into the kitchen, she poured herself a liberal glass of wine, and let the sadness have its way. She wanted him back, wanted to laugh with him again, and kiss again, and maybe even let it lead— After draining the wine in one gulp, she waited for the light-headed feeling that took over after one glass. All that came was an image of his smile and a throbbing ache inside of her. It didn't help knowing he'd soon be in her home. What had she been thinking when she said yes? There would be a gold mine of information waiting to be gleaned if Maks chose to invade her privacy. It wasn't only that that was making icy fear twist in her heart. The thought of him in her bed both thrilled and frightened her. She wanted to be there with him even though she had no idea who he was.

She hesitated, torn by conflicting emotions before running after him.

He was just opening the car door when she yelled out, "Maks, wait."

She gave Shane a look that translated to, *could they have a minute alone* and he was astute enough to read it. After getting into the car, he started the engine, the white plume of exhaust all but choking in the frigid air.

With arms crossed against her chest to keep the chill at bay, she faced Maks, her eyes downcast. She was going to ask him outright. What did she have to lose? If he told her, she could use it. If not, well she'd find another way. Helping him had become an obsession, he had become an obsession and she needed to know some truth about him.

A shiver coursed through her. The wind had picked up and was blowing her hair as if it were a wind sock. Letting it have its way, she placed a hand on his arm, and when their eyes met, she asked, "Who are you?"

His face was set in granite, his black eyes studying her intently.

After a few seconds, his voice cut into the silence.

"Maxim Zhernova. Is that what you need?"

She had a feeling she'd never get what she needed from him. It had to do with sweaty bodies, tangled sheets, and lots of skin. At the thought of that, she felt herself moving towards him, her hand moving behind his neck and bringing his face close enough that she could feel his breath.

"No, it isn't."

And with that, she brushed her lips against his, the jolt sending sparks in every direction. He didn't respond as she'd hoped. He accepted her kiss but did nothing to deepen it. Disappointment flooded through her and she knew she had lost something undefinable. She stepped back and let him go, swallowing back the tears that threatened to fall, not realizing until this moment that she had fallen in love with him.

As she watched the SUV pull away from the condo, she saw her future disappearing around the curve. Her mother spoke often about the magic of love at first sight. She'd never understood it, not until a Russian had answered the door to her knock. At first glance, she'd fallen head over heels. With no rhyme or reason, with no real understanding of why, her heart had decided. There was nothing to do with it now. She'd blown it, just like she had once before. The pain and recrimination of the past had nothing on this. This time, the pain was all encompassing.

⌒

Shane focused on driving as the car bounced down he rutted road but as soon as they hit the highway, he asked, "What was that about?"

Maks looked out the side window, still tingling from the kiss. He'd wanted to deepen it, take her in his arms again, but he still didn't trust her completely and he had to detach from the feelings she evoked in him. That they were as dark and deep as the Red Sea was troubling.

He scratched at the stubble on his face. He hadn't taken the time to shave this morning, wanting to get away from her and what he felt. Michelle had postponed the inevitable, but the time spent together made him want her that much more. He wanted to stay with her, yes, but it was more than that. He wanted to stay in one place for more than a night or two, wanted a country he could call his own again. The reality that he had no home came to him in stark, blinding colors. He'd never see the Urals again, never visit the town of his birth, never visit his father's grave. He'd never listen to the sounds of the Russian anthem as a patriot again, never love his country the way he had when he was younger. He wanted to find a place where he could belong, and he'd hoped— He forced those thoughts away reluctantly.

"She wanted to know name."

Shane spun his head to face him.

"Did you tell her?"

"I did. Might be mistake."

"Maks she's as professional as they come."

The question was, was she trustworthy? If he could believe she'd been in his room to check on him...but he couldn't shake his suspicions. He was back to doubting, second-guessing, mistrusting. Being on guard all the time was exhausting. He was bone-tired and he wanted this over with. Maybe she *could* help him with the application process.

"It is important for her to know name, so she can fill in blanks."

Pulling the visor down, the mid-morning sun glistening off the ice that lined the highway, Shane added as an afterthought, "It might have to do with the last case she worked for Nate. She bumped into some trouble."

"What you mean trouble?"

"She was sliced up by one of the French nationals seeking asylum. She told Nate not to call her again. Nate doesn't usually listen when he needs something, so his calling her didn't seem out of character, but I was surprised when he told us she'd taken your case. Russians are a lot more dangerous today than French nationals."

A picture of Nina came rushing back. This time the deathly pale face was Camille's. A shudder went through him.

He tried to swallow the lump in his throat, but it didn't budge.

"Sliced up?"

"Yeah. The woman she was representing ended up being a terrorist. Camille found her out, and when she confronted her, the woman pulled a knife, and...well, thank God there was an agent out in the hallway who heard the scream. They aren't normally assigned to those kinds of cases, but Camille asked one to accompany her to the apartment. When he got into the room, the woman had the knife at Camille's throat. Blood was seeping from a couple of cuts, one around her rib cage, another on her stomach."

Maks' hands closed into fists.

"She was hurt?"

"She was, not critically but...enough that she didn't want to take another one of Nate's cases for a while."

He cringed when he thought of her hurt and bleeding.

"The agent stopped this?"

"With Camille's help. She elbowed the woman when he charged in, sustained another cut for her efforts, but it gave the agent the opening he needed to take the woman down. She was deported, along with the other members of the cell, as soon as they could get them on a plane. Nate trusts her. She's thorough, otherwise we could have had an attack on our soil again."

"Does she think I'm terrorist?"

"I don't know what she thinks. We haven't given her anything. Neither have you. The upside about her taking the case was that she knows a lot about the racketeering, and all the deaths around the world at the hands of the Russian Mafia. I think it could also be a downside."

Could she believe the *reketiry* was trying to get to him and would go through her to do it? They weren't the ones after him, and that was worse. The mafia would stop at the border, others at the top of the regime would not.

"How long ago this happen?"

"From what I understand, it all went down at the end of September."

That was three months ago. Was that time enough to heal?

"Does she know I am on hit list somewhere?"

"You've got an agent with you and you're being moved from safe house to safe house. What do you think?"

"She put herself at risk with this. Why?"

"I don't have an answer for you. Alec gave me a heads-up about her because he wanted to make sure she was mentally ready for this. All I got was background on the prior case. And the warning that if I see her cracking under the strain, Alec is taking it to Nate to get her pulled."

He stiffened and swore. They were changing the people around him like he was the only one stuck in a revolving door. He needed continuity, especially if he began to trust those around him. He might have suspicions about Camille but...the thought of someone else asking him questions, bringing him dinner, making him breakfast, kissing him...She had become a fixture in this new life.

"I don't want new lawyer."

"Well, then you're probably going to have to share some of your story with her. At least reassure her she's not going to be killed in her sleep. By anyone."

"I'm not to say anything until after interview by Intelligence Committee."

"Did they explicitly tell you to keep things from your attorney?"

"They say no one."

"They assigned her to you for a reason. I'd go with your instincts."

"Instincts? I have instinct telling me to keep quiet about everything."

"You have to start trusting someone, Maks. It might as well be her."

He knew that on an intellectual level but on emotional one? Not easily done.

"Events of the past couple of years have, let me say, dented my ability to do that."

"I get it. But you're not there anymore. Do you trust me?"

"*Ja*, I do. That is reason I want you to stay bodyguard."

"Why?"

"You haven't given me any reason to think I shouldn't."

"Has she?"

He paused, wondering if he was being paranoid. Maybe he was, but it didn't mean she wasn't out to get him. A man could lose his life by trusting the wrong person. He couldn't quite take apart the puzzle that was Camille.

"She was in room. Don't know what she was doing there."

Shane looked over at him.

"Did you ask her?"

He hadn't had to. She'd given it before he asked, which made him wary.

"She said she was looking for me."

"And you find that hard to believe?"

"I would have called out, not invaded private space."

Shane's fingers began to tap the steering wheel. "She might have thought you were in the shower."

"She might have. Or else she went in looking for something."

"Like what?"

"Passport to see my name."

"Why would she ask you before we left if she already knew it?"

"Mind is too suspicious. I know this. But I can't help feeling she had ulterior motive."

"I think you should give her the benefit of the doubt. Trust her until she does something that proves she's not trustworthy."

He shrugged his shoulders, giving Shane the impression he'd think about it.

"Have you asked Alec about staying on as bodyguard?"

"He gave the okay. They won't let me work straight through, but I've been assigned as primary until you don't need a bodyguard. I told them I'll work through the Christmas shift so someone with kids can get the day with their family and then I'll have to take a day off."

"When is Christmas here?"

"A week from tomorrow."

"How you celebrate?"

"Santa, gifts, trees and tinsel, home-cooked dinners."

"You will have none of these?"

"I don't know. You're a chef, aren't you? I'm sure you could rustle up something good to eat."

"Where will I be?"

Shane slanted him a look, and he read regret there as if the agent knew what this was costing him.

"I don't know, Maks. They're still working on that. The agency seems to be swimming in refugees this month."

The inconsistency of his life was getting to him. He liked order, routine. He'd had neither since arriving. He leaned back, his chin in his hand as he looked out at the landscape speeding by. Stones and boulders lined the road, remnants of the mountain's fight with time. The trees were dressed in white, complementing the blacks and greys of the cliff. There was an eagle flying high in the sky, and he scrunched his neck to look up. He envied him. Free to come and go as he pleased, the sky his home, his cry unfettered. His thoughts drifted back to Camille as they so often did lately.

She'd been pissed at her mother for offering them the condo and it seemed it was a familiar beat for them. Michelle was gracious but there was a band of steel at her core. Camille had inherited it, although she would probably never admit it, and it was at the root of their disagreements. He thought they were a lot alike, not only in temperament but in looks, as well.

His mother, Sonya Zhernova, was different. More accepting of things. She'd lived with communism long enough to know you couldn't fight the system. And she didn't try. She'd been taught to keep her head down and stay out of trouble. Even when the regime had collapsed, she held to her belief, thinking the rule of law would last forever. It ended up she was right. Today they were more entrenched in a totalitarian type of government than before. Her husband had had more optimism. After the bloc was smashed into separate states and the rubble had cleared, he'd believed that the steps they were taking toward democracy would lead them out. He'd refused to keep his head down, refused to ignore the truth once he realized the country took a wrong turn, taking them backwards in time. His undiluted trust in the underpinnings of the political system had been his downfall. He hadn't seen the dangers that awaited him. Sonya's biggest regret was not arguing more strenuously with Petrov about leaving. If she had demanded they get out before the arrest, he might have listened. Maks had his doubts. Petrov had believed he was fighting for his country, that he was at war with the government, and he hadn't let the threat of death stop him from speaking out.

Living with Sonya through those dark days had made his life hell. Every time she came back from whatever prison he'd been moved to, she'd cry for what she'd left to chance. Insisted she was partly to blame. She'd gambled with their lives, with her ambivalence and her fear, and she'd lost. After the death, she'd become as much a vigilante as him. Was willing to buck the systems that had caused her husband's death. Petitioned the courts to review Petrov's death, and every time they were denied, she'd become more determined than ever to reveal the duplicity. When Maks had begun his hacking, uncovering things that spoke to how corrupt his government had become, she hadn't stopped him. She'd become his anchor, tethering him to a life underground, where he stayed below the radar. As his skills had improved and the material grew, she was the one who put together the dossier that he'd handed over to the FBI. She'd insisted he leave, knowing that it was the only way for him to spread the word. Staying in Moscow would have meant certain death. She was willing to risk her life to save his.

He missed her.

There were tears in his eyes as they came into a rest stop half way back to Boston. Wiping them away, he let Shane go ahead. He needed some time to compose himself. When he had re-bottled the pain of the past, he joined his bodyguard for a bowl of chili, and a coffee to go.

When they were back on the road, he asked questions about Shane's life, his work. What it was like working for the government here. What could they do and not do? What was tolerated by the top brass and what wasn't? He liked what he heard, for the most part. They were independent of the administration, and the head of the agency was a man of honor and integrity. Many were disappointed with the way he'd handled aspects of the election, but it didn't diminish the way his employees felt about him. He had already made strides with the Russian interference and he wasn't going to back down or kow-tow to anyone.

Shane admitted, "There are going to be some rocky days ahead, but we know what we have to do, and it will get done."

Maks could feel the commitment to revealing the truth. He certainly wasn't in Russia anymore.

Camille was glad she'd agreed to join her family tonight. Her escape had originally been about being alone, enjoying the quiet and getting some rest. Maks
had changed everything. Now that the condo was empty of his presence, she
should stick around, do some work, go to bed early. Think. It hadn't been
possible with Maks around. Now that he was gone—well, the memory of the
day was taking up a lot of space in her head. Or was it her heart? He'd been
totally uninhibited on the mountain. He'd laughed freely, talked to her about
his past, his first time on skis, his friends, and she had entertained him with
stories of her own childhood and what it was like growing up with Michelle
the Manipulator. She was getting to know him, and she wanted more. More
of everything. His laughter, his kisses, his conversation. All of him.

Did he sense that? Was that why he'd left, why he hadn't returned the kiss.

She groaned at her own forwardness. His lover was barely in the grave.
How could she have forgotten that when she reached out to kiss him?

She'd humiliated herself and she wasn't sure how she'd face him again.

After taking a shower, trying to wash away the disappointment, she
dressed for dinner and made the solitary drive to one of the wine-tasting chalet's where tonight's event was taking place. Her aunt Millicent and uncle
Harold would be there, along with their kids, Mike and Kim. They were staying at the house, which was why she'd gotten the condo. Her aunt was one of
her favorite people and the only one of her father's siblings who lived close
enough to visit from time to time. It was her aunt Millie who'd insisted she
get her grandfather's desk, knowing how close they had been and said it was
what Gaston would have wanted. Her father came from a family with five
children; her mother was an only child. Michelle's father had been one of the
last Frenchmen to die in Vietnam before the country pulled out of the quag-
mire and the United Sates stepped in. Her grandmother had died when her
mother was twenty-one, so she was alone in the world before her father found
her. She'd embraced the large Bissonnette family and had become one of
them.

As Camille entered the chalet, the sounds of the string quartet reached out
to welcome her. Glancing around, she saw people milling around each table,
tasting the wines that had been pulled from the family's private stock. There'd
be sleigh rides through the countryside and a candlelit dinner served by their
chef. She appreciated how beautifully the chalet was decorated. Her mother's
hand had created a warm and homey feel. Even with the ambience, there was

a sense of loneliness that accompanied her in. The melancholy had taken hold again.

Her mother came right over, put her arms around her, and squeezed. She didn't want it to, but it felt good. Her mother might be a busybody, but no one could deny she loved her children. Sometimes, it was a bit too much. Michelle thought she knew what was best for everyone. It sucked that she was right most of the time.

She broke away from the embrace, but her mother kept hold of her hand.

"You are unhappy he is gone. It is how I felt when your father dropped me back at home after our first date. It tells you all you need to know."

Michelle's ability to pick up on her children's moods was almost scary.

"Mama, please. I don't want to talk about it."

She couldn't without giving too much classified information away.

"He is good-looking, smart, and talented. What more could you want?"

"I don't even know him."

"I didn't know your father. It's what he makes you feel, *ma chere*. There is magic there. One can't miss it."

"He might not even be staying here. He hasn't decided where he's going to immigrate."

"He is here. Like me, he will go where his heart leads him."

"Not everyone is like you."

"And they miss out on real happiness. He's not stupid."

No, he wasn't. Smart but like a fox. Which meant wily as one, too. He'd avoid her for as long as he had to, giving her nothing while he stole her heart.

"Mama, please. Leave it. What will be will be. Isn't that what you tell us often enough?"

Ironic that her favorite saying was at odds with her constant interference.

"Yes, and this will be. Trust your heart. It will lead you in the right direction."

There were no further words about Maks or magic that night. Everything about him was internalized. He never once strayed from her thoughts.

CHAPTER EIGHTEEN

Maks was still thinking when Shane drove the car into the parking slot that had "number one" decaled in white. It had taken a few hours to get here, the traffic heavy off and on during the trip, and they'd hit that rest stop for food.

As he hefted his bags out of the back, he looked at the building that Camille called home. It was taupe color, very neat and trim. After walking up the four brick steps, Shane inserted the key, and they moved inside towards the door to the condo itself. Shane punched in the alarm code at the bottom of another set of stairs that led them up into a white kitchen with lots of counter space, the stainless-steel appliances gleaming in the sunlight streaming in through the windows. He couldn't help but smile. There were no smudges to be seen.

He let his eyes roam around every inch of the homey space. A coffee maker stood in the corner. Two ceramic containers held all kinds of utensils. There was a toaster oven, a cookie jar, and a block with knives. It was a pale ice-yellow with quartz counters, grey threads woven through it. He stepped into the family room, the bay window the focal point, to see a couch, two chairs, and a huge television mounted on a wall painted the color of smoke. A small round table sat to the side, graced with two chairs that he assumed was used as an eating area. There was a miniature Christmas tree in the corner, decorated with twinkle lights and an abundance of old-fashioned ornaments. A few wrapped presents sat beneath it.

Down the short hall was a bathroom, two other rooms. One had a bed, the other a beautifully restored desk, on which sat a computer, a pile of folders spread across the surface. There was a high boy that he investigated that held all her office supplies, envelopes, folders, computer paper. It gave him an insight into who she was. There was an organized clutter that spoke to a busy mind and an attempt to make order out of the chaos. Family pictures lined a long rectangular table set against a wall, and he gravitated to them. Bending forward, he fingered an old photo of a man with greying hair, a bushy moustache, wearing a uniform that gave away his nationality. It looked circa 1917, a World War I soldier who fought for his homeland. There was something familiar about the eyes, and he wondered if they were the same grey-green inherited by both Camille and her mother. Perusing the other dozen, he had the sense that she surrounded herself by family. He couldn't miss, it was important to her.

About to walk into her room, he stopped. It was too personal a step to take. The bed was unmade, a thick duvet of pale grey and white stripes pushed back as if she'd slipped out and left it. The matching pillows were scattered across the headboard, the indentation telling him she slept on her side. A grey armoire stood tall against one of the walls. Pictures lined another flat-topped bureau of pearly white. It was feminine in the same way she was, and he felt uncomfortable being in such sacred space. He backed away, calling out to Shane, "Why don't you take bedroom. I can sleep on couch."

Shane had already deposited his bag in the office and was back out in the living room, the TV remote in his hand.

"Nope. My job is to guard the exits. There are two of them and I'm not leaving you vulnerable to an attack."

Unable to take the final step in, Maks made a U-turn and moved down another hallway to the second entrance and peeked out. There was a deck and a fenced-in area.

"I found smoking spot."

He unlocked the door and opened it but he heard, "Wait up," and paused.

Shane went into the kitchen and rummaged around until he found an empty soup can in the recycle bin.

"Here's your ashtray. If you leave your butts out there, she won't be happy."

He didn't have to tell him who *she* was.

Maks took it from the extended hand and headed out to the large rectangular deck. There was a grill, covered in a tarp, and a couple of chairs that could withstand the winter weather. Camille loved the cold as much as he did, and he could see her taking a minute to come out, sitting down and breathing in the fresh, crisp air.

After pulling his pack out of his shirt pocket, he took the last of his Gauloises, the cigarettes he'd picked up in France. They weren't as strong as the Russian brand he bought, but nothing was. He struck the match, the smell of sulfur sharp and potent, watching the smoke curl and mix with his frosted breath. He rested his arms on the railing and looked out at the open space. He imagined a table and chairs come summer, the grill smoking from beef dripping with goodness, vodka or wine being passed around, friends chatting, making memories. Friends. Was he making them or were these people just accessories to this time in his life? He'd left two good ones behind in Russia. One was buried, the other an associate of his father who'd taken up the cause with them. He'd had no time for others. Not even at the restaurant had he found a connection. He'd worked, he'd gone home, he'd hacked, he'd slept. And repeated. There'd been women who'd come on to him, but he hadn't had time for such frivolousness. It was probably why he'd fallen into bed with Nina. It was a release and a short one at that. There were no loving words, no warmth, just a bodily exercise in getting the sexual energy out.

Grey-blue eyes looked out at him. He felt the gentle rise and fall of her breasts, the warmth of her caress, and the sweet taste of her lips.

He could see her here. Cooking, relaxing, sleeping.

It was the sleeping that hung him up. He didn't want to sleep in her bed. It would make him think thoughts that weren't healthy or safe. The kiss she'd given him before he left was still affecting his body.

He wished he knew what she'd been doing in his bedroom back at the mountain retreat. If she'd wanted to steal a look at his passport, she'd had the time. She could have been in and out while he was having his smoke. He'd left it out, not even thinking anyone would sneak in. He'd let his guard down. No way would he have done something so stupid before. He had to start paying attention again, take precautions, had to think about what he was putting at risk every minute. She had made him feel safe, something that scared him. Now?

When she'd come running out before he left, he didn't know what she wanted. When she'd asked who he was, he was conflicted. She hadn't asked what his name was. Had she already known? Was the question meant to confuse him?

If it was, she'd been successful.

Then the kiss. Unexpected and mind-boggling. Her lips so soft and full, those eyes pure blue, without a trace of grey.

What did she want from him?

What was he willing to give?

He put the cigarette out in the tin can and left it on the rail so it would be handy his next trip out and retreated to the warmth of the condo.

Shane looked up from his phone to see him re-enter.

"Still don't have a place. We'll stay here as long as Camille lets us."

"Hotel, Shane. Only one bed here and three of us."

"Alec nixed the idea of a hotel. Says it's too expensive if there's an alternative."

"No alternative."

"We'll see."

When Shane went back to the conversation, he took his bags into the room that reminded him so much of the woman who lived here.

⌢

Camille snuggled into the couch, a blanket thrown over her legs and opened her computer. She had a name and she'd been denying her curiosity all day. She was finally able to give in to it.

Typing in the name Zhernova, she waited for the results. The number of sites listed was in the thousands. She knew it wasn't going to be an easy search but culling through all the entries was going to take endless hours. The list to the side mentioned an Alexander, Victor, Rafail, Simon, Anna, Grygor, Petrov, Irina, Magdelyn. There were passport-like photos of some of them, short bios that helped her weed out the ones that didn't work.

There was no mention of a Maksim, but there was a Maxim Petrovonovich Zhernova. She knew the Russians used the father's name as their middle name, so this meant that Maks' father was Petrov. Re-scrolling up, she went back to the name Petrov Ivanevich Zhernova, the heading making her skin crawl.

LAWYER COMMITS SUICIDE IN PRISON.

As she scanned the story, her heart began to pound. Petrov was an attorney turned activist who had been arrested and charged with treason. Imprisoned for more than a year, he was found lifeless in his cell, the cause self-induced strangulation. The body wasn't returned to the family for over a week, the burial denied by the church. Russian Orthodox did not sanctify suicide.

He was laid to rest at an unknown location by his wife, Sonya and his son, Maxim.

She snapped the cover of her computer down and shoved it onto the coffee table.

Tears filled her eyes at the thought of what Petrov must have gone through. She knew what those prisons were like, had read numerous articles about others who'd been thrown in jail by the heads of state on trumped-up charges. Pursuit of the truth was enough to get you sentenced to certain death. How many had died at the hands of their jailers? Rubber batons, deprivation, health issues ignored. Her skin crawled knowing Maks' father had gone through that. Did this have more to do with why he was here than Nina?

Two deaths at the hands of his countrymen.

She thought of the movie *A Few Good Men*. She'd wanted the truth of who he was, but could she handle it?

She was already obsessed with Maks' asylum claim. She'd work even harder now to see it granted but not tonight. She had to settle her nerves, calm her emotions before getting back to it. She'd only touched the surface. What would be at the bottom of this swamp? And would her love for him cloud her judgment?

Hugging her arms around herself, she gave into the tears. She wanted to share her love with him, let him know he wasn't alone in whatever fight he was facing. Would he ever share it with her, or would she have to get all her information from the internet or the sources in Russia she was cultivating? It was so hard to know what was true and what was fake. The Russian government would put on the face it wanted the world to see. She doubted that Petrov had committed treason and she doubted he'd died at his own hand. Was Maks trying to prove it? Or get revenge as he'd suggested? She couldn't blame him. She knew of others who'd fought for justice, but it was always outside the borders. Nothing could be done from within. Was that why he was here?

Where was his mother? Was she still alive? Those were other avenues she'd have to pursue. But not tonight.

Tonight, she'd give into the grief and the sense of loss he must be feeling.

She was up before sunrise, unable to sleep with so many distorted images of Maks and his family invading her dreams. Dressed for the office, ready to go, she checked to make sure the coffee maker was off and rinsed, she hadn't left anything behind in her groggy state. Texting her mother, she let her know she was headed out.

She'd gotten her mother's standard reply. *Be safe.*

She didn't pay much attention to the scenery, her mind too busy with all she had to do today, not only picking up the thread of where she'd left off last night, but on her other dozen cases. She flipped through her mental to-do list, almost sorry she'd taken the weekend off, knowing full well if she hadn't she wouldn't have gleaned so much information about Maks. It had been worth it.

Even though it was never too early to go into the office, she took time to stop by her condo to check on things. Before getting out of her car, she texted Shane to let her know she was outside. She didn't want to be facing a loaded gun walking into her own home.

The first thing she saw as she started up the stairs was Maks in the kitchen. He was at the stove, the smells of peppers and onions wafting through the air. Where had he gotten the food? There wasn't much here when she left.

He glanced up at her entrance and smiled, which made her insides melt and the tears threaten.

She wanted to hug him, kiss him, feel his body close to hers but she had to stop the foolish hope that burned inside.

"I got an early start, so I thought I'd stop in to say hello. Did you find everything you needed?"

"I hope you don't mind. I fix breakfast."

Peering over his shoulder, she inhaled. "Not in the least. Where'd the food come from? The refrigerator was empty when I left."

"We stopped on way last night. Shane said we shouldn't eat your food."

"Can I eat yours?"

He glanced at her and a vaguely sensuous light passed between them. The peppers and onions weren't the only thing searing, and he put his attention back on the pan and stirred.

"You can share. Coffee is made. Shane is in shower."

She slipped out of her coat and hung it on the ornate coat-rack she'd picked up at an antique store and moved toward the coffee. She knew it'd be strong, and the caffeine would do nothing to unruffle the jitters at the sight of him, but she took a cup anyway.

"That will put hair on chest. No doubt. If I had known you come, I'd sacrifice taste."

"This is fine. I can pick up a normal cup on the way to the office."

"You start my application today?"

"More likely tonight. I've got a full day of appointments and meetings."

"All your asylum clients?"

"Yes, and I promised I'd speak as lecturer at my law school alma mater. The professor who teaches Immigration Law asks me to come in periodically, give the class some insights into how to handle refugees."

"From what I'm told, you are good at that."

"My mother's bias."

"Shane tell me, too."

He was splitting the omelet up, scooping it onto three separate dishes. She pulled open the fridge and her eyes widened at all the choices. She took the bottle of orange juice out. "You sure know how to stock up."

Shane came out, rubbing a towel over his hair.

"Thanks for giving me a heads-up. Not only so I didn't kill you, but I might have come out with nothing more than a towel."

That thought didn't even register. Nothing did other than Maks and his delicious offerings.

After disappearing into the bathroom, Shane came back out with dry hair and a hearty appetite.

Taking a seat at the table, he dug in to his food.

Maks handed Camille her plate and said, "You sit. I'll eat at counter."

"You're the guest."

"Also cook. We never sit."

Just as she planted her bottom on the chair, Shane upset her balance by asking, "Alec wanted to know if we could stay here for a while."

Her hands tightened together in a ball on her lap. It matched the ball of knots in her stomach.

"What's a while?"

"Through Christmas."

Her mind started racing. The condo wasn't big enough for three people, she hadn't gotten anywhere near the end of her Christmas list, she was going to Jelani's just like every year since she'd joined the firm. Seven days with Maks living with her. She didn't think her heart could take that much of a good thing.

"That's a week away. Where would you sleep?"

"I can get an air mattress in the office for Maks. I can stay on the sofa."

Maks leaned his arms across the counter, putting his two cents in.

"That is big imposition. Hotel."

Before forking in the piece of omelet he held, Shane reminded, "And I've already told you, we can't."

She could hear the warble in her voice when she offered another alternative.

"Take him to your place."

"Against regulations."

She could not have Maks here without... Now her voice sounded desperate to her ears.

"Why?"

Shane seemed to be thoroughly enjoying his food, because his fork never stopped.

"You'd have to ask my boss."

"No problem. I'll call him today."

For this he paused, and he gave her a smile.

"You're going to call the head of the FBI?"

She could feel the blood drain from her face.

"I thought you meant Nate."

"He doesn't set the regulations. Wish he did."

Camille was nibbling on her thumbnail, trying to think of an alternative. That her mind was blank except for a picture of Maks in her bed wasn't helping.

"What if I say no? What will he do then?"

"If you're thinking about throwing us out, then you'd be interfering with an on-going FBI operation. I think that's a jail-able offense."

"What?"

Maks interrupted with a brisk command. "You not going to jail her for wanting home back. We stay at hotel."

Shane put his fork down, putting all joking aside.

"Maks, I was kidding. We don't throw people in prison for that. Well, sometimes we do, but..."

He dropped the rest, putting his attention on Camille instead.

"Why are you so dead set against this? What would the harm be?"

"I live alone for a reason. You would be a major disruption in my life."

"Okay, I'll give you that. But I can get him out from time to time. He won't be underfoot all that often."

"If she doesn't want me here, Shane, we go."

Her eyes flew up to meet Maks'.

If he only knew that wasn't the reason. But she couldn't tell him that she wanted him, that it would be hard enough to see him periodically without seeing him morning, noon, and night. The spasms that started in her groin made her want to squirm, but she forced herself to sit still.

"That's not it, Maks."

She could feel her cheeks flame at the way he was looking at her.

Did he feel it, too?

Did she have the heart to ask him to leave? He didn't have a home, wouldn't until...who knew when. Would it be so bad sharing hers with him until he decided where he'd go?

She scraped the chair back and brought her uneaten food to the sink. After retrieving her coat from the rack, she put it on, but before she left, she said, "Fine. You can stay but there will be ground rules. Maks can sleep in the office but only after my work is done for the night." It didn't give him much in the way of privacy, but she'd be stripped of that coveted condition, as well.

Maks was staring at her. It was Shane who answered for both, of them.

"Thanks, Camille. We appreciate it."

She descended the stairs and left the condo wondering what the hell she'd just agreed to.

CHAPTER NINETEEN

Maks took a seat opposite Shane.

"This is not good idea."

"Why? You two certainly get along and I can protect you here as well as anywhere else."

They got along too well, in his estimation, but Maks wasn't saying that. All his mind could hold was the fact that she'd be sleeping in the next room. He'd toss and turn all night for sure.

"What about Boog and Smokey? We can't bring them into home."

"No, we can't. But we can go to them. They have a lab outside the city and I'm sure they'd let you work there. This way, you won't be cramped in one place twenty-four-seven."

That would be a nice change. He'd gotten used to being out in the world in the Notch and would hate to be back to four walls and no open spaces.

"We do today? I've lost much time."

"Yeah, let me make a call. See if it's doable. Then I'll help you clean up."

"I clean. You call."

⁀

After a twenty-minute drive, they arrived at what looked like a deserted factory building. Parking out front, Shane told Maks to stay put until he'd checked out the area. Once satisfied that it was safe, they walked inside the brick-front edifice and up two flights of stairs. At the end of the long hall, they entered a well-lit high-tech laboratory crammed with tables, and all kinds of computers: mainframes, desktops, laptops, and modems.

Boog got up from his seat at one of the desks and came toward them, a big smile on his face.

"Skoli, good to see you again. I've been waiting for you to pick up where we left off."

Maks couldn't believe how much equipment was in the space. He knew there were offices like this in Russia. It was where the hackers did their business, under the tutelage of the government. Hundreds of computer whizzes, given the job of interfering with the countries around the world, upsetting the dynamics of democracy. It had worked in Great Britain. France and Germany had been smart enough to work around it.

"How you wire?"

"We've got antennas and some satellite dishes up on the roof and a generator out back. We don't ever want to lose power."

"How you afford? This looks expensive."

"We check garbage dumps, then refurbish what we need."

"I built own. Better than what I buy."

"Good to know. Another hand for needed improvements."

Leading both Shane and Maks toward the work area, he explained, "Believe it or not, we started this whole set-up to play video games a few years ago. We met each other online, decided we wanted to get together, and found this place. Old factories are easy to come by, and this seemed to be off the grid enough that we could hide in plain sight."

"When did you become hackers?"

"Amazing how that word has morphed into meaning something good. When we began our journey into the dark web, it conveyed something sinister."

Maks was still examining the set-up, still amazed at what had been built here.

"It still does in some circles. Mention WikiLeaks and you don't think good thoughts."

"Too true. When we testified before the congressional committee on cyber-security, the reps just about shit their pants with what we told them. Amazing how leaders can be the least informed on the planet."

"It is a high priority where I come from. Citizens don't understand depth of damage being done to country by high-ranking officials in Russia. It is why I am here. I will testify soon. You will tell me what it's like?"

"Nothing intimidating. Some of them are dicks and will try to refute what you tell them, but you show them facts and they can argue all they want but it won't change the data. Come on, let me introduce you to the rest of the guys."

And he did. Smokey was there, as was Beers, Gateway 2.0, Rogue Warrior, Bean Pond, and Jellyfish.

"This is Skoli.on.Ice."

He still liked the name and gave them all a big grin.

"Needed new tag name. FBI made me give up the one I had in Russia."

"What was it? Maybe we heard of you."

He glanced over to Shane to see if he could reveal who he was back then. When he got the go-ahead, he said, "Matrixiator."

Boog's eyes went as wide as saucers.

"You're him? Holy shit, man. You're a legend. We wondered why he went dark."

"Didn't want others to follow him here."

They all began asking questions at once, and he tried to answer them all, feeling vindicated and at peace with where he was. The comradery was a welcome change after so much time seen as the enemy. It seemed his life was changing in increments and if he was honest, for the better. Maybe life here would give him what he was looking for. It wasn't only his decision to make, though. He had to make sure it was right for them both. That would come once he was finished with his work, with his testimony, and with his asylum appeal. Thoughts of Camille floated up, and he knew he was going to have to begin to trust her. At her job, if in no other way.

Maybe being with her for the week would work to his benefit. He could begin to talk about his past and what he faced if he stayed in Russia. The true story. Now that she had his name, she might already know what had happened, why he was here. Would it change her opinion of him?

Did it matter?

He was pulled out of those thoughts when Boog beckoned him to the table to begin another round of attacks.

Camille sat in her office, chewing her nail. She'd just told Em and Jelani that she wouldn't be spending Christmas with them this year. It had caused all sorts of questions, and Em left shaking her head, still not understanding the change in routine. She had a feeling that Em would figure it out sooner rather than later and she'd be in for another round of questions all having to do with her Russian.

Her Russian.

She was holding that thought close. He was hers for now, and she wouldn't leave Maks and Shane on their own that day. She wanted to pull out all the stops and make it a memorable occasion, like her mother had done, so that Maks would remember it long after he was gone.

She might only have this week with him, and she was going to do what she could to draw him out, get to know him better. Not only for the application process but for her own selfish purpose. If she'd fallen in love for the first time in her life, she wanted to spend as much time as she could learning about him. His past wasn't pretty. In fact, it was heart-breaking. She couldn't imagine what it must have been like to suffer like that, knowing your father was being tortured and being able to do nothing about it. As a lawyer, she didn't have to wonder how she'd feel if every avenue she pursued for his release was denied. It would have been maddening. Hate-provoking, and vengeance would have been first and foremost in her mind.

Was that why he'd begun his computer work? Hacking might be a better word for it if her intuition proved correct. What kind of information was he stockpiling? She was on the periphery of knowing why he was here and needed protection. If his father had been arrested for treason it meant Maks would be suspect for no other reason than familial connection. Any day, the police could arrest him as well and get away with it. Or was it because of the work he was doing? That would be classified as treason against the state, as well. Was he picking up where his father had left off? She was going to have to follow the clues she'd gathered and see where they lead her. She hoped it wasn't down some dark alley where danger lurked. Would he hurt her if she got too close?

At the knock on the door, she looked up to see Nell standing there.

"Got a minute?"

"Yes, sorry. Too many things on my mind."

"I think we're all under pressure lately. The anticipation of what's to come has got to be worse than the reality. Right?"

"If only. Come in, sit down."

Each of the four partners had identical office space. When the architect was drawing up the specs, it was something that both Mia and Arianna had insisted on. They wanted everyone on equal footing, and the offices were handed out as the women were hired. Jelani was first in, then Nell, Camille came next, and Em was the runt of the litter. But for how exact the dimensions were, every office was as different as the woman who worked from it. Hers had a French flair, with two Bergere chairs, rattan back and light tan linen upholstery. Her side table was French provincial, and she'd rewarded herself with a Louis the Fifteenth carved walnut and leather desk when she made her first million. There was something to be said for working around the clock.

Nell sat in her chair gingerly.

"How do you keep these chairs so clean? I wouldn't dare have something this color for clients."

Her space was much more functional, yet Bohemian, eclectic. Vivid colors, bright floral prints.

"I get them cleaned every now and then. I love the chairs, so I suffer the cost."

Crossing her long legs, Nell sat back.

"It's nice to just sit for a minute."

"I'm glad I got away for the weekend. Since I got back, I've been chasing a client all over the East Coast, had two interviews today I didn't think would end, and I missed lunch. I needed that time on the mountain. It's kind of transcendent."

"That's why my Fridays are sacrosanct. Being with Chloe does the same thing for me."

When Nell began playing with her charm bracelet, Camille sensed she was unsettled.

"Can I do something for you?

Dropping the charm, she clasped her hands together and said, "I just wanted to follow up with you on the case you're working. I met Jack this morning for breakfast, which I don't really want to talk about, so let's just say it's about him meeting Chloe."

When Nell began to fiddle with the charm again, Camille knew that topic bothered her, so she left it alone.

"Anyway, before I left, I asked him if the Intelligence Committee was interviewing any Russians on the cyber space issue. He asked why, and I told him I'd heard rumors. He said it was supposed to be classified but they were holding closed-door sessions on the election hacking as soon as the new Congress was seated. He says there's a mole called the Matrixiator who's been brought into the country to testify. Seems he has some conclusive evidence on people on both sides of the Atlantic. Does that mean anything?"

"It supports the supposition that he's a computer whiz. The Matrixiator. I've never heard of him, have you?"

"No, but then that's not listed among my skill sets. It might give you another avenue to pursue. If he's as valuable as Jack made him seem, there must be something on him, somewhere."

"I'm beginning to get a sketchy picture of what's happening."

If Maks was looking for proof that his father's arrest and death were a blatant perversion of justice, he could have stumbled on other kinds of information. Maybe it had been mixed in with the information he'd gathered for Nina. One answer uncovered a dozen more questions.

"If he's got evidence against the top officials in Russia, then his life would be in danger. How can I prove that if the FBI *and* Congress are keeping him under wraps?"

Would her probing bring him to light? She was going to have to find an ally in Russia, and she had no idea how she'd find one. She'd spoken to someone at the consulate and he was working on it, but she wasn't holding her breath waiting. There were too many people who ignored the danger, unwilling to upset the balance of powers. Next, she'd try the ambassador. Maybe a journalist? Another lawyer? She had her work cut out for her, but she wasn't backing down. She couldn't handle it if anything happened to him.

"Cami, it means you might be in danger, as well. Please, be careful."

"I will. And thanks, Nell. I appreciate it."

"If Jack gives me any more information I think you can use, I'll let you know."

Nell got up and left. Camille could tell she was going through her own version of hell from the purple smudges under her eyes. In just a few days, Chloe's dad had gone from being an unknown entity to a known one. Everyone at the office had turned on Jack Adams in a flash. She had a feeling it was going to take a heroic effort on his part to make things up to Nell, for them to give him the time of day again.

Before leaving for home, she spent an hour online, searching for someone known as the Matrixiator. She found a trove of information and couldn't quite believe it was her Russian.

Called a cyber warrior, extraordinary, unnerving, compelling, and hero. He'd been given accolades for pulling back the Wizard's curtain, to reveal the lengths Russia had gone to to skew the election. Most of it was unintelligible to her, more geek code than actual language, and she now knew how people felt about legalese. She was chomping at the bit to talk to him about all of this, but she'd have to hold herself back until she could coax the information out of him or get to know him well enough to share her find.

She could only do that by being with him, and as fate would have it, or her mother if she wielded that kind of power, he'd be staying with her for the next week.

When she packed up her briefcase for home, every muscle in her body tensed with expectation.

CHAPTER TWENTY

She texted Shane, letting him know she was on her way home. He'd thanked her and asked that she keep up the ritual.

After hefting her briefcase, her computer bag, and a couple of bottles of wine she'd picked up on the way home, out of the car, she let herself in and began her climb up the stairs. The next home would be on the ground level, not that the exercise wasn't good for her. She didn't get to the gym as much as she liked, often wondered why she kept her membership, but every time she thought of canceling it, her conscience wouldn't let her. Half-way up, her sense of smell kicked in. The same scene greeted her as it had this morning. Maks was in the kitchen, and the succulent aroma that enveloped her was something she could get used to. After dumping her things at the top of the stairs, she shrugged out of her coat and hung it up.

Walking into the small space, she asked, "What is that smell? It's heavenly."

"Rack of lamb. Never cooked before but sounded interesting."

He had a towel over his shoulder, his hair up in an elastic, beads of sweat on his brow. As he wiped his forehead, his eyes met hers and he smiled. "Just checked. Oven hot."

There was a pan of sautéed brussels sprouts and one on a gentle boil of fingerling potatoes.

"Where are you getting the food?"

"Shane order from store. They deliver. This is good about America."

She agreed and had never thought of that as an option. It would be a great way to get food into her refrigerator without taking the time out of her busy schedule for such a menial task. She'd just have to figure out how to get it inside. If they delivered on Sunday, she might be able to swing it. She looked over to where Shane sat in the living room, his computer on his lap. He gave her a quick smile.

"If you give me the name of the place you ordered from, I'll set up an account and you can charge the deliveries. I don't think Uncle Sam is going to want to provide such lavish meals on a regular basis."

"I paid out of pocket. Figured I'd get reimbursed at some point in the future. But you're right about the menu, so that would be great."

"Did you get everything in place?"

"We did. Your yoga mat was in the way, so I rolled it up and put it in the corner. Sorry about that but the mattress was bigger than I thought."

She walked the short distance to her office and peeked inside. He was right, and she sighed. She'd have to do some maneuvering if she wanted to get to her desk, and with Maks' bed right there, her thoughts would not be on work. She'd known this was going to be a test of will but not quite this challenging.

With a heavy sigh, she said, "I'm gonna change. I'll be right out."

She closed the door and leaned against it. What had she been thinking? Having him here was not going to be easy. She shook her head. No, it was his leaving that would be the toughest part. Especially if he cooked dinner every night and looked as appetizing as the main meal. She swallowed the saliva that had pooled in her mouth and stepped away from the door, shedding her pants and blouse on the way to her bureau. She glanced around trying to visually find a place to roll out her mat. She'd have to do her yoga in here but...

With jeans in hand, she dropped to the bed and drew them on. Her sweater came next and her Ugg moccasins. After tying her hair up in a messy bun, she picked up her discarded clothes and threw them on her chair. She'd get to them later.

When she came out, Maks was setting the table with two plates.

"I have a folding chair in the office closet we can pull out. You can't be eating at the counter every night while Shane and I get the table."

"No big deal."

But Shane had already taken it as a directive and went in to get it. They were crowded in the space, but at least they were all together.

Once everything was placed, they took their seats and began to pass around the serving dishes. He seemed to have found everything he needed, and she was glad he'd made himself at home.

"Your day? How did it go?"

"Busy, as usual."

"You find anything interesting?"

"About you? Possibly but I had several other clients I had to interview to-day, so I haven't been able to verify anything just yet."

She closed her eyes at the tenderness of the meat. She thought she'd died and gone to heaven. When she opened them, he was staring at her and she rephrased it. She knew she'd gone to heaven. She was almost getting used to the shivers that ran through her at the sight of him.

"Usually when I miss lunch, there's nothing to make up for it. This makes up for it."

He'd gotten up and opened drawers until he found the corkscrew. Pulling the cork from the bottle, he brought it to the table with three glasses and poured.

"You're having wine?"

"I'm getting used to taste with meal."

"Skoli stock is about to go down. I wonder if they'll survive it."

He looked thoughtful and then asked, "Is this joke?"

Shane volunteered, "Yes, and it's a good one."

"I have yet to get used to your jokes."

"She has what we call a dry sense of humor. What makes it funny is more in the way she says it than the actual words."

"We don't find much humor where I come from. Jokes can be taken for criticisms against the state. We don't dare make fun."

"The more time you spend here, the freer you'll feel. You can say just about anything you want and live to be censored."

"No rules like on Twitter?"

"On a social platform, maybe. It's more to do with common courtesy alt-hough respectful exchange seems to be vanishing. If I want to say fuck the president, I can. If I want to call members of Congress reptilian, cold-blooded assholes, I can. It's called freedom of speech."

"You just can't threaten them. There's the line you can't cross."

Shane obviously didn't want him to think there were no limits.

Maks seemed content to contemplate that and was silent for the rest of the meal. Once it was finished, Shane cleaned up and took his phone to the steps.

"I've got to check in. I'll be right outside."

⌒

Maks didn't know what to do once Camille retreated to her office. He channel-surfed for a while before deciding to do some work of his own. Going to the office door, he knocked before entering.

"May I come in and get computer?"

Without taking her eyes from the screen, she said, "Of course."

Maneuvering around the mattress, he pulled his bag up by the straps and went to leave when Camille swiveled around and asked, "Are you Matrixiator?"

He stared at her, completely unbalanced by her question. No one but a couple of government agencies knew about his connection to the hacker. Had they told her? If so, why was she asking him? Was it a trap? Did the agents want to see what kind of information he'd give up?

She looked curious, nothing more, but he was wary.

"Where you hear that name?"

She was staring at him, as if trying to figure out how to answer his question. She finally admitted, "I have a friend in high places and was told someone with the handle Matrixiator was going to testify before the Intelligence Committee. Is that you?"

"No one supposed to know this."

"The Congressional Intelligence Committee members would know."

"They leak information?"

She shook her head vigorously, as if to appease his state of panic.

"No. One of the partners at the firm is...close to one of the congressmen. I talked to her about you and she offered to ask him. He didn't really give anything away other than there was a hearing coming up with a Russian hacker giving testimony. I was the one that put two and two together."

"What else you learn about him?"

"He is an expert of the highest order, is respected around the world, and is renowned for his skills. Except, of course, in Russia. There he's known as a traitor. No mention of a name associated with the handle."

"He knows how to work system."

"When did you bury him?"

She knew it was him, so it was crazy to keep pretending she didn't. He was handing her the dynamite she needed if she wanted to blow him up. He had to trust, that as his lawyer, she wouldn't. It was like walking a tightrope across the Volga.

"Before coming here. Was told to."

"You have a new username now?"

He gave her a half-smile. "Skoli.on.ice." There were several others but this one had become his American handle.

He thought she'd find it humorous but the serious look on her face suggested otherwise.

"Is this you executing vengeance?"

All thoughts of humor fled at her question and he said with defiance, "Justice."

"For your father's death?"

He wasn't surprised she'd uncovered that. He'd known she would as soon as he turned over his name. There were many entries about Petrov, but most were damning, the headlines tilting from a Russian perspective. Would she believe he committed suicide? That he was a traitor? The phrase didn't seem an accusing one, just a statement of fact.

"His, Nina's and all others who have died at their hands."

She had closed the distance between them, her hand going to his cheek.

"I won't let them send you back, Maks."

It seemed she believed the truth without saying a word. The feel of her hand on his cheek sent crackling shocks down his body. The sense that she knew he was in danger and willing to help him softened his heart.

"That is good to know."

He stepped back, and she let her hand fall to her side.

"We will talk but not tonight. I need to straighten out thoughts. Was keeping quiet because I was told to. Now you know, I will tell you all."

"I'll be here whenever you're ready. And Maks, I'm so sorry about your father."

"He was good man. He died for nothing."

"If you can bring down the oligarchs, then he won't have died in vain."

"It is not oligarchs I want punished but I will not cry if they lose power. My country is lost to me. That brings tears."

He backed out, the look of abject pity on her face too much for him to bear.

After sitting down at the kitchen table, he opened his computer but could do nothing but stare at the screen.

Several hours later, he got ready for bed. In the bathroom, brushing his teeth, he heard thrashing on the other side of Camille's door. He held his breath. Should he go in and see if she was all right? Before he could answer his own question, she stumbled out of her bedroom. A vision, her blonde hair falling in soft waves past her shoulders, her blue nightgown feminine and alluring and the smoldering desire she saw in her eyes drew him like a moth to a flame.

"Are you all right?"

He was dressed only in his boxers, and the cross hanging on his chest.

"Bad dream."

He took a step toward her before he heard Shane call out, "Maks, is that you?"

He held her arm to prevent her from running away and yelled out, "*Ja*. I came out to get a drink."

After putting his finger to his lips, he put it out as if asking her to wait.

With even strides, he went out, got the water, and came back to her, hoping she'd still be there.

Hope won this time and when she cast her eyes in his direction, he could do nothing but lead her into her room.

As he closed the door behind him, he handed her the water and watched her drink it down, her eyes never leaving him. With her silent acceptance of his presence in her room, he took the glass, put it on the night table, and returned to take her in his arms. Holding her was like magic, the air pungent with her scent, the feel of silk under his fingertips sensually appealing, her face cradled in the crook of his neck sending chills through him. He moved his hand down to the hollows in her back, then to feel the curve of her hip. There was a hitch to his breath as he continued his exploration. He had never wanted anyone like this before. It wasn't just a physical coupling he craved but a spiritual one as well. She filled his soul with the type of healing he'd read about but had never experienced. It hadn't come through any intent on his part, but by a miracle of fate. Her soft curves were molded to his body, her breasts puckered, kissing his chest. He sought them out with his hands, and he brushed his palm over one with gentle circling motions. Her response invited more, and he took it, bringing his lips down to hers, hovering for long, torturous seconds before giving in to the feel of them. There was hunger there, not just his but hers, as well. He deepened it. Her arms twined around his neck, pulling him closer, as if she wanted to crawl under his skin. When she opened her mouth to him, he invaded the sweet interior, her breath giving him life, her sighs setting him on fire. Her tongue was like velvet, and it parried with his, suckling on it, driving him to the edges of ecstasy. He buried his hands in her hair, and began an assault on her mouth that left her lips puffy and full.

He fingered the strap of her nightgown off her shoulder, wanting to taste the sweetness of her flesh, and he nibbled her neck, and the soft down on her upper arms. She arched up against him, asking for more, and he obliged. He slipped the gown off and let it puddle to the floor, the inky darkness making his sense of touch more sensitive, his fingers making circular motions on her areolas, the creases telling him her nipples were ready and waiting. He took one in his mouth and drew it in, his saliva wetting it as he sucked the small nub, her breath labored now as she squirmed against him. He paused to kiss her again before lifting her to the bed where he could feast in full measure. After sliding his boxers off, he lay down beside her, his hand once again claiming her breast, teasing it, taunting himself with the pure pleasure of touch. His tongue caressed her swollen nipples, made a path down her rib cage, her stomach. He felt the ridge of a scar and she stilled. She pulled at his hair, trying to get him up and away from her. Instead, he held her down with gentle strength, pressed his lips against it.

Through the featherlike kisses, he said in a hushed tone, "Shane told me what happened. It pained me to hear. Let me love it better."

His kisses were enchanted, and as he spread them over her body, she felt a symbiosis that was other-worldly. She inhaled deeply. Her fingers brushed lightly over his back, the warmth of his skin intoxicating, and her heart swelled. If anyone had been hurt, it was him, time and time again, by the people in charge who were supposed to take care of their citizens, not send them to early graves. She relaxed into his touch, bringing him closer, kissing his neck, and burrowing into the heart of him.

He kissed away the tears that welled in her eyes at his tenderness. Here was the man she loved, every cell and drop of blood, and she'd almost pushed him away, a momentary panic stunning her into withdrawal. She took him against her, needing to feel him, become one with him. This was the magic her mother spoke of, the meeting of minds, hearts, and bodies. A flare of passion ignited inside of her, and she arched up, molten fire flowing through her blood. It clouded her brain, colored her world. Throbs of pleasure shot through her, and she positioned herself beneath him, her body begging him to take possession. When he grasped her hips and thrust into her, the penetration caused her nerve endings to explode in electric fire. She surrendered completely to this brand-new kind of passion, the spasms building higher and higher until they came as one.

He lay limply on top of her, needing time to recover from the explosion of feeling. This was something outside his understanding, a kind of power that went soul deep. If there were other lives lived, he'd lived them with her, always together, always connected, and he savored the feeling of satisfaction at their mutual pleasure. After wrapping her in his arms, he rolled to his side, keeping her close. He kissed her forehead, tucked her head in the crook of his arm. He could die now, having known such ecstasy.

She curled into the curve of his body, her fingers tracing his cross, and whispered, "This is old, isn't it?"

He lifted her hand and kissed the palm.

"Generations."

"It must have been so hard for you to leave."

"On one hand. Easy on the other. I have work to do here. If things change in country, I could go back."

Where that thought came from he didn't know. Suddenly, leaving her would be harder than leaving his homeland. Was he caught again, imprisoned this time by a woman? He had to keep his life clear of this kind of entanglements. He would enjoy her for as long as he could, tear himself away when the time came. There was another counting on him and she would have to come before all else. Even his heart.

When she kissed him again, his lips reclaimed her, and they fell into a more restrained coupling, even as the world continued to career off its axis. Their bodies were exquisitely in tune with each other, each touch a brand, and as she rose to meet him in throes of passion, he let himself be consumed by it.

CHAPTER TWENTY-ONE

When she woke, she was alone, the tangled sheets letting her know the night spent in each other's arms hadn't been a dream. It was almost too good to be real. She'd never known such tenderness, never experienced such an intense physical interaction. They had become one in every sense of the word, his spirit becoming hers. She closed her eyes and let the memory of his touch have its way with her.

She stretched, her body sore in places but still on fire, still in need. He had satisfied something so primitive that she was at odds on how to proceed. What if last night had just been a passing of time for him, something he didn't plan to repeat? How could she ever live without him now? It was as if he made her whole, and with him gone, she felt only half-alive. When she heard movement in the other part of the condo she stirred fully awake, and strained to hear what was going on out there.

Shane.

How could she have forgotten?

Was that why Maks had left before morning? Would he have stayed if their living arrangement was different, if there wasn't a watchful eye on them? Did last night mean as much to him as it had to her? Had he found this kind of love with Nina? It was a thought that pierced her heart.

After dragging herself out of bed, knowing she had a full schedule today at the office, she showered in the en suite and dressed for the day. Once her

make-up was on, her hair brushed to a brilliant sheen, she gathered her courage and opened her door to find Maks making his bed in the other room. He
looked up at her and smiled, a dark heat in his eyes. It gave her hope.

"Did you sleep well?"

He was perusing her from head to toe, the sensuous spark igniting a flame
that would be ever present.

"I did. Thank you."

"The thanks are mine to give."

The awareness of him as a man was potent. Needing to break the spell so
she didn't do something stupid by going in and stoking the fire, she moved
toward the kitchen.

"Any coffee?"

"There is. I made less strong. You should like."

"I appreciate it."

She passed Shane on her way through. He was reading the local newspaper,
the page turned to an article about the Electoral College meeting to put the
final stamp on the president-elect. She wondered if there'd be a miracle in the
making today, but doubted it. No one seemed willing to go out on that limb,
as if the founders hadn't put it out there for just this reason.

"Good morning."

"Same to you. Hope you don't mind I snitched your *Globe*. I noticed it
when I went out to check in."

"I don't usually get to read it until I get home, so knock yourself out."

She poured herself a cup of coffee, wondering where her breakfast was. She
was getting spoiled.

As she was looking around for some hidden gem, Maks came out, dressed
in ripped jeans and a Henley, and she couldn't help but laugh.

"What is funny?"

"You look so American. Except for the man bun. Do you watch *Game of
Thrones*?'

"No. What is it?"

"A television series. One of the main characters wears one of those. It's become the rage."

She was pointing to his head.

He fingered the knot on top of his head. "I saw man wearing one on air-
plane here. I thought good idea to keep hair off face. Alec bought me elastics.
Do you watch this series?"

"I haven't had time, so I'll have to binge one of these weekends."

"Binge?"

"Yeah. Take one whole day, sit in front of the television with a bottle of wine, a bag of chips or popcorn, and watch one show after another until I'm caught up."

"Sounds like waste of time."

"Only if you don't like the show. It's got a huge fan base and even the critics love it."

Shane looked up and added, "They're fanatical."

"Do you watch it?"

"No. I dated a woman who would rather be watching that than interacting with me. It wasn't good for the ego."

"There are some hunky guys on it."

As she glanced over to Maks, her breath hitched. She couldn't imagine watching the show over being with him. She'd give it up for life if...

Taking a sip of coffee, she asked, "Where's breakfast?"

"We already ate. You sleep in late."

"Late? It's not even seven thirty."

"I make you toast?"

"No thanks. I'll stop on the way into the city. I have a favorite bakery as my go-to. They have the flakiest croissants you'll ever taste."

"Not good for body."

"Maybe not, but they're good for the soul."

After pouring some of the coffee into her travel cup and twisting the cover, she got her coat on, hung her briefcase over her shoulder, and grabbed her purse. "I guess I'll see you tonight."

He was watching her, a smile dancing in his eyes. She wanted to kiss him good-bye, like they were...a couple. As if it might be the last time she'd see him. Instead, she fell into the dark depths and he held her there. Clearing her throat, she cast her eyes down and took the stairs out to the car. There was a reluctance to leave she'd never felt before. Usually she couldn't wait to get into the office, pick up where she left off, take on a new client, swap stories with her partners. She glanced up at the condo from the front seat of the car, wishing the day was already over and she was back. When the foolishness of what she was doing hit her, she started the engine and pulled away.

She was such a vision, he'd wanted to take her in his arms, kiss her good-bye, let her know he'd be thinking of her. Shane's presence offered the restraint he needed not to make such a foolish move. It wasn't that Shane didn't know what had transpired between him and Camille last night. As he'd reminded him this morning, it was his job to know. There was no judgment, but he was concerned. Reiterated that Nate and Alec would not be pleased, that they were getting into territory that might be tinged with prejudicial bias. They couldn't afford that at this late date. He was told it might also make any transition more difficult. He was going to be going to DC soon for his testimony, and who knew where they'd send him after that. He could be re-assigned to the agents in the capital, although that thought held no appeal for him. He was hoping after his visit to Congress, they'd let him be to live his life. What he had left of it. It was still anyone's guess as to whether the Russian operatives would let him. Once he'd testified, his intentions would be out in the open. It could go one of two ways. They'd kill him because he rattled the cage, or they'd let him live due to his exposure. If they assassinated him, people would know. The question was, would they care?

He collected his gear and poured the last of the coffee into another travel mug. It wasn't as strong as he liked it, but he wanted Camille to find it palatable. When he'd left Camille's bed before sunrise, he'd begun to organize his material. Working with Nina for a couple of years had given him the experience he needed to put it in a well-crafted document. He'd accomplished a lot last night, unable to go back to sleep without her. He'd forced his mind on the task. It reminded him of his mother, which helped delete the memories of last night. Usually he'd shut them down, like he did thoughts of his father. And Nina. It would do no good to agonize over something he couldn't change. At least not yet. But his day was coming. And then, he'd do what he'd come to do and find out what the future held.

It could not hold Camille. He'd been brutally forced to realize there were some things you couldn't will into being. A future with her was one of them. He couldn't offer her safety, couldn't promise forever, refused to take her into hiding with him if he was forced there. She had too much to give the world, too many talents to waste. He knew where bodies were buried, having lived through perestroika, witnessing the disintegration of the Soviet Bloc, being his father's son. He knew how things worked today. It had become a battleground where blood flowed in the streets. Where years of grooming had paid off. The Kremlin had worked hard to produce one of the biggest upsets in American history. He'd done his due diligence, found damning material that could prove collusion and the kind of *kompromat* the top officials could strike with. He was another in a long line of whistle-blowers, but the only Russian one to his knowledge. Some were afraid of the consequences, others were complicit, most were apathetic and didn't care what it all meant. It would prove important to see if Americans cared. If they would move to unseat the man who would become president. If not, then he would find another home. One where democracy meant something, where the people could tell the difference between true and fake, where the Constitution would be protected at all costs. Unlike many of his compatriots, he wanted the freedom to think. During the years of communism, the government had shut down all avenues to pursue knowledge. The social sciences were choked to death. Self-reflection was discouraged. The people were expected to follow as blindly as sheep. If a man wanted to learn and grow, he'd had to do it on his own. He'd done that at his father's knee and he refused to return to a world devoid of creative thinking, of innovation, where news was spoon-fed, where government officials were hand-picked, not elected by the people, and where the people allowed it to be so.

He'd dreamed of attending college here, or somewhere in the Western world where debate and free-flowing ideas were encouraged. Maybe become a lawyer, like his father, like Camille. Fight to strengthen the weakest link, defend the rights of others. Then, if his country recovered from the current blight, go back to fight there.

Today, the battle was here. When Shane dropped him off at the lab, he told him he was going home for a few hours. Another agent would be right outside, so he'd have protection.

He climbed the stairs, entered the brightly lit space, and got down to work.

He didn't have as much time as he would have liked. He was being interviewed by the FBI this afternoon, the first of many. Shane had given him a breakdown of what they were looking for, and he felt he was ready. He knew all the answers, had the resources at his fingertips. It was the first step toward his final appearance before the Intelligence Committee, which was set for early January. It was only a couple of weeks away. That was all the time he'd have with Camille.

At one o'clock sharp, he was led into the office of the lead supervisor at the FBI's Boston office, offered a cup of coffee and a seat. For three hours he was drilled on what he knew, how he knew it, and what proof he could provide them with. The agents in attendance had reams of their own intelligence, and it matched up with what he had. They touched on Lucky Strike, and the Cyber Two-Headed Dog, so named for the monster from Greek mythology and the Russian Laundromat, the moniker given to the agency that laundered money through American businesses. The difference was, he was Russian and had robbed the coffers buried in their adversary's own backyard. His backstory only added to the veracity of the testimony. There had been open channels the FBI had been able to access, foreign nationals who were under constant surveillance, the threat to national security a solid defense for the wiretapping. They knew that America was under attack in a war more dangerous than a traditional one. The methods and means for continued attacks were still in place, and until they had a game plan, anything could happen. He left the meeting, pleased with the welcome and the minds that were hell-bent on uncovering every chess piece played in the invasion. The citizens seemed to be asleep at the wheel, with only a small minority well-versed on the plot to take over their country. He would do what he could to wake them up. His country's life depended on it, as well. Only when the current president of Russia was gone could the country begin to heal.

Camille had spent a good portion of her morning tracking down someone who could help her get the documentation she needed for Maks' application. It meant being referred to someone on the ground in Russia. She'd need birth certificate, any paperwork that existed on Petrov's incarceration and death. The name she'd been given was not only a lawyer in Moscow, but one mentioned in an article on Petrov. She would not only be able to give her background on that case, but have some of the material she'd need at her fingertips. There was a running list Camille kept adding to. At the top was finding out what had happened to Maks' mother. Sonya might be able to shed light on other pieces she'd need to complete this before she was done. She'd poured over the application itself, filling in some of the missing pieces, like name, and origin of birth, parent's names, past addresses, schools, places of employment. Had he ever been charged with a crime, been arrested or jailed. She'd hoped he hadn't.

Camille left her office for a visit to the break room. There she joined Em, Nell and Jelani, who'd also dropped in for a late cup of coffee. Every one of them existed on it here, and there was always a fresh pot brewed and ready. The droop came for all four of them by late afternoon, when they knew they still had a couple more hours of work before trudging home. By the end of the day, they were physically, emotionally and mentally exhausted. It was a tough fight here in the trenches, but she knew that no one did it better than they did.

"I was wondering when you were going to take a break."

Em was pouring her a cup, adding milk and a fingernail of sugar. She gave her a tired smile and took the proffered cup.

"Just got off the phone with the detention center in New Jersey. They're giving me the runaround on Luisa. I might have to fly down and drag her bodily out of there."

Jelani was on overload with the DACA cases. The future of the program was unknown status, so everyone who could apply for it was coming out of the woodwork.

"I've had six interviews already today. I can't take another one. And yet—" she checked her watch,—"my seventh's due to arrive in fifteen minutes."

Arianna stuck her head in, and laughed. "Why did I know you'd all be here? We spend so much time together, we not only smell the coffee at the exact same moment of the day, but we get our periods at the same time of the month."

She stepped in and sighed. "I've got some new-hire interviews scheduled over the next couple of days. I want one or two of you in each one with me or Mia. Your input is a necessary evil. Let's work it out amongst ourselves so that I can move on with my day."

They all grumbled about it, but they appreciated the sentiment. One for all and all for one had become their manifest. When she put the schedule down on the table, each of them gave a time they could spare, and Arianna left looking pleased with herself.

Em offered a positive spin.

"It will save us time in the long run."

Nell moaned, "You know she'll give us each one to mentor. *In the long run,* might mean six months. Do you know how many clients we'll go through by the time they're up and running on their own?"

Jelani asked, "Don't know why she'd pair us up. We all work in very specialized fields. She's hiring to take up the regular slack. You know, all those feminist issues we started out with?"

The firm had been the first and foremost in violence against women, LGBT, women's choice, both reproductive and work-place policies, including sexual harassment. These had become back-burner over the last few years as more and more immigration cases came their way. Arianna kept complaining that they'd forgotten their roots, but they'd just expanded the practice. The percentage of women represented was still a high one.

Nell's shoes were off, her feet up on one of the empty seats. She was close to six feet tall when she had them on, adding at least three inches to her already tall build, but kicked them off whenever she could. They made fun of the idiosyncrasy, but she refused to give the Manolo's up, said they were her intimidator factor. Jelani was munching on pieces of one of the breakfast bars she'd brought in. Her cooking skills could rival the best, and she usually brought in something luscious every day.

Camille quirked a smile, thinking it might be fun to have Jelani and Maks face off, like in a *Chopped* episode. As she mentally ticked off a list of ingredients she could throw at them, caviar was the first one to go.

"Tell us, how's your Russian?"

She glanced up to see Em giving her an evil grin. "I talked to your mother this morning and she gave me all the details of your Mountain Man experience. He skis. Interesting."

She could just imagine that conversation although she couldn't imagine what had prompted it.

"Why the hell did you talk to my mother? Was she looking for follow up?"

Shaking her head, Em broke off a piece of bar and popped it into her mouth. After chewing, she explained, "I wanted some advice on what to get my aunt for Christmas. She gave me a few good ideas."

Getting up out of her chair, knowing she had a few more things to do before calling it a day, Camille walked to the sink to rinse out her cup. "I bet a ski vacation at Cannon was one of them?"

"No, that's on *my* wish list."

"I'm sure she invited you up to stay at the house any time you wanted."

"She told me there's always an open invitation. I think I might go up the weekend after New Year's. Make up for the one I missed."

"Rub it in."

Nell was slipping her shoes back on, Jelani refilling her cup to take it back to the office, and Em picked up the folder she'd brought in with her. They walked out together, each off to their own domain.

CHAPTER TWENTY-TWO

When she arrived home, Maks was huddling with Shane at the kitchen table. As soon as she walked in, they quickly wrapped up their discussion, his glance taking her in. She looked a bit more tired than she had this morning. Maybe it had more to do with the long night they'd shared than her work-load. He thought about tonight and whether they could share her bed again. She'd been on the edges of his mind all day, even during the interview with the FBI. He got up and went to the wine cooler. He extracted a white Riesling, un-corked it, and handed her a glass as soon as he'd poured it.

"This might help."

"Thank you, kind sir. It's exactly what the doctor ordered."

She took a sip.

"Um, good. It has a fruity flavor that satisfies the taste buds. Where did I get this?"

"Ordered today with duck. It is good pairing."

"It's good all by itself."

She began to walk toward her bedroom to change.

"Please keep the bottle so I can order more. I'll also send a case to my brother. He appreciates fine wine even if it isn't Mountain Man."

And then she disappeared. He continued to watch even when she was no longer visible. Shane must have been watching him.

"Are you going to tell her about the meeting?"

"Not sure. It is classified?"

"She's your lawyer. She knows how to keep things confidential. In fact, she should probably be with you the day you testify before Congress."

"That is good to know. I would like her there."

"I get the feeling you'd like her everywhere."

He ignored the statement. It was true but only temporary. He had to get away from thoughts that suggested otherwise.

"I have to check on duck. We will eat soon."

"Can I hire you on as my personal chef when we're done here? I can't pay much but you could consider it one of your patriotic duties."

"Not sure what I will do once this is over. There are many options here."

Shane followed him into the kitchen, where he began collecting ingredients for the spicy sauce.

"There are. I hope you stick around and take advantage of them."

He was thinking more and more about doing just that. Even if he could go back, he wasn't sure he wanted to.

"There is no future in Russia today. They are too mired in past."

He wasn't going back to driving a cab, which was what he'd been doing for the last year. Working at the restaurant meant fifty-or sixty-hour weeks. It gave him no time to do the work he'd prioritized after his father's death. He worked as he pleased, just enough to earn what he needed to live. Every other second was spent rooting around for dirt on the administration, and he'd found plenty. Until the current regime was gone, there was no looking across the ocean for a home. He might have to look for one here.

When Camille joined them, she looked refreshed. In jeans and a sweater, her hair up in a messy bun, she still gave off an essence of feminine beauty. Her feet were bare, her toenails painted a dusky rose. For some reason, it pulled at his groin.

Turning back to the stove, he put his unruly thoughts to their dinner.

It had been good to get back to the kitchen. Here he could play, wasn't under some other man's control. The chef he'd worked for had been a hard-ass ego-centric who bellowed if he didn't think you got his recipe the way he'd written it. Taking a sip of the wine on the counter he'd poured for himself, he was also enjoying the intense aroma of the fruity blend. Vodka was becoming a thing of the past, just like his country.

"Why don't I set the table tonight."

She was reaching in the cabinet for the dishes and then in the drawer for their utensils.

"What kind of duck are we having? It smells divine."

Shane laughed as he said, "You may not like the bill when you finally get it. Seems Maks has expensive taste."

"It's worth it. I haven't eaten like this…ever. Growing up, my mother cooked but more comfort food than French or any other cuisine. She said it was too rich for a daily diet. Like pot-pie was good for you with all the buttery, flaky goodness."

She hipped the drawer closed, before retrieving place-mats.

"Let's have some ambience along with our duck." Peering over his shoulder, she inhaled the spicy scent. "My brother would give you a job in a heartbeat."

"No more cooking as living. This I like. Working under someone, not again."

"This I like. I don't know what I'll do when you're gone."

Their eyes met once the words were out, each asking a silent question. His body was telling him he shouldn't leave, his mind telling him it would never happen.

"Back to canned soup."

"Ugh. Maybe you can make a couple of pots of homemade soup and I can freeze it in individual containers. Then…"

She wasn't going to say the word leave again. She couldn't stand the thought of not seeing him when she came through the door. He was her prize for the long days, something she hadn't realized was missing in her life.

She scurried to the table and began setting it.

Shane must have felt the tingling in the air, because he had the good sense to apologize.

"I'm sorry I'm a third wheel here, but it's too damn cold to sit in the car for a couple of hours to give you some privacy."

She could feel the blush creep into her cheeks. How could he not know how Maks affected her? The electricity was tangible.

Dinner was a quiet affair, as if they didn't know what to say, didn't know where to look, and when they were finished, Shane cleaned up and went to the TV.

Camille escaped to her office but Maks followed close behind. After taking the only other seat available, a chair in the corner of the room, he asked, "Is this too uncomfortable for you? Would you like us to leave?"

She spun around to face him, her eyes wide. The mere thought of his leaving burned a hole in her heart.

"No. I...like you here. Even if Shane is a third wheel."

"He knows...about last night."

Now her cheeks flamed.

"How—"

"He hears every little thing. It's his job. He says it's not good idea. Might make you...do your job wrong."

"It will actually help me do a better job. There's more at stake. You're not just another client...you're...much more than that."

"It is not good for other reason."

"Nina?"

"Nina? What she have to do with this?"

"She was your...lover. You must have—"

"No. We were just....How you say it? Sharing bodies. Not love."

"Are you trying to say that you're just sharing your body with me? Is that how it's done in Russia?"

"No, Cami. That is not how it is done. I cannot love anyone. Not now. Not yet. It is not right time for love. I have bounty on my head. It is not safe."

She got up from the chair and went over, crawled in his lap. She didn't want to hear that he couldn't love her. She loved him so much it hurt.

While putting her arms around his neck, leaning her head against his chest, she admitted, "I don't care about that. Don't forget, I'm your fighter. I'll help keep you alive."

Her eyes closed when he wrapped her in the cocoon of his arms. She felt so safe. She believed nothing could happen to them if they were together. How could she convince him of the truth of that?

"We do this for now, Cami. That's all I can give you."

She felt tears threaten but she forced them back. She couldn't tell him how she felt. It could make him turn away from her now and she'd take any time with him that he'd give her. After taking his face in her hands, she leaned up and kissed him. It was a slow, sweet kiss, and she lingered there. His lips felt like home, where hers belonged. There was a hint of tightly harnessed control when he stopped it. To fill the void that had come with the disruption, she began to trace the letters that she'd seen inked on his arm the second day she stopped by his safe house. Abruptly, she realized what it stood for.

"These are your father's initials."

He offered her a bleak, tight-lipped smile.

"They are."

"What is the significance of the numbers?"

The past came roaring back at him, the memories deep and dark. It showed in his expression as his smile twisted into a scowl, his eyes flashed with outrage.

"It was his prison identification number."

Her eyes fluttered closed and she hugged him to her, wanting to take away the pain of the past, but how could she when he'd indelibly inked it onto his skin? It must be a brand on his heart, as well. She wanted to hold him close all night, surround him in her love, but she'd unsettled him again and he pushed her away.

"You have work to do?"

She slid off his lap, adjusted her sweater, and returned to her chair, disappointed with his lack of response.

"I do."

She went back to her desk, pulled up one of her cases, hoping to get her mind off the rejection. She thought Maks would have the good sense to leave, so she didn't expect to hear his voice from the doorway.

"Shane tell me you will be at hearing with me."

She was trying to focus on the application she had up on the screen, Shia Muslims from Pakistani who were seeking asylum due to religious persecution. After several bombings that devastated their community, they'd fled to America and, as soon as they landed, made their request. They had chosen her name off a list of pro bono attorneys given out by the ACLU. It had taken very little work to get green cards, the application process now in its final stages. Maks' statement sliced through her efforts. She swiveled around to look at him.

"What hearing?"

"The Intelligence Committee interview."

Of course. Jack had said as much. She hadn't given it any thought in that context when Nell had told her. Now, there was a flicker of apprehension that coursed through her.

"I should be at all your interviews. Do you have any more coming up?"

His hand slipped into his front pocket and he shifted his stance.

"I met with FBI today."

She bolted out of her chair.

"You what?"

"I had—"

"I heard you."

She was already out the door calling out, "Shane. Where the hell are you?"

When Shane came running, she accosted him with a verbal assault.

"How dare you take him to that interview without me. Why wasn't I told about it?"

"It wasn't my decision."

She took three strides and was in his face, poking her finger at his chest.

"You are his agent-on-duty. You should have his back. Not only with the enemy but with all potential opponents. Was this Nate's doing?"

He took a step back.

"I'm not sure from how high up the decision came down."

"It will not happen again. I want a list of all scheduled meetings. If you can't give it to me, I'll be having a short battle of wills with Nate tomorrow. It may get bloody but I guarantee I'll win."

"You forget you work for the government, Camille." His voice was low, as if Shane didn't really want her to hear what he said.

A shimmering haze of fury clouded out all other thought.

"I quit. From now on I work for my client, Maxim Petrovonovich Zhernova. I will send Nate a formal letter of resignation tonight. If he thinks he can continue to railroad me or Maks, he's sadly mistaken."

"Let me talk to him. See if I can't work something out that benefits all parties."

"You can tell him for me that I want copies of those minutes of that meeting. I want to know exactly what was said and what questions were asked. I want to know who was in attendance and who wasn't."

Shane excused himself and said, "I think I'll make that call now."

"Good. I want a copy of that interview on my desk first thing tomorrow. Or else."

"Yes, ma'am."

Maks was enthralled. He'd never seen such a spectacular display of outrage. He understood better what she'd meant before. She was his fighter. It took that one split second as a witness to her passionate indignation for him to trust her with his life. He continued to study Camille's body, still coiled for a strike. Her hands were fists, her cheeks were spotted with color, and her eyes flashed in warning. She stood like an Amazon, at barely five feet five inches tall, and he couldn't stop himself from going to her. He cupped her face and, in one smooth movement, covered her mouth with his, the demand forceful, the need raw. She met him with the same kind of desperate fury, her mouth making love to him, her hands gripping a fistful of his hair. The kisses were hungry, and they consumed him. And when she drew him back to his room and down to the mattress, they feasted on each other, driven by a primitive force that could not be contained.

When the maelstrom was over, he could feel her heartbeat with every breath she took. He was a part of her now as he'd never been a part of anyone else. Had never wanted to be. With her, he wanted it all. He just wasn't sure he could take it.

CHAPTER TWENTY-THREE

She woke up the next morning still lying beside him. As it was his bedroom, she was probably the one who should have left, but once she'd fallen asleep, she hadn't awoken until the sun streamed in through the window. It had been a bottomless sleep, no knives, no inner trembling, no fear. When she nestled deeper, he pulled her close, his eyes still closed, a smile on his face.

She kissed his chest, smoothed her hand over the surface.

"Maks we have to start using protection. This isn't smart, and I've never been so careless before."

Her need for him made all thought beyond his body evaporate into smoke as the desire raged in a greedy fire.

"Where do I get this? Can I have delivered like food?"

She laughed into his shoulder.

"I don't think so. I'll try to pick up a couple of boxes today. I assume we won't be giving this up...for now."

He reached for her nipple, his thumb caressing the nub that didn't seem to sleep.

"That would be good assumption."

She sighed, the pulsing in her stomach spiraling down. She wondered if she'd ever get enough of him.

It seemed, at Shane's shout, she would have to save what she wanted to do for later.

"Camille, Nate's on the phone. He wants to talk to you."

"Tell him I'll call him back. I want to shower and change first."

She wouldn't be naked when she spoke to him. She needed to be in control and that would take time.

"He said he'll only be around for the next fifteen minutes. He has a meeting he can't skip."

She yelled her answer through the door, got up, stuffed herself into the clothes she'd shed last night and hobbled to her own room. After making quick work of the shower, she chose a dress that in one over-the-head movement fell in graceful lines past her hips. She'd save the make-up for later. Ignoring her audience, she picked up her phone from the counter, pulled out the plug for the charger, thumbed her contacts and punched in the call. Nate answered on the second ring.

"You're pushing things, Camille."

"Damn straight. He's my client and he's not answering questions without an attorney present."

"He doesn't have a right to counsel."

"Like hell he doesn't. He does and you made me it."

"There's a lot you don't know…"

"And that's going to change, as well. I want every shred of information you have on him and I want a list of every scheduled interview. He will not be answering any questions without my presence. If you want what he has, you go through me."

"Alec told me you were going to be trouble."

"I guess you shouldn't continue to think you know it all then."

"I have to run this by my supervisor."

"Then run away. I'm not going anywhere. And Maks won't be, either, until we have an agreement."

"Why do you women have to be so damn pushy?"

"You didn't just say that to me. Did you?"

"No. You must have been able to read my thoughts. A person can't get into trouble for his thoughts, can he?"

"You used to be such a nice guy."

"Sorry. I've got a lot on my plate lately. This Russian thing, the wreckage from the e-mail fiasco, the post-election crap going on, everything's gone haywire."

"Do you want me to quit and represent him pro bono on my own?"

"Not yet. Let me see what I can do to make things simpler. You're too good to be working against us. I'd rather you be on our side."

"I'd rather be there, as well. But I'll have no problem stepping to the opposition if forced to."

"I know that. You're doing well at the firm for a reason."

"We are a determined bunch of pushy women. Don't tempt me to get mean."

"I'll email you the minutes and get you a list of the upcoming sessions. There's six definites, with more to come."

"I appreciate it."

She ended the call before he could say anything else, and when she put the phone back on the counter, she looked up to see Maks and Shane both staring at her.

"What?"

Maks was the one who answered.

"You are...feisty."

"I have to be with the kind of cases I represent. Even more so because I'm a woman. People don't tend to take us seriously. I think Nate just got the memo."

Shane had the look of a scared rabbit, as if he was going to take the heat for her outburst. Maks had a smile on his face, as if he was enjoying this. Crossing his arms over his chest, he asked, "What memo?"

"The one that said don't fuck with me."

Now that the call was over, and she'd won round one, she announced, "I've got to finish dressing, then I've got work to do." As she walked past Maks, she stopped, looked him right in the eye and said, "Tonight, you tell me everything."

He nodded and glanced over to Shane.

"I'd do what the woman says. I think she's through being a lady."

As she disappeared through her doorway, the last words she said were, "I never was."

⌒

The brief was waiting on her desk for her as soon as she arrived. At least she could trust Nate to keep his word. She just didn't know how far the trust should go. Before sitting down with it, she needed coffee. The call had come before she'd had her two requisite cups and she'd need to fortify herself. The minutes might make her crazy.

Mia was already there, standing by the counter, waiting for the new pot to finish brewing.

Picking up her Nasty Woman mug that her mother had bought for her stocking last Christmas, she stood in line.

"I figure I better give you a heads-up. Your husband might have a few nasty comments about me tonight."

"What did he do now?"

Camille laughed. It didn't surprise her that Mia was already on her side and didn't even know what they'd argued about. Nate was a good guy, but he was a guy and he had a disparate view of the world. It sparked a memory of a YouTube video called A Tale of Two Brains that her sister had shared on Facebook. The comedian explained that a man's brain was made up of little boxes and although he had a box for everything, the boxes absolutely couldn't touch. If he wanted to talk about something, he took that box out and stayed on topic before putting it away when the conversation was over. If the subject was tied to an emotion, he shoved the box back as quickly as he could. A woman's brain was like a super-internet highway, made up of a huge electric ball of string, E-motion, the energy that kept it wired. Every topic was connected to every other topic. It gave them a much larger perspective of the world and the ability to dissect a number of different variables at the same time. Having sent the video to her partners as soon as she got it, all she had to say to Mia was, "He took out the wrong box," and Mia understood completely what had happened.

"I have to go back and watch that again. I need a laugh right about now. He's been a grouch lately with all that's out there and the tsunami that's coming. He uses his 'nothing' box more often than any other when he's home."

"And people think a man cave is a room. They don't realize it's just a state of mind."

They both burst into giggles that turned to snorts. With tears coming down her cheeks, Mia hugged Camille and said, "Thanks. I needed that," before going back to her office. After pouring herself a cup of coffee, Camille added her milk and sugar, hoping her good mood would last.

Back in her office, she checked the clock on her wall and estimated she had about an hour to read through the memo before her first appointment arrived for the day. There was nothing scheduled in her daily planner for tomorrow, so she could do a more intensive analysis then. She made sure to keep a day open every couple of weeks, so she could play catch-up, file paperwork, write her summations that would be attached to the files. It was on one of those days that Nate had snagged her to meet with Maks.

She sat down, made herself comfortable. The FBI log was staring up at her, its bold blue and gold insignia a chilling reminder of what she had stepped into. They were the ones, as the domestic intelligence service, who were entrusted with identifying and combating threats from foreign adversaries. Was Maks one of them? Had he committed a crime against her country or his? Was he a whistle-blower or an outlaw?

There was a nervous thrum of energy shooting through her as she picked up the minutes of the meeting and began to read.

Headquarters Boston, MA
Meeting Date: December 19, 2017
Meeting Time: 1:00 P.M.
Meeting Location: JFK Building, Boston, MA
Called by: Assistant Director of the F.B.I

In attendance: Special Agent Gavin Nicholson, Counter-Intelligence Division, Special Agent Collier Spade, Security Division, Special Agent Marcus Fromme, Criminal Justice Division, Field Director Michael Clinton, Boston Field Office, Senior Supervisory Intelligence Analyst, Jim German and Special Agent Nathaniel Fisher, Boston Field Office

Purpose:

This meeting was called to order to investigate the claims by one Maxim Zhernova, aka Matrixiator. Interrogated to uncover proof that a foreign country had tampered with the twenty-sixteen election. Inquiries into his methods, his investigative capabilities, and his knowledge of said cyber-attack were made by attendees.

This was the interview as it was recorded by the secretary taking notes.

As she read the breakdown of how the conversation had evolved, she was amazed at Maks' grasp of the situation, the depth of knowledge he had on the attack, the espionage activity he'd uncovered, and how far the web of intrigue reached. Her fear for his safety was magnified by the sheer amount of material he had acquired through back channels and invading secret communications. There was a breakdown of where billions of dollars was hidden within the immediate circle of family and associates. He also proved that the regime would stop at nothing to achieve its ends: a total disruption of democracy across the globe and the seeds of divisiveness sown wherever they found fertile ground. The ground here had been plowed, tilled and readied over the last two decades, and *kompromat* provided the fruit of their labor. Everything Maks had was now on record and there was no going back. Her job would be to provide the safety net of asylum, but she could do nothing about the spies among them who could do Maks bodily harm. His courage in the face of the threats received touched her soul and she felt tears fill her eyes. She'd seen courage before, in the eyes of those she represented, who had battled persecution for their survival. Maks was not only fighting for his existence, but for so many others'. He was no less a hero than Nina or Petrov, standing tall in truth, regardless of the consequences.

If she hadn't loved him before, this would have made her fall fast and hard.

Brushing the moisture from her eyes, she swore she would do everything in her power to keep him safe, even if it meant losing him to another state, country, or woman. She just couldn't lose him to death.

Collecting herself, she picked up her phone to find a bunch of missed messages. With her total absorption in her reading material, a dozen calls had gone to voice mail, her concentration untouched by the vibration of the phone.

Before she could return them all, Sikha announced her next appointment. After she took a few minutes to review the file of Nuella Uranta, the Christian woman from Niger was led into her office and offered a seat. The woman's eyes told her story, expressive and sunken from lack of sleep. For the next hour Camille listened to the tales of horror that had taken place in her country, stories Camille would never become immune to, the nightmare of events that took place when militants attacked her village, killing more than twenty people, most of them women and children. Every tale hurt her, and she grieved for every man, woman, and child who was persecuted for nothing more than religion, race, or gender. There was a plethora of material that Camille could use in Nuella's request for asylum and she promised she'd begin work on it immediately.

After three more interviews that rang the same mournful tune, Camille gathered up her things and left for home. She needed a glass of wine, a good cry, and a place to rest her head. She was hoping that Maks could provide the latter. But first she had to talk to him about all she'd learned today. It seemed like the long day was far from over.

Maks was pacing the kitchen, waiting for the rice to be done, anxious for Camille's return home. She'd been given the minutes of the meeting and he didn't know how she'd take his actions. Would she hate him for being a turncoat? Believe the facts uncovered about her own country? Would she write him off as being too much of a danger to stand by?

He wanted to believe she'd understand, help him. He needed her light, her optimism, and her strength. He'd come to realize he needed her, period. Would she be another hope dashed? He'd learned from experience if good came into your life, you had to expect the bad to follow. His country had proven that to be true. First there was *perestroika* and the hope for democracy and freedom, but over the last two decades, those rights and liberties were being taken away and replaced with what was there now. Whether it was totalitarianism, nationalism, Mafia-run, something not designated yet didn't matter. With the crackdown that had come in the last few years, nothing was too horrible for the government to do to its people. The bad had come like a raging river overflowing its banks. Not only that, but the head of the regime was waging an info war on Western democracy that got them tagged once again as the evil empire.

When Shane called out that she was in the drive-way, he automatically poured her some wine wanting it ready when she walked through the door. Maybe it would provide the magical elixir that would soften her heart toward him. He waited awkwardly for her to come in.

When she opened the door and looked up, her expression was an enigma, and he couldn't read what was written there. For the seconds it took her to climb to the top, his heart was frozen in his chest. When she dropped all her bags and reached for him, he greedily enfolded her in his arms and began breathing again.

"You do not hate me?"

He felt the shake of her head, as if she was unwilling to speak, unwilling to break the hold he had on her. They stayed wrapped in each other's arms, and he savored the feel of her against him.

A timer went off in the kitchen, and it was only then that he was willing to release her. He fingered the timer button on the microwave and handed her the wine.

"You seem to like a glass when you come in."

"I do and I need it more than ever today."

CHAPTER TWENTY-FOUR

They spent most of the night talking. He told her about his father, all the painful details of his arrest, imprisonment, and death, how he'd begun to dig for information on who was at fault, and all that he'd found. It hadn't started out as a quest for taking down his government. But the more he'd learned about the shadow events, the more he'd dug, finally reaching insanity point, trying to make sense of the ludicrous. His country was not only corrupt, they were engaged in a terror war, with their own citizens and various other countries. Russia could not let go of the idea that they had lost their satellites. When any of the former Soviet Bloc subjects had formed an independent and functioning government, shifted towards a Western point of view, sought a place in NATO, the president of Russia did what he could to turn the tide, infiltrating the country in question with insurgents, inciting violence, and blaming the resulting chaos on American- funded rebels. Lies infiltrated every level of government, and the media became a puppet in the hands of a few. Even the oligarchs who had amassed power were vulnerable. Several were stripped of their empires, jailed, or exiled. All media outlets now belonged to the state. The Soviet Union was back, only under a new guise.

They were in her room, lying on the bed, holding hands through the telling. When he was finished, he shifted, sat up, and faced her.

"The people live in a world of terror. There are no rules, everything is done at random, there is no logic behind any official act, all threats are unpredictable. It is crazy place to live."

"I'm beginning to think there are too many countries that govern the same way. I talked to four women today who could tell the same story. Why can't people get along? Why does there have to be so much tragedy in the world? I don't understand any of it."

"You see much misery. You have strong heart."

"I'm not sure about that. I was close to tears after every story I heard."

"It is good you don't lose that."

She pulled him back beside her and tangled her legs with his, held him close.

"I don't have any appointments tomorrow. I'd like to spend some of the time going over your application. I've been in touch with an attorney in Russia who is willing to help me put together a file on you."

He sat up so abruptly she was almost tossed off the bed. "No. It will not put him in danger."

Once she righted herself, her back against her headboard, she told him, "It's actually a woman. Irina Dresvyanin. From what she told me, she was one of your father's attorneys."

"She was but will not be safe if she does not stay within boundaries set for her. I cannot pretend that it would turn out well for her."

"I have to collect all the material I can about your past."

"Anyone willing to help you, or me, will be in serious jeopardy."

"She seems willing to take the risk."

"I will not allow it, Cami. I will not trade my life for hers."

She reached out to take his hand. What he'd said hadn't surprised her. It spoke to who he was as a person.

"You seem to be following in your father's footsteps. Truth above all. Even self-truth."

He'd stiffened as if she'd insulted him.

"No. He stayed. Didn't let anyone or anything hold him back. I feel like coward sometimes."

She cupped his face, his expression one of guilt, or was it self-derision?

"You are not a coward. You are fighting against a dangerous enemy, ready to come out into the light. You can do more good here than you could there. Leaving your home and your country took courage, accepting what Russia has become took courage, learning to trust when it has proven deadly takes courage. You are one of the most courageous people I know."

She'd almost let it slip. Almost told him she loved him, but he would not want to hear it. It wasn't the time. She wasn't sure it ever would be.

Distancing herself so she didn't do or say something she'd regret, she asked softly, "What was your childhood like?"

He seemed to relax with the change in topic. He probably thought she'd demurred to his edict, but she hadn't. She'd have to find another way to gather the material needed for his file, but she put all thought of it off until tomorrow.

"Born in 1984. March, the hardest month. Many food shortages, cramped apartment. When regime collapsed, my father thought things would be better."

"What was it like, living through that?"

"Many only felt chaos. There was no plan for transition. Under Soviet rule, people were taken care of, didn't have to think about life or jobs. They existed to survive. I've come to believe they didn't realize their country would no longer exist as they knew it."

"What did your father do back then?"

"He was lawyer. When I was seven, he went into politics, joined new movement thinking that change was possible. Moved to better apartment, but there was catastrophe looming. Food was scarce. Price controls did nothing to change that. My father was one of the local authorities who cooperated with stores and services, so our town grew, and although I won't say it prospered, it did better than most."

When she was seven, her life was normal. She was in second grade at St. Remigius, learning her catechism, spelling, geography. She knew the globe and learned that the Soviet Union was a communist country, a government the polar opposite of democracy. She ate well, was warm, and lived in a four-bedroom home where there was room for everyone. Growing up in a place where there was freedom of all kinds, how could she truly understand what the country went through?

"When did you move to Moscow?"

"In the summer of 1998. The president himself granted us an apartment in city. It was supposed to be mark of privilege, but filth everywhere."

"That would have been Yeltsin, right?"

"*Ja.* He had no idea how to improve conditions, and it was bad, but it all went to shit with his successor. It was soon after when my father became a rebel. Over time he realized the new president was taking us back instead of forward. It was no longer socialism with a new face, but a new face that represented a totalitarian way of ruling. He often complained that corruption was eroding the country, infrastructure was in disrepair, the justice system was corrupt, the constitution meant nothing, and that everyone had become the enemy. The enemy was actually the leader himself."

"Your father joined the protest movement?"

"Every day in some way. At first, it was legal and permits were granted, then they were banned. It didn't stop those who continued to fight for a better life."

"Did you ever think of joining him?"

"I went once. My mother was not pleased and fought with my father about my safety. She was determined to keep me alive, even if she couldn't affect my father's choices. I must admit I just wanted to live my life. I had no sense of how important his work was. Not until he was arrested and others were killed or exiled. Then I began to see the consequences of going along."

"What was she like?"

"My mother?"

She nodded.

"Raised to believe that you keep your head down and stay out of trouble. When he was arrested, she was angrier at him than with the police, but she had come to respect him and secretly believed all he fought for. She visited him every day and finally saw through the pretense as clearly as he had. With his death, she became as outwardly supportive of the cause. She helped me with what I started."

"Where is she?"

"I cannot say."

"You won't or can't?"

"I cannot say."

She traced his chin with her finger and decided not to push the issue. He was here with her and he'd just shared a good part of his life. She wanted to enjoy the warmth of the moment. She kissed him lightly, but he deepened it and they spent the rest of the night getting to know each other's bodies as well. She slept locked in his arms until the phone rang beside her.

It took a minute to come to grips with the sound. When she did, she reached for it and swiped to connect the call.

Sitting up quickly, she pushed her hair off her face and listened.

"I'll be right there."

Maks had come awake, his head leaning on his hand as he waited for her to finish the call.

As soon as she ended it, she swung her legs over the side of the bed and moved towards the bathroom, hearing him ask, "Where is it you have to go?"

Peeking her head out of the doorway, closing her eyes at the sight of him, not wanting to leave, she answered, "A woman from Myanmar landed at the airport and asked for asylum. Homeland Security took her to our detention center in Boston. That was the superintendent who called. The firm is on the list for pro bono work and I get the refugees."

⌐

She'd climbed in the shower, her hair in a cap so it didn't get wet. She didn't have the time to style and dry it. She began lathering her body in quick, short strokes when she heard his voice, from right outside the stall.

"Do you get three a.m. calls often?"

"On average, a couple of times a month."

"And you just go, no questions asked?"

"I do."

She stepped out, wrapping the towel that was hanging from the bar attached to the door, and began drying herself off.

"Myanmar's become a hotbed for violence and there've been a flood of requests for refugee status. This woman didn't ask. She just got on a plane and flew in. She was arrested on the spot and I want to get her out as soon as I can."

"You are a fighter for many. Not just me."

She kissed his lips lightly before she began dressing.

"You are not like the others. But yes, I fight for them all."

"You are as much hero as you claim me to be."

"My life is never on the line..."

His hand sought the scar just under her breast. "This tells different story."

"That was my fault. I got too comfortable with her. I let down my guard."

"You are doing same with me. It is not smart."

He was right. It wasn't, but her heart wouldn't let her care. She was standing in her bra and panties, and a feeling of vulnerability sliced through her. Her heart was like a battering ram against her rib cage when she looked up and into his eyes.

In a whisper she asked, "Are you going to hurt me?"

He took her face in his hand and held it gently.

"I pray I will not."

She stepped away, knowing he wouldn't hurt her physically but she could feel the guillotine hovering high over her head, ready to cut off the connection they'd begun to share.

After slipping on the skirt and the jersey top that went with the two-piece ensemble, she turned her back on him to get on the pantyhose. There was nothing graceful about the act and she hadn't given anyone the opportunity to observe it before. She felt awkward and was relieved when she gave them one last yank up. Once her feet were encased in her short boots, she turned to him again and gave him a kiss before leaving. "I'll be going right to the office when I'm done there, so I won't see you until tonight. I—"

She shut her mouth, shocked that she was about to tell him she loved him. It had just bubbled up out of nowhere, a natural extension of her feelings. Glad she caught herself in time, she scurried out without looking back.

⌒

He listened for the door to close behind her and pulled on his boxers and jeans and ambled out to the kitchen. Shane was awake and paying strict attention. The couch was a pull-out bed, but it was never untucked. He used a pillow and blanket but never undressed, never got more than snatches of sleep, his gun ready and loaded on the table beside him. He'd promised Maks he'd protect him, and he had done as promised. So far. He was sitting up, the blanket tossed to the side.

"Where'd she go?"

Scratching the accumulating stubble, Maks said, "Boston detention center."

"What for?"

"A new client."

"At this time of night?"

"It is not out of ordinary from what she says."

"My respect for her just grew."

"Mine, as well."

Although it was only three twenty in the morning, Maks was wide awake. Feeling guilty that he was going to keep Shane up, he apologized as he poured water for coffee.

"Sorry, I need coffee, then I'll let you get back to sleep."

"It's not like I really do. I've always got one ear open. Make enough for two. I'll join you."

Switching the machine on, he waited until he heard the drip before turning back to the man who had become a friend.

"I was wrong to make you stay. You need to take time off."

Waving away the directive, Shane got up and went to the bathroom. Maks got his cigarettes and stepped out on the deck. The snow was falling in soft sheets and it reminded him of home. There were days during the polar winter when the darkness didn't abate even during the daytime hours, adding to the depressive atmosphere. The moon was out tonight, illuminating the small yard, giving him hope that here was a chance for something better. He drew in the smoke, letting it fill his lungs with the cold, brisk air. He looked down at the burning paper, the desire to finish it gone. He stabbed it out in the can, stomped his feet, and returned to the kitchen.

Shane was holding a cup under the spout, letting the hot brew drip in.

"I didn't want to wait. Your cup is there."

Maks picked it up and took a sip.

"You call Alec. Get another agent to cover."

"I'm good, Maks. I've kinda taken this on as my job. Wouldn't feel right having someone else with the two of you."

They drank in contented silence until it was time to go. With showers behind them, they drove over to meet the gang, Shane sticking around to watch them.

CHAPTER TWENTY-FIVE

Camille was busier than usual over the next few days. At least from what she said. He hadn't known her long enough to make the comparison. He kissed her good-bye in the morning and didn't see her again until long after the sun went down. They'd spend the evenings going over his application, and as he told her about his life, she was filling in most of the blanks. They hadn't spoken of Irina since he forbid the contact, so he wasn't sure where she was going to get the information to back up his claims. If he stymied her, her failure would be his.

He lost sight of what that meant as soon as skin touched skin, finding solace in her arms.

Tomorrow was their Christmas, and she would have the day off. She seemed to like this holiday because every time she walked through the door, she had several more presents wrapped in bright paper and ribbons, a big smile on her face, telling him all about her bounty, what she'd gotten for who and why. He was coming to know her partners from the stories she told. Nell had a daughter, Chloe, who was eleven and who'd just met her father, the congressman. He was the man who'd given away his part in the upcoming hearing. Emilia was in love with Nick who was married to Saban. The Katsaros' had a son, Teddy, who was four-years old and the apple of Em's eye. Jelani was the social one, dating with the hopes of finding a mate, even though she'd deny it til her last breath. She wanted everyone to believe she liked the excitement of meeting new men, even though they all knew her well enough to know the truth. He'd helped Camille box all the presents up this morning as she described the women who'd be the beneficiaries of all she'd bought. She was giving them out today because she was skipping her usual plans, to be with him and Shane. He didn't want her to change routine for him, told her it was no big deal, just another day as far as he was concerned, but she refused to listen.

He was secretly glad. It would give him the pleasure of spending a day with her that was important. They'd planned the menu, and the food had been delivered yesterday, along with some other things he thought she'd need when he left. The day was soon coming when he'd be transferred to another house. The agent was worried that they'd been too long here, and Shane was more on edge than he'd been before.

They hadn't gone to the lab today. The group had dispersed to home bases for the holidays. It left him and Shane rambling around the empty apartment with nothing to do.

"I never asked if you wanted to go Christmas shopping. It's an experience here, one I think you'd appreciate."

"I thought it was because you were more nervous about being in same place."

"I am, so I asked Alec to come with us. We'll just stop at one or two places, get what we need, and come right back."

"It would be good to get out."

Shane's phone pinged, and he looked down to read the text.

"He's here. Grab your coat and think about what you want to buy."

"I have no money, Shane. Rubles all left for my mother."

"I know. I'll cover you. You can pay me back once you get a job."

"I could be dead before that happens."

"Not on my watch, buddy."

"I like this phrase, buddy. Is this bromance?"

Shane laughed as the doorbell rang.

"Nope. FBI agents don't do bromances. It would hurt the rep."

Shane became serious as he checked the door, making sure it was Alec before opening it up to let him in. Once inside, Alec stayed at the bottom of the stairs. "I have to admit, this was a good idea. I've been invited to Jelani's tomorrow with Nate and I want to pick something up for the hostess. Maks might know a good bottle of wine I can bring."

As he shrugged on his coat, Maks suggested, "You buy Mountain Man wine. It is good."

Shane followed behind Maks as they went down the steps.

"He's right, it is. The winery's owned by Camille's parents."

"Wine's not my thing, so that should be a safe bet. Now beer? I'd know exactly what to buy."

Alec stepped back out, his arm barring the way, making sure it was clear before Maks became the filler between his bodyguards.

They spent an hour in Downtown Crossing, going from one store to the next, the crowds of people not surprising. It was always crowded on the streets of Moscow, but the amount of goods sold here was unbelievable. He couldn't help but notice the way the men with him checked every face, every counter, every group of people that got close. It should have put him on high alert but instead, he felt safe and was able to browse the aisles for a present for his mother and for Camille. For his mother, he purchased a silk scarf that he knew she would love. The colors were the pastels that she favored, and he doubted she'd ever owned anything as expensive. Camille was a different story. He had no idea what she'd like, what she had, what she wanted.

"Maks, we have to get going. We've been here longer than I feel comfortable with."

"Just one more store. Please. I don't have anything for Camille."

Scanning the area, Alec gave a nod and they entered one of the bigger department stores in the outdoor complex. Walking slowly down the center, Maks glanced right and then left. And then stopped.

"There. I will get her that."

He was pointing to the china department. On the display case was a blue and white porcelain bowl that could have been sold in Russia. It was delicate like she was, and beautiful as well.

"Do we have money for that?"

Alec gave Shane the discreet nod to cover them before saying, "This one's on me. Until you get your first American paycheck."

When he handed the sales clerk his credit card, she asked, "Do you want it wrapped?"

It was Maks who answered, "*Ja*, please. With pretty bow."

"With a pretty bow."

When she handed it over the counter, he grinned, quite pleased with his purchase.

He hoped she liked it. There had been no celebrations over the last couple of years, nothing to celebrate since his father's arrest. It would be nice to share the day with two people he'd come to admire and appreciate.

⌐

Camille woke early and kissed him awake.

"Merry Christmas."

"Merry Christmas to you, as well."

She sat up, ready to pull him up and out.

"Come on, we have to get up. I don't want to miss one minute with sleep."

His finger traced one of her nipples as he said, "We start day in good way?"

Her body reacted as it always did, and she closed her eyes as the spiral of heat penetrated the core of her.

"Mhm, this would be a very good way."

She hadn't allowed herself to get in this deep with a man, didn't know it could feel so powerful. Her mother had been right. Again. When you found the one, there was magic in every touch and in every kiss. When his hand molded itself to her breast and his mouth sought hers in hungry abandon, she gave herself up to the passion that had begun to consume her. He continued to seduce her with hot, deep thrusts of his tongue before moving down to take each nipple in his mouth, pulling the nubs with his teeth, sending rippling sheets of pleasure through her. She squirmed beneath him, as he tasted the skin on her belly, his hands caressing her thighs as he made his assault on her senses. Then he was between her legs, spreading them open, dragging his tongue across her swollen clit. His hands slid beneath her bottom and he lifted her up to increase the pressure, his mouth now pressed against her, drinking her in. She could do nothing for the languid way he made her feel, except enjoy the intensity of the mating. He slowly moved his body along hers, until he covered her, his lips wet with her essence reclaiming hers. He fumbled with the drawer where she was keeping the protection and she helped him slide it on before he entered her. She gasped as he filled her up to the hilt in one smooth motion.

I love you, Maxim Zhernova. I love you.

The words echoed in her head as he took all she had to offer, silently demanding that she give him more. And she did, her body bombarded with sensation after sensation. When she felt the tightening of his muscles, she let herself be led to the precipice and they fell over it together. Unable to move, they stayed wrapped, body to body, and he whispered, "This is one Christmas I will never forget."

Neither would she. When loneliness came calling she would come back to this place in his arms and be forever grateful she'd found him, for even the briefest of moments.

Hearing Shane out in the other room, they were forced up but not before she brushed aside his sweaty curls from his brow and kissed him gently. He removed the condom and placed it in the wicker basket she used for refuse before returning the gesture.

"You shower, I'll start breakfast after cigarette."

She climbed out of the bed.

"One of these mornings I'm going to join you."

"Not good for you."

"Not good for you either but it doesn't stop you."

"Maybe the day I start to believe I have future, I give them up."

She trailed her fingers over his cheek, wishing she could guarantee he had one. She was committed to making sure he would gain residency here, and it was the best she could do. He threw on his jeans and a shirt, looked back at her once before leaving the room.

She stood for a moment, silently calling him back, her throat sore from holding back the words she so wanted to share with him. After stepping into the shower, she let the water pound her skin, attempting to wash away the sadness. This might be one of the last times she'd get to spend with him. She knew he was leaving soon. She just didn't know what it would mean for them.

How was she going to spend the rest of her life without him?

⌒

Maks stood on the deck, the need for the cigarette not as dire as he'd suggested. He needed to get out in the frigid air to think. Camille had become an obsession in his blood, one he knew he'd have to banish if he was to continue the journey he'd started. After the meeting with the FBI the other day, the government had offered to pay him to continue his work. He'd have money of his own. It was probably why both Shane and Alec had lent him the money to buy the Christmas presents.

The question was, would he take it?

It would mean living here in this city. He'd have Boog and the group to work with, he'd have time to spend with Camille, but would Sonya like it here? Should he try to grow roots before he knew what she wanted? Maybe she'd like to live in a warmer climate. She'd grown used to the cold and snow, but she might like to test the waters somewhere else. Florida? No. There were too many Russians who lived there, a congregation of radicals who would kill him in a heartbeat if given the opportunity. California? He'd heard it was nice there, but the high probability of earthquakes and fires was problematic. If only he could talk to her, get a sense of what she wanted. Boston wasn't an international type of city. It closed down early, but the people who lived here were liberal in a way that spoke to freedom and liberty. And he'd made his first friends here. Would his mother mind that he took the decision out of her hands? Hadn't she told him, as long as they could live near each other, in safety, she'd go anywhere? Anywhere that wasn't Russia. Could he summon the courage to live with Camille, or had his past made any chance at happiness inconceivable?

He stared into the morning light, wishing it would illuminate his path. But all he got was a painful reminder of why he was here. He could let nothing get in his way, not even the love for a woman.

When he heard her call his name, he turned to look at her. Love bubbled up, a love he couldn't stop but couldn't count on.

"Are you coming in?"

He tossed the filter into the can, having smoked very little of the burned-down butt, and walked through the doorway and into her arms.

After breakfast, Camille dragged the men into the living room to open presents. She'd handed out a couple boxes to each of them, and like a little kid, she clapped as they unwrapped the brightly colored gifts. She'd gotten Shane a money clip that was engraved with the words, BEST BODYGUARD EVER, a gift certificate to the grocery store they'd been ordering from, a GET OUT OF JAIL FREE that she'd fashioned on one of her business cards.

"Just in case, and if you never need it, which I'm hoping you don't, it can be transferred to a third party."

Shane seemed to like each of the gifts, telling them both he wouldn't have missed the assignment for the world.

Maks had opened one of the small boxes to find a couple of cards of elastics. They were in varying colors and thicknesses.

"For your man buns."

"It will be useful. I keep losing the two I have."

He lifted the bigger box, shaking it before setting it on his legs.

After untying the box, he ripped off the paper and took the top off to find a banjo. His eyes flicked up to see a look of doubt cross Camille's face.

"You said you played, but you haven't picked up the balalaika yet, so I'm not sure you still enjoy it."

"This is perfect. I have trouble with other. Too many memories. This will make new ones. Good ones. Thank you."

There were a couple of finger picks that he slid on and began to pluck away, the music upbeat and hopeful. When he was satisfied with the sound, he placed it down and handed Camille his present.

"I hope you like."

It sat on her lap, but her fingers were trembling, and she wasn't sure she'd be able to open it without him noticing.

She wiped her palms on her jeans, pulled at the ribbon and shimmied it off, putting it on the rug beside her. After lifting the cover, she fingered the tissue paper away to find a delicate white and blue porcelain bowl. It was exquisite, and she felt tears collect in her eyes. It was a version of something she'd find in Russia.

"Oh, Maks, this is beautiful."

"Until you go to country and cross off bucket list."

She glanced up, knowing any thought she had of visiting the country had been poisoned by what the government had done to him and so many others. She didn't love it anymore. Didn't need to see the Urals, the countryside, visit her great-grandfather's birth place. Not until there was another form of government, where the citizens weren't killed at the whim of their leader.

"To be honest, it's no longer on my bucket list. I can do without sanctioning what's being done by spending my money there."

Unless she could go with Maks, she didn't want to live the fantasy she'd had for so long. She'd been no better than anyone else, so mired in the past, her great-grandfather's past, that she didn't see the dangers. Instead, she'd go to France, see where he'd lived there, his new life, the family that was hers.

She lifted the bowl and brought it to the kitchen, where she placed it on the counter. It went well with her décor and she would have a daily reminder of the man who'd been hers for a short while.

CHAPTER TWENTY-SIX

Camille was grabbing her travel mug and filling it with a new coffee Maks had ordered, one with a caramel taste. She smiled to herself when she thought about yesterday. It was one of the best she could remember and had been filled with revelry, Maks entertaining them with his musical prowess, presenting a meal that would have made the angels cry, and pleasuring her at the end of it all.

When Shane came back in from his morning check-in, he brought earth shattering news. At least to her ears.

"Alec is replacing me for the next two days, and Maks is being moved to the place in Brighton. They finally solved the electrical problem, although if it had gone along other channels, rather than the governments, it would have been ready much sooner. You've got to pack up Maks. Alec will be stopping by within the hour."

It was as if she'd been hit in the head with a rock. Her senses were reeling, and her head was throbbing. Her eyes sought Maks' out to find him looking at her with the same disbelief.

"I will not have either of you for next two days?"

"You know Alec, Maks. He's better at this than I am, been doing it longer. He could stop a Mack truck with one hand."

"But will need to begin new routine. I don't like."

"We talked about this, Maks. You knew it was coming. You even made Camille several containers of soup she could eat when you left. She's still your attorney. She'll be at all the upcoming interviews, and she can still stop by to see you."

His eyes captured hers and didn't let go, speaking to her without words. They didn't have any to say to each other. They could only go through the motions of love.

"Won't be same."

Shane had picked up his duffel bag and was cramming things in.

"I know. But I don't think it's a good idea to let on that you and Camille are...a couple."

He pulled at Shane's arm, forcing him to look at him.

"When you are back, can she stay with me at new place?"

Shane stopped what he was doing, his expression suggesting the full force of what Maks was feeling was finally getting through. He looked over at her, then back at Maks.

"I can't promise that. Things are ramping up. We've got interviews all over the place in the next few weeks. You'll be flying down to Washington for a meeting with someone from the Department of Justice on the ninth, the Intel Committee hearing on the tenth, and a meeting with the Director of the FBI on the eleventh. Camille will be with you for all of them. Alec will be too. He has a higher clearance than I do."

"What if I make it part of agreement?"

"Like I said, you're better off keeping them in the dark about your relationship. They could pull her off the case completely if they think you've gotten too close."

She couldn't take it any longer. The ache was growing stronger and she knew it would soon be unbearable.

"Maks, he's right. I've crossed a line I shouldn't have crossed. You're my client and what I've done could appear to be unethical."

Saying it out loud, she knew there was no appear about it. She should never have let this happen but there was no guilt or regret.

"We hire new lawyer. You stay with me as...as..."

"Lover? I don't think that's a good idea. I've got irons in the fire that someone else couldn't manipulate. Let's get this finished and then we'll...decide what to do."

How many times had he told her it wasn't a good time to fall in love? Had he forgotten? Would he be willing to offer her a future? If not, she couldn't stay. She couldn't. Her heart would break every day he was unable to commit himself to her.

"You will come tonight? To where I am?"

"If Alec is okay with it. If not, I'll set up appointments with him to see you. There's still a lot of work to do and he knows we'll need to meet."

"You are good with this?"

She closed the distance between them and wrapped her arms around his torso.

"I am not good with this, but we're almost there. In a few weeks, we'll be able to see each other openly if that's still what you want."

His hands were in her hair, and his lips were on her mouth. The kiss was tender, and he lingered there.

Shane cleared his throat. "Come on, guys, I'm not supposed to see what's going on.

She extricated herself from his arms and gave him a look of longing before getting her coat on, picking up her briefcase, and walking out the door.

She sat in the car and the tears started falling. She couldn't help herself. She'd known the end was coming, but she hadn't been prepared for it to come at her like a speeding train. Not after yesterday, not after the way he'd loved her last night. Brushing the moisture away, she took a deep breath, took back some control over her emotions. She had a lot of work to do before this was over. She'd put out feelers in a couple of different directions, and she would see if her instincts proved accurate. She was going to play the game according to Russian rules. She just hoped they hadn't changed.

When she got to the office, she was back in control. As she entered the brightly lit space, the waiting room already filled with faces that looked peaked and scared. She checked in with Heather. The receptionist handed her over her call-back slips and asked, "Did you have a nice day yesterday?"

She gave her a wan smile, and said, "One of the best. Thanks. How was yours?"

"Great. Look, I'm engaged."

She showed the chip-size diamond as if it were three karats.

"It's lovely, Heather. Congratulations. Tom's a great guy."

"He is. We're hoping for a summer wedding, but it will depend on a venue being available. I hear you have to plan two years in advance."

"We have a lot of contacts. I'm sure we can put in a few calls if you need us to."

"Thanks, Cami. I appreciate it."

When the phones started ringing, three all at once, Heather managed them with the calm assurance that all their clients would feel well-served. She started down the hall toward her office and as she turned the corner, she bumped into Em, who was standing at her doorway talking to Jelani.

"Hey, you. We missed you yesterday. Was it worth it choosing him over us?"

"It was a nice day. Cozy."

Moving on, not wanting to get into how she really felt about the day, she dropped her briefcase on one of the chairs and went to the window.

Heather was engaged. She'd never felt such envy. Had never thought about it being an option for her, not with the way she kept every man at bay, but Maks...he brought out something she hadn't even known she had in her. What was she going to do when he was completely out of her life?

Alec had told her not to drop by after work. He wanted the night to go over what Maks had. She was going to have to go home to her condo to find nothing waiting for her. No wine, no smile, no conversation. She wasn't sure she could sleep alone, without Maks' warm body cuddling with her.

Her world had been just fine before he'd walked into it. She'd had her priorities in place, her friends, her family, and it had been enough. Or had it been? Well, her heart had been safe. There'd been a numbing acceptance with that. Now she was awake to what love could do. It had changed the colors of her life, making everything come alive. She'd been dead inside and hadn't even realized it.

"Are you okay?"

Em had come in and was walking toward her.

She glanced over, unaware that the tears were back. Em wasn't.

"Hey, what's wrong? Was yesterday a total shit show?"

She shook her head, unable to speak for fear of breaking down completely.

When she felt Em's arm go around her, she dropped her head onto her shoulder and choked out, "He's an eleven."

There was a moment of silence, as if Em didn't know what to say. Her friend would not only be surprised that she'd given into the temptation to find out but that it was making her cry. No man before had touched her in any way.

"And that's a bad thing?"

"He doesn't want a future. He says it's not the right time to fall in love."

She took a step away, looked Em in the eye, confused by that fact. "How do you stop yourself from falling?"

"I think I'm the wrong one to ask, hon."

"It's not just the sex, Em. It's him."

"The Russian thing?"

"No, although I'm sure that's what everyone will think. He's smart, talented, and he's got guts."

It didn't hurt that he anticipated her needs and met them every way he could.

"Is he still at the condo?"

"No. He's being moved today to somewhere in Brighton. Shane, the agent who's been with us, is taking a couple of days off. Alec Cleland is with him now."

"We met him yesterday. He's one of Nate's friends."

Jelani was just getting in, her briefcase slung over her shoulder, a pinched look on her face when she looked in on them. "He's a macho jerk if you ask me."

"Why the hell are you saying that? He was pretty well behaved for a fed."

"Too straight, like he's got a rod up his ass."

After the stories she'd heard about the state police in Russia, Camille didn't see the problem.

"It's a bad thing to have a by-the-book defender of the Constitution in government?"

"It belies common sense at times. There are too many ICE men out there who go by the book and it hurts people."

"He's not ICE, he's FBI."

"Applied for a job with the dick men, so he'll bring his ill-fitting by-the-book perspective to my area of the law. Don't like it, don't like him."

With that sentiment out in the public domain, Jelani hefted her briefcase and went a couple of doors down to her office.

"Whoa. Never knew her to be so effusive in her dislike."

"Has she ever met a man she wasn't willing to date?"

Em looked at her, and by the expression, she'd just made the same educated guess about Jelani's reaction. They laughed together. It made Camille feel lighter.

As soon as she left, Maks went and packed his bags. Handling the banjo with as much respect as he did his balalaika, he put them by the door to wait for Alec to arrive. He checked the refrigerator, where he'd stocked some of the soup, a container of pelmeni, the dumplings Russia was known for, and the butter and garlic sauce she could top them with. Wine was in the cooler, and she'd have enough for several days. He wished he had time to make her a couple of the dishes he'd made at the restaurant, the ones he'd come up with that the head chef had liked enough to add to the menu. They were more Spanish in cuisine than the heavy fare Russians enjoyed but it had been encouraged. The chef and his wife spent the winters in Basque country and brought back many new dishes upon their return. He knew Camille would have liked them, but he was too busy trying new things that he'd never had in the pantry or the freezer. The lamb, the roasted duck, the turkey he'd made yesterday with stuffing and cranberry sauce. He should have remembered that he had finite time with her. The agitation at being in new surroundings continued to build, and he tried to keep busy. He polished the stainless steel until it shone, and when he ran out of things to clean, he stepped outside for his final cigarette. This one he smoked like a man about to go before the firing squad. It felt like his heart had already exploded inside his chest.

Alec arrived right on time, and as they drove to the new residence, silence accompanied them.

As soon as they entered, Maks looked around with a grave sense of loss. There was no homey feeling here, no scent that filled him, and he felt as uncomfortable as he had those first few days with a different agent outside every few hours and the rooms empty of life. At Cami's, she was everywhere, even when working. Surrounded by her pictures of family, he had felt a part of it.

"Will Boog or Smokey be coming today?"

"Boog will be by later. He said he has something to show you. And Camille called, asked if she could stop by after work. She has some more questions for you. I figured you would have gotten a lot of the application completed with all the time you've spent together."

"It is far lengthier process than I imagined."

"It's never taken her this much time before. Even the last case..."

He stopped abruptly as if he'd almost given something away.

"Yes, I have heard of it. She was hurt."

"She told you?"

He speculated that Shane should not have shared that with him, so he looked for another explanation.

"At beginning, when I was not communicating, she said she was not putting herself in danger again. Told me some of it. Without giving away names and classified information."

"We had to convince her to take this case. *We* knew you weren't going to hurt her, but we didn't give her much to go on."

"Why you not tell her truth of why I'm here?"

"You didn't trust anyone, Maks. If she came in knowing everything, you would have seen her as an extension of us. You needed to get to know her as a separate entity, get comfortable with her. I assume you did, given that you bought her a pretty expensive Christmas present."

Maks let what Alec said sink in. It made sense in a convoluted way. He hadn't trusted anyone at first. He'd looked at everyone as an assassin, even the FBI agents who worked with him. It was a carryover from where he came from where it was the government you had to fear.

"I have. She calls herself my fighter."

Alec laughed. "I heard about her conversation with Nate. Let me put it another way. I was in his office when the call came, and I heard her voice from across the room. Nate didn't know what hit him."

Neither did Maks but something had. He felt he was in one of those cartoons where a character got hit with a hammer and stars, bells, and whistles circled his head. That's what Camille did to him. Now? Now, he'd be lucky if he saw her once a day.

"Camille will come today to ask questions?"

Alec was checking windows, peeking out through the curtains, making sure there was no one lurking.

"I told her it had to wait until tomorrow. I want to go over everything you've gotten in the last week so I'm better prepared for the sessions coming up. I'll be with you in DC and want every last detail of what you've uncovered."

Maks didn't think he could sink lower but when his stomach dropped, he had a sense that he'd just hit the bottom. How would he sleep without her? She'd become his talisman and he needed the warmth she offered. She freed him from his despair and now it was back with a vengeance. Vengeance.

He'd have it but it was going to be at a higher price than he'd thought he'd have to pay.

CHAPTER TWENTY-SEVEN

Camille spent the morning running down her contacts in Moscow. The ones she'd been given by the U.S. consulate in Moscow. She was finally getting somewhere, and her instincts had been on target. She was going to be able to get the information she needed, and it wouldn't involve anyone who could be put at risk by collaboration. When she'd made the promise to Maks to stay away from his father's lawyer, she was determined to keep it. Now, it seemed, she wouldn't need to worry over her decision.

She picked up the land line, wanting to keep her cell records clear of any call, and dialed the number. There was a eight-hour time difference between here and Russia and she hoped that Irina hadn't left for the day. She let out a breath when the receptionist put her through.

"Camille, it is good to hear from you."

"Irina, I am glad I caught you before you left for the day."

"I have much paper work to catch up on. The situation here becomes worse with time. How can I help you?"

"That's why I'm calling. I've been told not to bring you into this."

"By whom?"

"Maks. He was adamantly opposed to the idea and I've found other means to get what I need. I can safely keep my promise to him."

She refused to go behind his back and plow ahead full steam like she might have done when she was younger.

"I am not pleased with his edict. I don't like people telling me what I can and cannot do."

Camille gave a small laugh. "I know what you mean. I've been known to buck authority myself but this time I'm honoring my agreement. Like I said, I have found other avenues to pursue. I have his birth certificate coming as well as the files on his father's death. It was well covered at the time and there is a plethora of information I can use. And I've only made two calls."

"It is important for him to be granted asylum, Camille. For not only him. His mother is waiting to join him."

"Sonya."

"He tells you this?"

"No. He refuses to talk about her. I couldn't find anything on her death, so I assumed she was still alive. Was she the only one he left behind?"

Irina paused before stating, "As far as intimate family. There is aunt but that is all."

"Would she want to come as well? Will there be backlash for her?"

"She is thinking of possibility. Hasn't decided yet. She loves her country."

"Yeah, I know what you mean. So many people swore that if the in-coming president was elected, they'd leave, but it's hard to abandon what you love."

"It is the promise of something better that keeps us from going. It will take much for the people to win this fight, but they are beginning to protest again. The youth. That is the promise of a better future."

"Maks is giving us a chance to right the wrong. I wish it could help you, as well."

"He is good man. Too many of them are leaving, being forced out."

"Or killed."

"I do not want him to be one of them. Please, you must do all you can to see him safe."

"My heart is in it, Irina."

Not wanting to push an issue Maks wanted her to leave alone, she couldn't help but asking, "Is Sonya safe?"

"For now, but she is not silent. She still goes to Ministry every day to protest her husband's death. I warn her it is not good idea, but she has become true dissident. I will do what I can from this end. As soon as Maks is legal resident I will put her on plane myself."

"I'll begin the paperwork, so we have a head start on the process."

"You are good woman. I am glad that you have this in your hand."

"I am, too, Irina. Please stay safe."

"I will do best I can. You call if you...how I say it...hit bump in road."

"I appreciate the offer but like I said, I'm honoring Maks' wishes. You call me if you or Sonya get into trouble there. I'll do all I can to get you out."

"I will. Thank you. Good-bye."

After the brief conversation, Camille hung up a bit disconcerted. It sounded as if Irina had more at stake than just helping an acquaintance. She wished she hadn't promised Maks she'd leave it alone. She would have liked to pursue the relationship in more depth. Her fingers flew to her computer keyboard and she Googled the name Irina Dresvyanin and found hundreds of entries for the prominent attorney. Many relating to Petrov, but nothing relating to Maks.

She sat back, thinking.

As an attorney, she knew there were cases you didn't forget. If one of those clients called with a new problem, she'd go to great lengths to see that justice was served. Was that Irina's sentiment in this case? She'd do what she could for Petrov's son because of what was done to the father? Until new information was revealed, she'd have to go on that supposition and leave it at that. Knowing that Sonya was planning on joining Maks, she wanted to make sure they had somewhere to live, and she added that task to the already growing list of things to do. She had only a few weeks, and she'd need every spare minute to work on it.

With so many other cases needing her attention, she put Maks' file aside and spent well into the night juggling her hours so she could work on them all. It helped that she had no desire to go home.

She wondered at how strangely they had come together, how it fit so well into her mother's theory that people met their mates through the hands of circumstance. Was it the inevitability of fate that brought them together? What was it about Maks that fascinated her? Why was she willing to break the all the rules she'd put in place for herself? For him? There'd been an immediate all-knowing intimacy, as if her soul knew him at first glance, as if her heart had prepared a spot for him and it was just waiting for him to fill it. She loved so much about him. His courage. Or maybe it was the vulnerability that lay beneath the surface, that he let no one see, that was part of the allure. Out of pain he'd found the resolve to change his past, become a fighter for justice and truth.

She smiled to herself. She was making him sound like Captain America. He wasn't a superhero. He was a man, whose body fit with hers in harmony. Was that why making love with him scored an eleven?

There was a radiant truth about how she felt, and the empty condo was a reminder of what she'd lost.

As she was rubbing her tired eyes, Em knocked on the door.

"Cami, you can't stay here all night. Come on, we'll grab something to eat and you can vent."

Camille knew she was putting off the inevitable, but every time she thought of leaving, a vision of Maks in her bed would prod her to pick up one more file. She did need to get out of here, if only for a short time.

"You wouldn't want to stay over at my place, would you? Maks made some soup and I've got wine chilling in the cooler." Feeling off-balance, she admitted, "I don't really want to be alone."

"I'd love to. We haven't had a sleepover since Saban pinged me with her plans for their third anniversary."

"She's such a bitch."

"Yeah, well, your opinion doesn't count."

"I actually think Nick's finally realized and accepted it. I just wish he'd put her in her place more often than he does."

"Arianna's brother did yesterday, and there was a twitter all around."

"Even Nick?"

"I think that made Saban the maddest. He didn't come to her defense like he usually does."

Cami couldn't miss the puzzled expression on Em's face. She didn't know how to explain the change in behavior but didn't want to encourage Em any more than she needed to, so she made light of it. "Interesting. Seems he's growing some brains. I thought the cells he'd lost were lost for good."

Em rolled her eyes. "We're not going to spend the night picking on Nick. We've been doing that for years. It'll be nice to have a different man to roast."

"I'm not roasting him, Em. I'm going to be lonely without him and I just want some company."

Em gave her a brief hug, and a heartfelt smile.

"You've got it. I'm going to go home and grab some clothes for tomorrow and then I'll be over."

"Okay. I'll just finish this up. I'll meet you there."

"You better be there before me."

"I promise. Just one more detail and I'm out."

And she was true to her word. She was glad the cleaners had come in. It meant she didn't have to shut down the office suite for the night. Walking out in the dark was something that still made her uneasy. She'd lowered her guard with Shane around. She'd left the job of crowd control in his capable hands. Now, alone again, she was back to feeling apprehensive, scanning the hall, checking the elevator, walking with a brisk stride. Once she was inside her car, with her doors locked, there was a relief of tension. And only when she reached the highway did she feel free from the irrational fear.

⌒

Maks' mind was still full, as it had been all evening. He'd tried to clear it when he went out for his last cigarette of the day, a tumbler of vodka in his hand. Neither had done anything to clear the chaos of thoughts or soothe his soul. When he went to his room, he didn't even bother to climb under the covers. He knew he wasn't going to get to sleep, not without Camille.

Maks lay in bed, his hands behind his head. Most of the night had been spent updating Alec on his progress since arriving in Boston. He told him about the gains being made with the help of the Bunker Hill Group and Alec seemed surprised by the wealth of information he was handing over. He thought they had all they needed, reiterated that the bureau was willing to put Maks on the payroll, and suggested he might want to start giving some thought to where he wanted to live. Once the hearings were over and his asylum was granted, he'd be free of safe houses. If he was still alive by the end of the investigation, they hoped he'd stay alive. He'd just had to stay away from people offering him tea, or any kind of drink that might contain polonium. It was becoming a Russian go-to for mayhem and murder.

Boston had kept him safe. He'd kept under the radar so far, or the assassins had bigger fish to fry. But where? In the city itself? On the outskirts? He'd lived in three places so far and he liked Camille's the best. That could have more to do with the fact she lived there than the actual area. When he asked Alec, what condos went for outside the city, the prices seemed steep. For someone without a ruble to his name, he wouldn't have much in the way of spending power. Alec had told him that Camille's condo might have gone for almost a million dollars. A million dollars seemed like an insurmountable sum to come up with. Renting would be the only way for him to afford to live here, but even that was high. He'd been told the fed's would fund him for the first few months but after that, he'd be on his own.

He shifted, trying to get more comfortable, knowing without Camille it would be next to impossible.

Camille.

She was an odd blend of feminine grace and unfeminine tenacity.

He closed his eyes as her image came to him, the look on her face when Shane announced he'd be moving. She'd taken on a ghostly pallor, her eyes had been glimmering grey, and the expression suggested she'd been thunderstruck, as if she'd forgotten he would be leaving her. He wished he could have given her some guarantee that they'd be together again, but he didn't want to make a promise he couldn't keep. If she hadn't come over to hug him goodbye, he would have let her go without a word. And he would have been sorry.

He might have made it quite clear it wasn't the right time for him to fall in love, but it had happened. He didn't know when but thought it could have been the minute he'd opened the door to her the day she came to meet him. Lush lips, hair the color of sunlight, eyes that could change in an instant, calm, serene, feisty. So many shifts, so many different personalities. He wondered how many more there were and whether he'd ever get to experience them.

He leaned over to shut off his light. He wanted total darkness. The hope was that her image would fade into the inky blackness. It didn't work.

What was she doing?

The green digits of the clock told him it was eleven sixteen. They'd be sleeping now, if together, replete from a night of touching and loving, his legs tangled with hers, his hand on some part of her body. It had connected him to a safe harbor, and he'd been lulled to sleep every night with a sense of belonging he had never felt before.

Would she get another call from the detention center? Would she be handling another Russian soon? They were fleeing the country like lemmings, jumping into the unknown, following group after group of emigres blindly in a hasty rush to freedom. Or was it the ones staying who were the lemmings, on a suicide mission that could result in nothing short of death?

His father should have left. He would have done well here in America. He was a charismatic man, with a big frame and curly black hair. He was one of the reformers who wanted to take perestroika to its natural conclusion: where a liberal state would be directed by educated, Russia- loving, decent people. He hated anything that reeked of ideology, thinking it too narrow in scope. He preferred concepts and free-thinking ideas that expanded the consciousness of a people, instead of restricting them. He was part of the inner circle when Yeltsin was in power, scrupulously honest, a man of integrity, and he'd kept an arm's length from the men who had come to power through their manipulation of assets and the privatization of most of the state institutions. He didn't think that freedom could co-exist with oligarchs and he'd fought as hard as he could to take their status away from them. As his son, Maks had watched the fight from the sidelines. At times he'd thought Petrov stupid, at others reckless. Never did he think him a criminal or a traitor, which was the label he'd been branded with by his arrest and death, by the blatant lies the government was willing to tell, by the oligarchs who were too arrogant to see the writing on the wall. The news channels detailing his life in stark deception, his death announced over and over, deemed him a coward who didn't want to face his traitorous actions. Ironically, those who'd taken him down, were the next to go. He wasn't the only one who didn't fit into the plans of the future as the president saw it. One by one, the oligarchs' assets were taken forcibly or under duress. Some men were killed, others exiled. By the time the picture became clear, they had already lost what they'd bargained for.

It was only then that he'd seen what his father had. He'd been too busy living his life, taking advantage of the better times that seemed permanent, staying out of politics, staying out of the fight. But by then it was too late, and his father was dead.

He never again wanted to be that blind to what was going on around him. When he took up the cause, he got his first glimpse into the reality of life behind the curtain, rather than seeing it through the mud-stained glasses that he'd worn like everyone else. The words *apathy* and *fear* were crossed out of his vocabulary. With his mother's help, and Irina's, he'd begun the journey that brought him here. He would live it to the fullest, for his father as well as for himself. He would live up to the standards his father had set for him, not from words of wisdom or parental lectures but by the actions of a man steeped in decency and honor.

Could Camille live up to those standards? He could only be with someone who he could trust, who inspired honesty, and who helped those less fortunate.

She seemed to be all of that, and he was finding that life without her was colorless and drab. Emotionally she supported him, and physically she was every man's dream. He often used the phrase making love when discussing his past exploits, but it paled in comparison to what he found with her. She gave of herself completely and took everything he had to give. He'd never given so much of himself to anyone, and it set off a three-level alarm. The alarm was still sounding but he'd reached the point where he was willing to risk it. If he was hurt, or disappointed, he'd live. He would not let the word *coward* describe who he was.

CHAPTER TWENTY-EIGHT

Camille had gotten through the long night with Em's help and Alec had given her the go-ahead for a visit after work so she could catch them up on the progress she'd made. She wasn't mentioning the information she had coming, or how she was getting it. She'd keep it to herself. It wasn't like she was doing anything illegal, but she might be straying into some grey areas.

She wrapped work up for the night a little earlier than usual. The tingles shooting through her at the thought of seeing Maks had compelled her to move through her day with a nervous, frenetic energy. When she called out a good-bye to everyone still at their desks before she left, Em peeked her head out and whispered, "Good luck." She knew why it had been offered. She'd shared with Em the fear that Maks didn't feel the same way, that he might have moved on now that she was gone. Missing him could be a wasted activity if he didn't care whether she was there or not. Heading out to Brighton, she let the GPS lead her to a house close to the college that took up a good part of the city. She'd brought along some wine to have with dinner. When she'd spoken to Alec earlier, he said that Maks would be making food for them and it'd be ready for her when she got there. It wasn't the food that would satisfy her hunger. It was the man.

She stood on the stoop, waiting to see him, a ball of need bursting to life in the pit of her stomach. It was mixed with a primal fear that he'd act like there was nothing between them.

When Alec opened the door and stepped to the side to let her in, she saw him, and all time stood still. He was looking at her with the kind of longing she felt in her heart, which started beating again, in hammerlike strikes.

He wiped his hands on the towel over his shoulder and walked toward her, glancing at Alec, as if to tell her he couldn't do what he wanted.

"It is so good to see you again."

His voice was like soft velvet and she wanted to say something, but her tongue was lodged in her throat. All she could do was nod, never taking her eyes away from his.

After coughing out the frog, she said, "I brought some wine."

"That is good. I have missed it."

He went to take it, his hand caressing hers, and she knew she'd read between the lines correctly. It wasn't the wine he'd missed, but her.

"Take your coat off. Dinner will be ready soon."

"It smells good. What did you make?"

"A recipe I created for Seiveri. I think you like."

Alec was busy with the remote. She had heard the credits as the news program ended and, with every brief change in voices and sound, assumed he was searching for something more to his taste than a regional favorite. Thankfully he was too engrossed elsewhere to feel the energy that surged all around.

She walked to the stove, where she stood close to the body that was sending pings of shockwaves through hers, her hand going to his shoulder while she lifted the cover from the pot and inhaled the scent.

"It is paella with mussels and prawns. I hope you don't mind but I ordered from delivery service store. Only for tonight."

"You can use the service any time you want but I'm surprised they delivered out this far."

"I pay extra, or should I say, you did."

"It's fine. Anything you need, you let me know."

His heated gaze was like a sensual touch.

"I have need but cannot satisfy now."

"Me, too."

Alec had come in to see what they were doing, still totally oblivious to what was going on. She smiled, thinking Jelani might be right about the guy. Or maybe it was more simply a guy thing. His emotion box was shut tight.

Picking up a bottle of the wine, Alec said, "This is what I brought to Jelani's. I'm not sure she liked it, though. She never opened it. She's kind of a..."

Camille gave him a scathing look before he uttered the word. It was fine for Jelani to dislike him, but it was not okay for him to dislike Jelani.

He seemed to understand the danger and used a more acceptable word.

"...anti-social."

"Jelani? She's the most *social* of the bunch."

"That guy she had with her was a total jerk. He was so into himself he never expanded his views on any other topic. And the way he dressed...his pants were so tight you could see his junk."

Camille knew Jelani had felt the same way and the guy had become history that night, but she wasn't saying a word about that. Jelani had sworn off men the morning after, although she'd done that before. Nothing could keep her friend from pursuing her future, a future that held a husband and kids.

Alec was rifling through drawers, one after the other, until he came to the conclusion, that there wasn't any way to open the wine.

Camille moved toward her coat that was lying across a chair in the living room.

"I have a corkscrew in the car. I'll get it."

Alec stood, hand on hip, a look of surprise on his face.

"Why the hell do you have a wine opener in the car?"

"When your parents own a vineyard, you keep the essentials with you for times like these."

"Give me your keys and tell me where it is, and I'll get it."

She extracted them from her purse and handed them over. "It's in a travel bag in the back seat. There's stopper in there, as well."

"Not going to need one of those. I'm on duty and can only have a small glass but I've found wine doesn't last as long as a six-pack of beer."

"Suit yourself."

As soon as he was out the door, Maks pulled her close and settled his lips on hers, his hands threaded through her hair.

He was spreading featherlike kisses on her cheek as he murmured, "I couldn't sleep last night for wanting you."

"Me neither. I'm not sure I can last another three weeks without you."

"That long? Shane will be back soon. Then we can..."

They heard the door open and jumped apart, Camille fixing the hair that had been mussed by Maks' hands.

Alec came barreling in, holding the corkscrew high in the air. "Got it."

Dinner was served as the wine was poured and they ate as they carried on small talk during the meal. After it was done and her update was complete, Alec got up and announced, "That's great Camille. I think you're doing a great job. I am going to assume you'll have it ready in time for him to be cut loose?"

"And when exactly is that?"

"Right after the hearings."

"You'll give me until a week after. There may be things I have to alter due to the testimony."

"I'll talk to Nate. But it sounds reasonable."

He was getting her coat as he talked, telling her in his own interminable way that it was time for her to leave.

"I'll talk to the court and get the earliest date I can."

"Great. Let us know when and where. We'll be witnesses if you need us."

Maks came over and took her coat out of Alec's hands and held it in offering. She turned her back to him as he helped her on with it, brushing her neck with his fingertips. She felt a zap of energy flow through her and she visibly trembled.

And then she was gone, back to her empty apartment, cursing every G-man who ever lived, Alec specifically for general purposes alone.

⌒

Maks watched her walk out, his muscles stiff from holding in all emotion. When the door closed and she was no more than an apparition in his mind, he glanced over to see Alec talking on his phone, passing along the information Camille had relayed to them. He had given her most of the information, place of birth, previous home addresses in St. Petersburg, Novgorod, and Moscow, the schools he attended, his places of employment. It covered most of his thirty-three years, right up until he'd gone underground. Then his residential history disappeared. He stayed with other dissenters, some of his father's friends who had marched in protest with him, stood guard at the Kremlin with signs and chants, who'd been imprisoned and released. Moving from place to place had become routine, but it didn't mean the urge to settle and grow new roots hadn't taken hold. He knew this was his present, but he wanted a change in his future. Would he find it here? With Camille?

It had been good to see her. It would have been immensely better if he could have held her for more than the briefest of moments. He had worried that with the separation in locales, she would have detached herself, but her eyes had been filled with the same kind of longing he felt. He needed to get this over with so he could pursue any chance they had to be together. He'd been relieved to hear that she'd gotten her information from sources that wouldn't be at risk for aiding and abetting a traitor. She'd never once mentioned Irina or his mother although he doubted she'd even know where to find Sonya. They had her well-hidden. He didn't know where she would get the material needed to complete his asylum paperwork. There was an abundance of information on his father's death online but most of it was propaganda, lies to hide the truth. How would she get the facts straight and prove that he was killed, and the wounds were not self-inflicted? There were prison records, the autopsy report, the pictures showing graphic images of his body before burial. They told the grim story of how he'd spent his days in the rat-infested stink hole. Irina had it all documented, had pulled every detail into a file so if the future offered reparation for the deeds acted upon during the current reign of terror, they could collect on it. She had been a force to be reckoned in the after math. More than a friend from his old days in Novgorod, she worked side by side with Petrov during glasnost, helped him implement new policies and procedures that helped guide the residents through the rocky aftermath of the fall of the Soviet Bloc. She shared his values and ideas, and helped him express them through her legal expertise. When he turned away from the government, she had tried to lure him back with promises of better days ahead. He saw what she could not envision, and she'd been shocked to find out the government was exactly what he told her it had become, more fascist than democratic. She could only watch as the law of the land was shredded and cursed. After the arrest, she'd done everything in her power to get him out, even tried to work out an exile, but Petrov wouldn't hear of it. He'd sworn he'd die trying to shed light on what was happening to their country. She had also been his mother's most ardent supporter in the last two years and had taken great care of her life. If he'd allowed contact, she would have been the most efficient way for Camille to get what she needed, but she wavered on a fragile line between patriot and rebel and he wouldn't be the one who pushed her off.

Camille had warned him tonight that he would have to talk about his mother at some point. Background was needed on his parents and siblings, of which he had none. He was gearing up for it, getting ready for the emotional upheaval that would come with the description of events following his father's death, Sonya's depression, her tears, and the heartbreak that came when a loved one was no longer with you. Their arguments about her growing involvement with the protest movement when she picked up the sign he'd carried and walked along the bridge where people had been shot, blood lining the ridges and cracks in the pavement. Their verbal battles over how to proceed, how to retaliate, how to keep Petrov's memory alive. There had been no good-bye before he'd been whisked across the border to Finland, only a call to tell her what had happened and where he was going. There had only been one other since his arrival, the day Camille had driven him to the federal building. For as much as he longed to hear his mother's voice, he knew her calls would be monitored. He didn't want anyone to think she knew where he was. It would only be a few short weeks now before she could join him, and once she was here, some of the tension he lived with would abate.

Alec knocked on the door, telling him Camille was on the phone with some questions. He jumped up off the bed and opened the door, taking the cell from Alec's hand.

"Don't tie up the line for too long. I need it in case I need it."

He nodded hurriedly in agreement before putting the phone to his ear.

"I am here."

There was a slight pause before he heard Camille admit, "I don't really have any questions. I just wanted to hear your voice once more before going to bed."

"This is good. I like that, too."

"Will Shane be back with you tomorrow?"

"That is what I'm told. In another day they will be moving me again. I am not sure where. You will visit me?"

"As often and for as long as I can."

"Knowing that will make the night better. Is Em there again?"

"No. I have to learn to live alone again. I can't keep depending on her to keep me company."

"And I would rather be alone than with Alec. He is not friend like Shane. Does not share conversation."

"He goes by the book, from what I've heard. Shane and I have crossed a line we shouldn't have by getting involved."

"It helps me trust better. I hope it is not problem for you."

"I can take care of myself. And I won't tell anyone about Shane."

"I will not, either."

He could hear Alec's footsteps coming toward his room. "Alec is coming. He will want phone back. I will say good-night and I wish you pleasant dreams. Mine will be about you."

"And mine about you. Good night Maks."

"Good night, Cami."

He was waiting to hand the cell back as soon as Alec's face appeared at his doorway.

CHAPTER TWENTY-NINE

Their days became routine, with Cami at work all day, him going to the lab to work with Boog and the Bunker Hill Gang, and every night she would come to dinner, eat with them and go home. Alec was checking in more often now that the date of the hearings was rapidly approaching, and they never knew when he'd stop by, so they hadn't risked another night of passion. Maks had been moved a couple more times and was now residing in the city of Quincy. He hadn't been able to see the towns except from a car window. There had been no more outings since Christmas, so he still had no idea where he should set up residence. With the trip to DC less than a week away, he knew he'd have to decide soon.

That night, after dinner, when they retired to the living room, he brought the subject up.

"I will need own place soon. It will have to be affordable and close to subway. I won't have car and will need to get to work. I want it in safe place."

He still hadn't told Cami about his plan to have his mother join him. He still talked about Sonya as little as he could. The fear was too big for him to share it. Or maybe there wasn't enough trust to yet.

Camille looked up at Shane and asked, "Where will he be working?"

"As far as I know, at the JFK. That could change if he is transferred to DC"

He could feel a vein pound in his forehead. This was not acceptable.

"I will not go there. If I can't stay in Boston, I will find another job. Alec told me FBI will cut me loose after court date."

"If that's what he said, then I guess you can pick anywhere in the area."

"What is affordable?"

"I think you should focus on safe neighborhoods first if that's a priority. They will not be inclusive."

"What you say is I will pay more for safety. Then I will pay what I must." He glanced up at Cami and asked, "Will you let me keep delivery service? Then I can still eat."

He grinned at her, and she smiled back. He was learning to make jokes and he was enjoying it as much as she seemed to be.

"You can live with me for a while. Until you get your bearings."

"No. I will find place of my own."

"Is this Russian machismo for I won't let a woman support me?"

His features softened as if in apology.

"No. I would find pride in living with a woman of your talents. Money would not make difference."

She narrowed her eyes at him as if she wasn't sure he was telling her the truth. He knew there were many men who would not tolerate the woman being the more visible one. He'd learned that women had fierce wills and big hearts and he'd come to respect that.

"I'll take your word for it." She put her feet up on the stained coffee table that sat in front of the couch she was sitting on. "Let's see, I like where I live, obviously, but the rents are kind of high."

She glanced over at him sheepishly as if she were ashamed she could afford a nice place, then tilted her head as if in thought. "Charlestown is a nice place. South of the city might be doable. The MBTA runs all the time."

Shane interjected, "I live in Somerville and I've had no problems."

Her mouth quirked in a smile. "You're an FBI agent. Who'd screw with you?"

"Me, not so much. It's Alec who might give them pause."

Totally thrown off by the pronouncement, she said, "You live with Alec?"

"Yeah. For almost a year now."

"Why?"

"I know you're not overly fond of him, but he's a good guy, maybe a little straight-laced but that's not a bad thing. He took me under his wing when I joined the Bur, the bureau, covered for me if I made an FOB mistake. That's a rookie fuck-up. Laughed at me later. We used to hang out after work, grab a couple beers. When he broke up with the woman he was living with and I wanted to move out of my parents house we decided to get a house together and split the rent."

"You've got to be close to thirty. How the hell did you live with your parents that long?"

"Four years in college, two years in the army, then the academy means I didn't exactly live with them, I just didn't have my own mailing address. Now I do."

"You were in army?"

"Yeah. Stationed in Iraq fighting ISIS."

"Shit."

"Exactly. We ex-servicemen don't like sharing our experiences, so why don't we get back to the subject at hand. You've only got another week to figure it out."

Camille asked, "Do you want me to look around, see what's available?"

Maks figured he could look online as easily as she could, and he had more time to kill than she did.

"I can do that during day. I will need to know what pay grade is."

"You can ask Alec the next time he's here. He might be able to give you an estimate."

There was an idea introducing itself that Camille wasn't willing to share quite yet. She had a feeling Maks wouldn't like it, but it would give him some wiggle room and less stress if he wasn't making that much when he started work. She was going through her savings like water through a sieve, all for a good cause, so before she made any definite decision, she'd have to check with her financial advisor and see if the investment was doable.

"Do you want one or two bedrooms?"

"I watch Hunters for Houses tonight and make list."

"Don't get too crazy. It's too early in the process for you to become a spoiled American. That takes time and work."

"I make careful list. Three things that are important. Two bedrooms for sure."

She knew he'd need two bedrooms even though he hadn't mentioned anything about his mother joining him. Not wanting him to know about the conversation she'd had with Irina, she kept waiting for him to tell her, but he avoided the topic of Sonya as much as she'd let him. She was close to being finished with the packet and was scheduled to file the paperwork with the courts by this Friday. He'd have to sign off on them, which meant she'd have to go over everything she'd obtained. She knew he'd ask where she'd gotten it all. She didn't really want him to know.

A stream of concern flowed through her. They were keeping secrets from each other, and it meant they didn't have the kind of foundation they'd need if a relationship was what they were moving toward. It should be based on trust, something Maks had a tough time with. She had a sinking feeling that if he couldn't trust her with his plans concerning his mother, he wouldn't trust her with his heart.

Then what were they doing? Marking time, playing a game? There had been no more making love, and Shane had made it clear that he wasn't comfortable with them being affectionate in front of him. The apartment made privacy an issue and they were forced to steal kisses out on the front stoop when he went out to smoke. He seemed to miss it as much as she did, his searching hands under her coat fighting to find skin beneath all the layers. When he held her close, he took her back to the days when they'd found a home with each other, when their hearts had beat as one.

Did they still? Or was this just a momentary blending of hearts and bodies? Whatever time she had left with him, she'd grab with both hands. If it was a week, a month, or a year, she would be grateful.

⌒

Alec arrived a few days later to pick them up for their trip to Washington. Shane would be along as back-up, which made Camille feel better about the three-day stay. The first of the interrogations would be with representatives from the Department of Justice. How long they'd remain in their jobs was in question with the inauguration only a couple of weeks away. It's why Nate and his superiors had pushed for Maks to make his statements earlier than he might have. He was ready. She'd been with him the couple of times Alec and Nate prepped him. The questions thrown at him were a mixed bag of adversarial, civil, and amenable and she was impressed with his calm demeanor. They were unable to throw him. Maks knew his story, and he knew the most minute details of what he'd found. The information terrified her. Russia was at war, but the FBI was going to be hard-pressed to prove it to people still enamored with Fox News. There were actual troll farms, hundreds of hackers on payroll, working on various projects for the Kremlin on behalf of the president-elect, and targeting teens, hoping they could cause disruption in democracy over a generation. She saw the kinds of ads that they were buying on social media sites, promoting fake news and divisiveness. She'd never been privy before to what he'd been working on, and the repercussions could spell impeachment and jail for a lot of the people in office. There had been conspiracy, crimes against the country, and money laundering, to name a few. Would people believe it, even if he had hard data to verify his claims? In the current climate facts seemed to be irrelevant. It was as if black magic was being used to hypnotize the masses. She knew it mirrored what was going on in Russia. She just couldn't understand why. She was just glad she'd gotten a preview of what would be revealed in the hearings and meetings scheduled. Being well-informed would help her stay focused on Maks and not the collusion of so many to eradicate democracy.

He'd signed off on the asylum application the previous Friday. It had gone as she'd expected, with him asking her questions she had to skate around. That the file was over two hundred pages helped. He didn't have time to read the entire portfolio and he'd looked at her long and hard before putting his signature on the bottom line. He assured her he'd be reading the copy she'd given him, and although that set her on edge, it didn't stop her from filing it with the immigration court the same afternoon. His special circumstances, stated by the FBI supervisor in charge, prompted the judge to set an appearance date for a week from tomorrow. They were rapidly moving to the desired outcome.

Would it be the outcome she'd envisioned?

That question haunted her all the way down to the capital.

⌐

Maks examined the city from the back-seat passenger side of the SUV that had met them at the airport. It was much more congested here than in Boston, the traffic filled with hundreds of taxis, limousines, foot trucks, and street vendors. Even with the window up, he could hear sirens blaring and jackhammers piercing the air. They were sitting bumper-to-bumper, moving at a snail's pace toward the building that housed the DOJ. With three FBI agents in the car with him, he felt well-protected, but as the men shifted glances from side-to-side and back to front, he knew they were looking for trouble. It would probably come now if it was coming. He was here to reveal their secrets and they would know about it. Too many eyes and ears were here, the ambassador the most visible among them.

He squeezed Camille's hand which was hidden under his coat. He needed the connection to his safe harbor. She would keep him focused on what he was here to do, no matter what went down around him. Shane was on his other side, his head turned to read what was going on behind them. Alec sat shotgun and his head bobbled around in every direction, keeping tabs, his hand resting inside his coat as if he'd have to pull out his gun on a moment's notice. Linking his fingers in Camille's, Maks breathed in and calmed himself. He didn't want to die. Not today, not tomorrow. Not until he had some real time with the woman sitting beside him. It had been a fantasy in the making, and he wanted to see if there'd be a happily ever after.

She was here with him and that's all he needed to get through it. There'd been no smile since they'd left for the airport just after four a.m., her expression one of resolute determination. She looked the part of intimidating defense, dressed in a black suit, her pearls wound around her throat in a choker, her black boots heeled and dangerous. He felt her fingers grip his as they pulled up to the Robert Kennedy Judicial Building and he knew they'd arrived.

On the way in, she gave him her first warning.

"If I put my hand on your arm, it means don't answer until you've conferred with me. The panel will be made up of skeptics, and I want to make sure you don't walk into a trap."

"I understand."

Walking past the fountain in the cobblestoned courtyard, his body guards surrounding him like a glove, policemen walking the perimeter of the building, he was hurried up the stairs and into the lobby, where he was frisked and sent on his way.

In the Great Hall, the Spirit of Justice stood tall, her hand raised, her male counterpart the Master of Justice, by her side. Maks was impressed with the art, murals, and sculptures that seemed to be everywhere. "Are all buildings like this?"

"This has the largest historical art collection. The others are equally imposing. Marble floors and ornate ceilings."

"It reminds me of splendor of Russian architecture."

The flag told him he wasn't there anymore. It drooped in the warmth but stood proud in sentry.

They took the elevator up to the assigned floor, and he was escorted into what seemed more like a conference room than an interrogation room. A dozen chairs sat around the table, and he was told to sit, Camille taking a seat beside him.

Within minutes, several men walked in to join them, and he was introduced to the group who would examine his evidence, giving him a good idea of how things were done in America. Expecting a more confrontational audience, he was surprised that they were without rancor, there was nothing prejudged, no bias. He relaxed half way through the meeting. Camille did not. He felt her hand on his arm twice, and both times she gave him good counsel. He was beginning to trust that she was on his side.

Five hours later, the men seemingly satisfied with what he'd laid out, they dismissed him, with hearty hand-shakes and words of gratitude.

He had been well handled, and it made his decision to come here, to live here, more compelling. As they exited the room, Shane slapped him on the back.

"Great job, Maks."

Alec gave him a look that stopped him cold and wiped the grin off his face. Camille was stunned.

"What's the matter, Alec? Isn't it in the rule book to give praise?"

"That might be okay, but fraternization isn't."

"Jelani was right."

"About what?"

"Nothing you'd understand. You think she's anti-social. I'm beginning to think that describes you."

"My job isn't to become Maks' friend, it's to protect him with my life. If I'm willing to do that, I don't see what your problem is."

She didn't know where the sudden anger came from, but it was there in his tight voice. She could tell he was holding on to his control by a thread. His hands were fisted, his mouth in a twisted grimace. Staring at him for a minute, she searched his eyes, his stance and reality struck. The blush crept into her cheeks. How could she have had such a low regard for how dangerous his job was? He was right. He was putting his life on the line. She should just say thank you and not be so contrary.

"I'm sorry. That was out of line."

His facial muscles relaxed with her apology. "Let's get to the hotel. I'm starving and I'm sure you guys are hungry, too. We should have gotten you something to eat when we got in. You don't leave anyone in the Justice Department waiting, and we just made it to the meeting on time."

"I have vodka?"

"Yes, Maks. You're lucky enough that you can have a couple of stiff drinks. Us, not so much, but a good steak will suffice."

Once they got to Maks' room, they ordered from room service, and no one spoke again until they were replete, Maks guzzling two drinks down while she sipped her wine. Alec spent a couple of minutes going over the agenda for tomorrow before she was escorted to her room. The agent posted outside took a spot between hers and Maks'. The agency was providing dual protection. It brought back memories she thought had faded, and she spent a restless night, aware of every noise, every creak, every voice outside her room, waiting for some enemy to evade their guards and get them.

It meant the next morning she was not at her best. She'd have to a better job of controlling her emotions tonight. Dressing in another power suit, she met the men for breakfast. They were scheduled to arrive at the Longworth Building at ten for their closed hearing with the Intelligence Committee. Jack Adams would be there, and she wasn't exactly sure how to interact with him. Was Nell still upset with him? Were they working out their problems for Chloe's sake? She didn't want to be overly friendly, but she didn't want to snub him, either. He would be asking questions today and she wanted a level playing field, to give him no reason to antagonize her client. When they entered the room, there was a rectangular table facing the dais where members of the committee would sit. Several chairs were sitting at attention, and she looked around wondering if anyone else would be present as witness. There were name plates guiding them as to where to sit, and a microphone Maks would use when giving testimony. As she pulled her files out of her briefcase, Maks was looking around to get a sense of the place.

"We sit here?"

"We do."

"They ask questions from on high? They think themselves better, more invincible?"

She smiled for the first time this morning.

⌒

The meeting was gaveled into order by the chair of the committee, a member of the Republican Party and he said a few words of thanks and outlined the agenda set for the day. When the introduction was over, he came at him with his first question. Here was the animosity he had counted on. It was familiar, and he sat up straighter to face him down. Each member had twenty minutes of time for their questions. Some were less hostile, like the congressman from Massachusetts. Jack welcomed them both to the hearing, Camille by name, and thanked them for their service. Maks assumed this was Nell's acquaintance and the man who'd given away his username. His questions were pointed, and it seemed he understood the gravity of the situation. As Maks answered each question, he would direct his response to the examiner, but his gaze would take in the whole panel. As the morning progressed to afternoon, he noticed expressions changing. Some of the faces became clouded, some paled, some were outright livid at his audacity. But he kept his answers well-modulated, didn't allow anyone to unbalance him or make him angry. He produced reams of evidence, and he referred to Camille when he didn't understand the question. She would cover the microphone in front of him and explain what they were looking for.

Once she whispered, "He's being an ass. You've already answered his question, but he doesn't like the answer. He wants you to recant it."

He looked straight into the eye of the offender and said quite clearly, "This is how it is done here? I forgot for moment I wasn't in Russia."

There was a smirk on Congressman Adams' face and a buzz between two other members. Put in his place, not only by Maks but by some of his peers, the man passed his turn over to the woman who was next in line.

When the meeting was adjourned, several members of the committee came down to talk to him personally. Jack Adams was one of them.

"You've given us a lot of information to chew on. Along with concrete evidence of the subterfuge. Many of us are now going to hammer this home."

A woman on the panel, who he was introduced to as the representative from Rhode Island, shook his hand. "Thank you. Many of us appreciate that your put your life in danger by coming here. You've done our country a great service, and we hope we can alter the course we seem to be on."

Another announced, "This is war. The kind that Russia plays well. We've got to get our heads out of our asses and suit up. We can't win if we don't engage."

Alec had come over and led them out to a barrage of reporters and cameras that lined the hallway. Camille shielded her eyes as the flashbulbs popped, repeating the phrase *no comment* to no avail, as she all but ran to keep up with the agents who were hurrying to get Maks clear of any danger.

On the news that night, they watched as CNN showed a grim picture, faces showing signs of strain, the stark reality of Maks' testimony frightening the most astute. The others were cogs in the wheel of misfortune, willing to cover up anything to get their agenda through. *Party over country* had become a catch phrase that would galvanize the most ardent supporters of truth.

CHAPTER THIRTY

The meeting at the FBI was revealing. Maks would never have guessed that the bureau had so much of its own evidence, dating back to the prior year. His material proving the Kremlin had compromised the in-coming president years ago wasn't new to them. They confirmed what he was giving them would merely corroborate what was already on file. Hot mics had recorded damaging conversations, the intelligence community were monitoring international agents who just happened to be part of the president-elect's inner circle. They were building a solid case to present to the American people and their representatives. Shane had told them the scuttlebutt was, the director wouldn't last long enough to see the job done. The president-elect couldn't afford him to.

At the airport, as they waited for the plane to pull into the gate for their flight back to Boston, he picked up where he'd left off, reading the paperwork filed for his asylum case that Camille had put together. There was a dense amount of data that she'd put into almost prose-like structure. It read more like a book than a file. When he got to the piece that related to his father's death, he began scanning the document furiously. It was here. It was the original transcript of the trumped-up charges, the condemnation by the prison official, his father's defense. As he flipped through the rest of the file, he found more subversive material that could only have come from one source. His blood pressure rose, his blood now pounding in his temple. She'd betrayed him. He glared at her, could feel his face tighten in a mask of fury, his scowl freeze on his face. Striding over to where she sat, he lashed out, "Where did you get this?"

He was all but shoving the file in her face, the page turned to the documentation she had attached on his father. It wasn't anything she would have gotten online. It was the actual transcripts of several of the interrogations, along with the testimony of another prisoner who'd witnessed several of the beatings.

He didn't give her a chance to reply when he badgered her more forcefully, his voice a bellow.

"There is only one place you could have gotten this. I told you I did not want Irina involved."

She'd paled, looking more fragile than she had this morning after what he assumed was another night with no sleep. His heart almost softened toward her as it usually did, but the contempt at her betrayal pushed everything else out.

Her voice was so small and low he almost didn't hear her.

"I didn't get them from Irina."

"Then where from?"

A thin chill hung on the edge of his question.

He could hear Alec coming up behind him, as if waiting to hear her explanation as well. She was biting her lip, looking at someone just beyond him, who he knew had to be Alec and her face clouded with uneasiness.

"I promise I will tell you when we get back."

His temper snapped at her reluctance to set him straight. What was she waiting for? Why didn't she just come out and tell him? There could be only one reason for her lack of response.

"You are lying to me."

"No, Maks, I'm not."

Lies from his past flashed through his mind. Beautiful lies, steeped in confidence. They were, in reality, bullshit lies, meant to fool the people.

His father telling him everything would be fine, and he'd be out of jail in no time. Lie.

His government telling him that his father had committed suicide. Lie.

Leaders telling him that perestroika would work. Lie.

The television reporters telling him there were no troops in Ukraine, that Chechnya was the enemy of his people. Lies.

Perestroika had turned into a hopeless cause. Reform had brought empty shelves and black-market prices.

The president spoke to wanting the best for the glory of Russia, but what it had become was a third-world economy that still couldn't feed its people, corruption the marrow of its rotting bones. Russians were conditioned to believe that America was weak, the symbol of money and greed, that truth was Russia's strength. This was the ultimate lie, the polar, opposite of reality.

He'd thought Camille would be different, that she was on his side, his fighter. He didn't know she'd fight for him any way she damn well pleased and lie about it to cover her tracks. He'd spent the last two years digging up the truth, willing to die in the process if that's what it took. She was juggling her words, the sleight of hand no different than what he'd heard most of his life. It seemed everyone was a liar or thief.

She reached out to touch him, her hand visibly trembling. He jerked away as if scalded. She pulled her hand back, clasped it tightly in her other.

"I do not believe you. I cannot believe you. I no longer want you for attorney. All trust is gone."

She flinched at his words as if he'd struck her.

All it took was one step and Alec had him by the arm, all but dragging him over to the opposite wall of the small waiting area.

When Alec pushed him into a seat, he looked over, the bile settling back in his stomach. There were tears gathering in her eyes, but they no longer had any power over him. They were fake, meant to appease his outraged sensibilities.

Alec leaned down, speaking low into his ear.

"Maks, this isn't the time for this. We need to keep a low profile here. Please quiet down. You can work this out when we get back."

Maks took a breath, let the disillusionment go, and said in an even tone, "No, I do not want to work out. She went behind my back and I will not have her as attorney any longer. You get me new one."

Alec had squatted beside him, at eye level now. "We'll get you a new one if that's what you want, but you should think about this, Maks. Don't do anything you'll regret. She's done everything right to this point. She's been with you since day one and knows this case inside and out."

"I do not care. I am no longer client."

He locked his arms over his chest, closing the discussion, forcing down the misery that had erupted as soon as he read the first few lines of the transcript.

She'd promised him she would not put those he cared about at risk, and she'd gone and done it anyway. He could never trust her again. Not with his life, his case, or his heart. He'd known this would happen. It had been too good for the bad not to come pouring down on him. Had he learned nothing about life? About how the world worked? He would put this behind him, somehow, someway. He would not think about her again. His mother would arrive, and he would move them far away, to another state, where there was no one to remind him of what love might have been.

Camille sat, her body shaking, her breathing shallow. He didn't trust her anymore. Such a fragile thing, his trust, and she knew once it was gone, she'd never get it back, no matter how many times she explained what she'd done. She'd worked so hard to get what she needed, working around the restrictions he'd put in place. He didn't seem willing to give her the chance to explain. She'd counted on that, counted on the fact that he'd come to trust her at least that much.

Seemed she was wrong.

Maks wanted nothing to do with her. She'd taken the document he'd thrown at her and stuffed it away in her briefcase, promising herself she'd never look at it again. Not only were there too many painful memories that would go with it, the document itself was a violent saga of one man's journey through the Russian prison system. She had suffered through the reading and the retelling as she carefully crafted his application.

Everything she thought they had together had been smoke and mirrors.

At some point Alec had handed Maks over to Shane and had become her shadow. Unaware of her surroundings, floundering in a maelstrom of grief, she let herself be led to the gate, and onto the plane, her thoughts centered only on how she could have handled it differently.

Her entire body was numb, her mind equally so. Gratefully, she'd been given the window seat, and her gaze never faltered from the clouds that clung to the air around them. She'd lost him, through no fault of her own. She'd kept his edict in place, had run down different avenues to pursue, spent endless amounts of cash in the process. In the end, she'd gotten what she'd needed to set him free. Seemed it didn't matter in the long run. She could have gone the easy route and lied. He suspected her of that, anyway.

She kept her head averted so Alec wouldn't see her tears. She was fighting them back, the sniffles the only indication she was on the verge of crying her eyes out. She'd been so sure...that he was the one. The one her mother told her was out there somewhere waiting to meet her. His past would keep them from finding a home in each other's heart, a past filled with lies and betrayals. He looked for them now, created them out of fog and mist. Shutting down was the way he'd learned to deal with them all. Shutting her out would keep him safe. At least in his own mind. There was nothing she could do to change it, change his past, change the way he related to people and emotion.

Glancing up the aisle, she saw the top of his head, leaned back against the seat. He would never lay his head beside her again. They'd never touch, never kiss.

Desolation followed her off the plane and back to her condo. It was with a heavy heart that she let herself in. The stillness was welcome after the chaos of her thoughts and emotions. They had sucked the life out of her and she was as empty as the condo. He would never live here with her, now. Any talk of a future was dead and buried, and there was nothing that she could do, no matter how desperately she wanted him to believe her. She wouldn't attempt to convince him. It would only happen again unless he knew without question she wouldn't hurt him, wouldn't let him fall, wouldn't deceive him. She had to let him go.

She'd get Em to take over the case. She'd trust her to finish what she'd started.

She'd just climbed under the covers when her cell rang. She grabbed for it hoping...but when she saw the number, she bolted up and swiped to take the call.

The voice on the other end said simply, "I need your help."

She was back at the airport within the hour, waiting at another gate for another flight. It seemed she wouldn't be able to extricate herself from Maks' life just yet. Was fate intervening again? Was it offering her a way of redeeming herself? Not that she needed redemption, but she did need an opening to begin another dialogue. If he didn't want to be with her, she'd have to accept that. She wanted him to look back on their time together with something different than outrage.

The sun had come out, and Maks lifted his head, the smoke curling uninterrupted in the still air. He was smoking non-stop now, his nerves past being frayed. He'd been a wreck all week. The day after he'd fired Camille, he'd been told his mother had been arrested. Irina was doing all she could do get her out, and there was someone helping her through other channels. He'd never missed anyone so much as he did Camille. She would have been able to calm him, her quiet poise assuring him that all would be well. Nothing would be well again. Not if he lost both women, one to his own belligerent nature. Why had he started this fucking journey? Why did he thought he'd walk away unscathed? He would have been better off staying where he was. Death would have been preferable to the gaping wound in his heart. He'd never realized he could miss someone so much.

He put the cigarette out, let the door slam behind him when he re-entered the house. He'd been looking forward to this day, but it had dissipated like all hope did eventually. He paced, from kitchen to bedroom and back, waiting for his ride to the court house. He'd met Em yesterday for the first time, even though he'd been told days ago she was his new attorney. She'd gone over what to expect once he got to court, and how the judge might respond. Camille had already explained it, but he let Em ramble on, only half listening. She was professional but detached, her animosity easy to read. He knew the history between Cami and Em, knew they were good friends. He was convinced Em had been told about the firing, the insults, the accusations. He wasn't sure he could trust her to present his case, but he had no choice now. He'd let his fighter go.

"The car is on its way."

Alec was the agent on duty today, and he'd be accompanying him for his day in court. It would be up to the judge as to whether he'd be granted a residency visa, giving him the legal right to stay in the country. He almost didn't care one way or another. What would be would be. He was more concerned with the updates on his mother that Alec was passing on. Why had the police picked her up? Wasn't she in hiding? Was she being hurt? Was he to blame for her incarceration? Was Camille?

He tried Irina's number again on the phone he'd insisted on buying yesterday. He wanted his own connection, but she wasn't getting back to him. He'd almost broken down several times to call Camille. Just hearing her voice would have put him on a steadier course. But he couldn't. There was nothing between them anymore. She'd made sure of that. It might very well be Camille's willful disregard for his family that had set off a chain reaction. How could she have done that? Didn't she know it would create a problem for everyone he left behind? Hadn't he made that clear? Michelle's words came back to him, the ones that stated clearly that Camille had a propensity for this kind of thing, moving forward despite the repercussions. Camille had all but admitted, saying that it was always for her clients' benefit, but in this case, it had back fired on all of them. It was the first of a one-two punch to the gut, the second a ringing blow to the head. He'd gone down and hadn't gotten up yet. Today, if everything went well, he'd be a free man, but freedom could only be achieved when there was nothing left to lose. He'd lost everything he'd counted on when Camille...

Alec shouted back to him that the car was here, and his stomach churned as he picked up his coat and followed the agent out.

The ride over to the courthouse was spent in silence, all except for the tapping of Alec's fingers on the dashboard. Maks was looking out the window but seeing nothing except his life going up in smoke. Why had he done it? What had been gained? The FBI seemed to have had everything he'd given them, had all the information they'd need to move forward with indictments. He'd risked everything for nothing. All he'd gotten for his efforts had been a broken heart. The two women he loved were gone and he was powerless to get them back.

"We'll find her Maks. We've got some good people on the ground, and she'll be here tomorrow as promised. I feel it in my gut."

He glanced up, the man who he thought detached looking at him with sympathy. He'd trusted Camille and look what that had brought him. There was no way he'd trust again.

They pulled up to the courthouse and entered the building to find Em there, an accordion-style folder in her arms. All the components of his life were in it. From birth to death. The death of a dream he'd dared dream. Em wasn't as feminine as Camille. She was tall and thin, more athletic- looking like the tomboy he knew her to be. She looked exasperated, and he knew she didn't want to be here anymore than he did.

"Are you ready?" Her tone was brusque and to the point.

"*Ja.*"

"All right then, follow me."

He did as she'd asked, took a seat next to her in the gallery where they would wait for his turn.

He sat through dozens of appeals before he was called, each taking no more than fifteen minutes. The judge worked her way through the tall stack of folders on her desk. The term *speedy efficiency* seemed to apply, although people's lives were at stake and it seemed an insufficient amount of time given it. When the bailiff called out, "Zhernova docket number 9659678," Em got up, asking with her eyes that he do the same. He buttoned his suitcoat and rose.

The judge glanced up while flipping the pages of the brief before her.

"I've read over the finer details of the case, Ms. Spencer-Ronan, and it seems that I have no issue with the claims. I am granting Mr. Zhernova a residency visa. I hope he will follow that up with naturalization. It seems we owe the man a debt of gratitude."

When Judge LaRosa looked at him, he stood at attention out of habit. It was a habit he could break if he decided to stay.

"Mr. Zhernova, I commend you for choosing this attorney to represent you. The application was one of the most comprehensive I've seen. Good work Ms. Spencer-Ronan."

"Your honor, as you can see, it was Attorney Bissonnette who completed the application. Due to an unexpected trip overseas, she was unable to be here today."

The judge flipped to the back and looked up.

"I should have known. She always presents well-crafted briefs. This is no exception. Good luck, Mr. Zhernova."

With the bang of the gavel, they were excused. He'd barely heard anything past Ms. Bissonnette was overseas. Where? What was she doing? On another hunt for information for some other client of hers who needed documentation? Or...

As they were about to exit the courtroom, Maks quickened his steps to catch up to Em, who was all but running to get away from him. Taking her arm to prevent her from getting away, he asked, "Where did Cami go?"

Flushed with sudden anger, Em turned on him.

"Don't you dare call her Cami. Only people who love her are allowed to use that term of endearment. You are not one of them."

Chastised, admitting he didn't deserve the right but loved the way the name sounded to his ear, he asked, "Is she okay?"

"She'll be fine without you, if that's what you mean. You blew it big-time mister. You should have trusted her. You should have known she would never have betrayed you. She spent half her savings getting this information." She held up the folder indicating what she meant. "But you wouldn't know that. You never did let her explain."

His heart was racing, his mind exploding with the facts Em was presenting. "What you mean?"

With eyes burning into him, she said, "I...Nothing. I shouldn't have told you that, but I don't hold my tongue well when I'm totally pissed off. Have a good life Maxim Zhernova."

And with that, she was out the exit and racing down the steps of the judicial building.

He stood watching her retreating figure, trying to make sense out of what he'd been told. How could Camille have spent her savings? The only thing that came to mind was the term *bribe*. Nothing got done in Russia without them. Had she used the system to get what she wanted? Why would that have been so hard to tell him?

Pressing his fingers to stop the throbbing in his head, he went back to the conversation at the airport, when he'd accused her of contacting Irina. She'd denied it, said she'd explain it later. Why couldn't she have told him then? Was it because Alec was hovering so closely, knowing how straight he was and not wanting him to know the full story?

Had he assumed something because of his past dealings with the law? And if that was the case, where was his mother? Was it just coincidence that the two things had happened simultaneously?

Had he let the best thing that had happened to him get away that easily? Get away? He'd pushed her out. Half her life's savings? How much could this have cost her?

He had to speak to her and this time listen to what she had to say.

"Maks, are you all right? You got the visa so what's the problem?"

Alec had come over, his bodyguard days almost over.

"Problem is, I made mistake."

Alec's voice took on a darker tinge.

"With the testimony?"

"No. That was all truth."

"Then what?"

Alec's phone rang, and he answered it, turning away before Maks had a chance to answer him. When he turned back, what he said almost didn't register for the chaotic messages racing through his brain.

"Your mother is on a flight out of Minsk, flying to France. She'll be here tomorrow. Just like we promised."

His eyes shot up.

"How?"

"I'm not sure yet. We got word she was transported to Belarus and boarded a plane bound for Paris a little over an hour ago."

"This is good news."

"Yes, Maks. It is."

Tears collected in his eyes and he didn't care if Alec saw them. His mother was safe. He could stop worrying, start breathing again. Now there was one hurdle left to overcome before his new life could begin. Hope was sneaking back in and he let it.

He gave Alec a laugh. "Things do not need end up bad. Happiness can happen."

Alec gave him a couple of seconds to process the new information and then asked, "Are you ready to leave?"

"I am. Where we go?"

"One more night in our little safe house. And then, Maks, you're free."

He hadn't ever thought this possible. Hadn't made any plans, paralyzed with fear, not wanting to jinx himself by making plans that would go awry. He could have gone anywhere alone. Now, with his mother on her way here, he had to find a place for them to live. They'd have to stay in a hotel until he found something suitable, long-term. He'd been given a stipend of a few thousand dollars, and his first government pay-check would come in a couple of days.

"How long to rent apartment?"

"We could probably speed up the process if we had to."

"That would be good. Thank you."

All that was left was finding Cami. Telling her he was sorry. How would she respond? Would she spurn him? Forgive him? There were so many ways he'd short-changed her, so many secrets he'd kept from her. She'd overcome them all, along with his reticence, with her bold plan to play the game the Russian way. Who else would have thought of such a thing and who could have implemented it as well? His pride in her was a fresh, new experience. His gratitude that she'd done so much for him knew no bounds.

⌒

Her job was finished. She should be able to relax, but Camille was restless. What was she going to do with herself for the rest of her life?

Taking a play out of Maks' play-book, needing something to settle her, she opened the tiny refrigerator, took out a mini-bottle of vodka and drank it right down. It had been a mistake. Nausea roiled in her stomach, and she almost retched it back up, her body hungering for food more than drink. She swiped her sleeve over her mouth, years of good-manner conditioning right down the drain. Why couldn't she find some semblance of sanity? She'd done what she'd set out to do, and with her success should have come some satisfaction. But she felt nothing, not even numbness.

After going into the bathroom, she looked at her face in the mirror. She hadn't slept in over a week, couldn't for missing him. Threading her fingers through her hair, she pressed her lips together, trying to hold back the choke that was screaming for release, and leaned in closer. There were dark circles under her eyes, her skin looked translucent in the muted lighting, and her joints ached with every move she made. Dragging herself out of her clothes, she started the water, the steam soothing her face, the humidity taking her breath. The hotel she'd chosen was priced in the mid-range. It was clean and well-lit, picked at random. She didn't want to draw attention to where she was or who she was with. The last forty-eight hours had been a brutal regime of worry and wait. She wasn't sure she'd get Sonya out and she wasn't leaving until she did. The last of her available cash was gone, part of her investments liquidated, but it meant nothing to her. Money never had. It was a perk of her trade, and now that Maks was gone, she'd have only her work to fulfill her. Her finances would be healthy again soon enough. But would she?

After stepping into the stall, she lathered listlessly, as if all her energy was gone, pushing herself to wash her hair, do those mundane tasks she'd have to do every day even though she didn't want to. The day he'd sent her away, she could have crawled into bed and stayed there, the proverbial "woman dumped" eating ice cream and binging on television in the hopes that time would take away the depression, the pain. If the call hadn't come, who knew how she would have spent the last five days.

After pulling her hair up in one of the hand towels and drying herself off with the bigger one, she dressed in her sweats and a tee. One of his. One he'd left at her condo the day he left. She'd meant to return it, once it was washed and folded, but never had. It was all she had left. She raised the hem to her nose, inhaling the last of his scent. Hugging her arms around her, she walked to the window, looked out over the French city, the lights glaring and the traffic thick even at this hour. She thought about the women in the next room and a wan smile emerged. It had been worth every penny to get them on that plane. The knots in her stomach hadn't come undone until she'd seen them walking toward her. They'd hugged, like they were long-lost kin, and cried knowing how close it had come to a different ending.

The knock on the door startled her and she felt a splinter of fear slide up her body. After getting a hold of herself, she walked to the door and asked, "Who is it?"

"Irina. And Sonya. We would like to eat with you, yes?"

She opened the door and came face-to-face with Maks' family. All that was left of it. The love she had for him flowed around them and she invited them in.

"Room service might take a while. I can change, and we can go out and find a restaurant."

"I am out of Russia. Time is no longer my enemy. It will be good."

Sonya took her arm and led her to the bed and sat them both down on the edge.

"Irina has told me about you. I didn't know you helped my Maks."

"He was my client. I'm a sucker for that extra mile."

Sonya looked askance, as if she didn't understand.

"Sorry. It was a joke. Maks never got my sense of humor either."

"You go extra mile like this for all clients?"

"I couldn't afford to."

She tried to laugh but it fell flat.

"He is well?"

"He was the last time I talked to him."

"And that was?"

"Last week."

"Does he know you are here?"

"No. He...No."

When she'd left the airport, left Maks, after their flight from DC, she'd gone right home trying to shut down the voices in her head that were screaming at him to listen to her, believe her, trust her. It was only when Irina had reached out that night, told her that Sonya had been picked up and jailed, that she had a new purpose. Buying a ticket to Belarus, wanting to be close but not inside Russia itself, she'd begun to track down the people who could help get Sonya released. As long as you were willing to grease palms, you could get almost anything you wanted, including a dissident prisoner. Irina had done her part as Sonya's lawyer, picked up the wired money and delivered it to the block where Sonya was being held. With bags packed, they'd gone right to the small airfield where she'd had a private jet waiting to fly them to where she was.

"You thought of everything."

"That's my job. It's all in the details."

Irina reached down to cup her chin, lifting it so she could look in her eyes. "You are in love with my nephew."

Gulping back the truth, she said, "Goodness, no. I respect him. It took a great deal of courage moving to another country and forsaking his own, testifying like he did. He thought he'd reached the end of the nightmare. He didn't need for his mother to go missing."

Irina let her hand fall to her side.

"I was hoping. He is good man and I would for him to start new life, with good woman. It would make me happy to know you were with him at his side."

"He has his whole life to find someone. He will be free to do whatever he wants now."

It killed her to say that, think of Maks with someone else, but it was better to think that than pretend it could be different. She got up, and went to the desk, where a black binder was sitting. She leafed through until she found the take-out menu and they each decided what they'd have before she made the call. Once the food arrived, they sat and talked for hours, the food going down more easily with Maks so viscerally present.

CHAPTER THIRTY-ONE

Maks was waiting at the end of the airport rail, unable to go directly to the gate due to security regulations. He searched every face that came up the ramp, his gaze never faltering as he continued his vigil. Alec was with him, standing to the side, his normal posture keeping most people at bay. This would be the last time Alec would be with him as bodyguard. The agency wanted to make sure his mother and aunt arrived safely before ending the contract. He turned to see Alec, busy as usual, scanning the crowd, looking for who-knew-what.

He turned back to see Sonya and Irina walking briskly toward him, huge smiles on their faces. Then Sonya was running, and when she reached him, he scooped her up in his arms and held her as if he wouldn't let go, pulled Irina in for a three-way embrace.

"I am so glad you are safe. What happened?" Scowling at his aunt, he growled, "Why didn't you return calls?"

"I couldn't. Once we put plan into action we couldn't afford for anything to go wrong, and then we couldn't stop for fear we'd be delayed."

"What plan?"

"To get your mother out of jail."

"You were in jail? Was it because of me? Did they take you—"

"No, it was my fault. I went one too many times to ask about your father. They got sick of visits."

"It didn't help that you called them some unladylike names."

"They are pigs. If I don't tell them, who will?"

His mother was raising her chin at him in defiance, and it sent a shiver of fear through him. She could have been killed just because she was related to Petrov and to him.

"Ma, how could you do that? Especially knowing I am here revealing their secrets."

"I lost my temper. Shoot me."

His eyes gleamed with fury at his mother's recklessness. With a tight voice, he asked his aunt, "How did you get her here?"

Sonya tucked her hand in the crook of his arm as Alec began leading them out.

"A lovely lawyer. Irina reached out and she worked miracle. We flew to Belarus but had to wait until you were granted asylum. She had paperwork filled out, was waiting to put in place. Then we follow, how she say, on your coat tails."

His eyes snapped toward Irina.

"A lawyer? From where?"

"Boston. She's your lawyer, Maks, no? Camille Bissonnette."

"You reached out to her?"

"I did. She said if there was anything she could do for me, let her know. I took her up in it."

Had he been duped by Camille's friend? He'd been ready to apologize...had he been too eager to see a different picture than the one he'd drawn?

"When did she tell you this?"

"When she called to tell me that you wouldn't let me help in your defense. I argue with her, told her I had exculpatory evidence, but she refused. Said she made promise. Why did you tie her hands behind back, Maks?"

His voice thickened, the anger at himself for being so belligerent consuming him. He'd done it for their sake, to protect them.

"I knew what it could mean. I was not willing to risk lives."

"I am family. I was offended."

He gaped at her, knowing point-blank Camille had done nothing that should have earned her his ire. For verification, he asked outright, "You did not help her?"

"I told you, I did not."

Camille had protected them, too. In more ways than he could ever thank her for. What Em had told him was the truth. Camille had used the roulette system in place to get what she needed, at great financial cost to herself. Had flown to Belarus, gotten his mother released somehow and ultimately on a plane to Boston. But why? And why hadn't she told them he'd fired her, had let her go, had said unspeakable things he could never take back? She could have told his aunt to fuck herself, but she hadn't. The bottom fell out of his world when he realized she hadn't betrayed him. He'd betrayed her.

"Where is she, now? Did she not come back with you?"

Had she stayed in Paris?

"Yes, on same flight. She told us to go ahead, that you'd be here waiting."

His head snapped up as he began to scan the crowd, this time for the woman he'd left on her own, with no thought to what it could mean to her. Busy protecting his family, he'd forgotten Camille had become an important part of it.

Alec told him what he didn't want to know.

"She's already gone, Maks. She passed through while you were welcoming your mother."

He spun toward the exit, knowing he had to find her, talk to her, tell her...

Alec interrupted his thoughts.

"It's time to go. Have you thought about where that will be?"

No, he hadn't. He sputtered something about finding a hotel. His bags were packed and in the trunk of Alec's car. He should have made better plans.

Sonya asked sweetly, the radical dissident completely gone, "If we could go to the law offices of Woodley and Fisher, there are keys to a place Camille offered us."

Maks instantly stilled, not quite believing what his mother had said. Camille had even taken care of this last, not-so-small detail. Disappointment was something he was used to, regret and guilt as well, but what she made him feel was new, and he didn't know what to do with it.

Shaking his head, he wondered how he could have been so blind.

"She found us a place to stay?"

"Yes, she said she had investment property that was available. Said the keys would be waiting for us if you agreed. Is there reason you would be against this?"

⌒

"I might have led her to believe that I..."

"Didn't need her services anymore?"

They'd arrived at the car. He glanced over to Alec, who didn't know they'd been involved in a relationship. Should he give it away now? Could Alec do something that would get her in trouble? He didn't want to cause her anymore pain.

Alec gave him a sardonic smile.

"I'm not blind, Maks. I couldn't let it interfere with my job to keep you safe, but I know you had feelings for each other. I did my best to give you odd moments alone with each other without letting on what I knew."

"Is that why you told me to rethink my decision?"

"Part of it was that. The other part was she's a damn good lawyer."

Looking at his mother, who had come out of jail without a scratch on her, he had to agree.

His mother's eyes widened.

"You have feelings for this woman?"

"I do, Ma. But I made grave error. I accused her of getting information from Irina. I fired her, and walked away."

"It doesn't seem like she takes direction well."

His aunt was looking mighty satisfied.

"I fired my attorney. I never got around to firing my fighter."

Alec drove them farther into the city, to the offices of Woodley and Fisher in the center of downtown. After finding a spot in a parking garage, they walked the two blocks to the building and took the elevator up.

Irina was bedazzled by the lobby and waiting room, the large interior so professionally done. She turned in a circle, admiring the artwork that hung from the walls, as the phone rang furiously off the hook. Maks watched the receptionist handle every in-coming call, while managing clients entering and associates coming and going. In between tasks, she said in a calm voice, "Can I help you with something?"

Irina was the one who answered. He was still too wired to be of much help.

"Yes. Camille left keys for Zhernova's."

"She left them with her assistant. Let me get Sikha for you."

Within minutes, Sikha came around a corner a bright smile on her face.

"You must be the Zhernovas. Camille has told me all about you and I'm glad I'm getting to meet you."

"Is Camille not here?"

"I'm sorry but she did give me a note for Maks."

She handed him a small white envelope that was addressed to him in Cyrillic. He glanced up as if he didn't understand.

"She knows language?"

"She took some courses in college. She wanted to apologize before you read it. She says she's rusty."

Somewhat shaken, he slit open the flap and pulled out a card with her name embossed on the top in dark blue letters. Her printing was small, the first part in his native language, the second part in hers.

Dear Maks,

I hope the arrangements I made suit you. My cousin was gracious enough to furnish the basics, and there is food in the refrigerator. Please feel free to use the delivery service until you're on your feet. I'll use the fee I received from the FBI to cover all expenses.

I had a car delivered to the condo for your transportation needs. I know your mother and aunt will have to get to their lawyer's office to complete the residency application. I've given them a couple of names who can handle the process, and they will assist them as well as I could.

Your family is wonderful, and I'm glad I was able to arrange for their safe passage here.

Good luck. Hope all goes well for you.
Camille

With the note still in hand, he moved away from the group, retracing Sikha's steps. He walked quickly along a wall of offices to the left, where women were busy on phones, filing, working on computers. The cubicles were smaller than the ones on the right, so he focused his attention on those. Sikha was chasing after him, calling out for him to stop, just as he passed by Em's. Before getting another step closer to his goal, she came rushing out to stop him.

"You shouldn't be back here. Why don't you leave her alone?"

Em was standing in front of him, effectively barring his way, Sikha behind. It seemed he was right and that Camille was here. He hadn't anticipated she'd have her own bodyguards. He wasn't going to allow them to turn him back.

"I need to speak to her."

Em's hand went to his shoulder, as if she could prevent him from pushing by her.

"Sorry, you had your chance. You don't get another."

About to give an explanation, he looked up and saw her, standing on the threshold of her office. His breath was sucked out of him, she looked so beautiful. He was about to plead his case when she said, "It's okay, Em. I'll see him."

Her voice sent ripples of pleasure through his body.

Reluctantly, Em stepped aside.

He studied Camille's face, so pale. Exhaustion had taken its toll. He followed behind her as she moved into the room, so closely that he became her shadow. When she placed herself behind her desk, she erected a barrier between them. He had to find a way to breach it.

"I think I explained everything in the note. Are you here to argue about the condo?"

His Cami was gone and in her place was a woman devoid of all feeling.

"Yes, no. I...When did you get this investment property you speak of?"

"What difference does it make?"

"It makes difference if you bought this for us. I am good with computer. I can find record of purchase."

"I wasn't going to lie. I...figured it would be a good investment for the future, once you're settled. This gives you the time you need to decide where you're going to live."

Her shoulders drooped, and she leaned her fingers on the flat surface of her desk as if to stabilize herself.

"When do you realize Irina was father's sister?"

She sighed with exasperation.

"She told me during one of our phone calls."

"When she called looking for help?"

She looked at him in surprise, momentarily speechless.

"Yes."

He took a step closer and leaned into her, his hands almost touching hers on the top of the desk.

"And you dropped everything here for that."

"I didn't want your mother in jail. Not after all I'd learned about your penal system."

"And you knew by then that bribery got you everywhere."

"Yes."

She dropped into her seat. She couldn't stand anymore, she was so tired. She hadn't slept the night through since the day he fired her. Snatches here and there, but none at all since her trip to Belarus. Worried their plan wouldn't work, worried that Maks might not get asylum, worried someone would stop them, she'd held her breath until they touched down in Boston. She'd watched the reunion from a secluded place behind one of the pillars that stood as sentries along the corridor. Her heart was heavy, wishing she could celebrate with them, but she'd found some shade behind a group of tourists and made her way toward the exit and the office, where she hoped she'd find some healing. She hadn't expected him to seek her out.

"I've got a lot of work to catch up on. If you want to use the condo, fine. If not, that's fine, too. I'll get someone to rent it out for me. You need to leave now, Maks."

"You say in note you give recommendations for lawyer. They want you. You will take them as clients."

"I don't think that's a good idea."

He moved around her desk so quickly she didn't have time to counteract it. He was on his knee, took her hand in his, his eyes pleading with her to listen to him.

"I am sorry. I wish I could give good excuse, but it is same one I always use. I have learned not to trust. It made me do something wrong."

"It doesn't matter anymore. My job is done. You got your asylum. Your family is here."

"It does matter, Cami. I cannot have this good life you wish me if you're not in it. I would like that we go back to how it was."

She sought out strands of his hair that were in curly disarray. How she'd missed him.

"I can't, Maks. I'm not sure you'll ever be able to overcome your fears. I love you too much to always be on guard, wondering what you're keeping from me, what you believe, what you don't."

She squeezed her eyes closed. She couldn't believe she'd just told him what she'd kept so close. He didn't need to hear her declaration of love. It would only confuse things.

"It is good to hear that you love me. I want to spend life with you. Here, in Boston. I will work, and feed you. I will give you glass of wine after long day. I will kiss you good-bye in the middle of the night, when you are called out to help someone. I will ski mountains with you during winter. I trusted you with my life. It is time I trusted you with my heart. Please forgive me, give me second chance to prove I won't betray you again."

She studied him, wanting to believe him, wanting him back in her life with a desperation that scared her.

He stood, lifting her up with him and enclosing her in his arms. She could feel his heart beat hammering against his chest, his hand in gentle contrast as it swept down her hair.

"You are the good I thought never to have. I did not believe this possible. I cannot lose you now."

His lips found hers in a caress so sweet she felt tears fill her eyes. He brushed the ones that were falling away with his thumb, gazing at her with the love she'd always wanted, had never allowed herself.

"I love you, Cami. Tell me what I should do if you can't love me back?"

She kissed him then, a brief featherlike kiss that had her heart racing.

"I love you back, Maxim Zhernova. Have since the day you opened the door and didn't invite me in."

There was a semblance of a smile on his face. "This is joke?"

"More truth than joke."

He tipped his forehead to hers.

"You always tell truth. I learn to listen. And believe."

"I guess I have to trust that you'll at least try."

"Does this mean you will be with me again?"

"My heart will always be with you Maks, but I admit it's better when we're in the same place."

"We be in same place tonight?"

"I'd like that. Maybe I'll finally be able to sleep."

When she looked at him, his eyes so full of the love he spoke of, she amended that. She'd be getting very little sleep.

"I will go, get my mother and aunt settled in this place you bought for us. I will be at home after that, waiting for you."

A thrill went through her when he called her condo home. She kissed him again, with a little more pressure this time.

"I won't be too long. I just came in to tie up some things I was working on while waiting for your mother's release."

She began to walk him out, to find Nell, Jelani, and Em out in the hall waiting and watching.

Em said to the tight-knit group, "It looks like he has more brains than I gave him credit for."

Jelani sighed, as if she'd be jealous if it were anybody else finding her man. Nell, gave her a grin and a thumbs-up.

He smiled at all of them as Camille led him out to the waiting room.

Sonya jumped up and crossed the distance. "I didn't know what was keeping you. Do we still have place to stay?" Looking at Maks she added, "My son can be argumentative at times."

He was the one that answered.

"You do, but I will be staying with Cami. She has found it in her heart to forgive me. We live together."

The partners had followed them out to meet Maks' mother and aunt. She had been in constant touch with them, needing their expertise, their wisdom, and their friendship.

Em was the one who said, "You get to live, Maks."

He leaned in for another kiss. "I do."

CHAPTER THIRTY-TWO

Maks used the key to open the door to the condo Camille had bought for them. After walking in, his mother and aunt stood still, examining the newly renovated, open-concept living space.

Irina was stunned at what to them seemed like opulence. He'd gotten used to it, living with Cami.

"This is how Americans live?" His aunt's voice was filled with wonder.

"Some. The successful ones."

"Your Camille is successful."

"She is. As you have seen, she's very good at what she does."

She had a precious heart that only added to her wealth, and it was his. He couldn't believe his good fortune, but he promised himself he was going to accept that it was his to hold forever.

He walked into the kitchen, smiling, his hand sliding along the marble countertops. There were stainless-steel appliances, white cabinets telling him she'd made the kitchen a priority in her search. His mother had gone down the hall to the bedrooms and claimed one for her own, her small suitcase being placed by the door.

"The light in here is good. I have never lived so well. Irina, your room is here, yes?"

She'd chosen the one next door to hers. His thoughts went to all they'd been through since his father's death. These women might not be connected by blood, but they were connected by something stronger: tears and grief. He was glad that time in their lives was over.

"I will make you something to eat, then I am going home."

The word rang in his head and traveled to his heart. He would be going home, to Camille. He'd be able to hold her all night, something he'd thought he'd never get to do again. Even in his most painful moments, thinking she'd betrayed him, he couldn't get her out of his blood.

"You don't have to Maks. We know how to use stove. You go, now. Cami needs you. She has been rock, but now it is her turn to be taken care of."

He kissed them both on the cheek, taking a moment to appreciate the fact that were here, together and free from the curse of a malevolent government. Not all the people here were good. He saw murder and mayhem every time he watched the TV, but there were good people here as well, who would stand for you, who refused to allow for the persecution of others, and the government, although broken, still stood up to transgressors. Maybe some of the work he did would help them fix the system, casting out those who were more interested in money and power than the wellbeing of those who lived here.

He picked up the keys on the counter. There'd been a car in the driveway when Alec dropped them off, and he was glad it wasn't new. He wouldn't have felt comfortable. All he'd ever driven was a beat-up Citroen that had to be over twenty years old. It wasn't the most reliable mode of transportation, but It'd gotten him, and his passengers while taxiing, where they'd needed to go.

Looking back, he took in the scene, his aunt inspecting the food in the refrigerator, pointing out all the goodies stocked there to Sonya, who was sitting on a stool at the floating island. He was leaving them in good hands. Camille's.

He shrugged into his coat, a smile wide on his face, and pulled on his boots that he'd taken off before entering the pristine space.

Once outside, he looked at the Subaru and the smile grew bigger. He got behind the wheel, adjusted the seat for his frame and turned the key in the ignition. Then stopped.

He had no idea how to get to Cami's from here.

He reached for his phone, hit the app for the GPS, and entered her address. When the voice told him to take a right out of the drive-way, he followed her blindly.

⌒

Em had come into Camille's office as soon as the Zhernovas left. Nell and Jelani weren't too far behind.

"You forgave him."

It wasn't a question that Em needed answered, but Camille gave her one anyway.

"I made a mistake once. I wish I'd gotten a second chance to make it right. Why wouldn't I give Maks one?"

He'd seemed sincerely sorry for his rush to judgment. And the fates seemed to be in favor of a reconciliation. Hadn't they handed her a crisis to remediate that kept her in Maks' loop?

Nell mused out loud, "I wish I could make up my mind about that. Second chances. Sometimes they work, sometimes they don't."

Jelani, who probably had more intimate information, said, "You seem open to them. At least it seems you've been spending an inordinate amount of time with one congressman."

"Cami's slate is clean, mine not so much."

"Chloe seems happy."

"She does, which makes it a much harder decision. If it doesn't work out, what do I do then?"

Em frowned. "You learn to live with the impossible."

"I'm not as willing to do that as you are."

Camille knew Nell wasn't being sarcastic. Everyone here had said the same thing about Saint Emilia's tolerance level. No one here would be willing to pine over a lost love while entertaining the man and his wife at every turn. Masochism wasn't in their nature.

"Not many are."

Camille yawned. It wasn't the company. She loved these women as much as she loved her sister. Her stamina had been used up and she was drawing on the dregs.

Em got up from the seat she'd claimed when she came into the office.

"Why don't you go home, hon. We'll take all your calls. You need to get some rest. I don't know how you can even think right now."

"Thanks for the offer, but I'm good. I just have a couple of calls to make and then I'll go home. I can't thank you guys enough for all you've done for me this week. I couldn't have done it without you."

"Are you kidding? Our problem wasn't helping, it was worrying our asses off that you'd get back safely."

"I wasn't worried about me. I was worried about Sonya. All's well that ends well, as they say."

"Okay, you're using outdated proverbs. Get out of here. Go see your love. Get some sleep. You can catch up on the rest over the weekend."

"I think I will. The calls can wait until tomorrow."

Luisa was the one she'd needed to follow up on and she had. Her client would be arriving tomorrow, and she wanted to have a functioning brain during the pre-trial meeting.

After getting her coat on, her hugs from her partners, she clasped her briefcase in her hand and headed home. A thrill went through her at the thought she'd soon be seeing Maks.

⁓

She didn't expect to see him as soon as she opened the door. He hurried down to meet her and she collapsed into his arms. He lifted her up and didn't put her down until they were in the living room, sitting on the couch, her on his lap. It was the first time they'd been here together without Shane in residence. He didn't waste any time putting his lips on hers. His kisses were deep and satisfying and she returned them in kind, needing to share his body, his mind and his heart. Hungrily, they dispensed with their clothes and, skin to skin, made up for all their lonely nights. Carrying her into the bedroom afterward, he apologized for being so selfish.

"I should have carried you right to bed, to sleep, but I couldn't seem to put your needs ahead of my own."

He enfolded her in his arms, kissed her temple and rested his head against hers. Her eyes felt heavy, and with her body satiated, for now, she let them slide closed as she snuggled against him.

She awoke to the smell of something cooking. It drifted down the hall, and like a cartoon character, she followed the scent floating on air. He was in the kitchen, the towel over his shoulder, his head bent as he checked something in the oven. Her heart swelled at the sight of him.

When he looked up at her, he was smiling.

"I make you breakfast. You sleep well?"

She went over to him, blissfully happy, and took a morning kiss. He smelled of cigarette smoke and shampoo, and it mixed with cinnamon and whatever other spice he'd used, creating a sublime blend of aromas. She still couldn't believe he was here, and he wanted to stay.

"I did. And you?"

"Not so well. I stayed awake most of night watching you, afraid that if I closed eyes you would disappear. I cannot spend any more nights without you."

She cupped his face with her hands. "I don't want any more nights without you, either. I died a little each day thinking you hated me."

He fingered her hair, his face so close she could feel his breath. His words were whisper-soft.

"I never hated you. I loved you and that's what made me hurt so much. I should never have turned away without listening to what you had to say. I will not ever do that again. I should have listened to Alec."

"Alec? Why?"

"He try to convince me to rethink my decision."

"Mhm, my opinion of him just improved."

"He is now friend. No longer bodyguard."

"He is, is he? So are you going to grab beers some nights with him and Shane?"

"And leave you? A very large *nyet*."

"I work late some nights. A lot of nights, although maybe I'll change that. I think a ten-hour day is long enough."

"Come, have coffee and a Danish. It is flaky how you like."

He poured her some of the dark, rich brew and picked up one of the gooey sweets. When he offered her a taste, she smelled the warmth and steam, and bit into it gingerly.

"Oh, my God, Maks. That's delicious."

After putting it on a plate, he carried it to the table, pulled his chair close to hers, and took a bite of his own.

"What are you going to do now? FBI, computer geek, chef?"

"I would like to finish degree and go to law school. Be lawyer like my father. Like you."

"You'd make a good one. You'll appreciate how our legal system works, more than the average citizen. I don't think the spring semester has started yet. You could take a couple of classes at the community college near here and then apply to Boston University, Northeastern, UMass for the fall semester."

"I like idea. I work with FBI days, for money, go to school nights. You can do that here?"

"And there's online classes. I think you could manage that."

"You help me with application?"

She'd finished the Danish but needed more of his sweet samplings. After crawling onto his lap, she let the languid kisses they started with lead them to a more explosive kind.

⤙

During the next week, they fell into a routine, one where he did all that he'd promised. Greeted her at night with a glass of wine, cooked her dinner, after which they completed his applications for college, his attendance at the local community school already begun. They skipped the inauguration, spending it instead with his family, introducing them to Boston, strolling around Faneuil Hall, walking the historic Freedom Trail. It wasn't like the ancient sites they'd find in Russia, but there was an energy here that suggested revolution was a good thing.

That night they stayed over at the new condo with Irina and Sonya. The Women's March was scheduled for the next day, and they were planning on attending, along with the rest of the staff from Woodley and Fisher. Even Jack had agreed to go when pressed by his daughter that it was history in the making. Irina and Sonya were like little kids, anticipating the freedom to march in protest and not be in fear of arrest or punishment.

The day dawned clear and unusually warm for January. Dressed comfortably, light jackets rather than heavy coats, they took the T to the Common and met up with the rest of their party, Em and Chloe carrying signs. Everyone else brought attitude.

Irina had her arm linked with Sonya's, a huge smile on her face. "People march all over world, not just in Boston. This is amazing. I am here. Free. I like America."

"I wish Petrov could be with us. He would never believe this was possible."

"Yeah, Mama, he did. Possible, but where we come from, not feasible for the future."

"I am glad you are going into law. Will you work with Camille?"

"No. Her firm wouldn't hire me. I will work for public defender's office. Help people who don't have money to fight for rights."

Jelani reminded, "You better work for the right side. None of this ICE bullshit."

"I know where I need to stand. For people like my father."

Looking over at Camille, Jelani said, "I guess he passes the smell test."

"What is this smell test?"

He was sniffing himself, not realizing it was a joke. Until Camille burst out laughing.

By mid-morning, there had to be close to one hundred thousand people here and he'd never seen a crowd so big. Speakers were addressing those who had descended on the city, senators, other members of Congress. When Jack got up to speak, Maks listened to words like *shoulder-to-shoulder* and *letting our voices be raised as one*. He was a good speaker, charismatic, and he would vote for him when he got the chance. He only had to wait a year and then he could become a citizen.

He hugged his mother to his side as Camille applauded the speech.

Before the march began, they were asked to repeat an oath. As he said the words, "to protect, preserve, and defend the Constitution," he felt a seed sprout in his heart. These were fighting words, something the American people did well. As he was swept up with in the swell of protestors, he marched the one-mile route, holding Camille's hand, thanking his ghosts for leading him here, saying good-bye to revenge and hello to this brand-new life.

ACKNOWLEDGMENTS

There was a lot of research that went to the writing of this story. I had my pick from some informative books on cyberspace, the dark web, the Russian hacking and on Russia herself, that made *Skoli on Ice* come alive. I wish to thank all those authors whom I read, who are providing a crucial service, by letting us know what's going on in the world. It's up to us, as citizens to stay "woke" and to become active participants in our government. Democracy is our gift to the world and we have to safe guard it at all costs.

Thank you to my cover designer, Jaycee De Lorenzo for the fabulous covers she creates, Joan Frantschuk at Woven Red for my formatting needs. She also provides patience, advice and resources and I am ever so grateful.

To my line editor, Amy Knupp, a writer in her own right. She makes my lack of grammatical correctness seem insignificant. Check her out on Amazon. She's awesome.

Thank you to my friend, Bunny, for her enthusiastic support of the book. She was the first one to read it and couldn't wait to spread the word about the upcoming publication.

And thank you to the rest of my family, my husband Jeff, my daughter Kaitlin and her husband Juan, my son Justin, my five grandchildren; Jaiden, Jake, Jon, Dominic and Liam, my two dogs, Cooper and Molly and Isis the cat. They keep me grounded in a world full of make-believe.

ABOUT FAITH

Faith O'Shea is a contemporary women's literature writer who loves writing about strong women and the friendships they build. She throws in a little magic, a little romance, and develops unique personalities, and what you get are characters who come alive on the page. She's found that strong women need more than a happily ever after.

Faith lives in a small town in Massachusetts with her husband Jeff, dogs Cooper and Molly, and Isis, the Egyptian feline queen. Her children live close and are a big part of her life. In her spare time, she reads, walks Coop, dabbles in all kinds of cooking, and takes time to play with her grandchildren.

You can visit her on Facebook and Twitter or find her through her website at www.faithoshea.com.

HEART OF FIRE

Emilia Spencer-Ronan is finally ready to ditch her dream of marrying her soul mate. About time, too, because he was taken off the market years ago and for as much as she loved helping him out every once in a while, she was ready to move from Nanny, Inc to his four-year-old son, to over-him. About to close that door, and open a new one, disaster strikes, and she makes a promise she's not sure she can keep.

Nick Katsaros' life is a mess. His marriage is over, his son is hurting, and his best friend has turned her back on him. He doesn't understand why she's walking away when he needs her the most. She's always been his lifesaver and Teddy's go to when the chips were down. Funny thing is, she wants out, just when he's seeing her in a brand-new light, now convinced that she was the one right from the start. Is it too late for them to turn back the clock and start over?

CHAPTER ONE

Emilia Spencer-Ronan pushed through the double doors of the Woodley and Fisher law firm suite with a vengeance. She was pissed, and her scowl accompanied her into the reception area and down the short hall to her office. After throwing her briefcase on her desk, she picked up the phone and followed up the earlier call she'd made as she'd exited the courthouse. Having gotten nowhere with the attendant at the deportation center, she was now calling the superintendent to see what the hell had happened. Evalina Bazorga was scheduled to appear via video this morning during her court appearance. It wasn't bad enough that her clients couldn't face the judge personally, but when things like this happened, they missed their day in court completely.

Tapping her foot, then pacing, she waited on the line for the man in charge of the corrections facility to come to the phone. Instead of the head of the jail, she got his assistant.

"Ms. Ronan."

"It's Spencer-Ronan and you better be able to fix my problem or I'm taking it to the governor."

"I'm very sorry that the video equipment was malfunctioning. It doesn't happen often. From what I understand, you were able to get the judge to postpone."

"I did, but it means more time for my client in your beautiful center, and that is not acceptable."

The sarcasm was thick. They both knew the center wasn't beautiful. Better than most in the country, but a jail was a jail, no matter what you called it or how you sliced it.

"I'm aware of that, but if she had not broken the law—"

Her voice rose in direct proportion to her blood pressure.

"Broken the law? She is the victim here, sir. She was the one assaulted. She is the one with the broken arm. She was the one who was crawling out of that house to get away from the husband who was beating her."

There were witnesses to the brutality of the attack. Nick Katsaros, her best friend, was one of them. On patrol that day, he was called in by a frightened neighbor to stop the assault. He was the one who'd written the report she read over before filing a new petition to present to the court. Evalina had had no choice but to defend herself. Her life had depended on it.

Emilia had a hard time controlling her emotion.

"Are you telling me that a woman can't fight back against her abuser?"

"No, that's not what I'm telling you. But she's undocumented and now has a pending assault charge."

Undocumented residents could be summarily deported if they'd broken the law in some way. A woman was more at risk than other perpetrators.

"Against her abuser. What is it about that that you are having trouble with?"

Em caught sight of Cami standing at her door, her look suggesting she change her tactics. She knew her law partner was right. She wasn't going to get anywhere being belligerent with the person on the other end of the line. Taking a deep breath, she tried to tamp down her anger and approach from a different perspective.

"Assistant Superintendent Bayles, I know this was not done intentionally, but my client needs to get home to her children. Their father's already been transferred to the county jail. It's my job to make sure those kids don't lose both parents to this domestic abuse issue. I hope the video equipment will be fixed soon, at least in time for my next hearing."

"I can promise you that, Attorney Spencer-Ronan. We are sorry for the delay, but some things can't be helped."

"I'd suggest you get a back-up."

"I'll run it by our accounting department. Good day."

"Good-bye."

She let the receiver slip onto the cradle and plunked herself down in her chair, just as Cami came in and took one opposite her.

"What happened?"

"The damn video machine wasn't working, so Evalina wasn't able to..." she raised her hands to make quotation marks around the words, 'attend the hearing.' I sat outside the courtroom for over an hour waiting to be called and got the message right before I went in."

Prisoners were not guaranteed a day in court. Any petition presented by their attorney was done by means of a video conference. When the video failed to function properly, their pseudo day in court was postponed. It was no way to do business.

"What judge was presiding?"

There had been only one until the governor had assigned another to help with the backlog.

"Thankfully, it was Frechette. She was as angry about it as I was. Mumbled something about wasting the court's time."

The immigration courts were on overload, and judges were forced to give a bare minimum to each case presented. That she had read the brief meant she had lost five minutes, half the time she gave for each decision.

"Evalina's the one you got a restraining order for, isn't she?"

"Yes, for the amount of good it did her. Her husband walked right through it. The kids had to watch while their father pummeled their mother before they were whisked off to family services. It didn't help that Evalina tried to stab the son of a bitch with a kitchen knife. I went to see them yesterday and they're not doing well. The family they're with is great, but the kids are emotionally traumatized. They need their mother."

It wasn't the first time she'd handled domestic abuse cases, but when there were children involved, her hackles went through the roof.

"Where'd you get the case?"

"Saban. She was the one who got the initial call about domestic violence in the home and then got the kids into family services after the attack."

That had happened almost a month ago and now there'd be another week added to the sentence.

Cami studied her before saying, "I still don't get what Saban's doing in that capacity. From some of the stories you've told me, it's not her calling."

"It's not, but I think her supervisor has noticed. She's not working with families anymore. She handed off this case before her...demotion."

Saban Katsaros had been promoted to caseworker just six months ago and with each case handled, she made more of a mess than she'd started with. That she was back in her cubicle with paper and files was an improvement in the process. Organizational duties were more her thing than dealing with people, especially children. She didn't relate well to them. Her emotional stamina was critically low, so she created problems at the initiation of each case that had to be smoothed over. Em wondered why her supervisor had been so quick to step in. Usually the powers that be let the unqualified remain, to wreak havoc on those who weren't.

She told Cami, "She's being sent to court now as a resource. She knows her stuff, just can't put into practice with real people."

"She used to call you on a lot, didn't she?"

"Only when she needed an attorney."

"Or a babysitter."

Irritation pinched Em's eyebrows together. Nick had asked her to take Teddy tomorrow night, said he and Saban needed to talk. She knew their marriage had hit a rough patch, but it had hit a lot of them over the years. When would enough, be enough? And why was she still enabling him? She was his friend, not Nanny, Incorporated.

Her frustration meter had already been on high, and the problem with the video cam ratcheted it up a notch. It was probably why she'd handled it so poorly.

Camille slid her leg over her knee in such a graceful way, Em wondered how they'd become best friends. Totally feminine, Cami could have made her feel inadequate in comparison. Saban had the same effect and didn't go out of the way to disabuse her of that fact. Maybe if she had had that kind of allure...

"At least you don't have to work with her anymore. It must have been hard."

Shaking off the feelings that came with thoughts of the social worker, Em admitted, "Not really. She deferred to me on everything. She likes it when she can depend on someone else to do the job."

"Aren't you lucky she trusted you. Not only with her cases but with her son, as well."

With a large dose of disapproval in her voice, Em said, "Teddy's my buddy. Leave him out of this."

She didn't want to get into it. After the shit show at the courthouse, she'd didn't need to have an argument she couldn't win.

"Yes, ma'am. What are you doing tonight?"

Em released a sigh of relief.

"Just hanging out. You?"

"Maks and I are going up to the Notch. My mother wants to go over some of the wedding details."

Em sat back, a smile on her face. This was something she could feel good about. Camille had fallen head over heels with the man the FBI assigned to her right before the holidays. Cami's specialty was asylum, and the Russian had been brought into the country with detailed information about the election hacking scam that was still being investigated. The FBI was seeking data. Maxim Zhernova was seeking protection. Russians like him were being killed all over the world. Somehow, he'd managed to escape detection. Now? They hoped he'd be left alone. To think it had only been several months since they met, but the attraction had been strong, a love story, destiny, if you were to believe Cami's mother. They'd gotten engaged and the May wedding they'd planned was just a week away. She was thrilled to see her best friend so happy. That it made her own hollow love life more apparent didn't take away her feeling of contentment at Cami's upcoming nuptials.

Cami leaned forward; her features animated.

"Why don't you come up tomorrow. The snow is packed, and the skiing will be great."

Em steepled her hands under her chin and hesitated. Cami would probably lecture her about her plans. Knowing she couldn't get away with turning her down without a reason, she told her about keeping Teddy and the why behind it.

Cami's vexation was evident. "He has no idea that it must kill you to do that, does he?"

Camille was one of the few who knew her feelings for Nick went way beyond friendship. It might have started that way, but a switch had turned on somewhere over the years, and she'd developed even deeper feelings. Or maybe she was fooling herself and she'd loved him from day one.

Pulling at the corner of the file that sat atop her desk, Em sat with her eyes downcast. She didn't want to see the expression on Cami's face.

"It doesn't kill me. I love having Teddy. It's a preview of upcoming attractions when I finally have kids."

Leaning forward, Cami grabbed her hand.

"You need to fall in love with someone else to find that, Em."

After looking up to meet the intensity of the stare, Em gave her what she was looking for.

"I know. I'm working on that. I went out last week with a guy I met at Rissa's."

"And?"

"No chemistry on either side. But can't I get an A for effort?"

"I'll give you the A, but you can't quit now."

"I won't. If the opportunity presents itself, I'll take it."

She'd dated off and on over the years but hadn't found anyone that made her heart sing. With Nick there was a forty-fucking-piece symphony.

Cami rose from her seat, seemingly satisfied that she'd made the promise.

"We're taking off a little early, so I probably won't see you until Monday."

"Have a good weekend. Say hi to Maks for me."

"I will."

Cami disappeared into the office right next door, and Em heard the rustling of papers as she collected her things before leaving for the day. Em sat in the silence, wishing she could find a lasting love like her friends. Six months ago, Nell was alone with her daughter, Cami was alone with her fear, Jelani was alone with a burning desire to find her one and only. She was alone because she loved someone who wasn't available. She didn't know how to break the spell he'd cast the day they met. But she was sick of being in a one-sided relationship, especially now, seeing Nell and Cami with men they loved soul mates if she had to label it, just like her parents.

It was way past time to put it behind her and seriously think about opening another door.

When her cell rang, she checked caller ID and let out a staggered breath. How could she close this door if he kept pushing it open?

"Hi, Nick."

"Hey, I've got a favor to ask."

Of course, he did. It was happening more and more often, and she didn't know what she was going to do about it. She couldn't seem to say no. There had to be a dozen books on Amazon that would give instructions. Maybe it was high time to buy one.

"What is it?"

"Alec got a call about a canceled ice time, asking if we wanted it, and I was wondering...could you pick Teddy up at the rink and keep him tonight?"

It meant she'd be keeping Teddy for the weekend so Nick could play and take Saban out. Talk about having your cake and eating it, too. She was the one left cleaning up the crumbs. The fact that she loved the kid made it hard to turn him down.

She could resent this but decided that being with Teddy might chase away the blues.

"I guess. What time?"

"We need to be at the rink by eight. I'll feed him before hand, and if you want to stick around to watch for a while, he'd be up for it."

Would she? She'd attended quite a few scrimmage games in college and after, and although she didn't want to, she still enjoyed watching him play. He could have gone into the draft the year he graduated but didn't think he had the talents to make it for the long haul.

"That's prime time. Usually the big guys don't play until after ten."

"Don't know how he managed it, but I'll take it. I took on an extra shift tomorrow. This way I'll at least get some sleep."

"I'll have to go home and change, but I'll get there as close to eight as I can."

"Thanks, Em. You're a lifesaver."

She swiped to end the call, thinking he had it wrong. She was a one-pound whirly-swirl sucker.

www.ingramcontent.com/pod-product-compliance
Lightning Source LLC
Chambersburg PA
CBHW061942170626
46813CB00006B/2500